MOTION TO KILL

A NOVEL

JOEL GOLDMAN

Find out more about Joel Goldman at http://www.joelgoldman.com

Follow his blog at http://www.joelgoldman.blogspot.com

Sign up for his newsletter at http://www.joelgoldman.com/newsletter.php

Follow him on Twitter http://twitter.com/#!/JoelGoldman1

Follow him on Facebook at http://www.facebook.com/joel.goldman

Contents

For Hildy, the wife of my life

CHAPTER ONE

A dead partner is bad for business, even if he dies in his sleep. But when he washes ashore on one side of a lake and his boat is found abandoned on the other side, it's worse. When the sheriff tells the coroner to "cut him open and see what we've got," it's time to dust off the résumé. And the ink was barely dry on Lou Mason's.

The time was seven thirty on Sunday morning, July 12. It was too early for dead bodies, too humid for the smell, and just right for the flies and mosquitoes. And it was rotten for identifying the body of a dead partner. These were the moments to remember.

Mason's dead partner was Richard Sullivan, senior partner in Sullivan & Christenson, his law firm for the last three months. Sullivan was the firm's rainmaker. He was a sawed-off, in-your-face, thump-your-chest ballbuster. His clients and partners loved the money he made for them, but none of them ever confessed to liking him. Though in his late fifties, he had one of those perpetually mid forties faces. Except that now he was dead, as gray as a Minneapolis winter and bloated from a night in the water.

Sullivan & Christenson was a Kansas City law firm that employed forty lawyers to merge and acquire clients' assets so they could protect them from taxation before and after death. When bare-knuckled bargaining didn't get the deal done, they'd sue the bastards. Or defend the firm's bastard if he was sued first. Mason's job was to win regardless of which bastard won the race to the courthouse.

The U.S. attorney, Franklin St. John, had been preparing a special invitation to the courthouse for Sullivan's biggest client, a banker named Victor O'Malley. The RSVP would be sent to the grand jury that had been investigating O'Malley for two years. Sullivan asked Mason to defend O'Malley the day Mason joined the firm as its twelfth partner. Mason accepted and Sullivan spoonfed him the details of O'Malley's complex business deals.

Mason figured out that O'Malley had stolen a lot of money from the bank he owned. He was having a harder time figuring out how to defend him. Fifty million dollars was a lot to blame on a bookkeeping mistake.

Two days earlier, Sullivan took Mason to lunch and, over a couple of grilled chicken Caesar salads, casually inquired what would happen to O'Malley's defense if certain documents disappeared.

"Which documents?" Mason asked.

Sullivan studied Mason for a moment before answering. "Let's assume that there are records that show O'Malley and one of his business associates received favorable treatment from his bank."

Mason didn't hesitate. "That's what the whole case is about. There are too many of those documents to lose even if I didn't mind going to jail with O'Malley. Which I do."

"Lou, I only care about the documents with my name on them. Do you understand?"

Mason nodded slowly, wiping his hands with a white cloth napkin more than was needed to clean them.

"I'm not going to jail for you either. Show me the documents, and we'll figure something out."

Sullivan gave him the pained look of a disappointed parent and changed the subject. Mason knew then that he'd never see the documents. In the same instant, he also knew that his career at Sullivan & Christenson was over. He had failed Sullivan's test but passed his own. He decided to think it over during the firm's annual retreat that weekend, but he knew what he would do come Monday morning. Quit.

The retreat was at Buckhorn resort at the Lake of the Ozarks in southern Missouri. It was a long weekend of golf, drinking, and leering for the lawyers and staff.

Mason went for a walk after the Saturday night poker game, stopping at the beach, a kidney-shaped plot filled with sand along a retaining wall at the water's edge. A slight breeze rolled off the water, just enough to push the air around. A young couple was braided together at one end of the beach. He lay down at a discreet distance on the only lounge chair, turned his back to them, and felt the loneliness of the voyeur.

He didn't realize that he'd fallen asleep until a voice interrupted the recurring dream of his last trial before he joined Sullivan & Christenson. Tommy Douchant, his client and best friend, looked up at him from his wheelchair, eyes wild, tears beading on his cheeks, as the jury announced its verdict against them. Mason begged the jury to come back, to listen to him, as they filed out of the courtroom, their faces dissolving as a voice sliced through his dream.

"Excuse me . . . are you Lou Mason?"

Tommy rolled back into Mason's subconscious as he opened his eyes. The voice belonged to a woman standing over him, backlit by the glare of the morning sun. The glistening effect was a mixture of a Madonna halo and a Star Trek transporter. He thought about asking her to beam him up while he rubbed any leftover drool from his chin stubble.

The best he could do was a slightly sleep-slurred, "Yeah, I'm Mason."

Snappy repartee after spending the night on a bed of vinyl was sometimes the beginning and end of his charm.

"I'm Sheriff Kelly Holt. We need to talk."

"It's okay, Officer, I paid for the room."

Drumroll, please, he silently requested, satisfied that he was really hitting his stride.

"I'm sure you did, Mr. Mason. I'm more interested in whether you know Richard Sullivan."

Fully awake now, he stood so that he could see her clearly. Khaki uniform, Caribbean blue eyes, Pope County sheriff's badge, natural, no-sweat beauty, pistol on her hip. A shade shorter than his six feet, with honey-colored hair that draped the shoulders of a tanned, athletic body. She was a slap-on-the-cuffs dream come true, but her question flattened the fantasy.

"He's my law partner. Is there a problem?"

"I'd appreciate it if you would come with me. I'll meet you in the lobby in fifteen minutes. You may want to change first."

Mason looked down at his beer-stained T-shirt and gym shorts with a hole where the pocket used to be. He realized he was losing on banter and style points.

Doctors, lawyers, and cops all use the same technique when they give bad news. They tell you a little at a time. Knowledge is power—give it away all at once and the power is gone. Having done the same thing, Mason knew better than to press.

He was ten minutes late but smelled better and looked better in tan chinos, a green polo shirt, and deck shoes. The rest of him fit the clean clothes. Dark, closely trimmed hair and steel gray eyes that his aunt Claire always claimed darkened like thunderheads whenever he was angry. An anonymous flying elbow thrown during a muddy rugby scrum had left him with a speed bump on his nose just below eye level. He was clean shaven at seven a.m. but could expect a five-o'clock shadow an hour early. Good orthodontics bred a sincere smile that juries had found persuasive through ten years of practice in his first firm. It had yet to be tested in his new one.

Mason had had some luck and notable failures—his ex-wife, Kate, being foremost—with women. He knew it wasn't politically correct to immediately appraise Kelly as a social prospect, but it filled the time while he waited for her to tell him what was going on.

She showed no more interest in him than in any other out-of-towner she'd awakened on the beach, and she wasn't talking. So Mason took the first shot as they pulled away from the resort in her pickup truck.

"Listen, we can play twenty questions or you can just tell me what this is all about."

She shifted gears as she kept her eyes on the curving road

that snaked away from the lake. A two-way radio crackled with background static. He rested his head against the butt of a shotgun mounted on the rear window.

Kelly chose questions over answers. "When did you last see Mr. Sullivan?"

Mason rolled the window down and let the truck fill with the muggy morning air. The smell of summer flowers and long grass was a welcome change from midtown traffic.

Mason had sat across from Sullivan at last night's poker game, his first with his future former partners. For a ten-dollar buy-in, he spent the evening with a good cigar, a cold beer, and an open window into their psyches. Mason believed that poker made you win with your strengths and fold with your weaknesses. Luck always plays a part, but even the luckiest lousy card player will eventually lose it all if he gives the cards enough time. Sullivan was a good card player, but it sounded like he'd hit a losing streak that would spread to the other partners, who depended on the business he brought in.

"Last night around eleven. We'd been playing poker."

"Who else played?"

"Snow White and the seven dwarfs. All the regulars."

"You were better company before you woke up. Or is this just a phase of your arrested adolescence?"

"Tell me what happened to Sullivan. After that and eight hours of sleep on something besides vinyl, I'll charm your socks off."

She answered without a sideways glance or a hint of humor.

"One of the locals found a body this morning. It's been in the water overnight. The ID belongs to your partner. I want you to tell me if the body belongs to the ID."

CHAPTER TWO

Her voice was pure matter-of-fact, as if she had told him to check the tires and the oil. He caught a quick dip in her shoulders, as if she was dropping her burden of bad news in his lap. Still, she said it with a practiced weariness that convinced Mason she was used to violent death. He wasn't. He was accustomed to family deaths, natural causes, and ritualized grieving. Floating bodies were not part of Mason's life-cycle résumé.

Barring a freakish case of mistaken identity, Mason knew that Sullivan was dead. The odds of his ID being mismatched with a stranger were slim. Mason didn't know him well enough to grieve honestly. Partners are harder to get to know than spouses or friends. Agendas overlap only on narrow ground.

His emotions were a mixed bag that didn't include grief. He was more relieved than sorry. Sullivan's suggestion that Mason destroy evidence in the O'Malley case would be buried with him. Mason could stay at the firm if he chose. Yet he couldn't muster any enthusiasm for reversing his decision to leave. There was no glory in defending Victor O'Malley. His aunt Claire's warning that he wasn't cut out to fight over other people's money, especially when the money was dirty, echoed in his mind.

His recurring dream of Tommy Douchant's trial reminded him of unfinished business that he would have to complete on his own. Sullivan's death may have shown him the way out instead of the way back in.

The sheriff would have told him if Sullivan's death was accidental since there would be no reason to withhold that information. The likelihood that Sullivan's murder was tied to the O'Malley case and perhaps to the documents Sullivan had asked him to lose swept through him like a convulsion.

He was shaken by the twin possibilities that the killer might want to eliminate O'Malley's other lawyer and that the sheriff might suspect him in the crime if she knew what Sullivan had asked him to do. He felt his color drain and hoped the sheriff would attribute it to the grief he couldn't summon. It occurred to him that he was probably the least likely person to identify Sullivan's body.

"Why did you choose me?"

At last she surrendered a small smile.

"You weren't my first choice. We found a key to a room at Buckhorn. It belonged to Mr. Sullivan. The hotel manager gave us a list of the rest of the guests from your firm. You were third on the list. The first two checked out at dawn."

"Harlan Christenson and Scott Daniels."

Harlan Christenson sat next to Mason at the poker table. A shock of white hair hung loosely over his forehead, accenting his coal black caterpillar eyebrows. Shaped like a badly stuffed pillow, he filled his chair to capacity and grunted his bets with a Scotch-scratched voice. Only his head and hands had moved as he'd peeled back the corners of his first three cards, praying for aces.

He was a grandfatherly patrician of Kansas City society, opening doors that Sullivan never could have knocked on. Where Sullivan was brusque and kept everyone at arm's length, Harlan touched everyone. He shook their hands warmly and guided them to his office with his arm comfortably around their shoulders. Together they had built a powerful practice.

He was widowed and Mason was divorced, so he invited Mason to his farmhouse for dinner every couple of weeks after he'd joined the firm. They cooked out and tossed fishing lines in his pond, never really trying to catch anything.

Mason's other best friend and law school classmate, Scott Daniels, had sat on his other side at the card game. Scott and Tommy Douchant had flipped a coin to decide which one would be best man at Mason's wedding. Scott had called heads and won. Tommy claimed he'd used a two-headed coin, a charge Scott never denied.

Scott had started with the firm when they graduated and was now second in command in the business department, which Sullivan ran. Ten years after graduation, he still carried 175 pounds rationed along a swimmer's V-shaped frame. His eyes were robin's-egg blue with the shell's dull finish. Fine dark blond hair, slicked back, etched an undulating hairline along an angular, sallow-cheeked face.

Kelly asked, "Any idea why they left so early?"

"Scott had to get ready for a closing on Monday. Harlan said he had a noon wedding."

"And that left you, Mr. Mason. What were you and your partners doing at the lake?"

"Having our annual retreat. Lawyers, legal assistants, and administrative staff getting away from it all but not each other."

She pulled in at a marina called Jerry's Port. The water rolled with a slight chop stirred by the steady boat traffic of the lake patrol.

Mason's chest tightened along with his throat as he wondered if he'd recognize Sullivan's body. He remembered a wrongful death case he'd handled in which the victim had drowned. A body left in water long enough swells up like an inflatable doll, stretching the features into a macabre mask. The pictures of the deceased in that case had led to a rash of tasteless jokes in his office, none of which he could recall.

Mason followed Kelly to a sheriff's department patrol boat. She drove, while he hoped the spray off the lake would help him keep his cool. Soon she turned toward shore, aiming at a sign that read *Crabtree Cove*. The sides of the cove were lined with private docks. Modest lake homes sat above the docks, away from the water, which fed a shallow marsh at the heel of the inlet. Two other patrol boats were anchored across the back of the cove, forming a floating barricade. Kelly cut the motor to idle, and they coasted past the sentries until the bottom of the boat slid into the soft mud.

Knee-high grass had been tramped down into a rough carpet leading from the water's edge to a short, squat, rumpled man wearing dirty brown coveralls. He could have been half man, half stump, sitting on a log next to a tarp-covered shape that was roughly the size of a body.

"Mr. Mason, say hello to Doc Eddy, Pope County coroner," Kelly said.

"Damn shame, Mason, too bad."

He wiped his hands on his pants before pulling back a corner of the tarp. Sullivan's lifeless eyes stared unblinking into the still rising sun. Heat, water, and death had stolen his attraction and intimidation. Oily engine exhaust mixed with the swampy smell of brackish water and the sickly sweet odor of decomposing flesh. Mason's stomach pitched and yawed as he lost last night's dinner.

He stumbled a few yards away while the aftershocks rocked his belly, and his head slowly stopped spinning. Kelly appeared at his side and pushed a towel into his clammy hand. He was surprised at the softness of her skin when their hands brushed against each other.

"Listen, I'm sorry. There just isn't an easy way to do this. Is it Sullivan?"

The metamorphosis from "him" to "it" suddenly seemed natural. "Yeah, probably—don't know. You better ask his wife."

He was fresh out of smart-ass. Dead bodies, Mason realized, are hell on humor.

"We tried to reach her in Kansas City. No one answered."

"That's because she's here—at the lake. They have a place in Kinchelow Hollow near Shangri-La. We're having brunch over there at eleven this morning."

Kelly turned back toward the coroner. "Doc, we'll meet you at Listrom's Mortuary in an hour. Tell Malcolm to hold the body for identification. Counselor, you come with me to see Mrs. Sullivan."

Kelly aimed him toward the boat with a slight shove. He didn't need the help, but he got the point.

CHAPTER THREE

The path from Sullivan's private dock to the deck on the back of his house followed a switchback route up a slope landscaped with descending terraces set off by railroad ties and planted with a multihued variety of annuals and perennials. If Matisse had been from the Ozarks instead of France, he'd have painted Sullivan's backyard instead of all those gardens.

Kelly and Mason climbed the path while Pamela Sullivan watched them ascend toward her from the protective shade of a moss green canopy suspended over the deck. Mason had met her only once in the last three months. She was cordial but disinterested, a well-cared-for woman accustomed to the role of professional wife.

Mason wanted to protect her from the news that Kelly carried, even though there was no avoiding it. Protecting people when they were in trouble. That's what the law is for, his aunt Claire had taught him. She was his father's sister and the first lawyer, liberal, and hell-raiser in his family.

She wielded the law like a club for her clients, who were usually poor, disadvantaged, or just outnumbered. "There, that one," she would tell him when he was a child and she read the paper to him about the day's injustices. Then she'd be off on another mission.

She raised him after his parents were killed in a car wreck when Mason was only three. She tried talking him out of going to law school, telling him that he wasn't cut out for the only kind of law worth practicing. Her kind. He'd gone anyway, suspecting that she was right. He enjoyed the battle but didn't care enough about the war she never stopped fighting. When he graduated, he joined a small firm that specialized in representing injured people.

"It's the kind of practice where I can do good and do well at the same time," he told her.

"Go sell your slogans to someone else," she said.

Mason thought of Claire as the sun rose at their backs. She called Kelly the intrusive arm of the law—investigating, accusing, and punishing. She taught him that it's the lawyer's duty to shield the individual from that power. That duty drew her to the law. He understood the duty, but it had never held the allure for him that it had for Claire. Still, as they reached Pamela, he could hear Claire's voice telling him, "There, that one."

Pamela had the look of a handsome woman who did not miss the untarnished beauty of her youth. She carried herself with the confident assurance of someone who understood that age brings its own luster.

This morning, a lavender sweatband held back her chin-length chestnut hair. Her face was lightly made up, but not enough to cover the glow from a just-finished morning run. A trace of sweat darkened the scoop neckline of the yellow T-shirt that hung over her matching shorts. She stood with her hands on her hips, her full chest rising and falling with still settling breath, giving them a quizzical look as they topped the stairs.

"Oh my, excuse me. It's Lou, isn't it?" she asked him with sudden recognition.

"Yes, Pamela. I'm one of your husband's partners. We met a couple of months ago."

"Of course. Please excuse me. I wasn't expecting you or the police," she added, turning toward Kelly and extending her hand. "I'm Pamela Sullivan. But I expect you know that or you wouldn't be here. What can I do for you, Officer?"

Kelly shook her hand quickly and firmly. "Mrs. Sullivan, I'm Sheriff Kelly Holt. Would you mind if we spoke inside?"

"My, this is starting to sound quite official." Kelly didn't reply and Pamela's refined control showed the first sign of fraying as she held her arms folded across her chest. "Yes, it is a bit cool this morning, isn't it?"

It wasn't close to being cool, but Mason understood Pamela's sudden chill. There was no possible explanation for their visit that could include good news. As if she sensed their purpose, Pamela led them through a sliding door, taking her time to delay the inevitable a few seconds longer.

They followed Pamela through a sliding glass door and into the den. She eased herself onto a sofa, her careful movement underscoring the fragility of the moment. Uncertain of his status, Mason stood near the sliding door. Kelly sat on the edge of a chair next to Pamela.

"I'm sorry to intrude on you, Mrs. Sullivan," Kelly began in a soothing voice that quickly gave way to a crisp matter-of-factness. "A man's body was found this morning in a cove not far from here. A wallet was also found with your husband's driver's license and credit cards. The man generally matches your husband's physical description. Mr. Mason thinks it may be your husband."

Pamela held fast as her jaw tightened and her eyes widened at the implications. She shook her head in response to the inevitable question of whether she knew where her husband was. Kelly's request that she identify the body left Pamela mute and renewed Mason's protective instincts.

"Sheriff, I'll bring Mrs. Sullivan, but I would think my identification is sufficient."

Kelly acknowledged his offer without taking her eyes from Pamela. "You're welcome to come along, Counselor, but identification has to be made by next of kin if possible." Her soothing tone was reserved for the newly widowed. He was entitled only to her official voice. "You can bring Mrs. Sullivan in her car."

"I'm not a native, Sheriff. I'll need directions."

"I'm certain of that," she replied. "Take County Road F to Lake Road 5-47 and pick up Highway 5 south. Go across Hurricane Deck Bridge and take the highway all the way to Starlight. Listrom's Mortuary is on the square. I've got to return the boat, and I'll meet you there."

CHAPTER FOUR

Doc Eddy greeted Mason and Pamela at the mortuary. He introduced Malcolm Listrom as the finest mortician in Pope County, able to restore the departed to grandeur they had never achieved while among the living. He was so effusive in his praise of Malcolm's gift that Mason decided the coroner was in for a cut.

Malcolm basked in Eddy's praise while emitting appropriate solicitous sounds of sympathy for the bereaved. When Mason told him that the deceased was just passing through and would be buried in Kansas City, he became a waiter trying to turn his table. Kelly arrived a few minutes later and Malcolm led them to the room where he prepared bodies for burial.

Malcolm plied his magic in a ceramic-tiled, circular operating room dominated by two large surgical tables in the center. Glass-covered cabinets filled with unfamiliar solutions and tools lined the walls. The air was heavy with disinfectant that made their eyes water. Sullivan lay on one of the tables covered in an off-white sheath and adorned with a vanilla toe tag marked *John Doe*.

"I'm afraid I haven't repaired the damage, Mrs. Sullivan," Listrom apologized. "We're not allowed to prepare the body until the authorities approve."

Pamela nodded, but Mason wasn't certain she had really heard him. He stood behind her as Listrom pulled back the sheet.

"No, you bastard, not like this," Pamela said as she slumped into Mason's arms.

He half carried her into a waiting room and set her onto a sofa beneath a comforting portrait of Jesus, smiling beneficently, hands outstretched. Kelly followed them, murmured her condolences to Pamela, and motioned Doc Eddy and Mason to an adjoining office.

Mason asked, "Has anyone made a determination of the cause of death?"

"Can't tell yet," Doc Eddy said. "He's got a knot on the back of his head. May have fallen and hit something. Won't know for sure until we give him the canoe treatment."

"Canoe treatment?"

Eddy laughed. "The incision goes stem to stern. Just like hollowing out a log for a canoe. It's an old coroner's joke."

His crack made Mason punch up his defense of Pamela a notch. "I doubt if Pamela will want an autopsy. She's been through enough."

"An autopsy is required in the case of all suspicious deaths. Doc Eddy will do it this afternoon," Kelly said.

"Wait a minute! You just said he hit his head and fell in. He probably drowned. There's nothing suspicious or unexplained about that. There's no reason to put Pamela through that."

"A ski boat belonging to Sullivan was found tied up at the Buckhorn marina this morning. We found an earring on the boat, and your partner doesn't look like the earring type. I doubt if he hit his head, fell in, and the boat drove itself back to the marina. I'm betting someone helped him into the water. I'm sorry if that's hard on Mrs. Sullivan, but that's the way it is."

"If you're going to question her, you'll do it in my presence and you'll stop when I tell you."

He was drawing lines for a client who hadn't retained him. Claire would have told him he was finally showing some promise. He and Kelly eyed each other, trying to guess when the confrontation that was brewing between them would finally erupt.

"Take her back to her house, and I'll meet you there in an hour. Questioning is always more productive immediately following a death. I've been through this enough times to know that."

"Yeah, Sheriff, I'll bet that the lake is a real hotbed of murder and mayhem."

Her withering stare confirmed that he'd just made an ass of himself. He conceded the moment to her and shepherded Pamela to the car.

They made it back to Sullivan's just before eleven. Diane Farrell, Sullivan's legal assistant for ten years, was sprawled on the doorstep. She was leaning against a brown grocery bag filled with fresh fruit for the brunch, flicking ashes from her cigarette into clay pots brimming with red, pink, and violet impatiens. Pamela walked past her without comment, too dazed to speak.

Diane was plain and thick with a blocky face bolted to a rectangular body. Her hair was a washed-out brown matching the grocery bag. She had dark, wide-set eyes, a nose too small for her broad face, and thin lips on a downturned mouth.

She promoted and protected Sullivan as if he were her own. Try to go around her or behind her and you'd probably end up just going—to another firm. Office scuttlebutt had her madly in love with Sullivan, though no one could picture them together. Sullivan played only with beautiful women. Ordinary need not apply. But she had job security and a kinship with Pamela, who welcomed her as a link to her wandering husband.

"Mason, what's going on? Where's Sullivan?" she asked.

Mason knew Diane well enough to dislike her, and he disliked her enough not to soften the blow.

"He's dead, Diane. Someone found him floating in the lake this morning. Pamela and I just identified the body."

She studied his face for some hint that it wasn't true. Her eyes were like black holes, sucking in everything and emitting no light. When he didn't recant, she went inside, calling for Pamela. Her stoic response made him feel like a heel for smacking her with the news.

Mason spent the next twenty minutes telling his colleagues, as they arrived for brunch, that even though the firm's biggest producer was dead, everything would be fine. They didn't believe it and neither did he, but it was the sort of thing people said and accepted when bad news was too fresh to argue with. Some wanted to stay and help. But he told them there wasn't anything for them to do.

He was waiting for the sheriff. Claire's voice wouldn't let him leave Pamela to be questioned without a lawyer. When the last group drove away, he picked up Diane's fruit and went into the house.

CHAPTER FIVE

No one was in the den, and he was enough of a stranger not to knock on closed bedroom doors. Diane emerged a few minutes later, dry-eyed, with her normal shade of pale.

"How's Pamela?"

"Her husband is dead, so that's a bummer. Other than that, I don't know."

"The sheriff will be here soon to question her. I'll stay for that. You don't have to stick around."

"She expects me to stay, Mason. You play lawyer. I'll take care of Pamela."

One more reason not to envy Pamela, he decided.

Kelly arrived at noon. Mason introduced Diane, who studied Kelly's badge like it was counterfeit before saying that she would ask Pamela to join them.

Pamela had showered, changed, and added fresh makeup and appeared composed as she returned to the den. She and Kelly took the same seats as before. Mason stood at Pamela's left with Diane on her right. They were a mismatched pair of sentries.

"When did you last see your husband, Mrs. Sullivan?" Kelly began.

"Last night about seven o'clock. We were supposed to go to Buckhorn for dinner. We had a fight and he left."

Mason drifted away from Pamela's chair so that he could watch her face for any signs of weakness that would trigger his instruction not to answer any more questions.

Kelly continued. "What did you fight about?"

"I never remember anymore. We just fight."

"Where did he go?"

"He took the ski boat. I watched him from the kitchen window."

"Which way did he go when he left the cove?"

"Toward Turkey Bend."

"Do you know anyone who lives up that way whom he might have gone to visit?"

"No, we don't have many friends at the lake. We have a lot of visitors, and they either stay with us or at a client's condo."

"Whose condo is that?"

"One of Richard's clients has a condominium in a cove near here. I don't know who really owns it. Richard never talked about his clients. I only knew that he was able to use it for guests when we entertained at the lake."

"Did you have guests at the condo this weekend?"

"No."

"Do you water-ski, Mrs. Sullivan?"

"No, why do you ask?"

"Has anyone else used the ski boat recently other than your husband?"

"No, and he doesn't ski anymore either. He says his knees can't take it. He just uses the boat for transportation."

"Mrs. Sullivan, the lake patrol found your husband's boat at dawn. It was abandoned. I wonder if you can identify this earring that was found on the boat?"

Kelly handed her an evidence bag containing a single gold hoop earring. Pamela reached for her ear and removed one of her own clasp hoops.

"It's not mine, if that's what you mean. I've never pierced my ears."

Kelly's silence told Mason that she knew her business. She would learn more by listening than by asking. Pamela let the silence hang for a moment. She pulled herself upright, looked directly at Kelly, and answered with a last shot of dignity.

"The earring probably belongs to someone younger with a flat belly and firm tits and I don't know her name. Now, if you'll excuse me, it's been a long morning."

She rose and turned away. Diane padded behind her as they retreated into the bedroom.

"Son of a bitch!" Mason said.

"Seems likely," Kelly added.

"How about a ride back to Buckhorn, Sheriff?"

"Sorry, Counselor. I'm not running a taxi service."

"I wasn't planning on tipping you. You dragged me into this mess. You can't leave me stranded here."

"Yes, I can. Your partner's death isn't neat and tidy, and I like neat-and-tidy deaths. Now, if you don't mind, I've got a lot of work to do."

"Maybe I can help." Her arched eyebrows told him that she didn't think so. "Look, I admit I'm a reflex smart-ass. But I helped identify the body and brought you here. And I was just trying to protect Pamela."

Mason doubted that Sullivan had died of natural causes, as any decent asshole would have done. O'Malley's indictment on charges that he'd skimmed money from the bank that he owned was inevitable. Sullivan had done everything but confess to helping O'Malley steal the money when he asked Mason to lose documents that incriminated him. Mason knew that Sullivan's only chance to save himself would be to testify against his client. O'Malley couldn't invoke the attorney-client privilege to prevent Sullivan from testifying about their crimes. O'Malley's best defense would be a lawyer who was too dead to testify. Mason was the only other lawyer in the firm who knew what Sullivan knew—or who knew what Sullivan had intimated to him. If Sullivan had been murdered, Mason wanted to know sooner rather than later. His protective instincts were becoming self-centered.

"Who said she needs protection, Counselor?"

"Anybody who starts the day with a dead husband needs protection."

"Miss Farrell can take you back to Buckhorn. This is an official investigation. I don't need any volunteers."

"Don't worry. I'm going home today, but I've got an obligation to my partners to find out what happened." Though true, that was the least of his concerns. But it was the only excuse he could use until he knew whether Sullivan had been murdered. If Sullivan's death wasn't murder, telling Kelly that both his client and his dead partner were crooks would put him on O'Malley's hit list. "Just tell me what your next step is. Maybe I really can help."

Kelly sighed, as if he would accept her annoyance as an answer. His silence said not likely.

"Okay. I follow the most logical line of investigation. That means find out where Sullivan went and who he was with before he died. He left his house around seven. Mrs. Sullivan saw him heading toward a client's condo. I want to know where it is and who owns it."

"How will you find it?"

"I'll start with county records of property ownership."

"Perfect. I may recognize a name and save you a lot of trouble."

Kelly looked at him as if she'd just found a stray dog and couldn't decide whether to feed it or take it to the pound.

"I hope you're ready for a long ride home. I've got some stops to make."

"Sheriff, I'm like lunch meat; I'm always ready."

CHAPTER SIX

Kelly punched in a number on her cell phone as they pulled away in her pickup truck, leaving the call on speaker.

"Riley, it's Kelly. Get your lazy ass off your back porch and meet me at the courthouse in half an hour."

The playful teasing in her voice told Mason that Riley didn't have a lazy ass. He wondered what kind of ass Riley really had that caused Kelly to react that way.

"Listen, little girl. I got you that badge, and I can have it back in a heartbeat. Your daddy never woulda talked that way to me."

Riley's voice was filled with pleasure that said they'd played this piece many times before. Kelly's laughter was rich, lighting her eyes.

Mason was relieved that Riley sounded a generation removed. He was also surprised at his relief. He had lost track of the different emotional chords Kelly had struck with him in less than half a day.

"Friend of yours?" Mason asked.

"Riley Brooks has been the register of deeds since I was a girl. He talked me into taking this job until a new sheriff is elected in November."

"What happened to the other sheriff?"

"He got carried away with strip-searching women who ran stop signs. Someone had to finish out his term."

"Don't tell me you weren't first choice, Sheriff?"

Kelly gave him another annoyed glance. She seemed to have an inexhaustible supply.

"I was an FBI agent for ten years. My partner was killed last winter. I quit and came home. End of story. Now, tell me about the poker game. When did it start?"

Mason didn't blame her for being more interested in figuring out who killed Sullivan than in becoming his new best friend, so he didn't mind changing the subject.

"After dinner, about eight."

"Was Sullivan there when the game started?"

"No, he didn't get there until after nine."

"So we've got at least two hours unaccounted for. Give me the names of the players and, this time, leave out your imaginary playmates."

"Scott Daniels, Sandra Connelly, who runs the litigation department, Harlan Christenson, Angela Molina, Phil Rosa, and me."

"Who are Angela and Phil?"

"Angela is the executive director of the firm, chief bean counter, and administrator. Phil Rosa is an associate. One of the rising stars in litigation."

"Was Sullivan alone when he left the card game?"

Mason hesitated because he knew where she was headed. She was interested in more than tracking Sullivan's movements in the hours before he died. She was making a list, probably a short one, of suspects. Mason didn't know whether she would put his name on that list if she learned that Sullivan had asked Mason to commit a crime. He didn't want to find out. All he could do was steer her investigation away from the O'Malley case until he knew if Sullivan had been murdered. If he had been, Mason would tell her everything and put his faith in the system.

Kelly cut through his hesitation. "If you don't tell me, Counselor, someone else will. Someone always sees something, and they're always anxious to talk about it."

Mason knew she was right.

"Sullivan left with Cara Trent, one of the law school students who work for us during the summer."

"I'll need a list of the names, addresses, and phone numbers of everyone who was at the retreat, especially Cara Trent. I've only got the partners' names so far. Chances are one of them will know where Sullivan was before and after the card game."

"I've got a firm directory at the hotel. You can have it."

"Fine. Let's start with you. Where were you last night?"

The color rose in Mason's cheeks as he considered the tone of her question.

"I was in my room before the card game, and I spent the rest of the night on the beach where you found me this morning."

"Alone?"

"Alone. Before and after."

"Did you talk with anyone? Did anyone see you?"

"I had room service. You can check with the hotel."

"What about when you were on the beach?"

"Just a couple who were too busy with each other to notice me. You better take me in, Sheriff. I confess. The job was too good. I couldn't stand all the money."

"Let's hope everyone else is so helpful."

The corners of her mouth creased in a neat smile. *Well, even the Berlin Wall eventually came down,* Mason thought.

"Was Sullivan working on anything that might make someone want to kill him?"

He should have expected the question, but her smile had left him flat-footed. He had felt the same way in his last rugby match when a forward got past him with a fake pass. There was a reason that that move was called a dummy. And he was it.

"The firm has a lot of clients. They have a lot of problems, and they are unhappy about all of them."

"I spent the last ten years sifting through more double-talk than you can imagine. Make this easy on both of us and tell me if any of those clients might want to kill him."

"I'm not going to speculate about any client. If it turns out that my partner was murdered, I'll tell you everything I can. Until then, I can't tell you anything because of the attorney-client privilege. I'm sure the FBI has heard of that."

"Mason, I'll make this simple. If you withhold information in a murder investigation, I'll shove your smart mouth right up your smart ass. Are we clear on that?"

"They teach you how to do that at the FBI Academy?"

"The first day."

CHAPTER SEVEN

Kelly downshifted as they rolled into the center of the county seat, Starlight, Missouri. The Pope County Courthouse was a classic colonial edifice at least sixty years old. It rose from the center of the town square, with Missouri limestone columns guarding the entrances on all four sides. A Civil War cannon stood resolutely on the south quadrangle. Neatly manicured grass, still lush in spite of the midsummer heat, fanned out from the foundation, flanked by concrete sidewalks.

The courthouse reminded Mason of Tommy Douchant's case. It had been his job to do well and do good for Tommy, and he had done neither. His slogan had never proven to be so empty. Afterward, he went over every detail of the trial with Claire.

"Do it over again," she told him.

"I can't get a new trial without new evidence. You know that."

"Then get the evidence and quit feeling sorry for yourself and Tommy. I can't stand pathetic."

He promised himself that he would. It had been four months since Tommy's trial and three months since he'd started at Sullivan & Christenson. He'd discussed the case at the first partners' meeting he attended after joining the firm. No one was interested in investing time and money in a case that had already been lost. His promise was gathering dust.

Riley Brooks met them in the office of the register of deeds. He was well past six feet, with a skin-and-bones frame that made him appear even taller. A ring of gray hair circled his bald head like that of an ill-kempt tonsured monk. He sat on the edge of a table, his high-top sneakers tapping the linoleum.

"What'll it be, Kelly? Drug smugglers? Terrorists?" he asked, rubbing his hands together, hoping for both.

Kelly feigned irritation, but her eyes said she was glad to see him.

"Just property ownership records, Riley. I'll save the bad guys for regular office hours."

Riley, disappointed but dutiful, dug up the plans for the coves that included Sullivan's house and the four coves between it and the dam, which was the direction Pamela Sullivan had last seen her husband heading. The legal descriptions enabled him to print out the names of the owners from the county's computer system. Reminding Kelly to lock up when they were done, Riley left them alone in the courthouse.

"If we divide the records, we'll be done faster," Mason suggested.

Kelly tore the printout in half. "Recognize any names?"

Mason recognized one name and wasn't surprised when he saw it. He was willing to dodge her other questions, but he wouldn't lie to her.

"Just one, SOM, Inc."

"Who or what is that?"

"A company owned by Richard Sullivan and Victor O'Malley."

"I don't suppose O'Malley is one of those dangerously unhappy clients."

"He pays his bills on time."

"Thanks. I was beginning to think I'd have to torture you for information."

"Does this mean I get a deputy's badge?"

"Not yet. I don't want the responsibility if you injure yourself pinning it on. Let's go see if anyone is home at SOM's condo."

The condominium was two coves away from Sullivan's. The condo was part of a garden-style project with two units on each of three floors. SOM's was on the top floor. No one answered when they knocked. Kelly and Mason walked around to the back and peered through the sliding door on the balcony. They were about to give up when a woman appeared on the balcony of the other top-floor condo.

"It's about time you people showed up. I've been complaining for months."

She was short with the kind of fat that begins at the ankles and ends just below the ears. Her sundress billowed from her shoulders like a two-man tent.

"I'm Sheriff Holt. What have you been complaining about?"

"I know who you are, honey! I read the papers. Who's your boyfriend?" She ran her eyes over Mason, shaking her head, and whispered loud enough to make certain he heard. "Nice looking but soft. Stick to the local talent, Sheriff. Ozark men got better staying power."

Kelly swallowed her laughter and introduced Mason. Velma Marie Fouche invited them in for a cup of coffee and conversation, both of which were served in a living room furnished with one of the few remaining knotty-pine pit groups.

"I'm sorry, Velma, but I haven't been told about your complaints. Bring me up to date."

Velma warmed to Kelly's easy manner. Mason was learning that she had a style for every occasion.

"It's the women. Every week there's a new batch. It's disgusting!"

"Tell me about the women."

"Oh, you know. They're young and pretty and bouncy."

"Who are they with?"

"Men old enough to be their fathers!"

"Have they bothered you?"

"Nope."

Kelly smiled. "Then what's the problem?"

"My husband. He sees these sweet young things and gets ideas. Won't leave me alone, and I need my rest."

Mason choked on his coffee, but Kelly didn't miss a beat.

"I'll see to it that we look into your complaints. Did you see any of these people last night?"

"Well, I couldn't sleep, so I went out on the balcony for some air, and I seen two of 'em walk down to the dock and get in a boat."

"What time was it?"

"Close to midnight."

"What kind of boat?"

"One of them powerboats, like the skiers use. Can't stand 'em—they're too loud and they scare the fish off."

"Can you describe the people you saw?"

"She was a long-legged blonde. Busty and crawlin' all over him like ants at a picnic. He was one of the regulars. I couldn't see him too well, but I recognized him from all the times I seen him here. Jockey size and suckin' in his gut tryin' to look sharp."

"Did they come back?"

"Just her. Maybe an hour later. She was here and gone."

Velma didn't remember anything else. Kelly thanked her for the coffee and her help, gave her a business card, and told her to call if she remembered something more. They tried the rest of the units. No one else had seen the blonde or her jockey-sized companion.

"Sullivan fits the description of the man Velma saw," Kelly said as they drove back to Buckhorn. "Does Cara Trent fit the description of the woman?"

"As much as any good-looking blonde."

"Why was Sullivan staying at the hotel if he and his wife had a house at the lake, and he and O'Malley owned that condo?"

"The retreat is supposed to build camaraderie. Can't do that if we don't all stay in the same place."

"Maybe, but so far it doesn't sound like Sullivan spent much time in his room. Do you suppose that Victor O'Malley knew that Sullivan used their condo to cheat on his wife?"

Mason wasn't surprised that Kelly kept changing the subject. He used the same technique when questioning a witness. It kept the witness from getting too comfortable with the questions.

"I don't suppose anything, but O'Malley doesn't strike me as someone who would care."

"So why would O'Malley want Sullivan dead?"

"You don't give up, do you? You can't decide whether to arrest everyone in the firm or everyone the firm represents."

"People get killed for a lot of reasons, including not telling the police what they need to know soon enough to save themselves."

"I'll keep that in mind," Mason said.

CHAPTER EIGHT

They drove in silence the rest of the way to the hotel. Kelly parked her truck in the circle drive at the hotel entrance and got out.

"You don't have to come in," Mason told her. "I'll get the firm directory from my room and bring it to you."

"I'm more interested in Sullivan's room. And I've got the key."

"Don't you need a warrant to search his room?"

"Not if you let me in. Do you want the hotel maids to throw away any firm files Sullivan may have brought with him?"

Mason knew that Kelly could have asked Pamela Sullivan or the hotel manager to let her in. Neither would have refused. His refusal would only add to her suspicion that he was holding back information. He realized that she wanted to see his reaction to anything they found in Sullivan's room. Mason had spent the day reacting to events beyond his control, hoping to nudge the investigation away from O'Malley. It was like trying to hold back a rising river with a single sandbag.

They stopped at his room first, and he gave Kelly the firm directory. It listed every employee's name, direct-dial number, cell phone number, and e-mail address.

"Here's your list of suspects."

"Well, I can cross off one name."

"Whose?"

"Sullivan's. I don't think he committed suicide."

"That's very funny for a sheriff."

"Wait until you hear my good material."

She sounded coy, which confused Mason. He studied her for a clue. She offered none. She cycled through the good cop, bad cop routine so often that he thought she might be schizophrenic. If she was trying to keep him off balance, she was succeeding. Kelly was smart and attractive and gave fleeting suggestions that she liked him—all of which he could succumb to if she gave him a chance. But he knew that she'd put his head on a pike outside the village gates if she thought he was involved in Sullivan's murder.

She led the way to Sullivan's room and handed Mason the key. They smiled at each other and Mason fantasized for an instant that they had checked in for a more pleasant purpose.

"Not in your dreams, Counselor," Kelly said.

"If man doesn't dream, he has nothing."

"A man whose dreams will never come true still has nothing. Open the door."

Sullivan had a suite instead of the single room Mason had been assigned. A briefcase sat on a desk in one corner of the living room. Mason walked past a sofa and entertainment center and picked up the briefcase while Kelly checked out the bedroom.

He popped the latches on the briefcase, surprised that it wasn't locked. Once he saw the contents, he knew why. It was an inventory of insignificance: Friday's *Wall Street Journal*, the agenda for the retreat, a paperback copy of a John Grisham novel, a CD case titled *Johnny's Greatest Hits*, containing a lifetime supply of Johnny Mathis. He left it open for Kelly to see.

"Find anything interesting?" she called from the bedroom.

"Nothing. How about you?"

"Just this," she said as she returned to the front room, holding a letter-sized sheet of white paper by one corner. She set it on the desk next to the briefcase. "Don't touch it. Just read it."

It was a typewritten memo from Sullivan to Harlan Christenson dated two days earlier. Mason read it, aware that Kelly was watching each twitch he was fighting to control.

"Lou told me today that Victor O'Malley would be convicted unless we lost certain documents that he had found in our files. I

31

told him no. I'm not going to take any chances with him. I'll fire him on Monday after the retreat. There's no reason to ruin the weekend because of one person. If he tries to cause any trouble, I'll report him to the state bar and he'll be disbarred."

He looked up, expecting her to have drawn her gun and her Miranda card at the same time. Instead, he caught a glimpse of sadness before she resumed her official tone with a single question.

"Is it true?"

"I realize that we've only known each other a few hours, but do I look stupid to you?"

Mason slammed the briefcase shut, stood straight, arms half-cocked toward her, daring her to say yes.

"A lot of killers look pretty smart. They just do stupid things that get them caught."

"So how am I supposed to prove that I didn't have a conversation with a dead man?"

"Tell me about O'Malley's case and tell me you didn't advise Sullivan that the firm should lose those documents."

Mason let out an exasperated breath, clasped his hands behind his head, and did a quick circuit of the room. Kelly stood still, watching him orbit around her, while he decided how much of the truth to tell her. He decided to stick with what had already been reported by the press.

"Victor O'Malley was Sullivan's biggest client. Franklin St. John is about to indict him for bank fraud. I'm defending him."

"That's half an answer. Tell me the rest of it."

Mason didn't care about Sullivan anymore. Sullivan was dead and had set him up with the memo. But O'Malley was still his client, and if he told Kelly too much, he could lose his license. He drew a line only a lawyer could stand on without crossing.

"Sullivan and I had lunch on Friday and talked about the case. The rest of it is bullshit."

"And you won't tell me what you talked about because you're more concerned about attorney-client privilege than going to jail for murder. That memo reads like a good motive. You kill Sullivan and you keep your job."

"Give me a break, Sheriff. That memo reads like a good example of libel, which is a motive for a lawsuit, not murder."

"So Sullivan struck first and you struck back. Malice begets malice. Libel to kill."

"That's poetic, but, believe me, Sullivan wasn't worth it and the job wasn't worth it. I'd already decided to quit."

"Why? Because of your lunchtime chat with Sullivan?"

Mason stopped pacing. "That's only part of it. I've got a case that the firm won't take. I'm going out on my own so I can handle it."

"That's your idea of a defense?"

"I'll tell you what. You subpoena every memo Sullivan ever wrote about O'Malley. This is the only one you'll find, if he even wrote it. I've been through those files. Sullivan got things done. He didn't write memos. And he wouldn't wait to fire me or his mother because of the damn retreat."

"So why did he write the memo?"

"To set me up."

"Why wouldn't he just get rid of the documents himself? And why would he need to set you up?"

Mason didn't answer. He sat on the arm of the sofa and let her think out loud, nodding as she said it.

"If you get rid of the documents and get caught, the memo gives him plausible deniability. If you refused, he could get rid of the evidence and still blame you if anyone ever found out. In the meantime, you're gone."

"Now, you, Sheriff, you put on one hell of a defense."

"Then show me the documents."

"I can't."

"You've got to get over this privilege stuff. This is a murder investigation until the coroner tells me differently, and you're working your way up the suspect list."

"It's not just the privilege. I've been through those files. I don't know what documents he's talking about. Let me know when the coroner makes up his mind. I'm going home."

She handed him Sullivan's briefcase. "I'll let you return this to Mrs. Sullivan. Drive safely."

He hoped that she meant it.

CHAPTER NINE

Straight, flat roads are hard to find in the Ozarks. Two-lane county roads and state highways bob and weave like a punch-drunk fighter across and around the hilly countryside. Mason plugged his iPhone into the car radio, letting Bettye LaVette sing him home as he maneuvered his Acura in and out of small packs of slow-moving cars.

He took Highway 52 west through Eldon and on to the junction with Highway 5, where he headed north, hoping to leave the plodding traffic behind. Soon a black Escalade pulled up behind him, rode his rear end long enough to get Mason's attention, then bolted past him and another car, cutting back into the northbound lane just in time to avoid an oncoming RV.

The car in front of Mason turned off the highway a few minutes later. Mason caught a glimpse of the Escalade and closed the distance until a quarter of a mile separated them. Content to cruise at seventy, he let go the chase.

Ten minutes later, the Escalade slowed until Mason was within a couple of car lengths, the rolling grade preventing him from passing. They reached a level stretch of road when the driver of the Escalade stuck his hand out the window and waved Mason to go around.

He eased into the southbound lane and accelerated, pulling alongside the Escalade. He started to wave his thanks when he saw that the window was up and tinted so dark he couldn't see the driver, who was matching Mason's pace, freezing him in the southbound lane.

Mason pushed the Acura harder, unable to gain any ground and unwilling to drop back. He was hot enough, tired enough, and annoyed enough to keep pushing and not notice that the road had bottomed out like the trough of a wave. As they started back up the next hill, an air horn bellowed from a southbound flatbed tractor-trailer loaded with hay bales bearing down on Mason from the crest of the hill.

Mason answered with a squeal from his own horn, but neither driver changed course. At their combined speeds, he realized the truck would be in his lap before he could pass the Escalade. Mason hit his brakes, intending to swerve back into his lane behind the Escalade, only to see the Escalade slow down, hanging him out in the wrong lane, threatening to turn him into a hood ornament.

The truck was close enough that Mason could see the driver, mouth opened wide, screaming at him and waving his hand, telling Mason to get out of the way. Mason screamed back, unable to hear his own voice over the wind, the road, and their dueling horns. He felt as if he were flying and knew he would be when the truck hit him.

A thin strip of gravel separated the paved road from the tall grass alongside it. Barbed wire strung between steel fence posts marked the outer boundary of a farm. Cows on the captive side of the fence looked up as if they sensed that something was about to happen that even they couldn't ignore.

Mason pounded on his horn, screamed again at the driver of the truck and the driver of the Escalade. His hands slid around the wheel, greased by the sweat pouring off of him faster than the wind could dry it.

The Escalade cut off any retreat. The truck slowed, causing the trailer to shimmy and its load to rock sideways. But Mason knew the driver couldn't slow quickly enough, the certainty of the impending crash clear in the driver's stricken eyes.

Out of options, Mason spun the steering wheel hard to his left and jammed the gas pedal to the floor. The Acura bolted off the road and shuddered in the wake left by the truck as it blew past, their front bumpers exchanging air kisses.

The ground dropped off from the road, and in the next instant, Mason flew toward the cows like an unguided missile. The Acura landed hard and fishtailed clockwise. Mason fought the wheel, found the brakes, and rode out the spin until the car bounced to a stop against the barbed wire.

His airbag exploded, burying him in a fierce embrace. The jolt was no worse than the countless hits he'd absorbed playing rugby, though those blows were thrown in sport. This was a cold, calculated attempt to put him on the shelf—permanently.

Mason climbed out of the Acura and scanned the road. The Escalade had disappeared. He walked around the car, checking for damage. The barbed wire had etched an abstract pattern in the paint on the passenger side, but it was otherwise unscathed.

He leaned against the hood, waited for his heart rate to slow to suborbital speed, and tried to put the day's events into perspective. Richard Sullivan was dead, probably murdered and last seen with an attractive blonde, not his wife, at a condo he owned with Victor O'Malley.

Mason was defending O'Malley against criminal charges the feds were about to file. Sullivan had set up Mason as the fall guy in a scheme to get rid of evidence that had to incriminate both Sullivan and O'Malley. And someone had just tried to kill him and make his death look like the result of his own reckless driving.

It wasn't hard to connect the dots. The picture just didn't make any sense. He realized that he'd have to take a closer look at the O'Malley files in the morning. If he lived that long.

CHAPTER TEN

Mason lived in a neighborhood thick with large houses built during and just after World War II. The area was a magnet that held on to older people with old money and attracted boomers with new money. A fixer-upper easily ran half a million even after the recession knocked property values into the basement. The house belonged to Claire until she gave it to him when he graduated from law school.

"I lived in this house for twenty-six years before you came along, and now I'm fifty-five," she told him. "That's too long in one place for anybody. I need a fresh start. I bought a loft in a rehabbed warehouse in the Crossroads District. There's an artist on the first floor that uses his kitchen as his gallery. A couple of tech geeks took the second floor for their start-up something or other, and I've got the third floor."

Kate winced at the condition of the interior when she moved in.

"You've got Ethan Allen, futons, chrome and glass Scandinavian, oriental rugs so threadbare a moth wouldn't use them for a snack, Grateful Dead posters, and pictures of dead immigrants."

"Think of it as multigeneration chic," Mason said. "And the dead immigrants are my great-grandparents."

The mud-colored brick on the two-story Colonial had held up better than the weather-beaten white shutters. Kate stuck her fingers in the spongy, wood-rotted window frames and called a contractor.

The house was a block south of Loose Park, a sprawling green space perfect for walking with your girlfriend or running with your dog. Mason hadn't had a girlfriend or a dog since he and Kate got divorced a year ago.

They rescued a dog from the pound soon after they were married, a German shepherd–collie she named Tuffy because she was anything but tough. Mason spoiled Tuffy like an only child and the dog returned his affection. Custody of the dog was the last battle they fought in the divorce. Kate won when she dognapped Tuffy and dared him to complain to the judge.

Mason paid a guy to mow the lawn, rake the leaves, and shovel the snow, which he considered a fair contribution to urban gentrification. Still, most of the neighbors averted their eyes when they walked by, and he swore that a few crossed the street to avoid a close encounter. Maybe it was the untrimmed oak trees, whose low-hanging, heavy branches scraped the yard. Or maybe it was the blue floodlight he'd used to replace the burned-out porch light.

The only exception was Anna Karelson, who lived across the street. Anna and Mason were "wave and hello" neighbors. He waved and she said "hello." When Kate moved out, she began crossing the street to visit with him on the sidewalk, commiserating about her unhappy marriage as if that made them kindred spirits. Last week, she told him that she was going to hire a lawyer.

It was eight o'clock when Mason pulled into the driveway. He'd taken his time the rest of the way home from the lake, flinching every time a black SUV came near him.

Scott Daniels was pacing the sidewalk in front of his house. He and Mason had met during the first week of law school. Mason was amazed that Scott had already outlined the assignments for the first two weeks of class. Scott was amazed that Mason understood the material after a single reading. They studied together, Scott mastering the details while Mason painted the big picture.

The combination got them through law school in the top ten of their class. They shared an apartment in Kansas City after graduation until Scott got married. Mason was his best man, a favor Scott returned at Mason's wedding.

"I was at the office getting ready for my closing when Harlan called about Sullivan," Scott said as he followed Mason into the house. "Harlan has called a partners' meeting for eight o'clock tomorrow morning."

Mason dropped his bag on the kitchen floor and grabbed two bottles of Bud Light from the refrigerator, handing one to Scott and leading him onto the redbrick patio, where he slumped into a lounge chair.

"I helped Pamela identify the body. I can go a long time without doing that again."

Scott took a long pull on his bottle, wiping his mouth with his sleeve.

"Sullivan really knows how to screw up a good retreat."

"Better yet, the sheriff thinks he was murdered."

Scott stopped cold, his bottle dangling from his hand. "Get out!"

"She can't prove it yet, but his body was found in a cove on one side of the lake, and his boat was found at Buckhorn's marina. She also found a gold earring on the boat and Pamela says it isn't hers."

"That sounds more like adultery than murder. Who does he suspect?"

"I said 'she.' Her name is Kelly Holt. And she suspects everyone who hated Sullivan or stood to gain from his death. It's what cops do."

Scott drained the last drops from his bottle. "Well, if that's the test, I'll make her list."

Mason looked at him, wide-eyed. "Is that a confession?"

"Yeah, right. But you know that I hated the son of a bitch, and I'll inherit his clients. Sullivan was a total shit to work for. Nothing was ever right or good enough."

"That's not news. You've been complaining about Sullivan since the day you started. But you never complained about the money."

"Because I'm smart enough to know that I'm a good lawyer but a lousy salesman. I did all the work while he played golf. And I don't play golf. I guess I'll have to learn if I want to hold on to his clients."

Mason had listened to Scott complain for years. It was the one thing that had made him hesitate about joining the firm. He'd finally decided that Scott's grousing was just his way of dealing with the stress of his practice. Sullivan's death added an unsettling context to his complaints and put Scott on Kelly Holt's list.

"What happens to the firm without Sullivan?" Mason asked.

"Nothing good. You remember the death benefit I told you about?"

"Sure. If a partner dies, the firm has to buy out his ownership interest."

"Right. The firm bought life insurance on each of the partners to pay for the buyout."

"So the insurance pays off Sullivan's wife."

"That's the problem. Sullivan never took the physical exam the insurance company required. His death was uninsured."

"You mean the firm owes Pamela the money?"

"Exactly one million dollars, and we don't have it."

CHAPTER ELEVEN

"Well, that's great. What's the good news?"

"I think we can work out a deal with Pamela. I've done their estate work. She doesn't need the money. The real problem is what Sullivan didn't tell us about him and O'Malley. This afternoon when I was getting ready for my closing, I was in Sullivan's office looking for his copy of the contracts. I found this."

Scott handed Mason a subpoena demanding that Sullivan & Christenson produce all of its files on O'Malley before the federal grand jury at nine a.m. on July 17.

"That's this Friday. I'm defending O'Malley. Sullivan didn't tell me about this."

"It looks like Sullivan didn't tell anyone."

"St. John is getting ready to indict O'Malley. That's not a secret. The subpoena is just his way of putting on pressure. We'll claim attorney-client privilege. The judge will throw the subpoena out."

"Don't be so sure," Scott said. "St. John isn't just coming after O'Malley. He wants Sullivan and the firm."

He handed Mason a letter to Sullivan from Franklin St. John dated June 1. In a very polite fashion, the letter informed Sullivan that both he and the firm were targets of the grand jury investigation.

"That means the grand jury is going to indict Sullivan and the firm," Mason said. "Sullivan knew St. John was gunning for us and didn't bother to mention it! That no-good prick! No wonder he was trying to set me up!"

"Set you up? How?"

"We had lunch on Friday. He asked me to destroy documents that would incriminate him. I told him no. Then he wrote a memo to Harlan claiming that I had made the suggestion to him and that he was going to fire me on Monday."

"How did you find out about that?"

"The sheriff found the memo in Sullivan's room at Buckhorn."

"Welcome to the list of top ten suspects."

"Yeah, the sheriff thinks I killed Sullivan instead of suing him for libel. Don't worry, though. I've got a terrific defense."

"What's that?"

"Someone tried to kill me on the way back from the lake."

Scott dropped his empty beer bottle. The glass shattered on the brick patio. "You're shitting me!"

"Maybe. I don't know for certain. I was on Highway 5, trying to pass a guy in a black Escalade. This asshole held me out in the other lane until I was about to hit a truck head-on. I swerved off the road at the last second, or there would be two openings at the firm."

"You think there was a connection?"

"If Sullivan was murdered, his death is probably linked to O'Malley. At least, I can't think of anything else that could get him killed. I'm defending O'Malley. Sullivan tried to get me to destroy incriminating evidence. I refused. Sullivan set me up. Someone tried to kill me and make my death look like an accident. It makes as much sense as anything else."

"Did you report it to the cops?"

"Not yet. I'll tell the sheriff, but she'll probably think I'm making it up. I didn't get the license number of the guy who hung me out in the wrong lane. I can't prove it even happened."

Scott listened, nodding without agreeing. "I know this sounds trivial in comparison, but if St. John really wants to put pressure on the firm, he'll ask the court to freeze all our assets. They don't need a conviction to do that."

"You're right. I remember reading about a New York firm that got caught in an insider-trading scandal. The feds got an order freezing their assets and the firm disappeared overnight. Last one out the door turned off the lights. Any suggestions?"

"We've got to get out in front on this. Harlan will be overly cautious, too protective. We need someone to investigate the firm's exposure and get St. John to back off until we figure out what's going on."

Mason knew that Scott was right. Harlan was perfect for recruiting clients, but he was a conscientious objector to trench warfare. If St. John was coming after the firm, it would be a bloody fight.

"That'll require outside counsel."

"Bad choice. We'd never be able to control it. You've got to do it. You're new enough to the firm that you'll have credibility with St. John. You can offer him the dear, departed Sullivan and save the rest of our asses."

Mason wondered if the bottom of his beer bottle could explain how a simple weekend at the lake had managed to turn into such a nightmare. He was the wrong choice. This battle required someone totally committed to the firm. He wasn't.

"Listen, I hate to pile on the bad news, but I don't plan to be around long enough to handle this case."

Scott stared at Mason, eyes narrowed. "What the hell is that supposed to mean?"

"It means that I decided to quit when Sullivan asked me to destroy evidence."

"So what! Sullivan's dead, and you didn't destroy any evidence. That's bullshit!"

"Not to me. O'Malley's case is a tar baby that I'm not going to get stuck with. Besides, I'm going to try to get Tommy Douchant a new trial. The firm turned that case down. I've got to do it on my own."

"Tommy's case is a loser. You already lost it once. Don't waste more time on it."

Mason bristled at Scott's slam. "It's not a loser if I dig up evidence that will get Tommy a new trial. I owe him that much."

"What about what you owe me? I got you this job. You've got a year to file a motion for a new trial. It's been, what, four months since Tommy's trial? You've got eight months left. I need you now."

"You need someone from outside the firm, someone who's objective. Someone who won't be a suspect if it turns out that Sullivan was murdered."

"Wrong. I need someone I can trust. If Sullivan was killed, who's going to work harder to clear your name and mine? You or some hired gun that's got a dozen other cases he's got to keep track of? Besides, I'll make certain the firm lets you reopen Tommy's case."

Mason sometimes made poor choices when people made him feel like a badly needed, ungrateful shit. The last one had required a divorce to correct it.

"Okay. Let's see what happens in the morning," Mason hedged. It was a half promise Scott would make him honor.

He walked Scott to the front door and said good night. Closing it behind him, he stood in the front hall and looked to his right at the portraits of his great-grandparents—Aunt Claire's grandparents—on the dining room wall. Tobiah and Hinda Sackheim had immigrated to the United States from Lithuania in 1871. Tobiah, ignorant of English, couldn't tell the immigration official his name. Somehow, he explained that he was a stonemason, and the Sackheims of Lithuania became the Masons of Ellis Island.

From their perch on the wall, they guarded the silver candlesticks they had brought with them to America. Claire kept the candlesticks on the dining room table and, when Mason was little, she lit them each year at Passover and told him the story of the Jews' Exodus from Egypt.

Both stories, one of his people and one of his family, fed her passion for justice and had once fired his own. The flame still burned brightly for Aunt Claire but was little more than a flicker for him. Mason stared at the candlesticks and replayed the memories, searching for a spark he didn't find.

He returned to the patio, picked up the pieces of Scott's broken bottle, and lay down in the lounge chair. He watched the moonrise as his eyelids fell, wondering if sleeping on patio furniture was a sign of the early onset of dementia. He was jolted awake by the cordless telephone. Blinking, he focused on his watch. It was nearly midnight.

"Yeah?"

"Sorry if I woke you." Kelly Holt sounded too cheerful for the end of a long day.

"That's all right. I had to get up to answer the phone anyway."

Long pause. He couldn't believe his evil twin, the high school freshman, invaded his body every time he talked to this woman.

"Will you be in your office tomorrow? There are a few things I need to ask you about." She was all business and not interested in bonding through teenage humor.

"Sure. We've got a partners' meeting at eight that may go all morning. The afternoon will be crazy talking with clients. How about five o'clock—my office?"

"Fine."

"Any news?"

"Just one thing. Your partner was murdered."

CHAPTER TWELVE

Mason quit his old firm, Forrest, Mason, & Goldberg, a week after Tommy Douchant's trial ended. Tommy worked construction until one sun-drenched spring morning when the hook on his safety belt broke, bouncing him off steel I beams onto the pavement two stories below. Paraplegics don't work construction. Mason sued the safety-belt manufacturer, Philpott Safety Systems, and lost.

Tommy's case should have been settled, but he turned down two million dollars the day before the trial started. Mason told him to take it. He found out the day after the trial that his partner, Stephen Forrest, had met secretly with Tommy and convinced him to turn the offer down. Forrest didn't care that Mason had a tough case. He wanted to ride Tommy's broken back to a bigger payday and his share of a fatter fee.

Tommy's case wasn't the first one Forrest had sabotaged. Mason told him that he wasn't quitting because of the money; it was the lack of trust. It was like coming home and finding his wife in bed with someone else—again. It was the "again" part that Mason couldn't handle. Mason called Scott, and a week later he was the new gun in Sullivan & Christenson's litigation department.

His old firm was a six-person shop specializing in representing injured people.

"It's half a practice," Claire told him.

"How can you say that? We help the little guy, the person who can't afford to take on the big corporations on their own."

"Yes, you help the outnumbered. But it's all about the money, not noble causes. Every time I see a plaintiff's lawyer in a thousand-dollar suit driving a hundred-thousand-dollar car and living in a million-dollar house, I want to kick him right in his jackpot."

She'd been no fonder of Sullivan & Christenson. "That kind of firm has more rules than people," she'd cautioned Mason when he told her he was changing firms. "You're not cut out to join the army. Anybody can do what they do. Besides, there's no honor in stealing one thief's money back from another."

"Even a heartless corporation deserves a good lawyer," Mason said.

"But you're wrong for the job. You're not heartless. And that's the brutal truth."

Claire claimed all her truths were brutal or they weren't worth believing. Mason tried convincing himself that he took the job with Sullivan & Christenson for the change of scenery. The brutal truth was that he took it because he thought it was safer. He could live with stealing one thief's money back from another more easily than he could live with another Tommy Douchant. In the last three days he'd discovered that Claire was right. There was nothing safe and easy at Sullivan & Christenson.

Mason wondered how much of the firm's business for heartless corporations would be left after Sullivan's death as he cinched his navy and red tie beneath the collar of his white shirt and slipped on a gray suit. It was the lawyer's uniform. Appropriate for partners' meetings, funerals, and circumcision ceremonies. Today promised to roll elements of all three into one festive occasion.

Scott Daniels and Harlan Christenson were waiting for him in his office.

"Harlan and I want to go over a few things with you before the meeting," Scott said.

Harlan's face sagged under his silence. He had the connections that got the firm started. Sullivan had the backbone that made it a powerhouse. Without Sullivan, Harlan was lost.

"Before we get to that," Mason said, "the sheriff investigating Sullivan's death called me late last night. She said Sullivan was murdered."

Harlan muttered, "Dear God," and shrank farther into his chair. "How?" It was all he could manage.

"She didn't say."

"What's next?" Scott asked.

"She's coming here this afternoon to ask me some more questions. That's all I know."

"Why is she so interested in you?" Scott asked.

"How should I know? Either she thinks I did it or she can't resist my boyish charms."

Scott studied him for a moment. "Then we'd better focus on what we do know. I came in early this morning to get a look at the files the grand jury subpoenaed. Quintex Land Corporation was at the top of the list."

Mason said, "I thought Quintex was the company O'Malley used for his real estate deals. St. John is after him for bank fraud, not real estate fraud. What's the connection?"

"I don't know. Quintex has been around a long time, and a lot of assets have passed through it."

"Did O'Malley use Quintex for anything else?"

"A few years ago, he started using it for other investments."

"Were the deals clean?"

"Sullivan handled the real estate deals. I don't know about them. I handled the investments. They were all cash deals. No banks involved. St. John can't be interested in those."

"Maybe one of the other partners knows something that might explain some of this."

"We have to tell them about the subpoena, but I don't think we should put the details on the table yet. For now, we'd better keep this among ourselves. Harlan agrees with me."

Steady breathing was Harlan's way of saying yes.

CHAPTER THIRTEEN

The eleven remaining partners of Sullivan & Christenson assembled in the firm's south conference room on the thirty-second floor of the Grand Street Pavilion, an O'Malley Development Co. project, financed by O'Malley's Mid-States Savings & Loan and managed by O'Malley Properties. Sullivan insisted that the firm not exceed the developer's allowance for tenant improvements. "Wallpaper won't make you money," was his explanation. In this case he was right. Leasing from the firm's biggest client at market rates kept O'Malley happy by filling his building. There was no need to add to the expense.

The conference room, like the rest of the two floors the firm occupied, was finished in a nondescript blend of taupe, mauve, and teal hues woven through the carpet, woodwork, and grass-cloth wallpaper. Equally generic art decorated space that could be quickly vacated for new tenants. Twelve chairs surrounded the conference table, five to a side and one at each end.

Lawyers are pack animals with a clear pecking order reflected in office assignments and seats at conference tables. Mason had inherited a seat on the side with a view out the windows. Harlan took his customary seat at the far end of the table. Mason wondered if anyone would adjust the pecking order by claiming Sullivan's vacant chair at the head of the table opposite Harlan. Grabbing it too soon could send someone to the back of the pack.

Scott was the last to arrive and, without breaking stride, landed in Sullivan's chair, dropped a sheaf of papers in front of him, and looked around the table.

"Okay, Harlan, the day's gonna be a bitch, so let's get started."

Harlan described what was known of Sullivan's death, omitting that he had been murdered. Mason attributed the omission to Harlan's innate avoidance of unpleasant news. Harlan spoke of his shock, his sympathy for Pamela, announced that the funeral would be Wednesday at one p.m. at the Ward Parkway Episcopal Church, and turned the meeting over to Scott. The partners swiveled their heads in unison to the other end of the table.

"Harlan and I will contact Sullivan's clients and reassure them that their matters are being taken care of. Call any of your key clients who should be personally informed. Everyone else will receive a letter that should go out by the end of the day."

Mason was surprised that Scott also didn't disclose that Sullivan had been murdered. He wondered if Scott and Harlan would rather the partners read about it in the newspaper.

"Has anyone spoken to O'Malley?" asked one of the partners.

"He'll be here at eleven to meet with me, Scott, and Lou," Harlan said.

Scott pressed ahead before Mason could remind him that he hadn't agreed to stick around.

"That's going to be a tough meeting," Scott added. "I found out yesterday that Sullivan and the firm are now targets of the grand jury investigation into O'Malley. The firm's files have been subpoenaed for this Friday."

"How did you find out, Scott? Was that the surprise in your box of Cracker Jacks?" Sandra Connelly asked.

Sandra joined the firm as a partner a year before Mason did and was chair of the litigation department. She had been less than enthusiastic about hiring him. Scott told Mason that Sandra didn't think an ambulance-chasing lawyer was corporate litigation material. Scott told Mason not to worry about her opposition. She had the title but none of the power and didn't want the competition. She took her frustration out on Mason by alternating verbal jabs with a sterile indifference accentuated by calling him Louis, something no one had done since the third grade.

51

Sandra blended hard edges and soft touches. Her shoulder-length hair was the color of maple leaves in the fall. She had hazel eyes, high porcelain cheeks, and you-know-how-to-whistle-don't-you lips with a body to match. She'd made more than a few opposing lawyers want to thank her for slicing open their jugular.

Mason invited her to lunch during his first week at the firm. It was like the Arab-Israeli peace talks. No one spoke the same language. Scott told him that she'd never been married, didn't need the money she made, and was lethal in the courtroom.

Mason and Sandra hadn't worked on any cases together. He wanted to break through her refrigerated demeanor just to make her stop calling him Louis and because he considered her hostility a challenge to his natural charm.

Scott answered Sandra without looking at her. "I found a target letter from Franklin St. John and the subpoena in Sullivan's desk."

"You mean Sullivan kept this secret from the rest of us but just happened to leave the subpoena and St. John's letter lying around on his desk for the cleaning crew to read?"

"Sorry to disappoint you, Sandra," he answered, now looking at her. "I was looking for Sullivan's drafts of my closing documents when I ran across them. Now one of us has to deal with the U.S. attorney. Lou will be seen as the least tainted since he's only been here a few months. I think he should handle it. Harlan, what do you think?"

"Excuse me," Sandra interrupted. "His name is Lou Mason, not Perry Mason. Would you like to know what the head of the litigation department thinks about putting the future of this firm into the hands of a lawyer whose idea of a courtroom victory is selling a rear-end collision whiplash sob story? To say nothing of the verdict he got for his best friend in his last trial."

Mason felt everyone's eyes burning holes into him while waiting to see if he got up off the mat after Sandra's body slam. His were on her. She didn't flinch. Trouble was, angry as he was, she wasn't wrong. Vicious, yes. Wrong, probably not. That was the nature of brutal truth. Had she known Mason was quitting, she would have thrown him out the window. Scott saved him from having to respond.

"As a matter of fact, Sandra, what you think is not the subject of this discussion. The people who built this firm will make these decisions. Lou is the right choice."

"Sound judgment, Scott," Harlan added. "Lou, get started today. Sandra will cover your docket and reassign anything that's in need of immediate attention. You'll have our complete cooperation. Just get it done."

Bugging out now was not an option. Mason wouldn't let Scott down and give Sandra the satisfaction of thinking she was right.

"Not a problem. I'll take care of my other cases. That's why I get the middle money. But I'll need help on this."

"Sure, Lou. I'll back you up on the corporate side," Scott said.

"You'll have to stay out of it. You were too close to Sullivan. I don't want St. John to focus on you now that Sullivan is dead. I want Sandra and two associates, one from litigation and one from corporate. Sandra, let's talk after the meeting and make our choices."

Mason couldn't tell whether Scott or Sandra was more surprised, since both of them had stopped breathing.

"Look, Sandra," Mason continued. "I know you don't like me and you don't think I know what I'm doing. I can't help the first problem but you might be right about the second problem. If we work together on this, at least you can keep me from screwing it up."

Mason worried that he was in over his head. Putting Sandra on the team gave him a chance to solve both problems. Though it may not have been a good idea to ask someone to hold his safety net who would be just as happy to see him fall off the high wire.

Scott caught his breath and tried to change Mason's mind.

"Lou, I think we should try to keep this within as small a circle as possible . . ."

Mason cut him off. "Look, Scott, the stakes have gone up." Mason looked around the table, making eye contact with each of his partners. "The sheriff at the lake called me last night. Richard Sullivan was murdered."

He let the words sink in, watching the reaction of each partner. Most looked away as if to duck from Mason's announcement. A couple covered their hearts with their hands as if they'd been struck. Only Sandra, Scott, and Harlan held his gaze.

Mason continued. "This isn't about a partner who died in his sleep. It's about a murder investigation going on in the middle of a criminal investigation of this firm. If I'm going to run this show, then I'm going to make the staffing decisions. I'll lose my credibility if I lose my independence."

Scott swallowed hard. "You're right, of course. You won't get anywhere with St. John if he thinks you're shilling for Sullivan. Meeting adjourned."

CHAPTER FOURTEEN

Sandra Connelly followed Mason into his office and closed the door.

"Nicely done, Louis. I didn't think you had the balls."

"Thanks for the endorsement. I need you. You cut through the crap and get to the bottom line. I don't care if you like me. That's not required. Now, which of the associates do you think we should use?"

She folded her arms and gave him an appraising look as if she'd never seen him before. Mason wondered if she really thought he'd been ballsy or whether he put her on the team as a prelude to surrendering to her.

"Phil Rosa is the best litigation associate we've got. He's a workhorse and he never misses anything in his research. Maggie Boylan is the top corporate associate."

"Sounds good. Assemble all of the O'Malley files, including personal files from everyone's offices, in the thirty-first-floor conference room. Lock the door. Skip Sullivan's office. We'll do that together. There'll be no more solo searches."

"You may have some pretty big balls after all," she said on her way out.

Mason pounded down the internal staircase to the thirty-first-floor office of Angela Molina, the firm's executive administrator. Angela could figure more angles than Rubik's Cube had, and she used them to squeeze every penny of profit out of the practice and into the partners' pockets. Together with a legendary office intelligence system, she kept things on an even keel. Angela had jet-black wavy hair, olive skin, and a fiery disposition. She was attractive, divorced, and in her midforties. Office gossip linked her with Sullivan. But that story followed most women who worked for the firm.

She and Mason hadn't gotten off on the right foot when he insisted on bringing his custom-made furniture that had to be bolted to the wall. Angela objected because it limited her options for future office assignments, one of her chief patronage plums. The initial chill between them had barely thawed over the last three months.

"Angela, I need your help. This is absolutely confidential. The firm has—"

"—been named a target of the grand jury's investigation into O'Malley, and you're in charge of the cleanup. What do you have left to tell me, Lou?"

Her instant intelligence bothered him, but he'd learned a long time ago that there are no secrets in a law office, especially one managed by Angela Molina.

"Change the locks on Sullivan's office and the thirty-first-floor conference room. Sandra Connelly and I get the only keys. Don't have the property manager do it. I don't want any passkeys floating around."

"O'Malley's property managers won't like it if they can't get into that office to clean, and they'll complain about security."

"Your job is to make them like it, and I know you have the charm to do it. I want the locks changed by noon. Send out a memo that those rooms are off-limits except to authorized personnel."

"Who are?"

"Sandra Connelly, Phil Rosa, Maggie Boylan, and me. Anyone objects, tell them to talk to me."

Halfway out the door, he told her to send him copies of all the O'Malley bills for the last five years, including the most current, plus work in progress.

Mason's next stop was Scott's office. He was on the phone but waved him in with a signal that said to close the door. He hung up and unloaded.

"I thought we had a deal on how we would handle this. The last thing in the world I want is for that bitch Sandra to be involved. How could you pull a bonehead stunt like that?"

"St. John would rather have a live target than a dead one. You and Sullivan were joined at the hip, which means that you're available. I'm your friend. Sandra wouldn't piss on you if you were on fire. If she believes you're not involved, she'll have more credibility with St. John than I will."

"You're acting like you think I'm in trouble. That worries me."

"We're all in trouble. We've got to put some distance between you and our investigation. You and Harlan shouldn't be at the meeting with O'Malley except to make the introductions."

"Sounds like you've got it figured out." His shoulders drooped as if Mason had let the air out of him.

"Not even close, my friend; not even close."

CHAPTER FIFTEEN

Mason was ten minutes late to the meeting with Victor O'Malley. Scott Daniels and Harlan Christenson were huddled at the far end of the conference room with O'Malley, a dark-suited trio talking in hushed voices to add weight to their words.

O'Malley had a face like an inflated punctuation mark. A scarred, bulbous nose testified to the hard knocks he'd taken. He had crisp eyes that missed nothing.

Mason knew his story. O'Malley was awarded the Silver Star in Vietnam when he led his platoon in a successful bloody attack on a hill controlled by heavily entrenched Vietcong. He liked to say that's when he learned the importance of location, after he built a banking and real estate empire in Kansas City. And, he would add, the importance of being willing to risk everything to survive.

Sandra Connelly was seated at the center of the conference table, her back to the door. Mason recognized O'Malley's son, Vic Jr., leaning over Sandra, trying to make conversation while he stole a glance down the front of her dress. When she didn't respond, he wandered back toward his father, who kept his back to him, barring Vic Jr. from his inner circle. He pretended not to notice by picking microscopic lint off his black silk shirt.

Vic Jr. had not climbed out of his father's gene pool. He was round-shouldered, with a powdery complexion, a sharp nose, and close-set eyes. He had a nocturnal look, as though he preferred foraging at night to sitting in the conference room. He was a shadow alongside his father, for whom he'd worked since graduating from college a few years earlier. Mason had met them once before.

O'Malley had done the talking. Vic Jr. had done all the whining.

Mason cleared his throat. "Sorry I'm late."

O'Malley turned toward him, waving off any possible offense.

"Quite all right, Lou," he said, extending his hand as he walked toward him. "I was just telling Scott and Harlan how much I'm going to miss Richard. I depended on him very much. I don't know how to replace him."

O'Malley's two-handed greeting swallowed Mason's hand, though he struggled to return the intensity of his grip. At six-five, O'Malley took up a lot of space. His oversized ego filled the rest of the room. A heavy gold ring with the Marine Corps insignia flashed off his right hand.

"It won't be easy, but I'm sure Scott and Harlan will take good care of you."

"Of course, of course they will. So long as you keep me out of jail."

Harlan put his arms around Mason and O'Malley, forming a new circle. "Lou, I've told Victor that you and Sandra need to talk with him about the government's case and the subpoena for our records. Take good care of him. Victor has been very good to us."

They all laughed more than Harlan's comment deserved. Mason closed the door as Harlan and Scott left the conference room, then sat next to Sandra. Father and son took seats opposite them.

Mason led off. "Victor, did you know that Richard Sullivan and the firm were targets of the grand jury investigation?"

"Cut to the chase, eh? I like that, young man. Yes. Richard told me. He said it was a sign that St. John was desperate but that I didn't have anything to worry about. He said that you told him I was in the clear."

Mason studied O'Malley for some indication that O'Malley expected him to believe that story. O'Malley's face was a pool of calm water.

"We both know that's bullshit. You're smart enough to know how much trouble you're in. The U.S. attorney doesn't go after the defendant's lawyers unless he thinks he can squeeze them to turn on their client to save their own hides."

O'Malley didn't flinch. "Then suppose you tell me how much trouble I'm in."

"Here's what I know. Your bank loaned money to real estate partnerships you controlled that were in financial trouble. The bank never should have loaned the money because the partnerships couldn't pay the money back. You knew it and the bank knew it. The loans cost the bank fifty million. The government says that was criminal fraud."

"And my lawyer advised me that the loans were reasonable business investments that turned sour. That's not a crime."

"And I'm not the jury. Did your lawyer get any of that money before he turned up dead?"

"I'm sure Richard charged for his services and was paid."

"Did he collect for anything other than his legal fees?"

O'Malley offered a patient smile. "I didn't write the checks. You'd have to ask him."

"You begin to see the problem here, Victor. Richard Sullivan is dead. You haven't forgotten, have you?"

O'Malley's eyes narrowed and his congenial veneer evaporated.

"No, I haven't, young man. My friendship with Richard was the only reason I stuck with this firm and didn't hire a Wall Street heavyweight. I may have to rethink that now that he's gone."

"You may need a Wall Street firm sooner than you think. If the firm is indicted, we'll claim that we didn't know the true nature of your actions because you concealed them. The court will waive your attorney-client privilege, and we can fight over the movie rights."

O'Malley nodded. "All right. You've made your point. Better to hang together than separately. What else do you want to know?"

"St. John has subpoenaed our files on Quintex Land Corporation. I want to know why."

"I don't know. The bank didn't loan any money to Quintex."

"What does Quintex do?"

"I use it to buy and sell land."

"Scott said that Sullivan handled the real estate deals but that the company has made other investments besides real estate."

"Look, Richard set up more corporations for me than I could keep track of. I certainly can't remember every deal that I ever did. You've got the records. You figure it out and tell me if I've got another problem besides the loans."

Mason shook his head, realizing the struggle that lay ahead. O'Malley wasn't going to tell him anything he didn't have to. Mason couldn't blame him. They had met only once before. The lawyer O'Malley trusted was dead, and he hadn't decided whether he could trust Mason.

Mason and Sandra spent the next two hours hammering him on Quintex, but they didn't know enough to ask the right questions. They needed time to plow through all the material, so they scheduled another meeting for the following Monday afternoon.

"Well, what do you think?" Mason asked Sandra after O'Malley and his son left.

"No jury will ever believe that someone that successful could know so little about how he made all that money. He's not going to help us more than he has to."

"Doesn't he know that the harder he makes our job, the more likely it is that he gets convicted?"

"Maybe. Unless he's more worried about what the government doesn't know than what it does know. We better buy some time from St. John."

"Our appointment is at ten tomorrow morning. Let's have a look at Sullivan's office."

The locksmith was just finishing under Angela's watchful eye. She gave them the Girl Scout salute, handed each of them a key, and posted the *No Admittance* sign on the door.

"The office is secure, so let's leave it until tomorrow. Maybe we'll have a better idea of what we're looking for after we meet with St. John," Sandra said.

CHAPTER SIXTEEN

When Mason returned to his office, he found six banker's boxes stacked against one wall. Each box was labeled *Douchant v. Philpott Safety Systems*. There was a note from Scott taped to one of the boxes that read, *A deal is a deal. Save the firm and take care of Tommy. Then take the rest of the day off.*

Mason ran his hand over the boxes, deciding whether to open them. He knew that when he did, he'd have no more excuses to quit the firm or to blame the result in Tommy's trial on fickle courtroom gods. He used the letter opener Scott had given him for being best man in his wedding to cut the tape that held the lids on each box.

The first thing he saw was Tommy's safety belt, the Philpott Safety System logo embossed on the back. It was more harness than belt. Tommy wore it wrapped around his waist and between his legs. A six-foot rope called a lanyard was attached to the belt. A hook shaped like a giant safety pin was attached to the other end of the rope.

Tommy had been on a scaffold finishing cement on an elevator tower the day he was hurt. He hooked the lanyard to a steel loop that had been driven into the cement. Believing he was secure, he reached as far as he could to his right to smooth the fresh cement, when the hook slipped out of the bolt and he fell. There were no witnesses.

Mason picked up the belt, the metal cold in his hand. He worked the action on the safety hook just as he had in front of the jury, demonstrating how the slightest pressure caused it to slide open and how easy it was for Tommy to fall. He wondered again what he could have done differently to win Tommy's case.

Immediately after the accident, Tommy's employer gave the belt to Warren Philpott, the owner of Philpott Safety Systems, to examine it for defects. Philpott, to no one's surprise, claimed there was nothing wrong with it.

The expert safety engineer Mason hired said there was nothing wrong with the way the belt was made. It worked as it was supposed to. But the expert said the design was defective because it didn't have a lock to prevent the hook from opening and separating from its anchor.

Mason's lawsuit against Philpott was based on the unsafe design. A tough case to win since Philpott's experts said the lock wasn't necessary if the hook was used properly. Philpott had sold hundreds of thousands of the hooks. When a hook failed and Philpott was sued, he did what many manufacturers tried to do: settle if he could, the cheaper the better, and win the cases that went to trial.

Philpott's lawyers claimed the accident was Tommy's fault because he did a lousy job of securing his hook. They offered to settle because they were afraid that the jury would be sympathetic to Tommy's injury—especially with his wife testifying about life with a paraplegic.

"Two million bucks is a lot of money," Mason told Tommy the day before the trial. "After attorneys' fees and case expenses, you'll net close to a million-two. Between what your wife makes and what you can earn on that money, you'll be able to take care of your family."

Tommy didn't hesitate with his bitter answer. "It's not enough, Lou. Not after what those bastards did to me."

"Those bastards aren't paying you a penny. Philpott's insurance company will write the check. This isn't about revenge, Tommy. It's about taking care of your family. You can't take the chance that the jury will send you home empty-handed."

Tommy glared at Mason from his wheelchair. "I'm willing to take that chance, Lou. If you don't have the guts, get one of your partners to try the case."

Mason stiffened at his friend's challenge. "Tommy, this isn't double dare like when we were kids. It's not about my guts. It's about your brains. Take the money."

"Screw the money. Just win my damn case!"

Tommy didn't tell Mason that his partner, Stephen Forrest, had convinced him to roll the dice for a bigger payday. LeAnn, Tommy's wife, wheeled him out of the courtroom after the trial. They hadn't spoken since.

Mason put the safety belt back in the box and sat at his computer. Although it had been only four months since the trial, he wanted to know if there had been anything new in the press about Philpott Safety Systems. The only hit was an article in the *Kansas City Star* about the verdict.

Mason searched Warren Philpott's name. Again there was only one hit, a newspaper article published a week ago about a domestic disturbance at the Philpotts' home.

Ellen Philpott had thrown her husband out the front door and his belongings out a second-story window, both during a wind-lashed thunderstorm. Warren responded by pounding on the front door and throwing a rock through a window when she refused to let him back in. A neighbor called the police.

Ellen explained to the police that she kicked her husband out for cheating on her and that she threw his clothes out because she was doing her spring cleaning. When she added that they were getting divorced and that the judge had granted her exclusive possession of the house, the police ushered her husband away, leaving his clothes to soak in the rain.

When it stopped raining, she collected Warren's clothes on the patio, where she said they would remain until they rotted. Mr. Philpott declined comment.

Mason remembered Ellen Philpott, sitting in the courtroom for five days, first row behind the rail, far side from the jury box, a flexed smile fixed on the back of her husband's neck. Her own neck, thin-skinned and thick veined, bobbing and weaving with the testimony. She nodded at Mason each morning as they assembled, as if they shared a secret. Mason wanted to ask her what the secret was but knew that Philpott's lawyer wouldn't let him talk with her. That was then. Mason decided to work a visit to Ellen into his schedule, hoping to make an angry, wronged spouse his new best friend.

CHAPTER SEVENTEEN

Mason spent the rest of the day talking to clients. His secretary called at five fifteen to tell him that Kelly Holt was waiting to see him.

"Sorry, I'm late," she said as she sat across from him.

"No problem. I couldn't stand another sympathy call. Your timing was perfect. I apologize for acting like a jerk yesterday. It's not every day that I get to identify my senior partner's body."

Mason couldn't decide if she looked better in or out of uniform. She was wearing an indigo suit, an open-necked, lime blouse, and a ruby and jade striped scarf. A gold clip held her hair snugly in back. It was a toss-up. Better yet, she wasn't wearing a gold band to match her gold earrings and choker chain.

"Forget it. I never get used to the bodies either."

"Last night you said that Sullivan was murdered. How do you know?"

"Sorry, Counselor. It's my turn to claim confidentiality."

"Why? Am I still a suspect?"

"What do you think?"

"That everybody's a suspect until you catch the killer."

"Exactly. You can either confess or tell me who did it."

"I can't do either. But I doubt that someone would try to kill me if I was the killer." Mason told her about his drive back from the lake. "I'm parked in space number 110 in the parking garage. You can check the damage to my car and I can show you the place where I went off the road."

"I'll do that. Why would Sullivan's killer want to kill you?"

"Maybe the killer thinks I know something that would identify him or her. Or maybe the killer thinks Sullivan told me something he doesn't want anyone else to know. Or maybe it was just road rage."

Kelly answered with professional neutrality. "I can't protect you up here. Do you want me to ask the local cops to put somebody on you?"

Mason didn't know whether to be pleased or frightened that she made the offer. If she believed him, she might not suspect him. But if she thought he needed protection, he might be in real danger. He was used to fighting through a pile of muddy rugby players battling over a slippery football. But he'd never played against a killer, and the prospect now didn't seem real. And he didn't like asking someone to take care of him.

"Not yet," he hedged. "I'm defending O'Malley. I've got to deal with a difficult client and a U.S. attorney who wants to put us out of business. I won't have credibility with either if I've got a bodyguard following me around. Do you have any better suggestions?"

"Just one. This is not amateur hour. Get someone else to represent O'Malley and someone else to represent your firm. I don't want to pick up the paper and read that you've been fished out of the lake or sent up the river."

Before Mason could respond, Cara Trent knocked and opened his door, carrying O'Malley's bills in one hand and a coffee mug in the other. She was a lighter blonde than Kelly, soft where Kelly was sinewy, fragile where Kelly was tough.

"Oh, sorry, Lou, I didn't know you had someone in here. Angela said you wanted these. She had to leave and I'm right behind her."

"Thanks. Say hello to Kelly Holt. She's the sheriff from the lake who's looking into Sullivan's death."

Cara took a deep breath as she set her mug on Mason's desk and shook Kelly's hand. To her credit, it was the only part of her that was shaking.

"It's terrible. I didn't know him well, but he seemed like such a fine man," Cara managed to say.

"Yes, well, I'm certain it was terrible for all of you," Kelly answered. "I hope to visit with you about it in the next few days."

Cara looked away from Kelly's steady gaze. "Sure. I'll be around."

Kelly watched her leave, giving no clues as to her impressions of Cara. Mason assumed that Cara had known Sullivan a lot better than she would admit. He figured Kelly made the same assumption after he told her they had left the poker game together, but Kelly gave her no cause to suspect that. She picked up Cara's coffee mug by the handle, poured the contents into Mason's trash can, slipped it into the paper bag his lunch had come in, and dropped it into her purse.

"Mind if I borrow this for a few days?"

"Is that the way you take fingerprints in the Ozarks? What do you use for mug shots? Home movies?"

"Very funny. If Cara were at the lake, I'd ask her to come in and give me a set of elimination prints." Mason furrowed his brow at her explanation. Kelly continued. "I'd tell her that we found prints on the boat and at the condo and that we need to eliminate hers from those we found. Since I doubt that she's going back to the lake anytime soon, this cup will have to do."

"Be my guest."

She was gone before he could use one of his "How about a drink?" lines.

CHAPTER EIGHTEEN

Tommy Douchant bloodied Mason's nose when he asked Tommy's girlfriend to double skate at the roller rink. Crawling unseen under the table where Tommy and the girl were sitting, Mason tied the laces of Tommy's skates together while blood dripped from his nose. They were ten. Neither of them got the girl. Friendships are born in strange ways.

Tommy was Catholic. Mason was Jewish. Tommy was hotheaded. Mason was sneaky. Tommy joined his father's union. Mason went to college. Tommy broke his back. Mason lost his case. Friendships die in strange ways.

Mason thought about the parts of their lives that intersected and the parts that ran parallel to one another as he sat in his car in front of Tommy's house, engine running, a six-pack of Bud on the seat next to him. Tommy and LeAnn and their five-year-old twins lived in a small, two-story Cape Cod in Prairie Village, a suburb just on the Kansas side of the state line that divided the metropolitan area.

Tommy's subdivision was built after World War II, funded by low-rate mortgages for veterans. The house was originally a one-story ranch. Tommy finished the attic into a second floor, added dormers, and turned the ranch into a Cape Cod. Over the years, Mason watched him paint the inside and the outside, pour a new driveway, and rewire the house.

"Got a new project," Tommy announced with a kid's enthusiasm the week before his accident. "Gonna put up a basketball goal that I can raise and lower so the kids can use it. Wanna give me a hand?"

They were eating ribs and drinking beer at Bryant's Barbecue before catching an early-season baseball game. Tommy always asked Mason if he wanted to help and Mason always turned him down.

"You remember those skills tests we took in junior high school?" Mason asked him.

"Yeah. What about 'em?"

"You remember the section titled 'Works Well with His Hands'? My results came back 'has no hands.'"

"Then bring the beer and watch. You can't screw that up."

The bit was an old one they'd done dozens of times, still laughing at the punch line.

Mason studied the outside of the house, as if it could tell what had happened to the family who lived inside. The wheelchair ramp from the front stoop to the driveway was the only clue that things were different for them.

Fresh lawn-mower tracks partitioned the small front yard into neat twenty-one-inch slices. Day lilies, their blossoms leaning over like bowed heads, struggled in the heat beneath the dining room and living room windows on either side of the front door. A pink ball the size of a large grapefruit lay against the base of the basketball goal.

Mason looked at his watch. It was eight o'clock. LeAnn was probably giving the kids a bath, getting them ready for bed.

The front door opened. Tommy sat in his wheelchair, rolling forward and back over the threshold, as if he couldn't decide whether to stay in or come out. They looked at each other, neither waving, just looking. Mason sighed, turned off the car, and got out, carrying the six-pack of Bud. Tommy rolled his wheelchair over the threshold, onto the front stoop, and down the ramp. They met in the driveway.

Mason didn't know what to say. He couldn't bring himself to tell Tommy that he looked good, though his upper body was still strong and the muscles in his arms still rippled against his T-shirt. But his legs were out of place, muscles wasted. So Mason wouldn't tell Tommy that he looked good. Instead, he scanned the outside of the house again, stopping at the basketball goal.

"The kids must like shooting hoops."

"Gives 'em something to do."

"That's good."

Mason wanted to get to the point and skip the awkward small talk. But it was easier to talk about anything other than what they had to talk about.

"I built that ramp."

"Get out! Why didn't you call me? I could have helped."

"Remember those skills tests we took in junior high school?"

"Right. I brought the beer if it's not too late."

"Never too late as long as the beer's cold."

Mason handed him a bottle, took one, and set the six-pack on the driveway. They drank in silence, the awkwardness still lingering.

"You really built that ramp?"

"Yeah. The workers' compensation people sent somebody out to put one in while I was still in the hospital. There wasn't anything wrong with it. I just don't like other people working on my house."

Mason remembered that Tommy's workshop was in the basement.

"How did you get down to your shop?"

"Didn't have to. LeAnn moved my workbench into the garage. I cut the legs down so I could reach everything from my chair. When I finished cutting the boards for the ramp to size, she got me one of those little carts mechanics lie on to slide under cars and I just sat out here scooting around and hammering nails."

"It looks great."

"It looks like shit, but I built it. It's not much, but it's a start."

"What about vocational rehab? I thought workers' comp was going to retrain you."

"They tried. Told me I should learn computers. So far, I'm better at ramp building, but I don't know that there's much demand for crippled carpenters."

Tommy spoke without a trace of the bitterness he'd shown at the trial. He sounded more realistic than resigned.

Mason finished his beer as the last shadows of the day crept over them.

"I'm sorry about the trial—about the way everything turned out."

Given enough time, Mason knew he would probably apologize for every disaster of this century and the last. Tommy shook his head and waved off Mason's apology.

"I should have listened to you and taken the money."

"I should have done a better job."

"Quit kicking yourself. I was the one who screwed up. Your partner told me that Philpott would pay a lot more once the trial got started. I believed him because I was so mad about everything. You were right. All I cared about was getting even. It's too late now."

"Maybe not."

"What's that supposed to mean?"

"I want to reopen your case. But I've got to find evidence to convince the judge to give you a new trial."

"How are you going to do that?"

"Philpott cheated on his wife and she filed for divorce. I'll start with her. Maybe she's mad enough to tell me something that will help. After that, I don't know. I can't promise you anything, so don't get your hopes up. But I think it's worth a shot."

"Any hope is more than we've had for a while now. Do what you can."

Tommy pulled the six-pack up into his lap and rolled his wheelchair back up the ramp, his arms and shoulders flexing with the climb. When he reached the top, he turned and gave Mason a slight wave. *Not even breathing hard,* Mason thought. He smiled and returned the wave.

CHAPTER NINETEEN

Kate was sitting on Mason's front step, scratching Tuffy behind her ears, when Mason pulled into his driveway. Scott had been waiting for him the night before. He couldn't wait to see who would show up tomorrow. He didn't see Kate's car, which meant that she and the dog had walked from her apartment on the Plaza, about a mile away.

Tuffy liked to have the back of her ears scratched, and once the scratching started, she devoted herself to the sensation, refusing every distraction except for one—Mason. The dog was infatuated with him, which infuriated Kate. It was the reason Kate had stolen Tuffy when they split up. All of which he remembered with jealous clarity when he stepped from the car, clapped his hands twice, and caught Tuffy as she bounded into his arms.

"Never doubt a dog's devotion," Kate said with a spare smile as she joined them on the driveway.

Mason had the same reaction each time he saw her. He'd do it again even if it turned out the same way.

Tuffy finished licking Mason's chin and moved on to sniffing his shoes, pants, and crotch to confirm her master's identity. A squirrel jumped from a tree onto the driveway, daring Tuffy to give chase. She didn't disappoint.

"She's a very faithful bitch," Mason answered.

Kate shrugged off the irony in Mason's comment. He marveled at her ability to shrug off things and people. He attributed it to her disengagement gene. It was never more apparent than on the day she left the divorce papers on top of the sports section.

Mason tracked her down at her office, where she ran a web-design company.

"What the hell is this?"

He slapped the papers on her desk. She'd looked up at him, her perfect black eyebrows arched over her luminous blue eyes. They were the same eyes he was drawn to the night they met. They were an arresting blue that took him into custody on the spot. Then they seemed electric. Now they were ice.

"I'm done. That's all."

"Excuse me. You're done? Don't I get a vote?"

Kate pushed back in her chair, folded her arms, and shook her head like a teacher whose student just didn't get it.

"No, Lou. You don't get a vote. Love isn't an election. You're either in or you're out, and I'm out. Out of love with you and out of the marriage."

She said it without rancor. It was the way it was. She had disengaged.

It may have been simple to her, but not to him. They had been married three years. The first had been erotic and ecstatic. The second had been quiet and comfortable. The third had been dead and boring. Mason called it a slump. Kate declared it a dead end.

Afterward, he read an article by a marriage expert who said that successful couples developed rituals that helped bind them together. They had none. But he knew they had needed more than a few minutes spent lingering over coffee to trade stories of the day. After the passion, there wasn't enough purpose. He had been wracked by the breakup. She seemed to have dismissed it. That was the part he never got, though when she snatched the dog, he wondered if it was really just so much water off a duck's back.

"I need for you to keep the dog for a while."

They watched Tuffy tree the squirrel. A moment later, Tuffy lost interest when Anna Karelson whistled at her from her front yard and held a dog biscuit in the air. Tuffy flew across the street.

Anna's husband, Jack, had run off with a nineteen-year-old file clerk in his office and then resurfaced, begging her to take him back. She changed the locks. Worst of all, she wouldn't let him have his TR6, which she kept locked in the garage. Anna waved at Mason as Tuffy bounded back to his side of the street.

He scratched her behind the ears. "Not that I'm complaining, but why?"

"I'll be out of town for a month on a road show."

"You're going into show business?"

Kate gave him an exasperated smirk. "My company is very hot right now. We're one of the best in our space and we're starting to get national accounts. I'm going to a dozen cities to meet with potential clients."

"Umm. Sounds thrilling. Better sign them up before you lose interest and move on to something else."

"Keep drinking from that bitter cup and you'll give yourself an ulcer. I'll pick up Tuffy when I get back."

She walked away without a backward glance, arms swinging with a hunter's purposeful stride.

"Not if I see you first," he said.

CHAPTER TWENTY

At ten o'clock Tuesday morning, Mason and Sandra Connelly emptied their pockets for the deputy marshals guarding the federal courthouse before heading to Franklin St. John's sixth-floor office. Mason did a double take when the deputy gave Sandra a claim check for a three-inch knife she carried in her purse.

"I collect sharp things," she said in response. "It's a hobby."

"Ever hear of stamps?"

"No edge to it," she said with a shrug as they walked to the elevator.

Franklin St. John was a small, spare man, vain enough to comb the few remaining filaments of hair across his bald head. A high, shiny forehead dropped off to a narrow, long nose, thin lips, and a pointed chin. His upper lip curled into a sneer as he greeted them with a smile. Mason couldn't tell if it was intentional or a cruel trick played by involuntary facial muscles. He didn't look like a nice man, and Mason bet his face was a disappointment but not a surprise to those who knew him.

St. John was a career prosecutor from a political family whose connections reached to the White House. Originally from Kansas City, he'd been an assistant U.S. attorney in Chicago. When the U.S. attorney position opened up in Kansas City, he got the job.

He stood behind a massive desk, flanked by the seal of the United States and the official picture of the president. Tall floor lamps behind his desk cast an artificial aura behind him.

St. John introduced them to Gene McNamara, the FBI agent who was his chief investigator. McNamara's face was beefy, with a drinker's hazy red-veined pattern across his nose and cheeks. He nodded perfunctorily at them and took up a station at the end of the sofa opposite St. John's desk, his coat opened casually enough to expose the service revolver holstered under his right arm.

"We're all terribly sorry about Mr. Sullivan's death," St. John said.

Mason decided that the best approach was to make nice, put his cards on the table, and convince St. John that he wanted to cooperate.

"Thank you. We appreciate you seeing us on such short notice. We need your help sorting out several matters that Sullivan neglected to tell us about."

"My office is always pleased to cooperate, Mr. Mason. What can I do for you?"

"We just found out that you've subpoenaed the firm's files on Victor O'Malley and that we're supposed to turn them over to you on Friday and that Sullivan and the firm are targets of your investigation. We need some idea of what you're looking for and time to figure out what's going on."

St. John peered across the desk at Mason like a teacher whose student just told him that a squirrel climbed in his window and ate his homework.

"Mr. Mason, your late partner was O'Malley's gatekeeper, and we've been banging on the gate for two years. Did you really think you could make a fortune off O'Malley and not step in his crap?"

Mason was done with nice.

"We don't have the luxury of sitting around dreaming up conspiracies while sucking on the public tit. If Sullivan stepped on his dick, we'll deal with it."

"Stepping on his dick or your own may be the least of your concerns. Have the files here by five o'clock on Friday."

"Why don't we just go see the judge and ask him if he thinks an extension is appropriate since the person you served with the subpoena never told us about any of this and is now dead?"

St. John knew the judge would give them more time to respond and that he wouldn't win any points for being a hard-ass.

"Very well, Mr. Mason. How much time do you want?"

"Thirty days."

"Will that be all?"

"I want to know if you're tapping our phones. Once the press gets hold of this, I want to reassure our clients that their communications remain confidential."

"You're not entitled to that information, Mr. Mason, and you know it. But, in the spirit of cooperation—Agent McNamara, what's the status of our intercepts?"

"Holt handled the last round just before her partner was killed. Our authorizations expired after she quit. We don't have anything in their offices."

Holt's name made no sense.

"Kelly Holt?"

"Yeah, why?" McNamara asked.

"She's the sheriff investigating Sullivan's death."

"I wasn't aware that she stayed in law enforcement," St. John said as he glared at McNamara, reprimanding him for his oversight. "The paper said that Sullivan drowned."

"He died during our firm retreat. I helped identify the body. That's all I know. We'll have a response to the subpoena in a month."

Mason was silent on the walk back to the office, trying to piece together fragments that didn't match. Sandra waited to interrupt his thoughts until they were in the conference room, surrounded by the O'Malley files.

"Are you going to tell me what Kelly Holt has to do with Sullivan's death or do I have to use my knife?" No response. "Lou, it's a very sharp knife."

"Do you believe in coincidences?"

"No. I believe in chaos."

"O'Malley, Sullivan, and the firm are being investigated by the FBI. Sullivan dies and the sheriff who is investigating his death just happens to be an ex–FBI agent who just happened to be in charge of wiretapping O'Malley. Coincidence or chaos?"

He didn't add that the sheriff didn't tell him she'd been involved in the investigation. He hadn't had time to sort through that piece.

"Chaos—the rule of unintended consequences. Seemingly unconnected events run headlong into each other. It's like God is using people to play bumper cars. Sullivan drowned. Where's the connection?"

"Sullivan was murdered. That's not what I would call an unintended consequence."

Maggie Boylan and Phil Rosa pushed the door open, wheeling in a portable workstation with a PC, printer, paper, legal pads, calculators, and a lifetime supply of Post-its. Mason and Sandra exchanged looks, agreeing to table the discussion of murder.

"Do you have any idea how many trees will die before we're done with the paper in this case?" Rosa asked.

"I don't care," Mason said, "as long as you finish reviewing O'Malley's files by Sunday night. I want an analysis of all of the transactions we've handled for O'Malley. I want to know what each deal involved, who financed it, what changed hands, and the names of all past and present Sullivan & Christenson attorneys who worked on them."

"We could really use a legal assistant to set up a database for all that information. We've got the software to sort the data, but we need someone who uses it all the time if we're going to be ready for O'Malley on Monday," Maggie Boylan said.

"Sorry, we've got to keep this team as small as possible. I can't take the chance of leaks."

"She's right," Sandra said. "There are thousands of documents to review. Diane Farrell was Sullivan's paralegal. There can't be anything in these files she doesn't already know."

Phil stiffened at the suggestion. "That woman is the biggest pain in the ass in four states. If she wasn't screwing Sullivan, she had him by the short hairs some other way. Sullivan let her get away with murder. No one can stand to work with her."

"For Christ's sake, Phil," Maggie said, "can't we wait until the body's cold before we start shitting all over the grave? She knows this stuff inside and out. Besides, I'd rather have her where I can watch her than wonder what she's doing to get even for being left out."

Mason gave in. "All right, I'm convinced by this underwhelming endorsement. Bring her in, but tell her she's out of a job if she can't keep her mouth shut. Sandra and I will be in Sullivan's office."

CHAPTER TWENTY-ONE

Sullivan had a corner office with glass on three sides, giving him a panoramic view stretching from downtown to the horizon. Bookshelves mounted above file drawers stood behind his wraparound desk.

Mason tackled the file drawers and Sandra poked through the desk. When they were finished, they were no closer to any answers. There was nothing pertaining to O'Malley or St. John's subpoena.

"Scott said he found St. John's subpoena on Sullivan's desk. If Sullivan was hiding that from us, I don't think he would have left it lying around and I don't think he would have put it in his out basket so his secretary could file it. He would have hidden it, probably with whatever other files on O'Malley he didn't want anyone else to see," Sandra said.

"Makes sense, but it doesn't look like he kept them in his office."

"Maybe somebody got here ahead of us or maybe he kept them in an office at home. We should have a look after the funeral. I did find this DVD, but it's not labeled."

She handed it to Mason. He booted up Sullivan's desktop PC and inserted the disk into the CD/DVD drive.

"Man-O-Manischewitz," Mason said.

They watched as a half dozen naked men and women mixed and matched parts as if they were playing a deviant version of Mr. Potato Head.

"Look at those angles. I better take some notes," Sandra said.

"That's all the excitement I can stand," Mason announced. His face was flushed as he punched the disk out of the computer and returned it to its case.

"What's the matter?" Sandra teased. "Afraid to walk down the hall with Johnny Rocket ready for liftoff?"

She made a show of letting her eyes slide down his chest to his zipper.

"You are brutal. You know that? But watching a porno flick together is not my idea of bonding with you."

Sandra wouldn't let up. "You sure those big boys aren't making you insecure?"

"Of all people, Sandra, I thought you would know."

"Know what?"

"Like the song says, it ain't the meat. It's the motion." Mason enjoyed Sandra's silent, red-faced response. "Let's go," he added, grabbing the DVD. "I think I'll keep this so it doesn't show up in the stuff we turn over to St. John."

"Just a minute. Let's try a reality check with St. John." Sandra unscrewed the mouthpiece of the telephone receiver on Sullivan's desk. "You're going to love this," she said, showing him the miniature microphone attached to the mouthpiece.

Mason ripped the receiver from the phone and fifteen minutes later slammed open St. John's office door with Sandra and St. John's secretary on his heels.

"You really are a piece of work, St. John. Did you think we wouldn't check for bugs just because you said there weren't any?"

He jammed the mouthpiece under St. John's nose. Two deputy marshals ran into the office, weapons drawn.

"Sorry, Mr. St. John, but your secretary pushed the panic button," one of the deputies said.

"They didn't have an appointment, Mr. St. John. They wouldn't even let me buzz you first," his secretary said.

"It's quite all right, Paula. You did the right thing. Deputies, I'm sorry to trouble you. Mr. Mason and Miss Connelly will be leaving shortly, either with or without your assistance. It makes no difference to me."

Mason pretended not to notice the guards as they advanced

toward them.

"All I want is some answers, Frank. Why are you bugging our offices?"

St. John took the receiver from Mason, studied it, and handed it back to him.

"Mr. Mason, I'm afraid you may have more problems than either of us thought. Even those of us on the public tit can afford better equipment than this. It's not one of ours. Good day, Counselors."

CHAPTER TWENTY-TWO

Wilson Bluestone's friends called him "Blues," a name he'd earned playing piano in jazz clubs around Kansas City after he quit his day job as a cop. He and Mason became friends when Mason quit taking piano lessons from him at the Conservatory of Music.

Mason signed up for lessons a couple of years after he'd graduated from law school, and Blues was assigned as his teacher. At his first lesson, Mason told him that if he could play like Oscar Peterson, he'd think he'd died and gone to heaven. After four lessons, Blues told him to go home, listen to the metronome, and find another route to the pearly gates.

When Mason didn't show up for his next lesson, Blues called demanding an explanation. Mason told him he got the metronome message and Blues reminded him that he had paid for the first five lessons and that he ought to get his money's worth.

"Why are you giving up?" he asked when Mason walked into the studio.

It was a small, spare room furnished with an upright piano and a gray metal folding chair. Blues straddled the chair, his arms folded over the back. Mason took the bench, his back to the piano.

"Like I told you over the phone. I got your message. I wasn't born to be a genius jazz pianist."

"Why did you sign up in the first place?"

"I love jazz and I think the piano is God's gift to music."

"Yeah, but why did you think you could learn to play?"

Mason hadn't expected this question. "I just assumed anyone who wanted to play could learn to play."

"What do you like about the music?"

"The way it sounds, I guess. What do you want me to say? Is this some kind of exit interview for failing students?"

"That's why you'll never learn to play. It's not what you hear. It's how the music makes you feel. If it doesn't change the way you see the world, you're just in the audience. And the audience doesn't play."

"I guess you're right. I thought learning to play music was like learning a foreign language. First you learn the alphabet, then the grammar, and then you practice speaking. Keep after it, and you've got it mastered."

"I'll bet you don't speak any foreign languages either."

He was right, but Mason wouldn't admit it. "Is that all I get for my last lesson?"

"It's more than you got out of the first four."

"So is this all you do? Take people's money to tell them why they shouldn't take lessons from you?"

"Nope. I'm sort of a freelance problem solver."

"What kind of problems?"

"Some like yours. Help people realize that they're better off listening to music than trying to play it. I'm a private investigator. I find people who don't want to be found and I find out things that people want to know. All depends on what needs to be done."

He stood up and Mason realized that was the first time he'd seen Blues out of the folding chair. Watching that single movement, Mason began to get an idea of the other kinds of problems he could solve.

Blues was a solid six-three, probably went two-twenty. All of it sleek muscle. But he moved with such ease that it was clear he had power that didn't depend on size and strength. He had straight black hair and a complexion somewhere between tan and copper. His face was chiseled, with a square chin and dark eyes. The truth was, Mason hadn't paid much attention to who he was or what he looked like until that moment. And he couldn't figure who or what Blues was. The one thing Mason was certain of: Blues didn't belong to his synagogue.

"Mind if I ask you a question?"

"I'm half Cherokee, half Shawnee. That's what you wanted to know, isn't it? You'd do better not to stare."

"An Indian jazz piano player?"

Mason had said it without thinking, almost choking on the question.

"Used to be. Now I'm a Native American jazz piano player. Political correctness ain't strictly a black thing, you know. And if you've got more fool questions, don't ask them."

Mason took his advice and didn't ask any until six months later, when he needed help tracking down a drunk driver who had run over a client in an intersection and fled the scene of the accident. He hired Blues to find the driver.

A week later, Blues called and said he'd found the driver and asked Mason to meet him at Seventh and Pennsylvania on the northwest corner of the downtown. Mason knew the location. It was called the Lookout because it was on top of a bluff that overlooked the Missouri River as it wound down from the north before turning to the east and heading to its meeting with the Mississippi River in St. Louis.

It was the first week of October, and an early cold snap had sucked the last remnants of summer from the air, leaving behind a sharp, crisp sky overhead and small clouds of exhaust from the thousands of cars that flew past on the highways that wrapped around the base of the bluff. Mason parked his car and met Blues at the edge of the Lookout.

CHAPTER TWENTY-THREE

"Hey, good to see you," Mason said, his hand outstretched. It was a friendly gesture. Appropriate for greeting someone he hadn't seen in six months and who had agreed to help him out without even negotiating a fee in advance.

Blues ignored his hand, his gaze locked on the distance.

"What are you going to do to him?" Blues asked.

"Who? The guy who hit my client? I'm going to sue the son of a bitch."

"What do you know about him?"

"Nothing. That's why I wanted you to find him. I need to find out who his insurance company is so I can put them on notice."

Blues swept his hand across the view. "What do you see out there?"

Mason started to make a smart-ass remark, like "Not the guy you were supposed to find for me," when he remembered his last piano lesson. There was a message here and he wasn't getting it.

"I don't know. You tell me."

"Over there," Blues said, pointing to the west. "That's the Kansas River. The Indians called it the Kaw, and that spot, where it pours into the Missouri—right where the Missouri bends to the east—they called that Kawsmouth. Not very original. But it makes the point. Down there, where I-70 cuts across the downtown, that was all bluffs—just like this. Right down to the banks of the Missouri. Back in the 1870s, they dug out those bluffs to make the streets. At first they just cut the streets out of the bluffs, like gullies. They even called it Gullytown for a while, instead of Kansas

City. To the west, over there, in those old warehouses that are used for haunted houses at Halloween—that's the West Bottoms. More hogs and cattle were slaughtered there than you could ever imagine. Ten thousand people worked there when the meatpacking business was booming. Lot of people got rich. Not one of them an Indian."

"I know there's a point to this and I do appreciate the history lesson, but where's my drunk?"

Blues made another quarter turn to the southwest. "Over that way, back into Kansas—you can't really see it from here—is where the government put the Shawnee tribe to get them out of the way of all that progress. They kept moving the tribes farther west, each time promising them that they could have those lands forever. Course, it didn't work out that way."

"Look, if this is some kind of sensitivity test, let me know. I'll tell you the story about my Jewish ancestors sneaking out of their Lithuanian village in the middle of the night so that they wouldn't be killed in the monthly pogrom. They ended up here with a set of candlesticks and nothing else. My great-grandfather helped cut the stones they used for those streets and my grandfather slaughtered his share of those animals. Nobody said it was fair. I don't need for you to know about that or to give a shit. I just want to know if you found my drunk."

Blues looked at him with a half smile. "Just wanted you to know, that's all."

"Know what?"

"I've got more faith in my system of justice than in the one you're going to use to squeeze a few bucks out of your drunk's insurance company. I'll help you when I want to and you'll pay me. I don't like what you're doing or I decide I don't like you—that's it. That's my justice system."

"Fair enough. But if I don't get my drunk, you don't get paid."

"I've got your drunk. By the way," he added with mock surprise, "I didn't know Mason was a Jewish name."

Mason couldn't hold back his grin. "Yeah? Well, I guess that means we're even since I didn't know there were any Indian piano players."

Their arrangement had worked well over the years. Blues could find just about anyone who didn't want to be found and find out most things that people didn't want someone else to know. And he did it with a confidence and fearlessness that made it difficult for people to resist. When they did, they regretted it.

Blues didn't volunteer much about himself. Eventually Mason strung together enough bits and pieces to know that he'd been married and divorced before he was twenty, served in the army special forces, and spent six years as a cop in Kansas City.

He quit the police force after he shot and killed a woman suspected of smothering her baby to stop her from crying. Blues never went into the details except to say that the brass gave him the choice to quit or be fired. He quit being a cop but kept playing piano and moonlighting as a freelance problem solver.

Mason suspected that something more than reading history had shaped Blues's uncompromising solutions for the problems people brought to him. But Mason had yet to turn over that rock. Nor could Mason explain why Blues had agreed to help him with the drunk and his other cases he'd needed help with since he quit playing piano. The one time he'd asked, Blues told him it was the only way he could make certain that Mason didn't start playing again.

They met for breakfast Wednesday morning at a midtown diner where the upwardly mobile have breakfast and the down-and-out spend hours with a cup of coffee.

"Sounds like you and your pinstriped partners are in deep shit, man," Blues said after Mason finished telling him what had happened over the last three days. "You want me to watch your back until this is over?"

"You think my back needs to be watched?"

"Oh, I don't know. You've got one dead partner and somebody wants you to either join him or be convicted for killing him."

Mason couldn't ignore the warning in Blues's offer. His willingness to accept it after he'd turned down a similar offer from

Kelly was more than a little sexist. He resolved to work on his gender insecurity just as soon as people stopped trying to kill him.

"I've never had someone watch my back before. Is that a hard thing to do?"

"Easier than teaching you to play the piano."

"Do I get more than one hour a week?"

"I'll be around as much as I can. Most of the time, you won't know it, but I won't have you covered all the time. You'll have to be careful."

"I'll just talk into my collar so the bad guys will think I've got backup around the corner. In the meantime, I don't have a clue who planted the bug. St. John says it's not one of his."

"He's right about that," Blues said as he rolled the microphone in his palm. "Every low-life PI in town has a drawer full of these."

"Sullivan's funeral is at one o'clock today. The office will be closed. Find out if any more of these toys are lying around. Where are you playing tonight?"

"I've got a gig at The Landing."

"I'll see you there around nine."

"Any suggestions if someone decides to skip the funeral to catch up on paperwork?"

"Anyone who's there instead of the funeral will have more explaining to do than you. The elevator to our floors will be locked out and you'll have to use our access code." Mason handed Blues a slip of paper with a series of numbers on it. "Use that sequence on the elevator control panel. It's the only way to get to our floors."

"Why all the cloak-and-dagger stuff?"

"I hate being the last to know what's going on."

"What about your partner who found the bug?"

"Sandra Connelly. We agreed not to say anything to anyone else."

"But you didn't tell her about me, did you?"

"No, and don't start interrogating me. I'm being careful, just like you told me. See you tonight."

CHAPTER TWENTY-FOUR

Mason decided to skip the office and visit Ellen Philpott instead. He knew that dropping in on a witness unannounced was better than calling for an appointment. It was easier to hang up than it was to close the door in someone's face.

He had followed the same rule when he met Kate for the first time. He was at a lecture, which was thin cover for a chance to meet women who didn't like getting picked up at bars. He stared at her from the moment she walked in. She was slender and slick, with thick, wavy black hair. And she knew how to move. She didn't walk. She shimmied and shimmered. What she lacked in cover-girl credentials, she made up in mystique.

It was a combination of things; the arc of her smile, the promising cup of her hands, the scent that lingered on her very kissable throat. Some of these things he guessed at that night and some he discovered in the fever of their time together.

She didn't notice him that night until after the speaker had shared her life experiences, none of which he could repeat since he didn't hear a word the speaker had said. He introduced himself like a thirty-second commercial, probing her education, career, and relationship status, closing the sale by asking her out, figuring it was harder to say no in person than over the phone a couple of days later when she'd struggle to remember they'd ever met.

When she said yes, he peeled the name tag off of his sweater and stuck it on top of hers, making certain she wouldn't forget his name. Later that night, he looked at himself in the mirror, toothpaste still leaking from the corner of his mouth, and declared that Kate was the woman he would marry.

Ellen Philpott didn't surrender as easily. She didn't even come to her door. She summoned Mason from within.

The Philpotts lived in Crystal Lakes, a gated community in the suburbs of south Kansas City that offered neither crystal nor a lake. Gated community meant a high-dollar development enclosed by an eight-foot wrought-iron fence to keep out the 99 percent of the economic food chain that weren't otherwise admitted to visit or clean. *So much for surprise,* Mason thought.

Each resident's name was engraved on a burnished brass panel mounted on a limestone post outside the automated gate barring the private entrance. A white marble button was provided beneath each name so that a visitor could announce his or her presence. Mason pressed the button below the Philpott name and waited.

"Speak," a disembodied sharp-toned female voice commanded from the speaker.

"It's Lou Mason to see Mrs. Philpott."

"Of course it is. Third house on the left past the gate. I'm on the patio."

The first house on the left past the gate was a Country French limestone McMansion. The second house on the left was a pale pink Mediterranean stucco with a tiled roof. The third house on the left was a rounded two-story white brick structure that looked more industrial than residential. Flower beds were paved with lava rocks. Stainless-steel figure eights skirted the high-gloss ebony front door. *Home is where the bunker is,* Mason thought as he walked around to the back of the house.

Morning sun baked the inlaid Spanish tiles and red bricks that crisscrossed the patio. Ellen sat on a high-backed, red-lacquered oval stool, her slender shoulders ramrod straight, her wide eyes fixed on a canvas stricken with ill-matched strokes of black and blue acrylic paint, brushes and palette at her feet. Sodden men's clothes, reeking of mildew, were heaped in a pile behind the easel.

"Painting is supposed to soothe me, but I don't want to be soothed," Ellen said. She brushed her close-cropped auburn hair with both hands. "All things considered, I'd rather be crazy."

"Go with your strengths," Mason said.

She laughed so hard she slipped off the stool, stepped on her paints, cursed, and wiped her shoes on an Armani shirt at the edge of the pile. Warren Philpott may have been tough, Mason thought, but he couldn't compete with crazy.

"Now, that's real good advice," she drawled after catching her breath. Her Missouri twang was just another contradiction. Though he'd not heard her speak during the trial, Mason would have guessed that she was more city than country.

"Thank you for seeing me."

"That's not much to thank someone for. It doesn't take much effort and the payoff can be kind of skimpy."

"Mrs. Philpott, I'll be honest with you. I'm still working on the case against your husband's company for Tommy Douchant. I know that you're divorcing him. I was hoping you might be able to help me."

"Warren already kicked the snot out of you once. What makes you think I can help you or that I would?"

"I don't know if you can. That's what I'm here to find out. I read the story in the newspaper about your divorce and thought you might be willing to try."

She squared up and glared at him, hands on bony hips, elbows flared like a human pelican, the veins in her long neck pulsating. Captain Queeg would make a better witness.

"You must think I'm no better than he is. Yes, my husband did me dirty. Shamed me with women no better than twenty-five-dollar whores. And you want me to get my revenge by telling you his secrets. Betray him to get even. Is that what you want me to do, Mr. Mason?"

"Tommy Douchant is my best friend. He's got a wife and two kids who don't eat if his social security disability check is late. You can call it betrayal or getting even. I call it doing the right thing."

She gave him a calmer, more studied look. "Do you think I'm crazy?"

He laughed. "No, I don't. I think you're one powerfully pissed-off woman who's trying to figure out what to do with a pile of wet clothes."

"Are you married?"

"Divorced. My wife left me. She said she just woke up one day and was out of love with me."

Ellen chewed her lower lip, digesting Mason's answer. "I don't know which would be worse. At least Warren claimed he still had feelings for me. He said he just wasn't built to be faithful."

"I think the worst one is the one that happens to you."

"You are surely right about that." She picked up her palette and brushes. "What would you need to help your friend?"

"The jury decided that there was nothing wrong with the design of the safety hook on Tommy's belt."

"So wouldn't you have to prove that something went wrong when it was manufactured?"

"Exactly."

"So why didn't you do that at the trial?"

"My expert witness said that the hook was made just like the design called for."

"Then you'd have to prove that your own witness was mistaken, wouldn't you, Mr. Mason?"

Ellen Philpott's crazy act evaporated. Her country-cousin accent vanished. And her questions cut to the bottom line. Mason wondered if she was leading him along, hoping he would ask the right question and relieve her of the burden of outright betrayal.

"Not necessarily. Tommy's employer turned the safety belt over to your husband the day of the accident. I didn't see it until after I filed the lawsuit. If there was something wrong with the hook, he could have switched it for a good one and no one would ever have known."

"Why, Mr. Mason," she said, her drawl fully engaged. "That would be dishonest and deceitful. It would be the act of a man who had no honor."

"Would it also be the act of a man who would dishonor a fine

94

woman?"

Bending over, she reached beneath the pile of clothes and pulled out a metal cash box.

"Warren is a collector. He fancies bad women and bad hooks. I suppose a psychiatrist would have a field day tying those two passions together."

She handed the box to him. It contained ten hooks just like the one on Tommy's belt. Mason couldn't tell one from the other. He looked up. She was sitting on the stool, her back to him, adding strong brushstrokes of paint to her canvas.

"Is one of these Tommy's?"

"I don't know. Warren used to brag about switching the hooks. He said lawyers weren't very smart. These may not be the only ones."

"Does your husband know you have this box?"

"I doubt it, since I found it hidden in his closet. I suspect it's one of those personal things he keeps telling me he wants to stop by and pick up."

"Mind if I keep the hooks?"

"So long as you hang Warren with one." She turned toward him from her canvas, smiled weakly, and wiped a tear from her cheek. "Damn paint makes my eyes water. Good-bye, Mr. Mason."

On his way to Sullivan's funeral, Mason stopped at the engineering department at the University of Missouri at Kansas City. Dr. Webb Chapman, the chairman of the department, had been his expert safety engineer at Tommy's trial. He wasn't in, so Mason left him the box of hooks and a note asking him to call.

CHAPTER TWENTY-FIVE

The Ward Parkway Episcopal Church was a massive limestone cathedral more suited to the Old World than to Kansas City. It was filled with several hundred mourners, many of whom were attorneys paying their last respects before picking off Sullivan & Christenson's clients. Somber greetings and heartfelt condolences couldn't hide their burgeoning appetites.

Mason saw his aunt Claire signing the guest book when he walked into the church. She was tall and big boned. She considered her size an advantage. There was nothing diminutive about her, in either appearance or demeanor. He caught her eye when she turned around and she nodded in reply, waiting for him to make his way through the line and add his name to the book.

"Thanks for coming," he told her.

"I didn't know the man, but he was your partner, so I decided to show the family flag."

An older woman employed by the firm as a secretary interrupted their conversation and embraced Mason. "He's gone to a better place, to paradise," she said.

"I never knew a paradise that didn't have a snake in it," Claire said after the woman peeled herself away.

"That's not a heaven-bound theology."

"So what? I'm not heaven bound. Just plant me in the ground and call it a day. If I do enough in this life, I don't much care about the next. And, by the way, next time your senior partner dies, tell me before I read about it in the paper."

"Sorry. Things have been a little wild."

"The paper said the police are investigating. What's going on?"

Mason leaned into her to muffle his response. "It looks like he was murdered."

"By whom?"

"The official position is person or persons unknown. Only the living are suspected."

"Including you?"

"Including me." Mason spotted Sandra Connelly heading for the seats cordoned off for members of the firm. "I'll call you later."

Mason joined Sandra in the third row, behind the family. The Sullivans had no children. Pamela, Diane Farrell at her side, and an array of anonymous siblings, in-laws, and cousins made their black-clothed entrance as the congregation silenced itself.

The minister invoked a boilerplate eulogy praising Sullivan's many civic contributions, his devotion to family and church, and the tragic untimeliness of his death. When he left Sullivan one miracle short of sainthood, Mason figured they'd never met. Harlan Christenson spoke briefly but movingly of their years of practice and the brotherly bond that had held them together.

"What a crock!" Sandra whispered. "Harlan needed Sullivan, but Sullivan would have dropped him like a bad habit if he could have found a way."

Mason turned toward her, but his eyes found Kelly Holt slipping into an empty seat across the aisle. She smiled at him as she sat down before looking away. He kept staring.

"My mother always told me it's not polite to flirt at funerals. Who is she?" Sandra asked.

"Kelly Holt, the FBI agent who quit the bureau and landed in the Ozarks. What in the hell is she doing here?"

"Put your tongue back in your mouth before you ask her."

"No subtly, huh?"

"Zero. And it doesn't do much for my ego either."

"Remember what your mother told you."

Christenson finished, the organ played, and the congregation stood as the family followed the casket out of the church. Mason and Sandra left to join the procession to the cemetery and had reached their cars when Kelly caught up with them.

"Hello, Counselor. Got room for one more?"

Sandra stuck out her right hand. "I'm Sandra Connelly, one of Lou's partners. We're running the firm's investigation into Sullivan's death. Lou tells me you're handling the Ozark end of things."

"I wasn't aware of the firm's investigation. Perhaps we can help each other."

Mason opened the passenger door to his car before their serve and volley moved to the net.

"I'll just follow in my car," Sandra said, slamming her door closed.

CHAPTER TWENTY-SIX

"What was all that about?" Kelly asked as he pulled into the funeral procession.

"I don't think she likes you."

"She doesn't even know me. Do you?"

"What? Like you?" Kelly was bright, strong, and attractive. What wasn't to like? She was also direct and Mason usually wasn't, but he liked the question. "You're my favorite former FBI agent turned sheriff."

"Well, you're not my favorite smart-ass lawyer. But I'm getting used to you. Now, what's this about the firm investigating Sullivan's death?"

"I'm not investigating Sullivan's death. I'm trying to figure out how much trouble he left behind, and I'm starting to feel like the guy who follows the elephants around at the circus with a shovel."

"How deep is it?"

"Stop me if I tell you what you already know. Your pal St. John sends his regards. Why didn't you tell me you'd been investigating the firm?"

"Listen, Counselor. After all your talk about privileged information, you should be the last person to complain. But you may be able to help me."

"With what? You still haven't told me how you know that Sullivan was murdered. Tell me what's going on. Then we'll see who can help who."

"Whom."

"Are you always this annoying?"

"Are you always this insecure?"

"You just bring out the best in me."

"Maybe I should have gotten a ride with your partner."

It may not have been Romantic Comedy 101, but the banter was easy and the teasing friendly and promising.

"Okay, that's enough combat for one funeral. Am I still a suspect?"

"I checked the damage to your car. One of my deputies took a report from a farmer who was hauling a truckload of hay down Highway 5 when some idiot tried to pass another car in a no-passing zone going the other way. The farmer said the idiot flew off the road just before he was about to get creamed."

"You see? My story checks out."

"Wrong. It doesn't mean your story checks out. Passing in a no-passing zone makes more sense than your story that someone was trying to kill you. I could charge you with reckless driving."

She smiled as she said it, which comforted Mason. It wasn't the smile of a woman about to arrest him.

"Why didn't the farmer come back to check on me?"

"He had to go home and change his shorts."

"So I scared the shit out of him. Very cute. Have you been practicing your punch line all day?"

"Just since breakfast. Actually, the farmer does back you up. He said the other driver held you out in the wrong lane. And he did have to change his shorts. Did you?"

"Yeah. And I haven't stopped since. Now, what's the story on Sullivan?"

She faced him with a pure cop look that left no room for negotiation. "I want your complete cooperation."

"Do I get yours?"

"To a point."

"I'll take the same point. Deal?" Kelly raised her chin and grimaced, giving him her no-deal look. "I don't know who killed him or who tried to kill me, but nobody wants to find out more than I do. I can't give up a client unless I'm not worried about being wrong. And you're not going to tell me anything about St. John's investigation that could blow his case. So we both know what that point is. We're college graduates. If it gets tricky, we'll work it out. Deal?"

She slipped out of her cop look and put on her punch-line smile. "Deal. Sullivan sustained a blow to the back of the head. Probably not enough to kill him or even knock him out. Water in his lungs proves he drowned."

"That's not news. What else do you have?"

"Cause of death was drowning, but he had a heart attack first. The coroner says it was probably drug induced. He doesn't have all the lab tests back yet. But he does have one test back. Your partner was HIV positive."

"AIDS?"

"Not yet. Just HIV positive. We're not disclosing that information yet. I've got an appointment with the family doctor, Charlie Morgenstern, after the funeral, to examine his medical records."

"Any more surprises—maybe a birthmark that turned up missing?"

"Close. He had needle marks on the inside of his left arm and the inside of his thighs."

"Don't tell me he was an intravenous drug user too!"

"Intravenous user of something. That's what the lab tests are about."

"HIV explains one thing. Sullivan was stalling on the physical for the life insurance policy to cover his death benefit at the firm. Now I understand why. I wonder who gave him the virus and who he passed it on to."

"Spreading that news would not improve his sex life and might make someone angry enough to get even. The insurance policy is another motive. Who was the beneficiary?"

"Technically, the firm, since the money was to be used to buy out his stock. So I guess his wife ends up the real beneficiary. But what difference does that make? He never got the policy."

"Maybe his wife didn't know that. Maybe she only knew he had the death benefit."

"Where do you go with the information on his HIV status?"

"Missouri Department of Public Health. Morgenstern had to report the HIV diagnosis. The state may have tried to track down his sex partners to notify them."

The mental picture of Sullivan listing the names of his sex partners was too much. Mason would have bet money he asked for extra paper.

"Did you know Sullivan and my firm were targets of St. John's investigation?"

"No. St. John wanted O'Malley. We knew about Sullivan, but nothing I saw pointed at him or your firm."

"Well, something changed. St. John sent Sullivan a target letter naming him and the firm about six weeks ago. Then he served Sullivan with a subpoena for the firm's records on O'Malley. Sullivan was supposed to turn the files over this Friday."

"How did you find out?"

"Scott Daniels found the target letter and the subpoena in Sullivan's office on Sunday."

"That's convenient."

"Yesterday, Sandra and I met with St. John to buy some time on the subpoena. Your name came up when I asked about wiretaps. St. John said they weren't tapping our phones. Then we found this in the phone on Sullivan's desk."

He handed her the bug.

"Too cheap for the bureau. This is strictly amateur stuff."

"That's what St. John said. I don't think I'm on his Christmas list anymore."

"Did you find any others?"

"I'll know soon. Is that all I get from you, Sheriff?" he asked as they pulled into the cemetery.

"Maybe. Depends," Kelly said as they stepped out of the car.

"On what? I'll even buy you dinner."

"On what my pal St. John wants." St. John stood alongside his sedan a hundred feet away, motioning her toward his car. "I don't think I'll need a ride back. Dinner sounds great. I'll call you next week."

Mason congratulated himself on getting a date at a funeral and walked toward the grave site.

CHAPTER TWENTY-SEVEN

One thing Mason learned from Blues was to pay more attention to his hometown. After all, he was a fourth-generation resident in a city that at one time had been home to more hogs and whores than just about anyplace in the history of either commodity.

Kansas City was born as the last trading post before the pioneers' leap into the Great American Desert, later known as Kansas. It survived its adolescence as one of the most wide-open, swinging, corrupt towns of the twenties and thirties and matured into a five-county metroplex straddling the Missouri-Kansas state line, bragging that it had more fountains than Paris and more boulevards than Rome.

Following the funeral service, friends and family gathered at the Sullivan home in Mission Hills, the richest of the Kansas-side municipalities that grew into a seamless patchwork of neighborhoods, oblivious to the state line.

An out-of-towner couldn't tell where Jackson County, Missouri, ended and Johnson County, Kansas, began. But it was easy to tell where the money was, and a lot of it was in Mission Hills. This enclave of the locally rich and famous was five minutes and a million dollars west of Mason's house.

Huge homes sat on large, heavily treed lots, along winding streets that oozed an old-money ambiance. The Sullivan home was a handsome Tudor set back on a broad, carefully manicured lawn. The circle drive was filled with cars bearing Mercedes, BMW, and Lexus hood ornaments. American-made cars lined the street.

Two hours spent pumping the hands of colleagues who were

planning their pitches to Sullivan's clients was enough for Mason. He found Pamela in the family room, sitting on a small sofa next to a stern-faced, dark-haired woman who was holding Pamela to her breast and stroking Pamela's hair. The woman looked up at Mason with a defiant glare. Two half-empty cocktail glasses sat on the butler's table in front of them. Mason cleared his throat. Pamela raised her head and sat up. The woman brushed Pamela's lips with her own while Pamela brushed imaginary lint from the woman's breast. This was a post-funeral visitation, not a slumber party, he thought.

"I know this isn't a good time, Pamela, but I'd like to come back tomorrow morning. Richard may have left some firm files at home."

Her eyes were glassy. He couldn't tell whether it was grief or booze or both. She didn't introduce her friend, who kept her high-beam glare trained on Mason.

"Certainly, Lou. I should be up and around by ten."

Mason spent the rest of the day and early evening returning calls from clients and answering mail until it was time to meet Blues at The Landing.

The Landing was a piano bar in the northwest corner of the downtown in what used to be the garment district. The buildings that used to turn out dresses and coats had been rehabilitated as offices and lofts. One, however, still ground coffee beans, and when the wind was right, the aroma swept the streets like a runaway Starbucks.

The Landing occupied a three-story redbrick building on the northeast corner of Eighth and Central that felt as if it had always been a saloon. Maybe it was all the beer and whiskey that had been absorbed by the wood-plank floors and the bartenders who looked as though they'd heard it all. The food was good and the music was great. The bar was jammed when Mason arrived at nine, slicing his way through the crowd until he found Blues finishing his dinner in the kitchen.

"It's about time you got here, man. I go on in five minutes.

I'm gonna play 'Green Dolphin Street' no matter how many times those accountants taking inventory of each other ask me to play some hip-hop bullshit."

Blues was not a fan of professional people. In fact, Mason couldn't name many people Blues was a fan of, especially if they wore neckties and counted money for a living.

"How do you know any of them are accountants?"

"You go out there and watch how they move. Only accountants move like that."

Mason didn't want to hear his critique of lawyers. "How'd you make out at my office?"

"I didn't find any more bugs. It looks like somebody cleaned house."

"How could you tell?"

"The bugs have an adhesive backing to hold them in place. Two phones were sticky where they shouldn't be sticky."

"Whose offices?"

"Scott Daniels and Harlan Christenson."

"If someone was bugging all three offices, why leave the one in Sullivan's office?"

"Maybe they wanted to or maybe they didn't have time to pull it out."

"What's the range on these things?"

"Not much. Whoever was listening couldn't have been more than a floor or two away."

"I'm supposed to find out if Sullivan left any dirty laundry behind. It looks like I may be able to open a dry cleaners."

Mason left as Blues weaved through the crowd toward his piano.

The next morning, he told Sandra about Blues while they drove to Pamela Sullivan's house. She accused him of being sexist and patronizing for not telling her sooner. Mason told her she was right. Before he could lie and tell her that he was sorry, she told him that he was on his own if he left her out again and that he was invited to her place for dinner Friday night to show that there were no hard feelings. Mason was still trying to remember when she started calling him Lou when they pulled into Sullivan's driveway.

"Pamela, this won't take long," he said as she let them in. "We need to make certain we've got all of Richard's files on client matters."

"Of course, I understand."

"Before I forget, I have your husband's briefcase at the office. There wasn't much in it. Just a book, a newspaper, and a CD. I'll have someone bring it out to you."

"That's not necessary. I don't need it. Keep it or give it away. Can I offer you a Bloody Mary?" she asked, holding up her own tall glass. "I tried orange juice, but I needed something a little stronger. I'm afraid I'm not very good with death."

"Another time," Sandra said.

Pamela shrugged, set her glass down on a narrow table in the entry hall, and led them into a paneled, bookshelf-lined study with overstuffed furniture, a fine Persian rug, and prints of English hunt scenes on the walls. A high-backed chair sat next to a small table adorned with an inkwell and feathered quill. A pearl-handled letter opener lay alongside the antique writing instruments.

Sullivan's desk had six drawers that were devoid of anything related to his law practice. A credenza behind the desk contained tax returns, financial records, and a locked cabinet.

Sandra asked, "Pamela, do you have the key for this cabinet?"

"Try the desk drawer."

Sandra rifled the desk again with no luck. "Any other suggestions?"

"Well, perhaps."

Pamela walked over to the bookshelves, reached behind the six-volume Carl Sandburg biography of Abraham Lincoln, and pulled out a handgun. Before they could move, she calmly fired two rounds into the lock.

"There, that should do it."

They gawked first at Pamela and then at the gaping hole in the cabinet and then back at Pamela.

"Richard bought the gun for me after someone broke in last month. He said it might come in handy. He was seldom wrong," she said as she returned the gun to its hiding place.

The cabinet was empty except for an unlabeled CD case. Mason opened it and found another DVD.

"Do you mind if we take this to the office, Mrs. Sullivan?" Sandra asked.

"Not at all. But I would appreciate it if you could do a small favor for me."

"You name it," Mason said.

"Have someone let me know what to do to collect Richard's death benefit. When he told me about it, I never imagined actually getting the money. He didn't seem like the kind of man who would ever die."

She said it with a wistful, sad tone laced with genuine surprise. Her mix of anger and grief since last Sunday made sense to Mason, as did her drinking. Sullivan may have been a son of a bitch, but he was her son of a bitch. It was the way a lot of dead people left their survivors.

Still, her request felt as if she'd just fired another round from her revolver. Mason wasn't ready to tell her that her husband had been diagnosed with HIV and didn't get the life insurance policy to pay for his buyout and that the firm didn't have the money to pay her. He would leave that happy task to Scott after Mason warned him about her gun. But he did tell Sandra on the drive back to the office.

She looked straight ahead as she muttered through clenched teeth, "That no-good son of a bitch!"

"Seems likely," Mason said.

CHAPTER TWENTY-EIGHT

The conference room had given birth to a landfill. It was littered with half-empty coffee cups, Coke cans, wadded paper, and pizza boxes. Phil and Maggie had matching sets of bags under their eyes. Diane Farrell looked fresh, rested, and completely in charge.

They had rolled in portable erasable whiteboards to keep track of O'Malley's projects. Each project was cross-referenced to the others so that assets, ownership, and attorneys could be visualized at a glance. Diane was busily entering data on the computer so they could sort information into endless combinations.

"Diane, what do you know about these? We found one in Sullivan's office here and the other one at his house."

Mason handed her the two DVD cases.

"You found Richard's porno flicks—big deal." She turned back to her computer monitor. "What do you want—a psychohistory of a man who watched dirty movies on his computer? Give it a rest. Besides, we've got a lot of work to do."

"In case you've forgotten, Diane, you work for me now, so unless you want to peddle your bullshit at another firm, cut the crap. Make sure there's nothing else on these DVDs."

Mason wasn't certain he could fire Diane, but he doubted that anyone would fight to keep her now that Sullivan was gone.

"The king is dead. Long live the king. Would now be soon enough?"

For her, it was a surrender speech.

"That would be lovely, Diane."

She inserted each disk into her computer and pulled up a list of the contents on the disks. The only document shown on each was the movie title.

"Satisfied, boss?"

"How do you know if the list identifies everything on the disks?"

"That's what it's for."

"Can you put something on the disk that wouldn't show up on the list, something that you'd have to have a special password to access?"

"I don't know. Programming is not one of my areas. I just run the software on the system."

"All right." Mason turned his attention to Phil and Maggie. "How far have you gotten?"

"Phil and I are about halfway through the files. We should have the raw information compiled in a couple of days. Then we have to figure out what we've gathered. Some trends are starting to appear," Maggie said.

She stopped, waiting for them to ask her to continue. It was the nature of too many young lawyers not to speak unless spoken to, especially if they'd been to the Sullivan school of intimidation.

"Well, Maggie—we're waiting," Sandra said.

"Right. The real estate deals handled through Quintex look clean. The property values are backed up by independent appraisals."

"So far, so good. What else?" Mason asked.

"It looks like O'Malley set up a bunch of phony loans from the bank. The companies are mostly shells with no assets. The money ended up in his pocket."

"We've known about that for a while. That's what St. John has been pressing him on. Have you found anything else?"

"This may not be a problem yet. There's another set of deals by Quintex that involve the purchase and leaseback of store fixtures. I never worked on those and we haven't sorted them out yet."

"Fine. Stay after it and, remember, nothing leaves this room. If St. John can tie Sullivan to those loans, he may get the keys to our office as part of the settlement we'll have to make with the government."

Mason dreaded the stack of mail and messages that he knew would be waiting on his desk. His secretary, Cindy, had divided them into piles marked *Junk*, *I already stalled them until next week*, and *Ignore these and die*. Fortunately, the last group was limited to five calls and three letters, which he spent the next two hours answering. He was starting to review the O'Malley billing memos when Scott Daniels walked in and closed the door.

"O'Malley isn't happy."

Scott's pained expression meant that if O'Malley wasn't happy, he wasn't happy.

"I didn't ask him to be happy—I just told him to tell me the truth. If he can't do that, we've got serious problems."

"He'll fire us if you don't ease up. He doesn't want you digging up his life. Back off a little, just until things calm down. Let me deal with O'Malley. We can't afford to lose him as a client."

Mason wondered where Scott stood in all of this. They had been close friends for thirteen years. They had stood up for each other in their weddings and Scott had made a place for him at the firm. But someone had tapped Scott's phone. That had to mean that Scott knew at least some of what had been going on even if he wasn't directly involved. Mason decided to tell him parts of what he knew and let Scott's reaction guide him.

"Kelly Holt says Sullivan was murdered. Someone tried to run me off the road on the way back from the lake. St. John is on us like white on rice. Pamela wants her million bucks. O'Malley is at the center of all of this. I'm not backing off."

"You're making a big mistake, Lou."

He slammed the door on the way out just in case Mason missed his punctuation.

Scott's reaction to Mason's catastrophe checklist was near the top of the week's bizarre turns. No questions or comments about the murder of his mentor or the attempt on Mason's life, no concern for his own vulnerability, no solutions for the financial crisis they faced over Pamela's demand for payment. Scott either didn't care, which Mason didn't want to believe, or trouble with O'Malley was the only thing that really frightened him.

The door was still vibrating when Harlan Christenson opened it, looking as if he'd just been sent to the principal's office.

"St. John has upped the ante. I'm being audited."

"Harlan, lawyers are audited all the time. I doubt if St. John has the clout to single you out. Just give the IRS agent your files and your accountant's phone number and don't worry about it."

"It's not that simple."

Harlan picked up a pencil on Mason's desk and rubbed it between his palms.

"How hard can it be? You give the IRS agent your tax returns and answer a few questions."

"If all they wanted was my tax returns, there wouldn't be an audit. I file my taxes on time every year. They've got the returns."

Mason sat up straight, appreciating the seriousness of Harlan's situation.

"Have they asked for any specific records?"

Harlan didn't answer. He gripped the pencil with both hands, studying it as if the answer lay in the dull lead tip.

"They want records of my income outside the firm and my business expenses."

"Is that a problem?"

Harlan snapped the pencil in half and dropped the pieces onto Mason's desk. A thin trickle of blood dripped from the fat of his palm. He pulled a sliver of pencil from his skin and wiped his hand on his trouser.

"Lou, I can't pass the audit. I've been underreporting income and overstating my expenses."

Harlan shrugged his shoulders, stuck his hands in his pockets, and glued his eyes to the floor. He was a child hoping for his father's promise that everything would be all right.

"Who else knows about your tax problems?"

"Scott. I tried talking to him but he just got angry and told me to get out. Said I should have known better."

His eyes began to water.

"When's your first meeting with the IRS agent?"

"Monday morning at ten."

"Would you like me to go with you?"

Mason offered because he thought Harlan couldn't bring himself to ask. Harlan wasn't strong, but he was proud. It was a curiously sympathetic combination. Harlan was in trouble, which meant that Mason couldn't keep his nose out of Harlan's business.

Harlan straightened a bit and shook off the suggestion. "When the day comes that I can't handle some snot-nosed IRS kid, I'd better hang it up."

"That snot-nosed kid can send you away for a long time, Harlan. We've lost one senior partner this week. That's my limit."

"Don't worry. The government will always make a deal for the right price," he said before leaving.

Mason wondered what Harlan had to offer that would be good enough to wipe the slate clean on income tax evasion. He couldn't decide whether the question or the answer bothered him more.

CHAPTER TWENTY-NINE

Sandra Connelly stopped by Mason's office at three o'clock Friday afternoon. "Eight o'clock okay? Dress casual," she said.

His blank look told her he'd forgotten about their dinner date. Recollection came an instant too late.

"You forgot, didn't you?"

He didn't expect the disappointment in her voice. Sandra wasn't someone who let people know they'd hurt her feelings. She just found ways to remind them that paybacks are hell.

"Jesus, Sandra, I'm sorry. This has been a rotten week. I wouldn't be good company anyway. Rain check till next weekend?"

"Sure, no problem. You don't know what you're missing, though."

Her wolfish smile gave Mason a pretty good idea, but fooling around with a partner, even one as tempting as Sandra, was a low-percentage move. And he couldn't understand her sudden interest, since he'd never shown up on her radar before.

The worst thing was that part of him didn't object to the image of being taken advantage of by her. Which reminded him of the one and only piece of advice Aunt Claire ever gave him about sex: Think with the big head, not the little head.

Mason finished reviewing the O'Malley billing memos, checking them against the master index of matters Diane Farrell had generated. The firm had been billing O'Malley between a million and a million and a half dollars a year for four of the last five years. In the last twelve months, the billings had jumped to two million.

The only problem was that half a million had been charged to two matters that didn't exist except in the billing memos. O'Malley had paid five hundred thousand dollars for work that had never been done. Nobody could have pulled that off without Angela knowing about it. Mason called her and told her to come to his office.

"The staff reads all these closed doors like smoke signals," she said as she closed his. "They figure something big must be happening. It's one of the best sources of office intelligence next to monitoring radio traffic and troop movements."

"Yeah, I know. But this has been a closed-door kind of week. I've gone over these billing memos, Angela, and I—"

"—figured out that O'Malley was paying for work we didn't do."

"Do you always—"

"—interrupt and complete other people's sentences? Sorry, it's a bad habit. I knew you'd figure it out when you asked for the billing memos. No point in hiding it."

"I appreciate your candor. Why didn't you blow the whistle on Sullivan?"

"It's none of my business what the firm charges its clients."

Mason shook his head. "Angela, I've only been here a few months, but the one thing I know is that there's nothing that goes on in this place that you don't consider your business. Try me again."

"You're giving me too much credit. I'm a bean counter. That's all. My job is to make sure clients pay their bills so we can pay ours and that there's money left at the end of the year for my Christmas bonus."

"So you knew that Sullivan was billing O'Malley half a million dollars for work we didn't do and never once asked him why?"

"I didn't say that. You did."

Mason let out an exasperated sigh. "Okay, Angela. Let's play cross-examination. Did you talk to Sullivan about the bills to O'Malley for work we didn't do?"

She smiled at his frustration. "Isn't it fun to use all that education, Lou? Sure, I talked to him. He was the boss."

"And what did he tell you?"

"To keep my mouth shut . . ." She let her answer dangle, teasing him with the part left unspoken.

"Or else what?"

She eased back in her chair. "Or else he would have me arrested." She said it with sudden resignation, her bravado exhausted. "Sullivan was blackmailing me. I had cash-flow problems last year and I took an interest-free loan from the firm without asking. He figured it out."

"And if you told the partners about O'Malley, he'd—"

"—go to the police about my loan. I even slept with him, thinking that he might decide to forget about it."

Her eyes never left Mason's as she spoke. She'd been caught, but she was tough.

"What happened to the money you borrowed?"

"I paid it back with my bonus at the end of the year."

"Anything else I should know, like why O'Malley would pay us for work we didn't do?"

"Ask O'Malley. He's never given anything away in his life. I'll clean my desk out over the weekend."

"Why?"

"Oh, don't tell me I have to sleep with you too. You're good-looking enough and all that, but I've lost my appetite for lawyers."

"We need some continuity around here, and you're too valuable to lose. Stick around. I'll be straight with you if you'll do the same and let me—"

"—finish your own sentences?"

"Agreed."

Mason's phone rang and Angela excused herself. It was Webb Chapman.

"What am I supposed to do with these hooks? Decorate my Christmas tree?" he asked.

"Something simpler. Figure out which one was on Tommy

Douchant's belt."

"Why do you think one of them might have been his?"

"Never underestimate a crazy woman."

Webb listened without interruption as he told him about his meeting with Ellen.

"It's an entertaining story. But it gets you nowhere on identifying Tommy's hook. You'll have to give me a clue where to start."

"Do any of them look like they failed?"

"They all do. That doesn't prove Tommy was using one of them."

"Keep them anyway. I'll see what I can come up with."

Mason hung up as he pictured Tommy rolling his wheelchair back and forth across the threshold of his front door. He wasn't going back there with more bad news. His problems with St. John and O'Malley were screaming at him louder than Tommy. His would have to wait until he got them under control, or until he dreamt of Tommy's trial again. Whichever came first.

Mason and his team worked through the weekend. He told Sandra about the phony bills to O'Malley, but they found nothing in the files to explain the fees.

If she was angry with Mason for breaking their date, she kept it to herself. By Sunday night, they were the only ones left in the conference room. They had finished reviewing the files on O'Malley's loans from his bank.

"St. John has O'Malley cold," Sandra said.

"Ice-cold. He convinced the bank to loan money to dummy businesses that he secretly owned. The businesses couldn't pay the money back and had no assets for the bank to foreclose on when the loans went bad."

"Sullivan set up the companies, drafted the loan documents, sat in on the bank's loan committee meetings, and told everyone the loans were okay."

"So Sullivan was going down too."

"Not necessarily, Lou. Sullivan could claim that he was relying on information provided by O'Malley and that he didn't know the truth."

"Sullivan asked me to destroy documents that would implicate him. There's nothing here that St. John couldn't get from the bank and O'Malley."

Sandra gave him a look sharper than the knife she carried. "These details slip out of your mouth so frequently. Wouldn't it be just as easy to tell me sooner?"

"Yeah, but it wouldn't be nearly as enjoyable." He recoiled as she smacked him on the arm. "Fine," he told her, trying not to wince. "We had lunch last Friday. That's when he asked me. I told him no before he could even tell me which documents."

"Why wouldn't he just destroy the documents himself?"

"He may have. But by asking me, he sets me up to take the fall. If I agree, he owns me. If I refuse—which I did—he claims that it was my idea and uses it to get rid of me, which he tried to do."

Mason told her about the note Kelly Holt had found in Sullivan's suite at the lake.

"Sullivan wouldn't have gone to that much trouble unless somebody else knew about the documents," she said. "Otherwise, he'd destroy them and no one would know they ever existed."

"And we still haven't figured out the fixtures deals with Quintex. But we've got enough to talk to O'Malley about tomorrow."

"What if O'Malley doesn't come clean?"

"We quit and get ready to go to war with him and the feds."

"I don't like the odds," Sandra said. "We're outnumbered and surrounded."

"So we'll have to fight dirty," Mason said.

CHAPTER THIRTY

There was a message from Harlan Christenson on Mason's answering machine when he got home just before midnight. Harlan had left the message three hours earlier.

"Lou, it's Harlan. I know it's late, but I was hoping you'd come out to the farm. I need to talk with you about my meeting tomorrow morning with the IRS agent. I've got to make a deal. I just don't know how. Call me when you get home. Please."

Mason heard fear in Harlan's voice, the icy kind when a car slams on its brakes and shrieks to a stop at your feet. He dialed Harlan's number and listened to a recorded explanation that the number was no longer in service or had been disconnected. Thinking he may have misdialed, Mason tried again with the same result.

Harlan's farm was in Stanley, Kansas, twenty miles south of Mason's house and ten miles west of the state line. The nearest neighbor was half a mile away. City lights melted into inky blackness as Mason drove into the country, thinking about the hours he had spent tramping through the fields with Harlan, casting a line in his pond, catching nothing but good memories.

The farmhouse was black and silent beneath a distant canopy of stars, the darkness swallowing Mason when he stepped out of his car. The only sound was a distant train whistle riding the night air. As he approached the house, he could make out a faint glow leaking around the edges of a front window.

There was no answer when he knocked on the weather-beaten door. He squeezed the handle, his palm sweaty, cursing under his breath as the door swung open and he stepped into the entry hall.

He was fearless in the courtroom, willing to take risks others wouldn't because he was prepared and because he owned the ground, the battle one he'd chosen. Outside those walls, he'd never considered whether he was brave or what that even meant. Stepping across the threshold, he realized that bravery and stupidity were first cousins.

Mason called out to Harlan. He didn't answer. Afraid of what he might find, he hesitated, light-headed and breaking into a sweat from the sluggish mix of heat and humidity inside the house.

The entry hall led straight back to the kitchen and the light he had seen from the porch, a dozen steps. He took one and then another, stopping as the floorboards creaked beneath his feet, listening for what he didn't know, hearing nothing, starting again.

A man materialized out of the darkness, blotting out the light from the kitchen, and drilled his fist into Mason's gut. Mason folded in half as the man grabbed him by the back of his shirt and threw him headlong down the length of the hall and onto the kitchen floor.

Gasping for air, his eyes clenched, Mason rose on hands and knees, when a boot to his back put him on the floor. He curled into a fetal crouch, waiting for the next blow. When it didn't come and he heard the front door slam, he opened his eyes. Harlan lay next to him, tongue clenched between his teeth, bulging dead eyes staring past him into the fluorescent glow of the open refrigerator.

The silence was split by the cough of a grinding engine and tires spitting gravel. Mason crawled away from Harlan's body and huddled against the front door, shaking, waiting for the nerve to go outside. Moments passed before he stumbled out the door, slumped into his car, and called 911. He passed the time wondering whether to charge the call to the firm. Claire always told him that humor was the last thread of sanity. He clung to it.

The county cops responded. They were polite but suspicious. Why was he there? When did he get there? Who hit him? What did he see? What did he hear? Let's start again from the beginning.

Mason sat in the backseat of a stuffy patrol car, his sweat-stained shirt damp against his skin, answering questions in the dark. Every now and then, someone opened the car door, illuminating the spidery pattern of cracked upholstery on the back of the front seat.

The assistant DA on call for weekend bodies asked the questions. He was young and energetic and kept Mason on task. A deputy sheriff listened from the front seat, motioning to the ADA when paramedics emerged from the house, Harlan's body zipped inside a black body bag, laid out on a stretcher. They watched in silence as the paramedics loaded Harlan into the back of an ambulance and drove away, the headlights blinding them for an instant as the vehicle passed by.

"One more time, Mr. Mason. From the top," the ADA said.

Three hours and two detailed interrogations later, Mason stood under his shower, swearing never to spend another Sunday with his partners. Sleep was impossible. Sunrise wasn't far off, and he went jogging at first light. Another shower and he headed for the refuge of work. He decided to wait to announce Harlan's death to the staff until after he'd talked with Scott.

At eight thirty he looked up to find Kelly Holt smiling at him from his doorway, a soft-leather briefcase in one hand. Mason hadn't seen her since Sullivan's funeral. He wasn't expecting her, but he was glad to see her. Her smile didn't last long when she saw his face.

"Tell me about it," she said and closed the door.

It wasn't a question or a command. It was an invitation, and Mason gladly took it. She listened and asked questions that he answered with dull rote, having committed them to memory hours ago.

"Don't try to forget it. You can't. Don't try to understand it. You won't. Learn not to be afraid of it, and you'll learn to live with it."

"It's that simple?"

"Nope. The tough stuff never is. The good news is that you owe me for a year's worth of therapy. If it makes you feel any better, I've got more good news."

"I'll take it."

"I know how Sullivan was murdered," she said.

CHAPTER THIRTY-ONE

"I don't get cops. I'm in the middle of an epidemic of murdered partners and you're grinning like you just won the lottery."

"Professional pride. I like being smarter than the killer."

"How was he murdered?"

"An overdose of insulin."

"I didn't know he was diabetic."

"He wasn't. I doubt if he would have taken a fatal dose of insulin on purpose. Somebody injected him or duped him into injecting himself. That fits with the needle marks found on his left arm and thighs."

"How do you know it was insulin?"

"Lab tests. And it makes sense with the rest of the evidence."

"I thought he drowned."

"He did. The insulin overdose made him sick enough that he couldn't save himself when he hit the water."

"What did it do to him?"

"Probably made him sweaty and nauseated at first. At the end, his heart rate was in overdrive. That's what caused the heart attack. If he hadn't fallen in the lake, that's what would have killed him."

"When do you think it happened?"

"Could have been before or after the card game. The reaction can be fast or take up to a few days."

"What now?"

"I'm going to have a chat with Cara Trent. She was the last person seen with Sullivan."

"Why haven't you talked with her already?"

"I wanted to wait for the lab tests so I'd know what to ask her and so I'd know when she was lying."

"What makes you think she'll lie?"

"Everyone does at first. Or they leave things out, like you did."

Mason didn't argue since she was right about him.

"Mind if I sit in?"

He couldn't let one of the firm's employees be questioned about her involvement in a murder without a lawyer present.

"I'd have been disappointed if you didn't insist."

"Do you think she did it?"

"I don't know. Depends on what their relationship was really like. Murder is a strange business. It attracts the most unlikely people—friends, lovers, spouses—all kinds of partners."

They walked down the hall to Cara's office. She sat behind a wooden desk in her windowless office, twirling a pen between her fingers. She jumped when they knocked, as if they'd awakened her. Her face was slack, her eyes puffy. Mason guessed she wasn't sleeping and probably hadn't for the last couple of days.

Case files were stacked on both sides of her chair. The walls were bare. Her small office got smaller when Kelly showed Cara her badge and wasted no time with small talk.

"Were you with Richard Sullivan when he died?"

Cara pulled her chair up hard against her desk, a slight tremor passing along her jawline. "No."

"Mr. Sullivan was murdered, Cara. You were seen leaving the poker game with him on Saturday night, which makes you the last person seen with him. I'm certain you want to help us find out who killed him."

Cara looked at Mason for confirmation. She was struggling to keep her control as she wadded the edge of her legal pad.

"It's true," Mason said. "But you don't have to answer any questions. I'm sure you know that."

"No, Cara, you don't have to answer my questions. But I'd have to wonder why you'd refuse to assist in a murder investigation," Kelly said, holding Cara with her stare.

"You haven't given me a Miranda warning."

"You don't get a Miranda warning until you become a suspect. Are you a suspect?"

Cara crossed her arms over her chest. "I know my rights. You're not even in your jurisdiction."

"I'll make it easy on you, Cara. A neighbor puts you at the condo that night twice; the first time with Sullivan and the second time by yourself. And your fingerprints are all over Sullivan's ski boat. Now, be a good girl and tell me the truth."

"If you've got my fingerprints, you got them illegally. What's the matter, haven't they heard of the Fourth Amendment in the Ozarks?"

Cara turned ugly with her last shot, playing lawyer one too many times. Kelly counterpunched.

"Here, read this." She pulled Sullivan's autopsy report from her briefcase and tossed it onto Cara's desk. "Your boyfriend had a little secret he forgot to tell you about. He was HIV positive."

Cara turned chalky and started to shake. "You're lying, you goddamn bitch, you're lying!"

"I don't have to lie, Cara. The truth is a lot scarier than any lie I could tell you. Pick it up and read it."

Kelly's quiet insistence frightened Cara, who shrank from the report as if it were contagious.

"Pick it up and read it," Kelly continued, hammering her with a velvet glove. "You probably don't have AIDS yet since it can take ten years to show up. Now, read it and tell me what happened."

Cara picked up the report, quivering, tears streaming down her face. "Oh God, oh my God . . . ," she cried, and then reached for her trash can and vomited.

Kelly put her arm around her, now a soothing big sister helping Cara wipe her face with tissues from a box on the desk.

"Cara, you don't have to say anything else," Mason said.

He'd been transfixed by Kelly's performance and almost forgot why he was there. Kelly ignored him and handed Cara her coffee cup.

"It's okay," Cara said between gulps. "I know what I'm doing." Her voice was soft, childlike. "I wanted him to use protection, but he said I was the first one since his wife and I fucking believed him."

"Tell me what happened Saturday night," Kelly said.

"He said he was stuck playing poker with the partners. I was supposed to show up around eleven so he'd have an excuse to leave."

"When did you make your plans?"

"Saturday morning."

"Were you with him earlier in the evening?"

"No."

"Do you know where he was before the card game?"

"I just figured he was having dinner with his wife."

Kelly nodded at her to continue.

"He took me to a condo on the other side of the lake." She laughed dryly. "He said he felt lousy. He blamed it on his wife. As if that was supposed to make me feel better. Can you believe it?"

Kelly answered, sister to sister. "Yeah, men will really fool you. What happened at the condo?"

"Nothing. He couldn't even get it up."

"Did he have anything to drink?"

"Ice water. He kept saying he was dying of thirst."

"Did he take any medication?"

She took a moment to answer. "No. Not while I was watching."

"Were you in the same room the entire time?"

"Almost. He went to the john just before we left."

"Did you see any syringes anywhere in the condo?"

Cara gave Kelly a quizzical look. "What is that—a trick question?"

"Depends. Did you see any?"

"No. I don't do drugs."

"Are you on any medications?"

"Just the pill."

"How long were you there?"

"Long enough to know there was no helping his limp dick.

On the way back, we stopped in a cove. He must have been feeling better because he asked me to take my top off. He was a real boob man. Then he started shivering and stood up." Her voice rose an octave, and her eyes glazed with the telling of the rest. "He had this funny look, like he was somewhere else, and he was breathing so fast it was freaky."

"Tell me the rest of it," Kelly said.

"We were standing in the middle of the boat. I reached for him but he fell away from me, backward almost. He hit his head on something. I helped him up." She stopped.

"And then?"

"He took a couple of steps, like he was drunk, and fell in the lake." She shrugged as her voice dropped.

"Did you try to help him?"

"I can't swim," she whined, as if that too were someone else's fault. "The water was black—he never came back up."

"Why did you go back to the condo?"

"To look for an earring I'd lost. I was afraid what would happen if people found out about us, especially his wife. The firm would never give me a job when I graduated."

Cara looked at them, her eyes pleading for a way out. Kelly didn't open any doors.

"I found the earring, Cara. You left it on the boat. I'll be in touch."

CHAPTER THIRTY-TWO

Mason stayed with Cara after Kelly left. He suggested she hire a lawyer and didn't argue with her when she quit. He caught up with Kelly at the elevator.

"Cara resigned. Are you going to charge her?"

"I don't know. Poisoning takes a strong and patient personality. Those don't appear to be her strengths. And she didn't know Sullivan was HIV positive, so she doesn't seem to have a motive."

"Who did?"

"Look for the person who had the most to gain. Who loved him or hated him too much? Who envied him too much?"

"So many choices and so little time."

"Maybe not," she said.

"You've already got a short list of suspects?"

"I'll start with anyone who had access to insulin. You know more of the candidates than I do. Let's kick it around over dinner. How about six thirty at Brentano's on the Plaza?"

"Yeah, sure."

And she was gone. Mason started missing her as soon as the elevator doors closed. Maybe it was because he'd been overly celibate lately. Maybe it was because her badge turned him on. He wasn't certain, but he liked missing her.

He went back to his office. Scott Daniels walked in just as Mason answered his phone. When he hung up, Mason didn't know where or how to start, so he just plunged in.

"That was Pamela. She's been arrested for Sullivan's murder and, if that's not bad enough, Harlan was murdered last night."

They stared at each other, neither speaking, until Mason's secretary came in to tell him that Victor O'Malley was holding.

"Tell him something's come up and I'll have to reschedule."

"Pamela couldn't have killed Sullivan. That's crazy," Scott said.

"So far she's only been charged with conspiracy to murder Sullivan. They've taken her to the Johnson County Sheriff's office in Olathe and she wants me to represent her."

Claire would've flown to her side. Mason knew he had to go, but he wasn't in as big of a hurry as his aunt would have liked. He had no qualms about defending O'Malley in a white-collar crime case, but he was the wrong lawyer to save Pamela from the death penalty.

Scott lost interest in Pamela's problems. "Tell me about Harlan," he said, his gaze on the floor while he shrunk into his chair, trying to crawl inside his three-button suit.

"I got home late last night. Harlan had left a message on my machine asking me to come out to his farmhouse and help him prepare for his meeting this morning with the IRS agent. I called him back but his phone was dead. When I got out there, he was dead too."

"What do the police think happened?" Scott asked without looking up.

"They didn't confide in me. They just asked a lot of questions, nodded when I answered, and then asked the same questions again." Mason changed the subject. "Let's send the staff home for the day. We better have another partners' meeting in the morning and figure out how we keep this operation afloat."

Scott agreed, and they gathered the staff in the thirty-second-floor lobby and broke the news of Harlan's death. He was a man no one could dislike. The lawyers and staff were dazed, many weeping openly, as they staggered from the office. Angela volunteered to stay and man the phones.

Mason waited until everyone except Angela and Scott were gone before leaving. Victor O'Malley Jr. nearly ran over him as the elevator door opened. Mason was in no mood for O'Malley-lite.

"Sorry, Victor, I wasn't expecting you. My secretary told your father that we had to reschedule. We've got a couple of real emergencies."

"We never needed an appointment with Sullivan. He understood how to treat important clients."

Weasels were lousy at intimidation, Mason thought. And he was fresh out of client suck-up.

"I'll remember that when you're the client. Maybe your father will let you sit in on our next meeting so you can practice."

Scott rounded the corner in time to hear their exchange. He was redefining pale but managed to welcome Junior with a conciliatory smile.

"Vic, we're all in shock around here," he said while taking him by the arm. "Somebody broke into Harlan's house last night and killed him. The police think it was a burglary that went sour. On top of that, Pamela has been charged with Sullivan's murder. Lou is on his way to the courthouse to see her. I just talked to your father and he understands about the appointment."

"We've all got problems, Scott, but we need to talk about the fixtures deals."

Scott cast a quick glance at Mason as he stepped onto the elevator, then took Vic Jr. by the arm and led him to his office.

The Johnson County Courthouse was in Olathe, Kansas, another once sleepy small town that had grown into a virtual suburb of Kansas City, even if it was twenty-five miles southwest of downtown and on the other side of the state line. On his way there, Mason left a message for B.J. Moore, a good friend and a better criminal defense lawyer.

He first met B.J. when they shared a client who had been charged with embezzling three million dollars from his employer at the same time he was making a workers' compensation claim against the company. The client pled guilty to the embezzlement charge and the DA agreed not to prosecute him for what turned out to be a fraudulent injury claim.

B.J. returned his call as Mason crossed the state line into

Kansas. He was already at the courthouse on another case and would wait for Mason. Thirty minutes later, they were ushered into an interrogation room in the county jail across the street from the courthouse.

The room was a bleak display of tax dollars at work, off-white walls, white ceiling tiles, and green linoleum, wooden table, four chairs, and no windows. They excused the deputy sheriff who was there to protect them from Pamela and then listened as she declared her innocence and screamed at them to get her out of the goddamn jail.

"If I'd have wanted to kill that no-good bastard, I'd have shot him with my own goddamn gun!"

Jail was a true class equalizer. Dressed in an orange prisoner jumpsuit, her hair tangled, her makeup smeared, and reeking of bad breath, body odor, and stale booze, Pamela had morphed from an upscale Mission Hills widow into a drunken bag lady charged with murder.

"We'll try to get you out of here as soon as we can," Mason said, "but I can't represent you."

"Why not?" she snapped as she threw herself into one of the metal folding chairs.

"Because I could be a witness. You need the best lawyer you can get, and that's why I asked my friend B.J. Moore to be here."

B.J. was pear-shaped and shaggy haired, and his suit looked as if he had picked it up where he'd dropped it the night before. Women liked him because he was cuddly. Men liked him because he was without pretense. He had a knack for making people comfortable with him.

"Please don't take offense, Mr. Moore," Pamela said, "but I don't know you, and I'd rather have someone I know."

"Mrs. Sullivan, I'm more interested in how you feel after your case is over. Let me figure out if I can get you home for dinner. If you're still here at breakfast, you can hire somebody else."

B.J. looked into Pamela's eyes as he spoke, holding the gaze until she softened, fussed with her hair, and dipped her chin.

"Okay," she said.

B.J. took her hand. "Good. Let's get started."

CHAPTER THIRTY-THREE

Kelly was waiting in the hall.

"What's she doing in a Kansas jail for a murder she supposedly committed in Missouri? And why was she only charged with conspiracy?"

"She was arrested in Kansas. The DA went for the conspiracy charge because he wanted to grab her and the headlines. It's easier to back off of that than a murder charge if he can't make the case."

"Doesn't sound too bright to me."

"That's never been an obstacle to elected office."

They walked across the street and sat in the shade of the gazebo in the center of the Courthouse Square. Mason nodded at the few familiar faces passing by. A groundskeeper rambled away, leaving them alone except for the yellow jackets feasting on the flowers planted nearby.

"The sheriff's detective on Harlan's case says it looks like a burglary that went bad," Kelly said. "They're trying to find out if anything's missing. Where's his family?"

"Two kids, one on each coast. His wife died a couple of years ago. Do you really think Pamela murdered Sullivan?"

"I didn't arrest her. The Johnson County DA is up for reelection, and he's grandstanding. That doesn't mean she didn't kill him, but I wouldn't have gone for the arrest until I had better evidence."

"I thought it was your case. What happened?"

"I needed a search warrant for Pamela's house. The DA had to get it for me because I'm out of my jurisdiction. We may have found something, and he decided to charge her with conspiracy to commit murder so he could hang on to the case."

"Based on what?"

"We found a syringe and a vial of an unidentified substance. If it turns out to be insulin, he'll claim she planned the murder in Johnson County, which gives him his conspiracy count."

"What happens to the murder charge?"

"The crime was committed at the lake. We'll charge her there and Kansas will extradite her so we can try her on the murder charge first. The DA still looks good when he ships her down to us."

"Which gets me back to my first question. Do you think she did it?"

"He was cheating on her and she knew he had exposed her to HIV—not bad for a motive."

"How did she find out that Sullivan was HIV positive?"

"Sullivan's doctor, Charlie Morgenstern. Sullivan tested positive for HIV last year during his annual physical. He told me that he threatened to tell Pamela if Sullivan didn't."

"So she had a motive. What about the means?" Mason swatted away a bee that threatened to land on her sleeve. "Let's walk."

They brushed shoulders as they stood, letting the contact linger for an extra moment, smiling and admitting that they'd taken a small step.

"She's been volunteering at a hospital, which means she could have had access to insulin. We're checking it out. And she fed him his last supper, so she had the opportunity."

"That doesn't explain how she could have given him the insulin. I doubt if she sneaked up on him and stabbed him with the needle or talked him into letting her inject him with a fatal dose. Did you question her?"

"She's watched a lot of TV. When we arrested her, she called you and didn't say another word. How is she?"

"She's actually quite well except she says that orange is not a good color on her."

"Okay, I deserved that. Are you going to represent her?"

"No. That's one case of malpractice I'm not going to commit.

She's talking with a friend of mine, B.J. Moore. He's topflight. If she did it, why would she keep the vial of insulin lying around? She can't be that stupid."

"The jails are full of stupid criminals. That's why cops have job security."

He looked at her for some sign that she'd give him an honest answer to his next question, but he kept getting lost in her eyes.

"Do you have another question, Counselor?" she asked, grinning as if she could read his mind.

"Yeah," he answered, clearing his throat and losing his nerve. "What are the odds that both named partners of a law firm under investigation by the Justice Department will be murdered within a week of each other in unrelated crimes?"

She lost her grin, glaring at him for an instant. "I thought of that, but there's nothing to connect them. Pamela's not strong enough to snap someone's neck, and I don't know of any reason she had to kill Harlan."

"That's my point. Maybe someone had a reason to kill both of them. That would exclude Pamela."

"That's the problem with you amateurs. How do you explain the syringe and the vial we found in her dresser drawer?" She couldn't hold back a satisfied smile.

"How do you explain that there were break-ins at both homes?" He enjoyed her annoyed, tight-lipped response. "That's the problem with you pros. You're too smug. Pamela told me they had a break-in about a month ago."

Their teasing had the familiar ring of a mating dance. They didn't know each other well enough for serious emotions. But chemical reactions were as good a place to start as any.

"Don't get cocky. I'll follow up on the burglaries. If you've got any better suspects, you'd better tell me at dinner. If I don't like them, you buy."

"You'd better plan on a lengthy interrogation."

"I warn you, Counselor, I'm very persuasive."

She gave him a long, promising look before returning to the

jail. He rode that look all the way back downtown.

CHAPTER THIRTY-FOUR

Angela was planted at the receptionist's desk, reviewing bills between phone calls, when Mason arrived at the office.

"How's the radio traffic and troop movements?" he asked.

"Vic Jr. left with Scott about ten minutes after you did."

"That kid is like a pimple on your butt. He'd be a lot less irritating if you could just squeeze him until he popped. Where's Sandra?"

"Locked in on thirty-one."

Mason took the stairs two at a time. Sandra was leaning back in a chair, feet up on the conference room table, staring out the window. He sat next to her, propping his feet alongside hers.

"Your eyes look fixed and dilated."

She turned to him, frowning. "And you are positively glowing; hardly the look of a man whose partners are being picked off one by one. Tell me, Lou, is it her uniform or her handcuffs that have turned you to jelly?"

Mason laughed with none of the nonchalance he wished he had. "I'll let you know when we get past the initial frisking. We're having dinner tonight."

"Does this mean you're going to stand me up again this weekend? I'll wear a uniform too if that will help."

He was still trying to figure out Sandra's interest in him. Mason was willing to believe that any woman could be attracted to him, but Sandra wasn't on his list of Most Likely to Swoon. Maybe a murder investigation was the key to her heart. He enjoyed the attention, but Sandra had an air about her that said "look before you leap." Still, the leap was very tempting.

"Come on, Sandra. Things have gotten pretty crazy around here lately. I don't know if I'm coming or going."

"Well, I definitely recommend coming before going."

"Yeah, well, that's good advice, but we better sort out this firm scandal before we start on the next one."

Mason walked behind her, forcing her to change positions. She made him wait but finally put her feet down and swiveled her chair toward him. He gave her the rundown on the charges against Pamela.

"And she wanted you to represent her?"

"Until I told her I couldn't and introduced her to B.J. Moore."

"Just as well. Mooning over the finest sheriff from the Ozarks in front of the jury would look bad."

"Okay, okay! Our partners are being knocked off like Kewpie dolls on the midway while gorgeous women beat a path to my door. I don't know why the fantasy has to be screwed up by the nightmare."

"Sometimes that's the difference between dreaming the fantasy and living it."

"So, you're a philosopher and a tease. A combination not found in every law firm."

"I'll take that as a compliment."

"Believe me, it is. I like you. You're smart, you're tough, and your legs make it very hard to concentrate. But there's only so much I can deal with at one time. Let's stay on track and figure out the rest when this is over."

"Well, I'll consider that a 'not now' instead of a 'no.' Fair enough?"

"Fair enough. So where are we?"

She switched from shameless flirt to killer litigator without breaking stride.

"We know that O'Malley has the loan limit problems, but it seems like there should be something else to bring all the feds' firepower down on us."

"I think you're right. Maybe there's some overall picture we've missed. Where are Diane's summaries?"

Diane Farrell had written summaries of the O'Malley transactions on poster-sized post-its, one for each of the seven years they were investigating. Sandra stuck them to the walls in chronological order.

The summaries set out the date each transaction closed, the name of the project, a description of the assets involved, and the Sullivan & Christenson lawyer who handled the deal. She highlighted in yellow each deal involving Quintex.

"Who are the shareholders, officers, and directors of Quintex?" Mason asked.

"Vic Jr. is the president, Harlan was secretary, and Scott is treasurer. Father and son are the only shareholders and directors."

He noted her correct usage of the past tense to describe Harlan.

"Were they the original officers?"

"I'll have to check." Sandra leafed through the Quintex corporate minute book. "The corporation was formed in 1984. Daddy was the sole shareholder, director, and president. Sullivan was the secretary, and there were no other officers. Fast-forward to 2008 and the current slate is swept into office."

"Look at the transactions since then. Sullivan was the lawyer on almost all of them until early 2008. Then Scott took over and all the transactions are fixtures deals. What are they about?"

"Quintex bought fixtures and leased them back to someone else."

"What kind of fixtures?"

"According to the lease documents, display racks, countertops, stuff like that. Phil Rosa did an analysis of the key deal points."

She handed him Rosa's memo. He studied it and the summaries on the wall.

"That explains what but not why or who. Quintex bought from one corporation and leased back to another. All those companies have alphabet soup names like NKC Corporation and EPT Enterprises."

"I'd say that someone on one end or the other, if not both ends, wanted to make it hard to trace the connection between them."

"We're focusing too much on the deals and not enough on who was making them. I want to know who the real players are, and I'll bet the O'Malleys know."

"The two might not have anything to do with each other. Vic Jr. may be doing his own deals just to prove to his father that he can make it on his own. Vic Sr. may not be involved in or know much about what he's doing."

"Yeah, but Scott and Harlan were involved and they would be a direct pipeline to O'Malley."

"Not necessarily. Scott wants out of Sullivan's orbit. Harlan's slipping further behind Sullivan every year in the amount of business he's generating for the firm. They both need a boost. Maybe they're working with Vic Jr. and don't want Sullivan or O'Malley Sr. to know what they're doing."

"If you're right, there's no connection between Senior's loan problems and Junior's fixtures deals."

"No intentional connection—but remember chaos?"

"God and bumper cars."

"Exactly. We know St. John is investigating Quintex, but we don't know if it's Sullivan's side or Scott's side or both."

"Meaning anything is possible. Great theory."

"You don't get it, Lou. We're assuming that things are happening for reasons we understand. But we may be completely off base."

"And we don't know what Sullivan knew and we don't know what Harlan knew, since they are both conveniently and permanently unavailable."

"All I'm saying is we have to be willing to look at things a little differently," she said. "We have to look for the unintended connections, not the grand conspiracies."

"Fine, but I'm sticking with what we know and what we don't know. And we don't know enough about the fixtures deals, and I'm going to change that."

Mason called Angela. "Find Diane, Phil, and Maggie. I want

them back down here as soon as possible. Tell them to plan on a long night. Then call Victor O'Malley and tell him I'll be in his office in twenty minutes."

He hung up before Angela had a chance to remind him that she wasn't his secretary, and gave Sandra her instructions.

"Tell the troops to peel the onion and find out who owns those corporate layers and what kind of businesses are using those fixtures. I want you to talk with Vic Jr. about these deals. We'll compare notes in the morning before the partners' meeting."

"Don't you think we should synchronize our watches, Commander?"

"I'll settle for as close to seven as you can make it. Listen, Sandra, two people are dead already. We may step on the wrong toes with all of this, so please be careful."

"Lou, I'm touched."

"Let's just say that beautiful legs are a terrible thing to waste."

CHAPTER THIRTY-FIVE

When Mason started working on Victor O'Malley's case, he asked Sullivan why O'Malley paid rent instead of moving into one of his own office towers. Sullivan explained that O'Malley had the space tied up at rock-bottom rates through a series of long-term options, which was better than losing out on market-rate rents on his own property. Mason recalled the conversation as he walked to the Union Energy Building and took the ancient elevator to O'Malley's twentieth-floor office, knowing that his client was a man who didn't miss a trick.

O'Malley shook Mason's hand with both of his, patting Mason's back and smiling like a proud father. He ran his empire from a scraped and scarred desk too small for his frame. The walls were lined with photographs of his projects, leaving no room for pictures of his family or any other sentiment.

His office faced south and west, overlooking the site for the new performing arts center that would open next year. A fierce battle had been waged in the corridors of city hall by competing developers, each of whom had invested in pockets of property on the southern fringe of the downtown in the hopes that the city would choose their site for the project. Millions of dollars had been at stake, with each contestant promising to build a world-class facility. O'Malley outprepared and outfought the competition. Gleaming and buoyant, he drew Mason to the windows to show off his victory.

"Goddammit, Lou, just look at that! It's magnificent! Five years ago that land south of the highway was worthless. Half the buildings were abandoned and the few businesses that were left were thrilled to sell so they could pay their back taxes. You know what their problem was? No vision. No ability to look down the road and see what might happen—and not enough balls to take the risk they might be wrong."

He put his arm around Mason as they turned from the windows and eased themselves into cane-backed chairs facing each other across a small round conference table opposite his desk.

"I'm still in shock about Harlan," O'Malley said in low tones, slowly shaking his head. "He was a good man, not the brightest lawyer that ever practiced, but good and loyal."

Mason was surprised at the speed with which the news had spread.

"How did you find out?"

"The press. It's how I find out everything about myself these days. All I have to do is wait for St. John to leak his latest story and the phone rings off the hook. That's why I was calling you this morning—I figured you'd want to reschedule our meeting."

"Scott said he told you about Pamela's arrest."

"I don't know which is more of a shock, Pamela and Sullivan or poor Harlan. Murder—that's too far beyond me to even seem real. Can I get you something to drink?"

"No thanks. We know that St. John has been focusing on the loans by the bank to companies you controlled. If you're convicted, that can mean anything from civil penalties to jail time. But there are two other problem areas that I need your help to figure out."

O'Malley looked at Mason without expression. "What are they?"

"One of your companies, Quintex, has been involved in a series of sale and leaseback arrangements. The return cash flow was tremendous in comparison to the amount invested. Your son put those deals together. St. John may be interested in them and I need to know why."

"And the other?" O'Malley prodded.

"Sullivan billed you half a million dollars for work the firm didn't do. You paid us and I don't think you're that generous."

"Lou, I appreciate all you've done, but with Richard Sullivan and Harlan both gone, I've decided to change counsel. Under the circumstances, I don't think we should be discussing specifics."

Mason fought the urge to tell O'Malley that he was a no-good slime ball who'd decided to can them because they were too close to figuring out what he was doing. He didn't look forward to telling Scott they'd been fired. The murders of Sullivan and Harlan, an unfunded million-dollar liability to Pamela, the FBI investigation, and the loss of their biggest client would be too much for the firm to handle. Clients would abandon them in droves if the staff didn't beat them to it. He was tired of being pushed around and he was ready to fight back. He hadn't suddenly fallen in love with the law or the firm. He was just in the mood to step on someone's throat.

"I understand your concerns, but I thought we'd agreed that we're both better off trying to work through this together. Besides, it'll cost you a fortune to bring someone else up to speed. This is the wrong time to make that sort of a decision."

O'Malley's eyes narrowed to cold bands. "I've made the decision and it's simple enough that even you should understand it. You're fired. I want a final bill on all my matters tomorrow morning, and you'll be paid by noon. Have my files delivered to this office within twenty-four hours." He stood to signal the end of the meeting.

Mason remained seated. "You'll have the bills in the morning. If we aren't paid by noon, the lawsuit for our fees will be filed by five o'clock."

Then he got up. O'Malley's face darkened as Mason walked to the door. He wasn't used to people talking to him the way he talked to them.

"And," Mason added, "the files belong to the firm, not you, but you're entitled to copies. It'll probably take a couple of weeks for a job that size, and we'll require payment in advance. Have a nice day."

Mason smiled as O'Malley slammed the door in his face.

Back at the office, he explained to Angela, Maggie, Phil, and

Diane what had happened.

"Angela, how many copiers do we have?"

"Three upstairs and one down."

"That won't be enough. Call one of the copy companies and have them bring over as many portables as they can. Get as many staff people as you need. I want every scrap of paper in the O'Malley files copied by morning."

"Do you want them bound and organized like the original files?" Diane Farrell asked.

"No, just stacks of paper in expandable folders with the name of the matter on them. Copy the attorneys' notes and memorandums sections, but don't include them in O'Malley's copies. We'll hold on to those until a court tells us O'Malley is entitled to them."

"There's no way we can finish that tonight. It's already four o'clock," Angela said.

"O'Malley will probably file a lawsuit against us first thing in the morning. We'll give him the copies tomorrow. His new lawyers will spend weeks figuring things out. In the meantime, we can start looking out for our own asses. I'm outta here."

"Where the hell are you going?" Diane asked. "You leave us with the shit work and head for the nearest bar! No way!"

"Just do your job while you still have it. I have a date with a cop."

CHAPTER THIRTY-SIX

Mason liked the cocky grin staring back at him in his rearview mirror. It had been a while since he'd felt the jolt of a new relationship, and he was savoring the sensation as he headed for the Country Club Plaza, six square blocks of Spanish architecture and high-end shopping in the center of the city.

Mason was glad that Kelly had chosen Brentano's, a comfortable, sophisticated restaurant with an attentive but discreet staff. Tables buzzed with conversations that remained private.

He found a seat at the bar, positive that the rest of the world was revolving around him. He waved nonchalantly to Kelly, who brought the sun inside with her.

Mason signaled the bartender for two cold bottles of Boulevard Beer. As he raised his to his lips, a thin stream splashed down his chin, splattering in his lap and washing away his reign as the king of cool. Hope and humility were restored when Kelly laughed and pressed her napkin against his thigh, soaking up the beer.

Over dinner, Kelly told him about growing up in the Ozarks, in Pope County. Her mother wasn't ready for marriage or motherhood and walked out on her and her father when she was an infant. Her father was killed in a farming accident when she was sixteen. She lived with relatives until she went to college at Missouri State in Springfield. The FBI recruited her during her third year of law school at the University of Missouri. When she went to Washington, D.C., for her training, it was her first trip out of the state. Since then, she had seen the country's underbelly in tours with the organized-crime strike force in New York, the gang strike force in Los Angeles, and the drug strike force in Chicago. Her last assignment was Kansas City's financial fraud unit.

"What was your partner's name?" Mason asked.

Kelly paused, looked at the bottom of her glass. "Nick. Nick Theonis."

"Did you ever find out who killed him?"

Her eyes shone with a coldness he didn't expect. "It was a drive-by hit. I saw the shooter's face. His left eye was only a slit—like he'd been cut. His smile was the worst. He enjoyed it."

"Could you identify him?"

"Jimmie Camaya. He's from Chicago and started out there working for the Jamaicans as a drug courier and graduated to freelance killer. The mob likes him because he takes risks nobody else will. The FBI's shrinks say he gets off on it."

"Why hasn't he been arrested?"

Kelly laughed. "You really are a Boy Scout, aren't you, Counselor?"

"I just figured the good guys are supposed to win a few."

"Yeah, well, we do win a few every now and then. But Camaya stays a step ahead. He goes underground after every hit, and no one sees him again until the next victim goes down."

"So who hired Camaya to kill your partner?"

"That part's just speculation. We were working in Chicago. After he was killed, we found out that Nick was taking bribes to tip off the mob about drug busts. Nobody was suspicious because we nailed enough of the lower-level dealers to keep the bureaucrats happy."

"How'd you find out?"

"After his death, Gene McNamara searched Nick's apartment and found records of the payoffs. He put me on administrative leave until he finished the investigation to make certain I was clean."

"Gene McNamara? St. John's lapdog?"

"We were all in Chicago together. St. John was appointed U.S. attorney right after Nick was killed. He wanted McNamara to be his chief investigator and McNamara wanted to keep his eye on me until I was cleared or indicted."

"What did McNamara come up with?"

"Carlo D'lessandro runs the Chicago mob. Nick was on his payroll. Carlo must have gotten worried about Nick's loyalty and had him hit. The bureau didn't want to hang its dirty laundry out in public. So Nick was dead and Camaya disappeared. I quit the day McNamara gave me the report."

"But you were exonerated."

"McNamara said I was cleared because they couldn't pin anything on me—not because he thought I was innocent. I'd have spent the rest of my career in Alaska."

"Charming guy. Which reminds me. You never told me about your ride with St. John after Sullivan's funeral."

"Vintage St. John. He wanted to know what I knew about Sullivan's death and reminded me in his usual subtle way that I had left under a cloud that could rain on me at any time. He promised me sunny skies if I kept him informed."

"What did you tell him?"

"I suggested that he and McNamara try some anatomically impossible dance steps."

"Did you suspect Nick was moonlighting?"

She played with her spoon, swirling the remnants of her coffee. "You've got to trust your partner completely or it doesn't work. I'd invested an awful lot into the relationship. It bought a lot of loyalty, maybe the wrong kind." The mist in her eyes said there were layers of meaning in her words.

"Were you in love with him?"

"Sometimes."

"I don't mind."

"Do you always have to be so damn sensitive?"

"I'm just not jealous of the dead."

She laughed and swept her hair back. "So much for sensitive. And I just thought you were trying to get in my pants!"

"How am I doing?"

"Well, rehashing old murders is an interesting approach. Does that normally work for you?"

"I never know what works for me. Might as well give it a run."

CHAPTER THIRTY-SEVEN

They left, strolling past the outdoor sculptures, weaving in and out of the crowd that jammed the shop-filled streets. Mason remembered the first night he walked on the Plaza with a girl and tried to hold hands with her. They were sweaty-palmed teenagers whose fingers accidentally brushed together. He was so proud when she didn't pull her hand away.

Kelly slipped her hand into his like they'd done it a thousand times before. Mason squeezed her hand and told her about life in his aunt Claire's house. When he tried to make excuses for screwing up, Claire cut him off, insisting that life was about causes and not becauses. She spent more time feeding him values than vegetables, setting the bar high and expecting him to do backflips over it. He ended up with her house, great memories, and a lifetime supply of rules to remember.

"Ever been married?" Kelly asked.

Mason gave her the highlights on Kate and turned the questions back to her.

"Why did you go back home after you quit the bureau?"

"I wanted out of city life. I know that the country isn't pure. But it seemed like all I ever saw in any city was the dirt that people did to each other. But with this case, it looks like my exit strategy has a few holes in it."

They wandered to the eastern edge of the Plaza, hands intertwined, arms swaying slightly to their newfound rhythm. Sitting on the edge of a fountain, they watched as the mist fractured the fading sunlight into miniature rainbows. Last week's heat had marched east, leaving the city host to a cool front. The air cleared as the temperature dropped, turning the evening into one that demanded sleeping under the stars.

Their life stories exhausted, they filled the space with a stream-of-consciousness zigzag through baseball, modern art, and celebrity look-alikes.

"So who do you look like?" she asked.

"When I was eighteen, older women said I looked like Dustin Hoffman. Fifteen years later, a girl at Baskin-Robbins told me I was a dead ringer for Tom Cruise. Go figure."

"They saw what they wanted to see. Who do I remind you of?"

"No one I've ever known."

"Now, there's a good approach, Counselor."

First kisses are promises. Hers was moist and soft. Second kisses are offers. His was plain. Third kisses are answers. Hers would have to wait.

"So who's on your short list of suspects?" she asked, pulling back.

"You really know how to keep a guy's interest."

"I told you I was a tough interrogator. I was just softening you up."

"Soft is not where I was headed."

The fountain lost its magic, and they started walking again—west this time.

"Come on," she said, consoling his hormones. "A deal is a deal. I paid for dinner and now you turn in all your friends."

"Pretty funny for a cop. I don't think Pamela did it. Sullivan wouldn't let her inject him with anything—he wasn't the type."

"So who does that leave?"

"You mean other than the unnumbered women whom he exposed to AIDS?"

"I want the short list, not the long list."

Mason took a deep breath and jumped in. "Angela Molina says Sullivan was blackmailing her because she embezzled from the firm."

"Angela qualifies."

"Angela also says that Sullivan billed O'Malley half a million bucks for work that was never done—and O'Malley paid for it."

"Add O'Malley to the list. Anyone else?"

Mason hesitated. Scott Daniel's name was the next obvious one. He struggled to find a reason not to add it to the list. Loyalty was the only one. On almost any other day, that would have been reason enough. But Mason's suspicion of Scott was growing like a bad seed. Mason hoped he was wrong.

"And Scott Daniels. He hated Sullivan and wants me to convince St. John that Sullivan was the only bad guy in the firm."

"Was he?"

"I don't know. Scott handled a series of transactions for O'Malley that we haven't figured out yet. They may not pass the smell test."

"With Cara Trent and Pamela Sullivan, that's not such a short list. Do any of them have access to insulin?" Kelly asked.

"Pamela's the only possibility I can think of, based on what you said about her volunteer work at the hospital."

"There's always money. What do you know about Sullivan's estate?"

"Not much. Scott wrote the estate plan. He say's Pamela's in good shape, but I haven't seen the will."

"Where is it?"

"Probably in the safe at the office. I'll check with Pamela and B.J. Moore. If they don't object, you can come by tomorrow morning and I'll go over it with you."

"Tell me more about your review of O'Malley's files."

"O'Malley fired us today. Other than that, I can't talk about it because it's privileged."

"Don't give me that. This is a murder investigation."

"Come on, Kelly. You went to law school. The privilege belongs to the client and lasts forever, even if he fires us."

"Except your firm is a target of a criminal investigation. If your defense requires you to disclose client confidences, the privilege is waived. Talk to me, Counselor."

"The firm hasn't been charged with a crime yet. Besides, the waiver may only apply to that case and not yours."

"Unless Sullivan's murder is related to the grand jury's investigation. There's a long history of witnesses who die on the eve of testifying."

"You're fishing. Pamela was arrested this morning because the DA thinks she killed Sullivan because he exposed her to AIDS. Now you want me to violate my client's confidences to prove he killed Sullivan to prevent him from testifying before the grand jury. Tell me what's wrong with this picture, Sheriff?"

"I'll tell you what's wrong with it, Counselor. There's an idiot named Lou Mason in the middle of it who thinks this is either just another game of cops and robbers or a law school hypothetical."

Her interrogation lasted long enough to get them to the Tuscany restaurant. Jammin, a jazz bar, was in the basement, and Blues played there on Monday nights. They chose a table near the stage beneath a black painted ceiling ringed by a violet neon ribbon. People were packed around small tables and along the bar. A middle-aged, heavyset man was stuffed in a chair, his chin on his chest, his fingers wrapped around an empty wineglass. The man was either dead or asleep. They would find out when the waiter brought the check.

Blues was finishing his first set. The man knew Oscar Peterson—heard his voice and spoke his music with his fingers. Mason always liked watching him play. He could tell when Blues was playing for the crowd. The music was there but he wasn't. When he played for himself, he moved from top to bottom. His shoe tapped and his face danced, all in time to the music. He'd look at his hands, eyes wide, eyebrows arched with surprise that they could do what they were doing—as if they had a life of their own. The sweet melancholy of "Autumn in New York" faded to appreciative applause. Blues brought three frosted long-necked bottles to their table.

"Man, you look like shit!" he said to Mason.

"Kelly, say hello to Wilson Bluestone. He gave up being a cop to play a mediocre piano."

Blues looked at Mason as if he were measuring him for a pine box. "You're the one who found Harlan Christenson? Newspaper said it was one of his partners but didn't say which one. Figured it was you."

He listened like the cop he used to be as Mason repeated the story, adding that they now knew that Sullivan had been murdered as well.

"You've got a real unhealthy practice. If I was you, I'd find another place to hang your shingle."

"I can't prove anything, but I've got to believe the murders are connected."

"Let the cops figure it out."

"She doesn't buy it," he said, nodding at Kelly.

"So what? I said let the cops figure it out."

"Sheriff, show Blues your badge and he'll be more polite."

Kelly smiled and showed him her badge—and her gun.

"Damn! What are you doing out with a cop instead of a nice Jewish girl?"

"Is this guy really a friend of yours?" Kelly asked.

"Yeah. He's just intimidated by heavily armed women."

"Well, Sheriff, do you think it's just bad luck that Lou's partners get whacked on back-to-back Sundays?"

"So far, that's all there is to connect them. It would help if Lou would tell me what his clients have to do with this."

"He's not going to tell you. It's privileged, and even though you've got his tongue dragging next to his shoes, you're on the other side."

"That's what he says—that it's privileged, I mean."

"Don't worry. He'll tell me, and I'll tell you."

"Why will he tell you?"

"Because I'm watching his back, and I can't do that if he doesn't tell me."

"But why will you tell me?"

"Because I'm likely to need help."

154

Mason was about to argue with both of them, when he realized that Blues was right. He would tell Blues. Blues would tell her, and Mason was in heat.

"So you're the one who searched the office for more bugs," she said to Blues as Mason drank his beer in silence and listened to them work the case.

CHAPTER THIRTY-EIGHT

By Tuesday morning, the thirty-first floor had become an obstacle course of copy machines, banker's boxes, and stacks of files. Phil Rosa was asleep in the conference room, stretched between two chairs, snoring softly under a Pizza Hut box planted like a teepee over his face. Mason picked up the box, waving away Phil's pepperoni morning breath, the fresh air enough to wake him.

"Any survivors, Phil?"

"Barely. Two of our copiers went down after midnight. We ran out of paper at three. Maggie and I tried to organize the leftovers. Everyone else went home."

"How far did you get?"

"About two-thirds of the way through. We'll have to send the rest out to be copied if we're going to get the files delivered to O'Malley today."

"I don't like it, but we don't have a choice."

"Well, well, the prodigal partner returns. I hope you can find some new assignment to keep us challenged today," Diane Farrell said as she sauntered in.

"Diane, I'm glad you're here. Phil—take the day off. Diane will finish up."

"And the horse you rode in on, boss," she said.

"I didn't know you were an animal lover, Diane," Mason said on his way out.

Sandra stood him up for their seven o'clock meeting. He hoped that meant they were even. At nine, Mason's secretary delivered a memo announcing that the partners' meeting had been moved to one thirty. Scott's secretary answered Mason's call to his office and told him that Scott wouldn't be in until noon.

"Do you know where he is?"

"No, sir."

"Can you check with the other partners?"

"Sorry, Mr. Mason. You're the only partner here."

He should have seen it coming then, but he was too busy to pay attention to the firm's radio traffic and troop movements.

Kelly was a welcome sight when she walked into his office. He knew when he had a crush on someone. In high school, he called it being in deep like. In his twenties, he called it magic. Now in his midthirties, he called it dumb luck and hoped it would last long enough to fill the crater Kate left.

"Wait here," Mason told her, motioning to a small, round conference table. "Pamela and B.J. gave me permission to show you Sullivan's will. I'll be right back."

"Your office is too masculine," she told him when he returned. "You need some flowers."

"Since when is masculine a bad thing?"

"It's almost my favorite thing," she answered. "But you need more hormonal balance."

"I'll rent you space," he said, pulling his chair next to hers.

"The will was signed on August 31, 1997," Kelly noted as she began reading.

"There's a trust agreement that runs twenty-five pages. Fortunately, Scott included a summary."

"What's the bottom line?"

"Sullivan's estate is worth about twenty million dollars. Pamela gets half, and half goes to charity."

"Unfortunately for Pamela, ten million dollars is a hell of a motive for murder."

Mason started to put the will and trust back into the file when a sealed envelope he hadn't noticed before slipped out. Kelly grabbed it and tore it open before he could claim another privilege.

"I don't get it," she said as she handed it to him.

Mason studied it for a few minutes. "I don't get it either. This is a codicil, an amendment revoking his will."

"So he died without a will?"

"Which makes no sense. He might change his will. But he'd never revoke it. That would cost his estate a fortune in taxes. He'd spent his entire career making sure his clients avoided taxes. I wonder if Scott knew about this."

"What happens to the estate now?"

"In Kansas, if you die without a will, the entire estate, after taxes, goes to your heirs. Your spouse gets one-half and your kids share the rest equally. Pamela and Sullivan didn't have any children, so she gets it all."

"And the charities get screwed. Just in case ten million bucks wasn't enough to see her through her golden years, now she gets twenty million. I think the DA's case just got a little better."

"Not if Pamela didn't know that Sullivan revoked his will. In Kansas, a spouse has to give written consent to the terms of the other spouse's will, which Pamela did. She didn't have to consent to the codicil, and she didn't."

"Who witnessed the will?"

Mason flipped to the last page and read the names. "Maggie Boylan and Sullivan's secretary."

"And the codicil?"

"Diane Farrell and Angela Molina."

"I'll talk to them later," Kelly said. "The hearing on Pamela's bail is this afternoon. Let's have dinner at J.J.'s. Blues told me he's playing there tonight. Meet me at seven thirty?"

"Are you serving dessert?"

Third kisses are answers, and Mason didn't have any more questions.

After Kelly left, Mason's secretary told him that Sandra was waiting for him in her office.

"Sorry about this morning, Lou. I had a late night," she said.

Sandra's desk was an oval-shaped slab of blood-veined marble supported by shiny silver pedestals at each end. The effect was simultaneously cold and passionate. *We are our furniture,* Mason thought as he sat across from her.

A bookcase held a collection of reference books. He noticed a copy of the *PDR*, the *Physicians' Desk Reference*, which explained how drugs acted, how they should be used, and the risks of misuse. The library at his old firm had a copy, but no one at Sullivan & Christenson had ever chased an ambulance.

"Do you have any personal injury cases?"

"No, why?"

"I just wondered about your *PDR*. I didn't know anyone around here had one."

"I sold pharmaceuticals and medical equipment before I went to law school. It's a leftover from those days."

Her long legs, crossed at the ankles, reached under the marble slab. She dropped a dangling shoe and brushed her toes against his pant leg, the effect swimming upstream against the lingering sensation of Kelly's kiss. Mason decided to ignore her toes.

"O'Malley fired us. I hope you had better luck with the son."

"Vic Jr. isn't so bad if you keep his hands busy. I'll know all his secrets by the end of the week."

"That's not a fair fight."

"And I don't like fair fights. He's picking me up for lunch. I'll be back in time for the partners' meeting."

The receptionist called, announcing that Vic Jr. had arrived. Mason walked with Sandra to the front desk, where Angela was pretending to be entertained by him. He left her hanging in midsentence when Sandra flashed her melting-point smile before taking him by the arm and heading for the elevator. He was grinning as if he'd just gotten a date with the homecoming queen.

"Don't tell me?" Angela said.

"Yep. Hard to believe, isn't it?"

"How can she stand the creep?"

"She put a leash on his dick and told him to heel."

Turning around, Mason saw Scott watching Sandra and Vic Jr.'s dating game from inside the conference room behind him.

Scott shifted his gaze to Mason for a moment before turning away, his eyes as cold as Sandra's marble slab.

CHAPTER THIRTY-NINE

Diane Farrell was waiting for Mason in his office. "You want to talk about the fixtures deals or try and figure them out on your own?" She was sitting in the chair Kelly had occupied an hour earlier, holding a sandwich in one hand and a bottle of root beer in the other. "I brought you a sandwich. Consider it a peace offering," she said as she shoved a brown paper bag toward him.

"Do I need a food taster?"

"Don't be such a tight-ass. Try living on the edge. It's turkey and horseradish on rye. Same as me." She took a bite of her sandwich and washed it down with root beer.

Mason examined the sandwich and resisted the temptation to sniff it before he bit into it. "Thanks," he managed to force out before the horseradish lit a fire in the back of his throat.

Diane laughed, reached beneath the table, and produced another bottle of root beer. She twisted the top off and handed it to Mason.

"You don't like me, do you?" she asked him.

Mason wiped his mouth with the back of his hand. "Nope."

Diane laughed again. "Good. I don't like you either. Makes us even."

"Then why did you buy my lunch and offer to help me with the fixtures deals?"

"Sullivan was my boss. I still work here. It's my job. Take your pick."

"Works for me. Tell me what I need to know."

"Quintex started investing in these deals in 2008."

161

"How many deals?"

"Twenty. In each transaction, Quintex purchased fifty thousand to seventy-five thousand dollars' worth of fixtures."

"What kind of fixtures?"

"Retail store and entertainment fixtures. They could be used to display merchandise, serve food, or house televisions and stereos in bars and restaurants."

"What were the economics?"

"Quintex leased the fixtures to other companies for thirty-five hundred to six thousand dollars a month on a ten-year lease with two ten-year options. Quintex usually got its money back in eighteen months. Ten of the deals have paid back the initial investment and just over half a million dollars in profit in the last year."

Mason finished his sandwich and his root beer and jotted some figures on a legal pad.

"At an average of sixty thousand dollars per year per lease, Quintex will make twelve million dollars over ten years on an initial investment of around a million and a quarter. Who did Quintex buy the fixtures from?"

"I can tell you the names of the companies, but they won't mean anything. They're just shells. A parent corporation owns each one. Each parent owned five of the seller corporations. Two holding companies owned these four and a final holding company owned these two. All the companies were set up in Nevada."

"So what?"

"I forgot you don't do corporate work. Nevada doesn't require shareholders and directors to be identified in state records. It lets the companies keep their ownership secret. Kind of like a Swiss bank account."

"Somebody must have signed the papers?"

"Lawyers in Chicago had power of attorney. The firm is Caravello and Landusky. They represented the companies that sold the fixtures and the companies that leased them."

Mason tore off the page of figures, wadded it into a ball, and fired it at his wastebasket.

"Somebody has gone to a lot of trouble to hide the ownership. If the Chicago lawyers are representing the sellers and the lessees, they could be one and the same. Otherwise, the lawyers would have a conflict of interest." Mason glanced at his watch and realized he was late for the partners' meeting. "Gotta go, but thanks for the information and the sandwich."

CHAPTER FORTY

Mason walked into the conference room in time to see Scott fidgeting with a stack of papers, stopping long enough to glare at Sandra from Sullivan's old chair while she smirked back from Harlan's former seat. None of the partners would look at him. Scott cleared his throat and began the meeting.

"I received a very disturbing call from Victor O'Malley last night. He's fired us because of the way Lou handled the grand jury subpoena." He spoke with real regret, underscoring with understatement the gravity of their situation.

"Bullshit!" Mason said, slamming his palm on the table. "He fired us because he didn't want to tell me how he hung us out to dry for St. John. We're better off without him anyway. Now we can concentrate on our own defense."

"Lou, you're dead wrong," Scott said. "I trusted you with this job out of friendship. I tried to warn you—told you to leave O'Malley to me. But you wouldn't listen. You had to do it your way. Now the firm's existence is in jeopardy."

"Come on, it's not that bad."

"You haven't been here long enough to understand the relationship with O'Malley. Everyone here except you and Sandra grew up with this firm. We've never had a problem like this."

"The two senior partners have never been killed in the same week either. O'Malley isn't blaming me for that too, is he?"

"That's part of your problem, Lou. You think that a few wisecracks will solve everything. The rest of us don't find any humor in losing our practice because the new kid on the block turned out to be a loose cannon."

"Look, we were going to have to dump O'Malley anyway. We've got a conflict of interest with him that even a Republican could recognize. Let's move on and figure out what we're going to do next."

"We've done that already. This wouldn't have happened if we were as close-knit as we used to be. We have to make changes if this firm is going to survive."

The picture Scott was painting was finally coming into focus. Sandra and Mason were the only outsiders—the only partners who weren't born into the firm after law school. They would be the sacrifices to O'Malley.

"Let me guess. You and the other partners had a meeting with O'Malley and he promised to keep the lights on for you if you canned Sandra and me. Don't you remember our discussion Sunday night when I told you that I had decided to quit before Sullivan was murdered and you begged me to stay and save your sorry ass? Or did you forget that when you were convincing our loyal partners here that Sandra and I were the real problem?"

"I met with Victor last night. He didn't promise anything. As for Sunday night—I should have let you quit then. Once you told me you'd lost your nerve in the courtroom, I should have known that there was no way you could handle something like this. I guess I thought I was doing you a favor—giving you another chance. But you blew it. I should have known you would."

Scott had told the worst kind of lie—one that had a kernel of truth in Mason's own admission that he had been ready to walk out on his partners; one that they were eager to believe; and one that he couldn't disprove. It was cruel and effective. Mason knew that his close relationship with Scott sealed it for the rest of the partners, ensuring their sympathy for Scott as the friend Mason had let down. It was over. Sandra rose with Mason as he stood to leave.

"Leave your parking garage access cards on your desks," Scott continued. "We'll forward your final paychecks and refunded capital contributions as provided in the partnership agreement. Your personal belongings will be sent to your homes. I want you out of these offices now!"

Scott tried to pull it off as Sullivan would have; the secret meeting to line up the votes. Appeal to old loyalties. All topped off with a ruthless finish. But he had one problem that Sullivan never had. Scott was scared. There was more desperation than anger in his voice and more fear than threat in his eyes. Sandra had been silent throughout the coup, but her closing shot clearly hit the mark.

"It's too bad really, Scott," she began. "It was such a nice speech, and I'm certain you worked on it very hard. But you're too late. You can't stop what you've already started."

Mason didn't understand what she meant, but Scott did, clenching the edge of the conference table in a white-knuckled vise. Before he could answer, Angela Molina opened the conference room door, letting in a deputy sheriff.

"Which one of you is Scott Daniels?"

"I'm Daniels. What do you want?"

"These papers are for you, Mr. Daniels."

He handed Scott an envelope with the seal of the Jackson County Circuit Court on it and left. Scott scanned the pages, losing color with each page before dropping them on the conference table. He walked out without another word.

Sandra picked up the papers and Mason read them with her. It was O'Malley's lawsuit against the firm seeking half a million dollars for work the firm charged him for but didn't do, plus fifty million dollars in punitive damages. The kicker was a court order appointing a temporary receiver to manage the firm's affairs until a hearing could be held on July 28 to consider the appointment of a permanent receiver.

Mason stopped in his office and filled his briefcase with the reports Diane Farrell had prepared and his copies of the O'Malley billing records. He tossed in Sullivan's X-rated DVDs and his Johnny Mathis CD as a reminder of happier times. Sandra met him at the elevator and they rode down together.

"Was Scott telling the truth?" she asked.

"About me wanting to quit?"

"All of it."

"The truth is, I did tell Scott that I had decided to quit. I didn't give him a reason, and I'm not certain I could explain it. That jury of our partners and peers wouldn't have believed any reason except the one Scott gave them. So the rest doesn't matter. What did you mean by your crack about Scott being too late?"

"Vic Jr. told me about the lawsuit at lunch today. And a few other tidbits."

"All that over lunch? What did you order?"

"Room service."

"Tell me you didn't."

She laughed. "Give me some credit. It was enough that Junior thought it possible."

"And the tidbits?"

"He bragged about all the money he was making that his old man didn't know about until he told him last week."

"Did he tell you where the money was coming from?"

"That was on the menu tonight. But it looks like I've been dumped."

Franklin St. John and Gene McNamara were waiting when the elevator opened.

"Well, Mr. Mason," St. John said. "You'll save me the trip upstairs. I'm sorry to hear about Harlan Christenson. He seemed one of the few decent people in your group."

"I'm touched that you came all the way over to express your condolences."

"Actually, I've got more important business. The federal court has frozen your firm's assets to protect the taxpayers' interests."

CHAPTER FORTY-ONE

St. John handed Mason an order issued an hour ago freezing all of Sullivan & Christenson's assets pending a hearing on July 27. Mason gave it back to him with his most gracious smile.

"You are ever diligent, but you'll still have to take a ride upstairs."

"Are you refusing to accept service of the court's order?"

"Sorry. It's not my firm anymore. But I'll sleep better knowing that you're watching over my interests as a taxpayer."

Mason smiled, and he and Sandra left them standing at the elevator. Out on the sidewalk, he tilted his face to the sun, soaking in the warmth.

"You know something, Sandra? I may actually enjoy unemployment."

"I know. There's something liberating about it, at least until we don't get our next paycheck. You know what? Screw it! Let's celebrate! How about dinner?"

"Wish I could. I'm meeting Kelly Holt at J.J's."

She grabbed his arm. "Perfect! I can't wait to see the look on her face when we tell her what happened. I'll see you there!"

Under normal circumstances, Mason would have enjoyed the prospect of dinner with two attractive women, both of whom were showing more interest in him than he deserved, but there was nothing normal about the circumstances. Kelly had asked him to dinner to talk about Sullivan's murder, but they both knew that was a pretext, thin cover for what happening between them. There was no room at the table for Sandra, but she had outmaneuvered him.

Sandra was waiting for him outside J.J.'s, wearing a dress with a plunging neckline and thigh-high slit that would cheer up the fleet. Mason took a deep breath and opened the door for her. The hostess led them to the table where Kelly was sitting with Blues, who was between sets.

"Nice to see you, Kelly," Sandra said, extending her hand. "Lou invited me to join you for dinner. We both got fired today, so we thought we could cheer each other up."

Kelly took her hand for an instant as she interrogated Mason with raised eyebrows.

"It was a bloodless coup," Mason said. "Scott Daniels lined up the votes in a secret meeting this morning after O'Malley fired the firm. He blamed everything on me. Sandra was guilty by association."

"Well, at least you've still got a job," Blues said to Kelly.

Sandra interrupted. "I'm Sandra Connelly," she said to Blues.

Blues looked up at her from the table. He had a thin sheen of sweat, more like a glow, from the set he'd just finished. "That's fine," he told her, giving her a long and appreciative look. "That's very fine."

She returned his stare with her own. "And who are you and what do you do?"

"I'm Blues. I'm just the piano player."

"That's very fine," she said and sat next to him.

Kelly rose and signaled Mason to follow her to the bar.

"I'm afraid that my day didn't turn out any better than yours. The vial we found in Pamela's dresser drawer was saline solution, not insulin. The DA decided there weren't any votes left in the case and dropped the charges."

"Does that take Pamela off your short list?"

"No. She lost a husband with HIV and found twenty million dollars. That's a combination that will keep anybody on my short list. Did you really ask her to join us?"

Mason put his hand on the small of her back and pulled her toward him. "Not a chance. She just tries too hard."

169

Kelly put her hands on his chest. "Don't make the same mistake."

When they finished dinner and Blues finished his last set, the four of them left together, walking around the corner to a side street where they had parked. Mason and Kelly held hands, Blues and Sandra behind them, their arms locked, two couples riding a soft wine buzz. They stopped on the sidewalk at Mason's car when Kelly screamed.

"Gun!"

She shoved Mason to the sidewalk as a black Escalade sped toward them, a man leaning out the backseat window, spraying them with automatic fire. Mason looked up long enough to see the slash on the shooter's face where his left eye should have been.

Blues lay on top of Sandra, shielding her. Kelly returned fire as the Escalade made the corner turn and disappeared.

"You okay?" she asked Mason.

"Yeah," he said, shaking as he stood. "That Escalade—I'd swear it's the same one from the highway on the way back from the lake."

"Stay here."

Kelly made a wide circle, flashing her badge and motioning bystanders who'd rushed onto the street to back up, protecting the crime scene. When the first police officers arrived, she handed the scene off to them and joined Mason, who was leaning against a tree, his heart slowing to a normal rhythm.

"You recognized the car. I recognized the shooter. It was Jimmie Camaya."

"The guy gets around. Who was he after? You or me?"

Her eyes were red, her jaw clenched. "Do you have a preference?"

"Yeah," he said, taking her in his arms. "Me. It's not even close."

"I'm sorry," she said, taking his hand. "I didn't mean that. This case is tough enough. If Camaya is involved, it's only going to get uglier."

"Boogeymen and ghosts."

"Yeah, and I didn't hit either one of them."

A tall, beefy, barrel-chested man wearing an olive gabardine suit, his shirt damp around the collar, interrupted them. His face was large, round, and uneven, like a pumpkin.

"Lou, what are you doing in this mess?"

Mason smiled and clapped him on the shoulder. "Damn, Harry! Am I glad to see you! It's a long story. I'll let her tell you. Sheriff Kelly Holt, say hello to Detective Harry Ryman."

"Kansas City Police Department, ma'am," Harry said.

"Kelly Holt," she replied. "Pope County Sheriff."

"Harry's like family," Mason explained.

"What he means is, his aunt Claire and me been together long enough to be family. So what's this about?"

Kelly gave him a quick rundown on the murders of Richard Sullivan and Harlan Christenson and her ID of Jimmie Camaya. Harry took notes, then turned to Mason.

"Your aunt is worried about you—you know that, don't you?"

"I do."

"And this cluster isn't going to help any. You get yourself killed and I'll never hear the end of it."

Mason laughed. "I'll do my best to keep you out of the doghouse."

"I'd appreciate that." Harry pointed to Mason's Acura. The car was peppered with bullet holes. "It's evidence. We'll have to tow it in. I'll let you know when you can have it back."

Blues and Sandra joined them. Harry and Blues barely acknowledged each other.

"Evening, Detective Ryman," Blues said.

"I should have known you'd be in the middle of this mess, Bluestone," Harry said.

"Lou and his friends stopped in for dinner. That's all."

"There's no such thing as 'that's all' with you. You were trouble when you were on the force, and nothing's changed." Turning to Mason, he added, "I'll get someone to take you home."

"Save it, Ryman," Blues said. "I've got him."

CHAPTER FORTY-TWO

"Let's caravan to Sandra's," Blues said after Harry left. "Make sure she was just in the wrong place at the wrong time."

"Makes sense," Kelly said.

"Anyone want to know what I think?" Sandra asked. They looked at her. "I think it's a hell of a good idea."

Mason rode with Kelly while Blues took Sandra home. "What's the history between Harry and Blues, besides bad?"

"Blues blames Harry for getting him kicked out of the police department and Harry thinks Blues should be in jail."

"Who's right?"

"I wasn't there, and I'm not picking sides."

Kelly parked in front of Mason's house, Blues nosing in behind her. The front door was open, the blue porch light off.

"You leave the door open?" Blues asked him.

"No."

"Are you strapped?" Kelly asked Blues.

He raised his shirt, showing her the holster on his hip.

"I'll take the back," Kelly said.

Blues nodded his agreement. "You wait here," he told Mason.

"And do what if Camaya pays me another visit while you're inside?"

"Fair point. Stay behind me and keep your mouth shut."

The deadbolt on the door was splintered. Blues eased the door the rest of the way open, crouching as he stepped inside, sweeping his gun through each room on the first floor, meeting Kelly in the kitchen. Tuffy stood next to her, wagging her tail.

"I found the dog hiding behind the firewood on the patio," she said.

Mason scratched her behind the ears. "Your German shepherd ancestors would be very embarrassed."

They checked the bedrooms and the basement and found no one lurking behind shower curtains or behind closed doors. All they found was a mess. Everything soft was sliced open. Everything solid was broken.

The wreckage was systematic, purposeful. The photographs of Tobiah and Hinda lay on the dining room floor amidst the shattered glass that had covered them. Tobiah had a scratch beneath his right eye. Hinda was fine. Their candlesticks lay close by, unharmed. Someone wanted something. Mason didn't have a clue what it was.

"Call it in," Kelly said to Blues.

Harry Ryman was there minutes later. "Your aunt isn't going to like this. She loves this house. That's why she gave it to you. And she's more than partial to you. I'll have a couple of uniforms out front."

"That's not necessary. I can't sleep here tonight anyway. I'll stay with Blues."

"Then get out of here and let me do my job." He shot Blues a hard look. "Anything happens to him, Bluestone . . ." He didn't have to finish the sentence.

When they got to Blues's house, Mason flopped in an easy chair with Tuffy curled at his feet. He tried to make sense of a day in which he'd lost his job, his car, his home, and his possessions and nearly lost his life—all for reasons he couldn't fathom. He thought of his great-grandparents and their escape from the pogroms. They had lost everything they had held dear, except for a pair of candlesticks. Yet they recovered, starting a new life in a new world. He still had their candlesticks, but he wondered if he had their courage. Kelly and Blues were in the kitchen, deciding his future.

"What will he do now?" Kelly asked.

"Only thing he can do. Start over."

Mason spent the night flip-flopping between half-fetal and

half-pretzel positions in Blues's easy chair. When he woke up, Kelly was asleep in the kitchen, folded onto the butcher-block table.

The sun made a cameo appearance on the eastern horizon before bowing out to the vagaries of a Kansas City summer that breeds thunderstorms faster than time-lapse photography. By the time they gathered at the breakfast table, a fleet of towering thunderheads had formed in the distant southwest sky, readying for an assault on the city. The hum of the window-unit air conditioner bolted in above the kitchen sink added a strained chorus to an already tense morning.

"I still say one of us should be with him at all times. We'll take twelve-hour shifts," Kelly said.

Red-eyed and wrinkled, she slid a half pint of milk across the table. Blues stirred a tall glass of iced coffee, declining the milk and the suggestion.

"If Jimmie Camaya is hunting our boy, and he's half as good as you say, it isn't going to do any good to walk Lou across the street even if both of us hold his hands. Besides, you're a sheriff who's a long way from home."

Kelly pushed away from the table and threw the game plan back to Blues. "What do you suggest? Call Camaya and tell him to meet us on Main Street at high noon?"

"No. Not yet, anyway. Lou needs to take a trip."

Mason pulled an orange into two sections as juice squirted on his T-shirt.

"Wrong," he said. "Drive-by shootings are the summer's top team sport. Besides, if this guy was Camaya, he was probably after Kelly to finish off his last job. I'm just an unemployed lawyer. Nobody's mad at me except MasterCard."

"And the people who trashed your house were just an overzealous cleaning crew," Kelly said.

"Random chance. Odds are the same as winning the Publishers Clearing House Sweepstakes—just my lucky day."

"We'll put that on your tombstone," Blues said. "Somebody's decided to reestablish the pecking order with you at the bottom."

"Look, I've lost my job, my car, and my La-Z-Boy recliner. I'm not going to be run out of town."

"So, Counselor, what are you going to do?" Kelly asked. "Print résumés and go door-to-door? Be sure and tell the receptionist that the guy who's shooting at you is really aiming for someone else."

"I'm going to go home, shower, and change. Then I'm going to the office and get some answers from Scott. You could do one thing for me that I would appreciate."

"What? Pick up your dry cleaning?" Kelly asked.

"That too. I left my briefcase in my car. Can you find out where the cops towed it?"

"What's in the briefcase?" Kelly and Blues asked in unison.

"C'mon, guys. Pens, paper. Stuff from the office. Nobody would try to kill me for that."

"What's in the briefcase, Lou?" they repeated.

Mason raised his hands in surrender. "Okay, okay. Copies of the memos on O'Malley and his billing records. Nothing somebody couldn't get with a lot less trouble than shooting up a neighborhood and pillaging my house."

"Buddy of mine handles impounded vehicles. I'll check it out. Kelly, take Clarence Darrow home, and I'll call you there."

CHAPTER FORTY-THREE

Two uniformed cops parked in the driveway of Mason's house greeted them.

"Any more company?" Kelly asked them.

"Just a nosy neighbor from across the street," one of them said.

"Good. Who's that?" Kelly asked, pointing to a man getting out of a sedan parked across the street.

"I'm Nelson Sloane," the man said, waving at them. "Senior casualty adjuster for the American Casualty Insurance Company. You must be Mr. Mason." He handed Mason his card. "Well, Mr. Mason, I've seen worse. Vandals can't hold a candle to a good old-fashioned hurricane."

He looked up at Mason from thick black-framed glasses. A pencil rested above his right ear, a clipboard clenched under his left arm.

"How'd you find out about this? I haven't turned in a claim yet."

Sloane consulted his clipboard. "Telephone report of the claim came in last night about eleven. Source was a Mr. Bluestone. I asked him how he knew to call us and he said he's your landlord and you asked him to find your insurance information in your office and make the call for you. The police let me have a look at your car this morning. It's totaled. A few bullet holes can be hammered out and painted over, but your car looked like someone used it for target practice. Let's have a look inside. I'm sure we can agree on a figure for your household contents."

Kelly turned to the uniforms. "When he's done with the

adjuster, take him downtown."

"Where are you going?" Mason asked.

"Public health department. I'm going to have a look at Sullivan's records."

Mason led Sloane inside, going room to room, wide-eyed at the destruction. No piece of furniture had been spared. Shattered stereo equipment and televisions lay on the floor. Cabinets and drawers were emptied and upended. Even his dishes had been broken.

The bedroom he'd converted to a study was a shambles. The only item untouched was his computer.

The lining of his suits and sport jackets had been sliced open. The rest of his clothes were scattered all over the floor of his bedroom. It reminded him of when he was sixteen.

"No regard, no regard," Sloane said, taking notes on his clipboard. "I'll wait for you at my car."

Mason sifted through the piles until he found a pair of Dockers and a polo shirt in good enough condition to wear. Thirty minutes later, he was showered, shaved, dressed, and ready for Nelson Sloane.

Sloane laid out the claim form on the hood of his car and handed Mason a check.

"That's for your Acura. Kelly Blue Book says that's all we can pay."

Mason looked at the check. "Ten thousand dollars? You've got to be kidding me."

"The car was eight years old and, even without the bullet holes, in poor condition."

Mason glared at Sloane, but the adjuster was unmoved. "I'm afraid things aren't as simple with the damage to your personal property."

"Let me down gently. It's been a bad day already."

"Well, sir. It's classic good news and bad news." Sloane rocked back on the balls of his feet, a comedian dying for his straight man to deliver the setup.

Mason sighed. "Okay, Sloane. Give it to me. Both barrels."

"I put your loss at fifty thousand dollars, Mr. Mason. But you're only covered for twenty-five thousand. You should have increased your policy limits instead of trying to skimp. Never pays to skimp on insurance, Mr. Mason. No, sir, it never pays."

"That's it?"

Sloane stuttered. "Umm, well . . . actually, you are entitled to a hundred dollars a week for temporary living expenses for five weeks. Brings the total to twenty-five thousand five hundred. I can give you a check right now and we'll have everything picked up and sold for salvage. Gives the company a chance to get some of its money back, if you know what I mean."

He winked at Mason, who resisted the urge to yank Sloane's eyelids down over his chin.

"Does that mean I get my premiums back too?" Sloane squinted at Mason, trying to decide if he was serious. "Forget it. I'll keep my clothes, the pictures of my great-grandparents, their candlesticks, and my computer. You can have the rest."

"Splendid, Mr. Mason. Splendid indeed!"

Sloane showed Mason where to sign, handing him checks for his car and his personal property as Anna Karelson strolled down her driveway and joined them.

"My goodness, Lou. What happened? Where's Tuffy?"

She was wearing flowered capri pants and a halter top brimming over from a firmer time in her life. Her frosted hair was piled on top of her head. She'd been lying out in the sun but was one of those people who splotched instead of tanned. Mason felt a sudden sympathy for her husband, Jack.

"It was some crazy kids, Anna. They trashed the place. Tuffy and I are staying with a friend of mine. Anything new with you and Jack?" he asked to change the subject.

"The SOB still wants me to take him back. He just wants that damn TR6."

Mason lusted for the car as much as Jack, but she'd ignored his hints in their previous conversations that he'd be happy to take the car off her hands.

"Why don't you sell it?"

"Can I do that?"

"The car is titled in both of your names. You can do anything you want with it."

"But I wouldn't even know what to ask for it."

Mason knew what he was doing, and he was only mildly ashamed of himself.

"Let my adjuster tell you. Sloane, what's the Blue Book value on a low-mileage 1976 TR6 in excellent condition?"

Sloane consulted his book. "Ten thousand dollars."

"Anna, you've let this car come between you and your husband. If you have any hope at all of reconciliation, you have to find out if he wants you more than the car."

She looked at him with the pleading eyes of one who was lost and was about to be found. "Yes, that makes sense."

"I need a car. Normally, I'd spend a lot of time researching in *Consumer Reports* and haggling with dealers. But I don't have time for all that. Anna, we can help each other."

Fifteen minutes later, Mason had endorsed his check for ten thousand dollars to Anna, she had signed the title to the TR6 over to Mason, and Sloane had sold Mason a policy on his new car. He was halfway to Sullivan & Christenson's office, top down, wind in his hair, when he realized that he'd forgotten his police escort and that he hadn't heard from Blues.

CHAPTER FORTY-FOUR

Mason felt weirdly self-conscious riding the elevator up to the office he'd been thrown out of the day before. There weren't many places he had been thrown out of, especially ones that he wanted to leave anyway.

Yesterday, he had been angry and embarrassed. Today, he was angry and scared. He half hoped to be met by a welcome-back committee of former partners, led by Scott saying it had all been a mistake. It reminded him of kids who fantasized about their divorced parents getting remarried. His fantasy dissolved when a security guard wouldn't let him off the elevator. He rode back down and walked outside looking for a can to kick.

Mason needed to talk to Scott. He still believed in the rule of reason, and he still trusted in the loyalty of friends, even when the friend had cut him off at the knees. He'd been trained to be a creative problem solver, but his training was for a different game, and he was running out of patience.

It was only eleven a.m. If Scott stuck to his routine, he'd spend the noon hour in the pool at the Mid-America Club, a couple of blocks from the office. Mason decided to wait for him there.

The Mid-America Club was a venerable Kansas City institution, which meant that it hadn't been decorated since Eisenhower was president and didn't accept Jews, blacks, and women as members until it didn't have a choice.

Scott was the lone lunch-hour swimmer. His normal stroke was powerful, controlled, and precise, but today he was beating the water. Mason waited for him to surface at the shallow end. Five laps later, Scott stopped, pulled his goggles above his eyebrows, and shook his head at Mason.

"What do you want, Lou?" He sounded tired, as though he'd been worn down by something tougher than a mile swim.

"Answers. What's going on with you and O'Malley?"

"You're out of it. Keep it that way. It's for your own good."

"Okay. Let's try something else. Why did Sullivan revoke his will?"

"What in the hell are you talking about?"

"Don't tell me you didn't know. I checked his file yesterday. He executed a codicil six months ago revoking all prior wills."

"He never said a word."

"Have it your way. Somebody shot up my car and ransacked my house last night. I'm starting to take this personally. You owe it to me to tell me what in the hell is going on!"

Scott didn't answer. He shook the water from his face, wiped his bloodshot eyes, and pulled his goggles down, pushing off and clawing at the water as he kicked away from Mason.

Leaving the club, Mason grabbed a sandwich at the food court in another downtown office tower. He suppressed his fear of a repeat of last night's drive-by shooting with the myth that there was safety in a crowd. He didn't think Camaya would risk a shootout between McDonald's and Panda Express.

He kept a watch for people shooting at him from speeding cars while he walked to the county courthouse. He checked the court file on O'Malley's case to see if anything new had been filed. Nothing. It was the same story at the federal courthouse with St. John's lawsuit. He decided to pay another unscheduled visit to St. John.

"Mr. Mason, you're going to have to learn to make an appointment just like everybody else," St. John said as Mason walked past his secretary.

McNamara was in his usual spot on the couch. Mason was beginning to wonder if he slept in a kennel at the foot of St. John's bed every night.

"Look, Franklin, I don't feel much like everybody else lately. I'd like some information."

"Gee, Counselor, don't you like getting shot at?" McNamara grinned, enjoying his keen wit.

"Can't you housebreak this guy?" McNamara started to get up, but St. John pointed to the couch. "Good boy, Gene, that's a good boy."

"Mr. Mason, don't press your luck. You may not have enough to go around, from what I understand."

"I don't understand any of this. Maybe you can educate me."

"You've obviously aggravated the wrong person. Given your charming demeanor, I know you find that hard to believe."

"What do you know about Jimmie Camaya?"

McNamara's ears pricked up. Mason pictured him with his tongue out, humping St. John's leg.

"No one's ever been able to pin anything on him. He enjoys a rather celebrated reputation. If he's involved, you're in way over your head. We can give you protection if you'll tell us what you know."

"I'll tell you anything you want, except that I'm dumber than dirt. Kelly Holt thinks he's the guy who shot up my car last night."

"If Camaya was shooting, he most assuredly wasn't aiming at your car. My reports are that Holt returned fire. He's not used to that."

"Does he do floors and windows too?"

"I heard about your house. My sympathies. Such a violation. I assume that whoever did that and Camaya have the same employer. Why are you attracting all this attention?"

"I got into this mess when Scott Daniels asked me to check the firm's exposure from Sullivan's relationship with O'Malley. It's been downhill since then."

"Help us with that and maybe we can help you."

Mason considered the implications of the offer. St. John thought Mason could help him nail O'Malley and the firm. Mason had mixed emotions on the subject. He didn't like the idea of being a moving target. But he couldn't get excited about putting himself in St. John's hands.

"Thanks for your time. I'll think it over."

Mason tried the county courthouse again in the hopes that he might run into Kelly at the public health department. The clerk told him that he had missed her by an hour.

He started to call her when he realized his cell phone was on silent and he'd missed a message from her yelling at him for leaving without his police escort. There was also a message from Blues that he had retrieved his briefcase. He hung up and called his landline at home, checking his messages. There were three hang-ups. He couldn't think of anyone who would call and not leave a message. Unless they just wanted to be certain he wasn't home.

CHAPTER FORTY-FIVE

Mason decided to try his luck with Angela. He was certain that he hadn't been restored to the office guest list, so he waited for her in the parking garage. It was a confusing maze of levels going up and down in opposite directions at the same time that even a cheese-starved rat couldn't navigate, but it made a great hiding place.

He waited in a dark corner near Angela's car, until she had her back to him before approaching her as she opened her car door.

"How's the radio traffic and troop movements, Angela?"

He caught her elbows when she jumped, falling backward into him.

"Jesus Christ, Lou! You scared the shit out of me."

He may have, but that didn't explain why she was pressing her bottom against his crotch instead of running away.

"Sorry. I'm just trying to be more careful in my efforts to reach old age. Can I buy you a drink?"

She turned around but didn't back up. "I don't think that's such a good idea. You've got official leprosy, and it may be contagious."

"Don't worry. I've had my shots. And we made a deal. I'll be straight with you if you'll be straight with me."

"Okay, get in. But I pick the bar."

She chose a place called The Limit on downtown's West Side. Dim lighting left him almost blind until his eyes adjusted. He was the only man in the place. The chalkboard sign at the door announced a seminar on alternative treatments for AIDS.

"Surprised, Lou?"

"I didn't think anything could surprise me after the last few days, Angela, but you are full of surprises."

"Because I brought you to a lesbian bar?"

"It's not something I would have thought—or thought about. You just seem so interested in men."

"I am. Exclusively. I come here when I don't want to be bothered by men. These women understand that and respect my privacy. Besides, there's not much chance of running into Scott here, is there?"

They both laughed, breaking the tension. A waitress took their drink orders, beer for Mason, a martini for Angela.

"What's happening at the office?"

"All hell broke loose after you and Sandra left. Scott and St. John had a real pissing match."

"We ran into St. John on our way out. He had a court order freezing the firm's assets."

"That's what was so funny. The two of them were fighting over whether the federal court order freezing the firm's assets trumped the state court order appointing a receiver to run the firm."

Mason smiled at the image. "Who won?"

Angela giggled. "I did. I told Scott we were screwed either way."

"You have the wisdom of Solomon."

"And very big ears. After St. John left, Vic Jr. showed up again. He and Scott had their own screamer in the conference room."

A waitress brought their drinks. Mason sipped. Angela finished hers in two gulps.

"What was that one about?"

"I only caught bits and pieces, but it was mostly about the fees we charged his father for work we didn't do. In the meantime, half the staff has quit and the clients are panicked. Scott hired the security guard to keep out the press."

"And me."

Mason signaled the waitress to bring Angela another round. Several women waved at Angela from across the bar. She caught their eyes and waved back, all smiles. The waitress set another martini on the table and wiped up the water ring left by the empty glass.

"Angela, I need some answers."

"Don't ask me questions I can't answer."

"Can't or won't? Someone is trying to kill me, and it has something to do with the firm. You know more about what's going on there than anyone else. You've got to help me."

"You give me too much credit. All I know is what I read in the papers."

Mason waited, not wanting to press too hard. The volume of the bar's background music had picked up, prompted by the arrival of the after-work crowd.

"Do you remember when Sullivan changed his will last winter? You were one of the witnesses."

"Sure. Diane asked me to be a witness. What's that got to do with anything?"

"Did you know what changes he made in his will?"

"C'mon, Lou. That was six months ago. I don't remember what I had for lunch yesterday."

"I'm not interested in your diet. Just do your best. Was Sullivan in the conference room?"

She hesitated, realizing that his questions were serious ones and that he expected serious answers.

"No. Diane was the only one there. We waited about ten minutes, but Sullivan didn't show up. Finally, she just gave me the document and told me to sign it, and she would take care of the rest later."

"So you never actually saw Sullivan sign it?"

"I know that's against the rules, but we do it all the time with notary signatures."

Mason hoped she was loosening up, so he decided to take the plunge. "Angela, do you remember our conversation the day after Sullivan's body was found—"

"—when you did your big-shot impression and told me you were in charge?"

She couldn't resist the chance to tease him. He smiled without taking his eyes off of her.

"Actually, that was old news by the time I got to your office. You already knew, and I've been wondering how you got the word so quickly."

She reddened, swirled the ice cubes in her glass, and drained it. She looked down the length of the bar as she answered.

"Like I told you, Lou, radio traffic and troop movements."

"I don't think so. Only Scott, Harlan, and I knew before the partners' meeting. I was the first one in your office after the meeting. Try me again."

No answer. Mason took the telephone bug out of his pocket and dropped it on the table. Angela's death grip on her glass was answer enough.

CHAPTER FORTY-SIX

"You had me going for a while, Angela. You followed the first rule of the con artist. Tell the truth you have to tell. A little honesty buys a lot of credibility and makes it easier to lie about the important stuff."

She wouldn't look at him, but she looked her age for the first time since he'd known her. She shrugged, as though it was no big deal.

"All I wanted was something I could use to bargain with Sullivan. I knew that he'd hold my unauthorized loan from the firm over my head forever. There weren't enough blow jobs to pay that debt off."

"So why bug Scott's phone and Harlan's phone too?"

"I didn't care where I got the information as long as I could use it."

"When did you find out about the subpoena?"

"After the retreat. I came to the office every Sunday night to check the tapes. Scott had called someone, and they talked about it."

"Who did he call?"

"It was a man's voice that I didn't recognize."

"Why did you remove the wiretaps from their phones and not Sullivan's?"

"God knows I wanted to. I was afraid what Scott might do if he found out. I didn't want to deal with another partner who could blackmail me between the sheets or anyplace else. So I got rid of the ones in Scott's office and Harlan's office first. I was going to take out Sullivan's, but the cleaning crew showed up. I didn't want someone saying they'd seen me in Sullivan's office, so I left. I planned on getting rid of it on Monday, but you ordered his office sealed before I could."

"What did Scott and the other man talk about?"

"Scott told the other guy that Sullivan was dead. Then Scott told him that he'd convinced you to handle the grand jury subpoena. The guy got mad, but Scott told him that he could control you. Then the guy told Scott to find some documents and hung up."

"What documents?"

"I don't know."

"Where are the tapes, Angela?"

"In a safe place."

"Does anyone else know they exist?"

"No. An FBI agent interviewed me last week. He asked about the wiretaps but I didn't confess."

"Did he interview you at the office?"

"At home. He said he didn't want to disturb me during the day because he knew how crazy things must be at the office."

"Why didn't you tell me?"

"He said the FBI's investigation was very confidential and that I should keep quiet. Otherwise, the suspects could be tipped off. Since I knew who had done the taping, I wasn't about to open my mouth."

"What was the guy's name?"

"I don't remember, but he gave me his card." She fumbled in her purse and produced Gene McNamara's business card.

"Angela, I need the tapes. Someone tried to kill me. The tapes may help me figure out what's going on."

"Sorry, Lou, but I'm not sticking my neck out. They'll find out who did the taping, and then I'm finished."

"Just give me the tapes, Angela, or at least let me listen to them. I'll make certain your name stays out of it."

She stopped stirring her drink and looked at Mason as if about to answer. Her gaze went over his shoulder to the front of the bar and froze.

"Oh, shit!"

She looked down, but it was too late. They had company. Mason turned around.

Diane Farrell took a long drag on her cigarette, dropped it on the floor, and ground it out with her heel. She began a slow walk toward them, stopping along the way to kiss one woman and squeeze the butt of another.

"Well, Lou, are you coming out of the closet or are you just curious? Really, Angela, I thought you had better taste."

She dismissed Mason with a pathetic sigh, gave Angela a sympathetic pat on the shoulder, and headed for the bar.

"Let's get out of here," Angela said. She left a twenty-dollar bill on the table and he followed her out.

"Sorry, Lou," she said hurriedly as he caught up to her. "You'll have to walk back to your car."

"I don't get it. It's no big deal when you take me into that bar. Then Diane shows up, and you can't wait to get rid of me."

"You're right, you don't get it."

"Then what is it?"

"You're the problem. Scott told the staff that we weren't supposed to talk to you or Sandra. I've got enough problems without losing my job. Don't do this again."

"We can help each other."

"I don't think so. Good-bye."

The air was thick and still. The peaks of the thunderheads were no longer visible as clouds rolled over the city. People quickened their pace. Mason marched in double time, watching the clouds and the cars.

Anna and her wayward husband were holding hands on their front porch when Mason pulled into his driveway. Any guilt he had about the TR6 vanished with Jack's friendly wave. At least something was working out.

The salvage crew had swept through his house, leaving a card table and chairs in the kitchen and his computer and bed frame upstairs. A pile of underwear and socks was on the floor of his closet. The rest of his clothes were piled in one corner of the bedroom.

There were three messages on his landline. Blues said he was tired of Mason not answering his cell phone and to meet him for dinner at eight at Constantine on Broadway. He checked his cell. The ringer was turned on, but for some reason his calls were going straight to voice mail. The second message was from Kelly, saying she had to go back to Starlight and would call him tomorrow. The third call was from Sandra Connelly. He replayed her message twice.

"Lou, it's Sandra. I'm meeting Vic Jr. at seven thirty tonight at a bar in the West Bottoms. The address is 312 Front Street. Meet me there. I want a witness."

Mason wasn't crazy about the idea, but he figured it would still be light out, and Vic Jr. had never struck him as dangerous. Besides, even if Sandra did carry a big knife, he knew she was counting on him to be there. He'd be only a few minutes late for dinner with Blues. The first drops of rain were beginning to fall as Mason left.

CHAPTER FORTY-SEVEN

Mason's grandfather, Mike, was a butcher in a slaughterhouse in the West Bottoms. He was also a saloonkeeper and a ward healer and anything else that would put food on the table during the Depression, all of it in the West Bottoms, a floodplain that drank in the overflow from the confluence of the Kansas and Missouri Rivers.

His last career had been in the wrecking business. When Mason was a boy, his grandfather took him to work on Saturday mornings at MM Wrecking Company. The office was on the first floor of a warehouse that stored the leftover, cast-aside guts of buildings and businesses that Mike Mason somehow turned into cash. Mason spent the mornings hunting for magnets while his grandfather shuffled papers.

Mike Mason got his start in the wrecking business through Tom Pendergast, the political boss who ran Kansas City and a good part of Missouri during the Depression. Bagnel Dam had just been finished, damming up three rivers and creating the Lake of the Ozarks. Pendergast's concrete company had provided the cement and Pendergast doled out the leftovers, one of which was the scrap that had been salvaged from the project.

Mike Mason asked Pendergast if he could gather the scrap and sell it. Pendergast gave his blessing and waived his usual cut as he often did for his boys who made sure the voters turned out and voted Democratic. MM Wrecking outlasted Pendergast.

Mason played with his memories as he pulled alongside Sandra Connelly's BMW. She had left it in the parking lot of a five-story, redbrick warehouse that backed up to the Missouri River, *Hamlein Furniture* painted in faded yellow above the windows on the fifth floor. A loading dock dominated the front, steel-paneled garage doors closing off the dock's three bays. There was an entrance on the west for walk-in traffic. The bar was across the street, a half-lit neon sign in the front window promising free beer tomorrow.

He wondered why Vic Jr. had arranged the meeting here. Scott had given orders to the firm's staff to stay away from Sandra and Mason. O'Malley had probably told Junior the same thing. Only Junior couldn't resist Sandra. Mason was not unsympathetic.

Sandra's car was empty, giving Mason a fleeting panic attack until she called to him from the doorway of a nearby storage shed that faced the parking lot about a hundred feet south and east from the dock. Two large commercial trash containers flanked the shed.

"Where's our boy?" Mason asked as he joined her in the shed.

It was a ten-foot-square aluminum can littered with discarded scrap metal and the lingering odor of tenants who'd been too careless for too long with food, booze, and tobacco.

"He's not due until eight o'clock. I wanted time to figure out what we're going to do."

"Does he know I'll be here?"

"No. He said he would only talk to me."

"In that case, I'll move my car."

Mason parked the TR6 in an alley half a block away.

"Say something," she said as he stepped back inside.

"This is a bad idea."

"Don't tell me you're afraid of Junior."

"These days, I'm afraid of my socks. Whose idea was it to meet down here? What's wrong with Starbucks on the Plaza?"

"Vic Jr. insisted. He said he wasn't supposed to talk to me and didn't want to take the chance that we might run into someone who knew him."

Sandra was wearing a hooded, navy nylon pullover, blue jeans, and running shoes. She pulled a slender handheld recorder from the front zipper pocket of her shell and replayed their brief conversation. Mason's voice was muffled but understandable.

"I don't want any questions later on about who said what to whom," she said as she tucked the tape recorder back in its hiding place.

It wasn't too noticeable. Besides, Mason figured that Junior would have something else on his mind if he started talking to her chest.

"When did he call you?"

"He left a message late this afternoon."

They compared notes since last night. Sandra had also met the security guard at the office. She ran into Phil Rosa at the courthouse while reviewing the O'Malley lawsuit. His summary of office conditions matched Angela Molina's.

They decided that Sandra would keep the meeting outside in the warehouse parking lot. If Vic Jr. insisted on going inside, Mason would just have to wait outside the bar. Otherwise, Vic Jr. would see him.

Sandra went back to her car and stared hard at the window on the front of the shed, trotting back to tell Mason he was invisible as long as he hung back in the shadows.

"Be careful," he said.

"Always."

The on-and-off rain was off again when a familiar black Escalade pulled into the parking lot. That meant Jimmie Camaya was inside or close by. Mason was desperate for a way to warn Sandra but ran out of time before he could think of anything.

The Escalade stopped ten feet from Sandra's car. Vic Jr. stepped out the driver's door and walked toward her. If she recognized the Escalade, she gave no indication, leaning against the hood, one foot on the fender, thumbs in her belt loops. She thrust her pelvis at him just enough to be an invitation. He took her arm and guided her toward the Escalade.

"Shit!" Mason said, wishing she could hear him. "Don't get in the car. Whatever you do, don't get in the fucking car!"

Junior opened the passenger door and shoved her from behind.

She threw her arms against the doorframe and tried to turn and run, but someone inside the car grabbed her by the shoulders and yanked her in.

Another guy, broad and thick, appeared from the far side of the Escalade, hit Junior in the back of the head, hoisted him by the belt, and threw him on top of Sandra and slammed the door.

CHAPTER FORTY-EIGHT

Mason had a flashback to Harlan's kitchen. He never saw the face of the man who threw him across the floor, but he recognized the swing. The same man climbed into Sandra's BMW and followed the Escalade to the warehouse entrance.

Two men got out of the backseat of the Escalade, one twisting Sandra's arm behind her back as they disappeared inside the building, joined by the man who'd driven Sandra's car. The Escalade rolled back into the street and disappeared into the night.

It happened so fast that Mason had no chance to stop them. He tried his cell phone but couldn't get a signal. He considered going for help but was afraid of what might happen while he was gone, so he picked up a foot-long piece of steel pipe and ran toward the warehouse as the sky erupted in blistering sheets of rain.

Hugging the exterior wall of the warehouse, he ran around to the back looking for another entrance. On the north side, overlooking the river, he found a narrow flight of concrete stairs that led down to a darkened landing.

He bolted down the steps only to find that what had once been a door at the bottom of the stairs was now a brick wall. He slumped against the rail, rain soaked, his chest heaving. He looked up, blinking against the rain, the wall seeming to sway.

Mason rubbed his eyes and climbed the stairs, reaching ground level, when familiar hands lifted him by his collar and tossed him against the wall. His back absorbed the force of the throw as his steel pipe clattered back down the stairs. He gathered himself in a crouch, promising himself that this time would be different.

Mason launched himself at the bigger man's gut, his lunge catching the man by surprise. Shoulders down, he drove the man backward. All he wanted was running room. What he got was a knee in his belly.

Mason sucked in his breath, wrapped his arms around the man's knee, and kept coming until the man fell on his back and Mason rolled off, gasping for air. The man jumped to his feet and planted a boot in Mason's ribs, putting him in his place—back against the wall—and ending the round with a gun pointed at Mason's mouth.

The man was dark, with hair braided into shaggy cornrows. He had a couple of inches on Mason and at least thirty pounds of muscle. It wasn't close to being a fair fight.

He prodded Mason inside the warehouse, where the only good news was that the roof didn't leak. The front was a long rectangle bathed in fluorescent light, a waist-high counter cutting it off from rows of shelves rising to the ceiling. The aisles were too dark to make out their contents.

Sandra sat on a wooden stool, glaring at an invisible spot on the wall, more angry than scared, which Mason figured was just about the opposite of how he looked.

Two men stood in the far corner. The one facing him was coal black and cut from the same mold as the guy who'd captured him. He studied the floor while a short, heavyset man, his back to Mason, chewed him out, leaving no doubt about who was in charge.

The boss's head was a caramel-colored, clean-shaven dome with a crease in the back as if it had once been cleaved. He turned, studying Mason with his one good eye, the other folded into an angry scar that ran from his eyelid to the corner of his mouth.

"Mason," Jimmie Camaya said, holding Sandra's recorder in one hand and a pistol in the other, "I'm glad you could join us. You've saved me a lot of trouble."

He wore a cream-colored tropical wool suit and a pale blue silk shirt accented by a hand-painted tie. The contrast wasn't lost on Mason. A short, fat guy with a good suit and a big gun was one serious motherfucker.

Mason knew what to do in the courtroom when the opposing lawyer was hammering his client into submission. Take control. Fire back with enough objections to make him back off. And never let him see you sweat. He hoped the same technique worked with killers.

"You should have waited at my house last night. You just missed me."

"So you know I've been lookin' for you. Good for you. Julio here will keep an eye on you and Miss Sweet Cheeks until I get done with some other business. He pointed to the man who'd brought Mason in out of the rain.

"If you want me, you don't need her. Let her go."

"Need got nothing to do with it. My customers place orders and I fill 'em. Customer says you two die. You die. Up to me how. That's all."

Supply and demand. Serving the marketplace. Jimmie Camaya was just a businessman, an entrepreneur. Mason felt Adam Smith's invisible hand at his throat. But he was determined to keep Camaya talking. Words were Mason's weapons. The longer their scrimmage lasted, the better he liked his chances.

"So who's your customer? Victor O'Malley?"

"Mason, you must think I'm a real dumb fuck, you know that? My business ain't none of your business."

"Cut the crap. You shot up my car and trashed my house. You want something you think I have. Tell me what it is, and it's yours."

Camaya's stomach shook as he laughed, a deep rumbling gurgle, like a satanic Santa Claus.

"Mason, you are a funny man," he said, wiping his good eye. "I wasn't shooting at your car. I was shooting at you."

"Don't give up your day job. You're a lousy shot."

Camaya stopped laughing. His bad eye disappeared into his scar as he walked toward Mason. He stopped a foot away, his head upturned. Bay Rum cologne lay heavy on him. His breath was sweet. Death had many faces. Mason never thought his would look like this.

Mason couldn't help the tremor in his thighs. It crept upward, washing over his groin and twisting his gut. He looked at Sandra. Julio gripped her shoulder, clamping her to the seat. She struggled a moment, then quieted, whispering to him that she was sorry.

Camaya raised his gun to Mason's face, brushing it across his cheek, probing his ear with the muzzle, then past his ear, under the base of his skull, and then pulling the trigger. The bullet shattered the sheetrock, Mason's hearing, and his fear. He held his ground, depriving Camaya of the collapse he wanted.

Camaya's voice turned stone cold. "So you got a pair, huh, Mason? Well, guess what? Tough guys die slow, real slow. You'll piss your pants and cry for your mama, and we'll just be getting started."

A cell phone rang, breaking the moment but not the sweat that dripped down Mason's neck. Julio answered and handed the phone to Camaya, who listened without talking and hung up.

"Julio, tie them up. I'll be back soon. When I'm done, you can play with them."

CHAPTER FORTY-NINE

Mason took his first good look at Julio, amazed that he hadn't killed himself when he tried to run over him. With his thick neck, heavy muscled arms, and concrete body, Julio could have played nose tackle on the all-steroid team.

He bound Mason's and Sandra's hands behind their backs and wrapped another length of rope around their waists, leaving them sitting on the floor, tied back-to-back.

"Check the rest of the warehouse. Make sure it's buttoned up tight," Camaya told him, leaving with the rest of his crew as the rain swelled to a pounding downpour.

"Help me tip us over on my right side," Sandra whispered as soon as Julio was out of sight.

Mason didn't know what she had in mind, but he was open to suggestions. They rocked side to side until their momentum carried them over. Mason still wasn't sure if this was progress.

"Put your hand inside my jeans," Sandra said.

"Great idea, but I hate getting aroused when I'm all tied up."

"Do what I tell you, and we might get out of this!"

It wasn't easy, but he was able to slip three fingers inside her jeans. No underwear. No surprise.

"Lower!"

Her demand reminded him of an old joke he was about to repeat when he felt a slender object wrapped in tin foil pressed against her rump.

"Pull it out!"

It was enough to make him forget that he was about to be

killed.

"It's coming, it's coming!"

Sandra dug her nails into his back, convincing him to shut up.

"It's a number-ten surgical knife blade."

Mason didn't need any more instructions. He peeled the foil, felt the razor-sharp edge, and sliced into the first rope he could reach. It was an awkward angle to wield a blade. Sandra flinched when he caught her skin, but she didn't complain when he cut through the rope on his next pass, pulled his arms around in front, and cut the rope around their waists.

They scrambled to their feet and headed for the door. Exploding thunder muffled the sound of Julio's return. He tackled Mason for the second time that night just as Sandra opened the door and vanished into the storm.

They rolled across the floor and crashed into a workbench, showering them with tools. Julio straddled Mason, hands clamped around his throat, lighting a fire in his lungs and blurring his vision. Mason grabbed a pipe wrench from the tools that had fallen on the floor, aimed for Julio's temple, and opened a gusher that rained down on him. It took two swings, but Julio's fingers relaxed, and he fell off, stunned but still conscious.

Gasping, Mason crawled to his feet. Julio was kneeling between him and the door, blocking his escape. He took another swing with the wrench as Julio pulled a gun from his waistband. He adjusted his aim for Julio's hand, knocking the gun to the floor. When Julio dove for the gun, Mason threw the wrench at his head, missed, and ran into the darkened aisles, searching for another way out.

"Gotcha!" Julio shouted when he turned the lights on and opened fire.

"Not fair, asshole!"

Mason ran down a junk-filled aisle in the middle of the warehouse, zigzagging as bullets ricocheted around him, until a bone-rattling blast of thunder shook the walls and a lightning strike lit the windows and knocked out the power. He tripped in the dark over a pallet of five-gallon cans, banging his head on the way down. Rolling to his knees, he felt something warm and sticky on his forehead, guessed it was blood, the only question whether it was his or Julio's or both.

He knew he couldn't hide from Julio forever in the rows of junk and that the power could come back on in an instant. He had to find a way out, which meant getting to the exterior wall and feeling his way toward an exit. The lightning's unpredictable strobe light guided him.

The building was square shaped. Mason groped along the wall, hunched over to shrink Julio's target. If he didn't find a way out, eventually he'd get back to where he started. Julio would figure that out too and would be there, waiting for him.

He made it to a back corner and felt the wall jut out as his hand bumped into a doorknob. He drew a deep breath, quietly opening and closing the door. Stale, sour urine. He was hiding in the john, a wooden partition separating the sink and stool.

The power returned, the flash of the naked bulb dangling from the ceiling blinding him for an instant. He turned the light off and stood astride the stool with his back pressed against the wall, his heart pounding against his ribs.

He had trapped himself. Julio would check the exits to make certain they were still locked. He'd walk the aisles and not find him. The bathroom would be next. Julio's footsteps slapped against the concrete floor and stopped outside the door, making him a prophet.

"Come on out, man. I won't hurt you."

Mason was surprised that Julio's voice was soft, almost feminine, but he wasn't tempted.

"Have it your way, man."

Five shots smashed through the door, splinters flying, Julio kicking the door off its hinges. Mason lifted the porcelain tank lid off the back of the stool, lowered it in a two-handed grip, counted off the two steps from the door to the partition, and swung for the fences, catching the center of Julio's face, driving his nose into his brain.

Julio crumpled as Mason's swing carried them forward into a heap, Mason on top, Julio not moving. Mason pushed himself to his feet and turned on the light. Julio's eyes were wide open and fixed. His nose had vanished into his face, blood trickling from his ears and the corners of his mouth.

Mason heard more footsteps running in his direction. Julio's gun had skidded beneath the sink. Mason reached for it, hoping there were a couple of rounds left, giving up when he heard a familiar voice.

"Freeze, shitbag!"

Blues stepped into the bathroom, gun drawn.

Mason looked up at him and smiled. "Sorry. I forgot to tell you. I'll be late for dinner."

CHAPTER FIFTY

"Fuck you! What the fuck you think you're doing?"

Sandra pushed her way into the bathroom and knelt at Julio's body, searching for a pulse.

"He's dead," she said. "How'd you do it?"

Mason stood. "I hit him with the tank lid."

"I don't fucking believe it. You killed the son of a bitch with a toilet!"

Blues shook his head and walked out. Mason and Sandra followed him.

"Let's get out of here before Camaya comes back," she said.

"They took Sandra's car. Where's yours?" Blues asked as they stepped outside into the driving rain.

"In an alley. What do we do about Julio?"

"Let Camaya clean up his own mess. Follow me back downtown. We'll leave your car in a tow zone."

"Why do we have to leave it anywhere?" Mason asked.

"You're getting out of town. You can't go back to your place. The cops will tow your car and at least you'll know where to find it."

Mason parked the TR6 in a handicapped spot in front of city hall and got in Blues's car, smiling when he saw his briefcase. Blues had made good on his promise to retrieve it from Mason's Acura.

"Thanks for that," Mason said, pointing to the briefcase. "How did you know where to find me?"

"I was minding my own business, waiting for you to show up for dinner, when Sandra called and told me what happened. I swear to Jesus, both of you are too stupid to live! What in the hell were you thinking? Never mind. I know the answer to that question. You weren't thinking!"

They knew better than to argue so they kept quiet as he wound through a maze of inner-city side streets, doubling back several times to make certain they weren't followed, before finally reaching the interstate.

Wiped out by the post-adrenaline letdown, Mason closed his eyes, thinking about the fraternity of killers he'd joined. Camaya was a charter member. He'd just been initiated.

When he woke up, they were at the intersection of Highways 50 and 65 in Sedalia, Missouri. Blues turned south on Highway 65 in front of a sign that pointed to the Lake of the Ozarks.

Blues called Kelly, told her what had happened and that they were on their way to the lake. She met them at one a.m. on Highway 5 just after they crossed the Camden County line south of Laurie, Missouri.

Mason rode with her as she led Blues through the woods. Her stony silence told him all he needed to know. She crushed the one attempt he made at explaining with an attack on civilians who tried to play cops and robbers.

They stopped at a cabin so isolated and hidden that Mason half expected it to be a bed-and-breakfast run by the seven dwarfs. After handing out blankets, Kelly left, threatening more than promising to return in the morning.

They drew straws and Sandra won the only bedroom. Blues claimed the couch, and Mason got the wooden floor. Claire had always claimed that sleeping on a board was good for a bad back. Mason decided that she must have cheated and used a mattress. He woke up at first light, heard Blues snoring, and stepped outside.

The only log cabins he had ever seen were on bottles of maple syrup. Studying this one was easier than thinking about Julio.

Rough-hewn logs, sculpted at each end to mate with another log, were laid one on top of the other. Gaps between the logs were filled with mortar made from clay and mud. Windows and doors had been cut into the logs, each ninety-degree angle sharp and precise. The roof was made from split rails raised to a modest pitch that extended over the front porch, a limestone chimney on the south side adding a homey finish.

The cabin was set on the side of a hill in a clearing ringed by trees. The untamed grass formed a green belt roughly a hundred feet wide between the trees and the cabin. Long-stemmed purple stalks, sunflowers, and deep blue pansies painted the grass in a natural palate.

A fifty-gallon propane tank on the north side fueled the hot-water heater, kitchen appliances, and an electrical generator. Along with the bathroom, they were the only concessions to modern living.

Mason sat on the wooden bench on the front porch, letting the rising sun warm him as he relived last night. Hallmark has a card for almost every occasion. There's one for birthdays, remembered or forgotten, comings and goings of all kinds, friends and loved ones gained or lost. There's even one for Mother-in-Law's Day, but he was certain there was no card for killing someone. After all, what would it say? *Congrats on hitting the big one!* Or maybe, *The bigger they are, the harder they fall!*

He was just tugging at the fringes. He didn't know how this was going to feel now or in the future. He knew three things for certain. The first was that he had responded to the most basic instinct of survival. The second was that killing came more easily than he would have ever imagined possible. And the third was that the threat was still there.

Everything began with Sullivan's death. Harlan's murder and the latest efforts to add him to the obituary list connected events since then.

Sullivan had been poisoned, which is a chancy way to kill someone. The killer can't be certain that the poison is going to be consumed or that the dose is sufficient for the size of the victim. Unless the poison acts instantly, there is always the possibility the victim will fall ill and get to a hospital before it's too late.

Sullivan had been poisoned with insulin. According to the autopsy report, the reaction time can vary from a few hours to a few days. Even if the killer was present when Sullivan took the fatal dose, he or she could not have known where he would be when the stuff hit him.

Poisoning was like drawing to an inside straight when compared to the pat hand used with Harlan. His neck had been snapped like a dried branch. Nothing left to chance. Poisoners and neck snappers weren't cut from the same cloth. The difference was enough to convince Mason there were two killers. Probably.

Someone in a black Escalade tried to run him off the road. The next time he saw it, Jimmie Camaya was shooting out a window at him. The last time he saw it, Vic Jr. was driving it but Camaya was in it. That was enough to convince him that there was a connection between the two killers. Probably.

He didn't have a favorite on the short list of suspects he'd given Kelly. Pamela Sullivan had enough motives for a miniseries and probable access to insulin.

Without his own clients, Scott Daniels's best chance of securing his future was to inherit Sullivan's practice. Angela was squirming enough under Sullivan's blackmail to risk bugging the offices. Either one—or both—could have rented a ski boat, met Sullivan at the condo, and poisoned him. As long as Sullivan agreed to sit still while they injected him with a fatal dose of insulin.

With the feds closing in, O'Malley may have decided Sullivan was the weak link in his defense—or maybe he really didn't like paying for work that nobody did. He wasn't at the lake when Sullivan was murdered, but he was the type who hired people to cut his grass, shovel his snow, and do his killing.

Even if one of them killed Sullivan, Mason couldn't guess at a reason to kill Harlan or—better yet—to hire Camaya to kill him. What did he have that was worth killing for?

Mason thought about it as if he were preparing for trial. Putting a case together meant building a puzzle, tearing it apart, and putting it back together again until any jury can understand

and believe it. No matter how many times he prepared a case, he always worried that he'd forgotten something that would unravel his case faster than a loose thread on a cheap suit. This case was all loose threads—each one leaving a hole when he pulled it out.

CHAPTER FIFTY-ONE

The rumbling growl of an engine in low gear scattered his thoughts. Mason resisted the urge to run for cover, not believing Camaya could find him in the wilderness.

The engine belonged to Kelly's maroon, middle-aged Chevy pickup. She swung the truck in a tight arc, braking so that the Chevy's nose was pointed downhill.

She climbed out, took four brisk strides to the porch, folded her arms across her chest, and glared at him. The dust hadn't settled around the truck tires. She was ready to pick up where she'd left off last night when Blues opened the cabin door. He was wearing a ratty T-shirt and boxer shorts and was engaged in the male morning scratching ritual when Kelly turned her high intensity eyes on him.

"Morning, Sheriff," he said. "Glad you could join us for breakfast—hope you brought enough for everybody."

With an easy stretch and a wide yawn, he pivoted half a turn and slid back inside.

"Well, you can take the cop out of the country but you can't take the country—"

"Save it, Counselor! It's going to take a lot more than smart-ass punch lines to clean up this mess."

Kelly was back in uniform, body and soul. She had a real knack for spoiling magic moments. Mason pulled himself up from the love seat and followed her inside.

Blues had brewed coffee, and the aroma filtered into the bedroom, bringing Sandra back out with it. Mason had never developed a taste for coffee and still felt like a kid when he was the only one sucking on apple juice. Since the cabin didn't have a fully stocked minibar, he rinsed his mouth with tap water while the others drank their attitude adjustment.

They each stood their ground in the cramped kitchen, no one talking, sorting their muddled feelings for each other and their circumstances. Kelly stood at parade rest, shoulders drawn back, fingers of both hands wrapped around her mug, eyes fixed on a watermark on the wall. Blues hunched over the sink, humming something unidentifiable under his breath, pausing only long enough to take an occasional sip. Sandra lounged against the refrigerator, drawing invisible circles on the hardwood floor with her bare toes. Mason filled the doorway between the kitchen and the den, bottling them up. Steam rose from coffee cups. Nothing else moved.

"Kelly—," Blues began, his back still to her. "Lou and Sandra were in a jam. We had to get them out of there before Camaya came back."

"Goddammit, Bluestone! You were a cop! How could you be so stupid? You let him run around until he almost gets himself and Sandra killed and then you leave the scene of a homicide! And just for kicks, you drop the whole mess in my lap!"

Blues placed his cup on the Formica countertop and watched a pair of squirrels chase each other in the grass.

"You called it in, didn't you?"

"The body, the one you called Julio? You knew I would the minute you told me what happened."

"Kansas City cops or the feds?"

"Kansas City—it's their jurisdiction."

"They told you someone had already called it in."

"Yeah. How did you know?"

"Because I called it in from the car. You call them back this morning to find out what went down?"

"Yes." The edge was gone from her answer.

Blues turned around, facing Kelly, and raised himself onto the counter. "And they told you they checked it out and didn't find a body."

Kelly's face softened as she nodded her reply.

"Wait a minute!" Mason said. "I killed that son of a bitch and his body disappears?"

He dropped onto the lone kitchen chair, a metal-backed model with torn, red vinyl upholstery.

"I told you Camaya would clean up his own mess," Blues said to him. Turning back to Kelly, he continued, "Camaya was coming back to finish up with Sandra and Lou. If the cops got there first, it was Jimmie's problem. If he cleaned house first, it stayed private. Either way, Sandra and Lou had to get out of town."

Satisfied for the moment, Kelly changed course. "Camaya isn't the only one looking for you, Lou. Gene McNamara called first thing this morning wanting to know if I knew where you were."

"What did Fido want with me?"

"Victor O'Malley's son is missing. McNamara wants to talk with you about that. I told him I would let you know the next time I saw you."

Mason knew that if he talked to McNamara, he would have to tell him all about last night. Body or no body, he'd killed a man. He knew it was self-defense, but he also knew that he wasn't ready to talk to McNamara about it. He'd probably end up on the receiving end of one of B.J. Moore's comforting chats. Trouble was, if he didn't tell McNamara what he knew about Junior's disappearance, he could be in more trouble for obstructing justice. While that sounded fairly puny compared to homicide, it appealed to his lawyerly sense of duty. Since McNamara had sent his question through Kelly, he decided to use her for the reply.

"Tell him to look for a black Ford Escalade. Last time I saw Junior, one of Camaya's boys was loading him in the back like a sack of groceries."

"I don't suppose you noticed the tag number?"

"It's an Illinois plate," Sandra said. "I caught the first three numbers—735—before they put me in the car."

Kelly looked at Sandra, unable to thank her for the information or fire a shot across her bow. She was saving her ammunition for Mason. She wrote the information down without a reply before stuffing her notepad into her shirt pocket

"You'll have to talk to him eventually; you know that."

Anger takes a lot of energy to sustain, especially if the other side won't fight back. She'd had all night to work herself up. Mason hoped that her anger was partly out of concern for him. That, plus the realization that he'd screwed up big-time and was lucky to be alive, kept him from firing back.

"Yeah, I know. Only not yet. You can tell him everything I know, which isn't much, and his investigation won't be stalled."

CHAPTER FIFTY-TWO

Mason didn't want to go home until he had a lot better idea who his friends were. The only way he knew to figure that out was to put this puzzle together from the beginning.

Kelly agreed not to arrest Mason for homicide, obstruction of justice, illegal parking, or any of the other offenses he'd committed in the last twenty-four hours. With a look that said she knew she would regret it, she went outside to call McNamara. She returned a few minutes later with a briefcase she tossed on the sofa and a sack of groceries she deposited in the kitchen.

"What did he say?" Mason asked.

She didn't answer until she had emptied the contents of the sack on the table. A dozen eggs, butter, a pound of bacon, a gallon of orange juice, a loaf of Ozark Home Style Honey & Wheat Bread, and a jar of strawberry preserves.

"I like my eggs scrambled and the bacon crisp. Butter the toast lightly. I'll get my own orange juice."

Mason saluted and went to work.

Kelly continued. "McNamara accused me of harboring a potential suspect in a kidnapping investigation and threatened to have my badge. I told him he could have it if I got to pin it on." Her mouth opened in a half-moon smile, her first of the day.

Mason negotiated an "I'll cook and you clean" package with Blues and Sandra. Within minutes, the small cabin was brimming with the fragrance of Ozark smoked bacon snapping in the frying pan. *Fresh air, hot food, and being alive,* he thought. *Things could be worse.*

213

He sat on the sofa with Kelly while the dishes were washed. The fabric was rough tartan wool. The springs had long ago given up. The ones that still had some punch were pointed at odd angles guaranteed to poke where the sun didn't shine. The floor was looking better to Mason all the time.

Mason retrieved his briefcase from Blues's car and started reviewing the O'Malley summaries, looking for a thread to tie everything together. He was seeing the words without reading them. They were too familiar to him. He glanced at Kelly. She was equally glazed over, thumbing through reports she'd read a dozen times.

"Listen," he suggested, "we both need a fresh approach. Let's trade files. Maybe we'll see something the other has missed."

Kelly handed him her folder. Sullivan's medical records from Charlie Morgenstern's office were on top. The chart was organized chronologically with the most recent records on top. It was like reading Sullivan's life story in reverse. He already knew the ending. He just hoped there was something useful in the past.

The first entry was impersonal. *Patient died in boating accident, Lake of Ozarks, July 3—date estimated—await autopsy from coroner.* No hint of a twenty-plus-year friendship. Mason hoped when his doctor made his final entry for him that he at least rated a "poor Lou" instead of the anonymous "patient died."

There were weekly entries since Sullivan's diagnosis of HIV, regular blood work and prescriptions. Mason expected to find records of multiple injections, but there weren't any. He'd assumed that the needle marks found at autopsy were treatment related, but the records didn't support that. He started writing a list of questions on a legal pad, beginning with *Needle marks?*

Prior to the HIV diagnosis, Sullivan's records were routine and uninteresting. His weight fluctuated between 150 and 160 pounds. His blood pressure was generally around 120/80. He never showed any signs of masses or lumps. His chest X-rays were clean. He rarely had a cold and had never been hospitalized in the twenty-two years that Morgenstern had been his doctor.

An entry dated September 29, 1987, caught Mason's eye—
Sample drawn and delivered to Comm. B. B. The next entry was
three days later and was written in physician shorthand that he
could only partly decipher: *TC from Dr. Ashland, Comm. B. B.—
pt's sample 95%+.*

"Kelly, what do you think this means?" Mason handed her the
chart and pointed out the entries.

She studied the entries, knitting her brow, double-checking
for anything that would shed light on their meaning. The cabin
resonated with the mixed scents of pine logs, remnants of breakfast,
and musty upholstery. The potpourri couldn't hide her fragrance.
It was subtle, spicy, and elusive. He inhaled deeply and realized his
last shower had been a day and a half ago. Not wanting to spoil the
moment, he edged away from her.

"The records don't explain it," she said.

"Let me have a look," Sandra said. "I used to spend half my
time reading medical records. 'Comm. B. B.' is probably the
community blood bank. My guess is they tested him for something
and the results were ninety-five percent positive."

"Most doctors send their lab work out, but not to the community
blood bank. Why would Morgenstern use them?" Mason asked.

"Could be a lot of things, I guess; hepatitis, special blood
counts, paternity. The easiest way to find out is to ask Charlie
Morgenstern."

"I'll make the call," Kelly said. "In the meantime, Lou, do us all
a favor and take a shower."

Mason coaxed a thin, lukewarm stream from the single-setting
showerhead. Julio's boot had left an angry inkblot on his left side.
Raising his arm above his head, he peered at his side, examining
the yellow and purple tinges that were forming in the blood pooled
beneath his skin. He fingered the area gingerly, afraid to discover
what fractured ribs were supposed to feel like. He was encouraged
when his palpations didn't produce shivers of pain.

An odorless scrap of soap was stuck like a piece of gum on the
underside of the soap dish. It yielded a pale film that was harder

to rinse off than it was to scrub on. The total effect was like an economy car wash—one pass without the undercarriage blast. Putting yesterday's clothes back on made the entire effort a break-even proposition. He was half clean, uncombed and unshaven, and starting to blend in with the logs.

When he came back into the front room, Kelly and Blues were deep into the O'Malley papers. They had spread the summaries on the floor and were taking notes. Sandra was rereading Sullivan's medical records.

Kelly's phone rang, interrupting the study group. She listened, said thank you, and hung up, smiling. This one was wide, toothy, and satisfied.

"That was Dr. Morgenstern. Sullivan took a paternity test and passed. He's a daddy."

CHAPTER FIFTY-THREE

"So who's the lucky heir?" Mason asked.

"He doesn't know. In 1987, some woman contacted Sullivan and claimed that he was the father of her ten-year-old child. Sullivan didn't deny it but wanted a blood test to confirm it. Afterward, he never mentioned it again."

"Call the blood bank," said Blues. "They keep their records forever."

"Forget it," answered Sandra. "I've dealt with them on other cases. You won't get anything out of them voluntarily. They're too worried about confidentiality. You'll need a court order."

"That's what assistant prosecuting attorneys are for," Kelly said.

She grabbed her phone, punched in a number, and asked for Tina DeVoy, telling what she wanted and that she wanted it yesterday. Even though they could hear only one end of the conversation, it was easy enough to piece it together.

DeVoy followed standard rank-and-file procedure, explaining why she couldn't get the order before Monday and why it would take another week to get the records after she got the order.

"Not good enough," Kelly told her. "You'll get the order, serve it, and bring me the records before the sun comes up in the morning or you'll spend the rest of your career plea-bargaining traffic tickets. Are we clear?" Kelly listened and nodded. "Good. I'm sure you will."

"That prosecutor surely knows you aren't her boss, doesn't she?" Blues asked when Kelly hung up.

"She's brand-new and figures that anyone who yells at her

might also sign her paycheck. She'll get the order today, but we'll be lucky to get the records before Monday. But at least it's a start."

Sullivan's blood tests triggered a memory from Tommy Douchant's trial. Tommy's hip was lacerated by one of the I beams he hit on his way down to the pavement. Mason had used his bloody clothes as trial exhibits.

"How long will dried blood last?" he asked.

"Why? Are you planning to start a collection?" Sandra asked.

"Just trying to revive a lost cause. Any ideas, Kelly?"

"There are too many variables to generalize. Depends on the surface, the temperature—a lot of things."

"Who would you use in Kansas City to analyze a safety hook for dried blood?"

"Virginia Norville. She's the county medical examiner, and she does freelance forensic work if it's interesting enough."

Mason called Webb Chapman, leaving him a message to take the box of hooks to Dr. Norville for analysis. Sandra grabbed the phone as Mason was about to hang up, telling Chapman to also have the hooks checked for fingerprints.

"Good enough," Mason said. "Let's see if we can figure anything out in the O'Malley records. The fixtures deals are the key. Quintex invested in a series of sale and leasebacks of store fixtures. Scott Daniels did all the legal work."

"Who signed off on the deals for the corporations?" Blues asked.

"A Chicago law firm with power of attorney for the corporations. The real players are anonymous."

"What's the name of the law firm?" Kelly asked.

"Caravello and Landusky," Mason said.

The light drained from Kelly's eyes as she grabbed Mason's file and tore through the pages. Dropping the file, she balled her fists under her arms and paced around the room.

"What's the matter? It's only a law firm. Did they turn you down for a job?"

She stopped with her back to the stone fireplace, her expression grim. "Caravello and Landusky is Carlo D'lessandro's personal law firm. They don't sharpen their pencils unless it's to cover for the mob. Jimmie Camaya has always been freelance, but D'lessandro is one of his best customers."

"What else do we know?" Blues asked.

Mason answered. "Quintex invested fifty thousand to seventy-five thousand dollars in each deal. Annual rent was around sixty thousand. The first group of deals have recouped the initial investment and threw off about a half million dollars in the last year."

"Anything else?" Kelly asked.

"In the last twelve months, O'Malley paid Sullivan & Christenson a half million dollars for work it never did."

"Who controlled the billing?" Kelly was boring in.

"Angela Molina on the administrative side. She planted bugs in Sullivan's, Harlan's, and Scott's offices to try and get something she could use on them."

"Where in the hell does that news come from, and when were you planning on telling me?"

Kelly strapped her arms down with her hands to keep from strangling Mason. Blues just grinned, enjoying the show.

Even Mason couldn't believe that he hadn't told them everything he'd found out. Then he remembered that he'd spent most of the time since he talked with Angela being beat up and shot at, hitting bad guys with toilets, and sneaking out of town in the back of a car. It was easy to forget petty stuff like blackmail, wiretapping, and fraud when he got caught up in the fun and excitement of dodging bullets. Still, he felt sheepish—well, actually, stupid, but he thought he could sell sheepish easier than stupid.

"Okay, look. I've been kind of busy the last couple of days, what with being beat up, held prisoner, shot at, rescuing Sandra, and killing a guy. I know I should keep you guys more up to date, and I'll try to do better from here on out."

Blues grimaced as if he had gas. Sandra stuck two fingers down her throat. Kelly wasn't buying any of it. All he could do was finish the story.

"Okay. Here it is. Angela and I had a drink at a gay bar called The Limit. She admitted the bugging and said the recordings were in a safe place. She was about to tell me where when Diane Farrell showed up."

"Sounds like somebody is laundering money through Quintex and the law firm," Kelly said. "Probably drug money. We need to talk to someone who can tell us if the lease payments are way above market value. If they are, I'll bet that's how they're washing the cash."

"Might be easier to trace the money after it leaves the law firm than try to backtrack it to where it started," Blues said.

"How do we do that?" Mason asked.

"The first thing to do is examine the firm's expenses. Are there any new, large expenses that aren't easily explained? Do they match up in time with the receipt of the fees from O'Malley?" Kelly explained.

"We'll have to get into the firm's records to figure that out. I doubt if Scott will just turn the books over to us," Mason said.

"That's assuming he's still running the show," Sandra added. "Last we heard, the firm was the prize in a dogfight between St. John, with his federal court order freezing the firm's assets, and O'Malley, with the receiver appointed by the state court."

"Don't leave anything else out, Counselor," Kelly said.

"There is one other thing. Diane Farrell had Angela witness Sullivan's codicil revoking his will, except Angela never saw Sullivan sign it."

"So we charge Angela with murder, wiretapping, and falsely witnessing a document. Great." Kelly said.

She picked up Mason's file and started to return it to his briefcase when she hesitated, reached inside, and pulled out three CDs. "I thought you said you told us everything, Lou. What are these?"

"Souvenirs from Sullivan," Mason said. "Two porn DVDs and the Johnny Mathis CD that was in his briefcase when we searched his room at the lake. His wife didn't want them, so I kept them."

"Why? You like a Johnny Mathis soundtrack with your porn?"

"Yeah, the moaning and groaning get old after a while."

"Where did you find the porno DVDs?"

"One of them was in Sullivan's office and the other was at his house."

"Tell me again how you know that there isn't anything else on them."

"Diane Farrell looked at them for us."

Kelly's eyebrows rose with each word until Mason thought her forehead would vanish. He realized again how lame some things sounded when you tried to explain them to someone else.

"This is the same Diane Farrell who told Angela to witness Sullivan's codicil without Sullivan's signature and who showed up just in time to stop Angela from telling you where she was hiding her wiretap tapes?" Kelly asked.

Mason decided to treat her question as rhetorical.

"Yeah," Blues answered for him. "My money says these disks will get you more than a rise in your Levi's."

Kelly picked up her phone again.

"Riley, it's Kelly. Meet me at the courthouse computer center as soon as you can, and be prepared to do some hacking."

"Who's Riley?" Blues asked.

"He's the register of deeds," Mason said.

"And, he set up the county's new computer system," Kelly said. "If Sullivan hid something on these disks, he'll find it. And, Lou, another shower wouldn't hurt."

CHAPTER FIFTY-FOUR

"There's got to be something hidden on those DVDs that will unravel this whole thing," Kelly said over the wind whipping around the open windows of her pickup.

She worked the stick shift as if it were a natural extension of her arm, engaging the four-wheel drive when they hit a particularly rutted stretch of road that rose and fell like a poor man's roller coaster. The road was barely wide enough for one vehicle.

"Something worth killing Sullivan, Harlan, and me for?" Mason asked.

Humid morning air, heated by the rising sun, filled the cab and softened the stiffness in his back and neck. The rough ride loosened the tougher kinks that remained from sleeping on the cabin floor. Kelly was pushing the pickup at a fast clip that would have been suicidal for someone unfamiliar with the road. Blues and Sandra followed at a distance in his Trans-Am.

"Not Sullivan. Camaya doesn't poison people. He shoots them or breaks their neck or runs them off the road. Sullivan may have been on Camaya's hit list, but somebody beat him to it."

"Even if you're right about that, those DVDs are still pretty pricey."

"Camaya is the only one who thinks about how much it's worth. That's how he makes payroll. Price didn't matter to whoever hired Camaya. If you have to ask how much it costs, you can't afford it. Whatever is on the DVDs could explain why. You and Harlan may have just gotten in the way, known too much."

"But I don't know anything."

"Yeah, but the bad guys think you're a lot smarter. The rest of us know better. You've got the DVDs and that's enough to make you a target."

Mason braced his hands against the dash as the pickup splashed through a washed-out patch of road and leaped over a hilltop. Kelly let out a whoop as she put the truck into a hard right onto smooth blacktop, where it fishtailed before leveling out. She slowed until she caught sight of Blues turning onto the road.

"Your cabin isn't exactly on the AAA scenic route."

"That's the idea. I'm the only one who knows where it is. That makes it private for me and safe for you."

"If there are two killers, maybe Sullivan's murder set off a chain reaction that's out of control. Sandra calls it chaos theory—the rule of unintended consequences."

"We can't rule out anything yet. We haven't accounted for Sullivan's movements during the time he was most likely poisoned."

"Angela Molina has Scott Daniels on tape talking to someone about Sullivan's death and St. John's subpoena the same day Sullivan's body was found," Mason said. "Scott left the lake before you woke me on the beach. How did he know that Sullivan was dead?"

"You said that Angela didn't recognize the voice on the other end of Scott's call. That rules out anyone in the firm. So who was Scott talking to?"

"I don't know. All I do know is that Scott has been more worried about O'Malley than anything else. When O'Malley fired the firm, Scott lost more than a client—he lost Vic Jr. and Quintex. I'd sure like to find out where that half million dollars in bogus fees ended up."

"That may be another link to Harlan's death," Kelly said. "If he was getting laundered money, I doubt that he would have reported it on his Form 1040. He may have been willing to give up the whole scheme to stay out of jail. Somebody figured Harlan would deal and killed him to shut him up."

"That makes Angela a link between both murders. She knew

about the fees. She bugged the phones. She witnessed the change to Sullivan's will."

Mason wondered whom Angela was covering for on the phony bills. He had assumed it was Sullivan because O'Malley was his client. He thought back to his conversation with her and realized that his questions assumed that it was Sullivan. Angela had never said that. Mason had. He remembered the advice he always gave his clients before the other lawyer questioned them: "If he hasn't got the facts straight, that's his problem. We're not here to help the other side."

Scott and Harlan were the lawyers on the fixtures deals—not Sullivan. Angela could have been covering for them as easily as for Sullivan. The dirty money that was being washed through Sullivan & Christenson's books may have financed her "loan" from the firm. Her story about Sullivan blackmailing her could have been just that—a story.

Angela had always been one to play every angle. She said the tapes were in a safe place. Mason hoped she had one picked out for her.

Kelly interrupted his thoughts. "The paper trail on the fixtures deals leads to a Chicago law firm that fronts for the mob. Jimmie Camaya works for the mob. Scott and Harlan wouldn't know how to make those kinds of connections."

"So they were drawn into the fixtures scam with Vic Jr. He was the O'Malley involved in the fixtures deals, not his father. Camaya used him as bait to grab Sandra, and now he's missing."

"Who knew you had the DVDs?"

"Plenty of people. Pamela Sullivan, Sandra Connelly, Diane Farrell, Angela Molina, Maggie Boylan, and Phil Rosa. They'd all seen me with the disks. I'm sure everyone else in the office had heard about them."

Mason finally understood the reason his house had been trashed—to find the disks. That's why they left his computer intact. It was a calling card—a message that they knew he had the disks and they wanted them. And they didn't know whether he had found what was hidden on them. When in doubt, kill first and ask questions later.

CHAPTER FIFTY-FIVE

Riley Brooks was waiting for them in the computerized nerve center in the basement of the county courthouse. What was once a deteriorating, mildewed graveyard for closed files and ancient furniture was now a gleaming, climate-controlled tribute to high-tech government.

Riley stood in the center of it all, beaming at the gadgetry spread around him. Kelly introduced Sandra and Blues. Each of them was greeted with an enthusiastic handshake and clap on the shoulder.

"All right," he said to Kelly. "What have you got that old Riley's supposed to break into?"

He rubbed his palms together and his face shone with excitement as Kelly handed him the DVDs and the Johnny Mathis CD. Mason laid out the essential pieces of the puzzle. Riley listened thoughtfully, tugging occasionally at one of the gray wisps above his ears.

"What do you think, Riley?" Kelly asked when Mason finished.

"I like Johnny Mathis. Always made the missus melt. Mind if I keep it?"

"Be my guest. What about the movies?" Mason asked.

"It's easy enough to hide data on a disk so that an amateur won't find it," he answered as he tapped one disk against the palm of his hand. "But I'm no amateur."

"Diane Farrell told us she checked the list function and didn't see anything else on them," Mason added.

"May not have been on the same program as the video. I'll

check it out through the utilities program. That should identify everything on the disks. If someone was really clever, they could hide the data from that too. It may take time, but I'll find it if it's there."

They left and Kelly took them to the shops ringing the courthouse square. An hour later, Blues, Sandra, and Mason had clean clothes. Their next stop was the showers in the county jail; Mason telling the others that it pays to have connections when traveling.

Clean and dressed, he found his way to Kelly's office on the first floor of the courthouse. She sat in front of her desk digging through six inches of in-basket, shoving it aside when he pulled up a chair next to her. A faint breeze wandered in the open windows, adding the smell of freshly cut grass.

"Blues and Sandra are checking in with Riley. Where do we go from here?" he asked.

"You don't go anywhere. Stay out of it. You don't know what you're doing, and I don't need any more bodies showing up on my doorstep."

She answered without looking up from her papers. Her message was clear. Take off.

Mason wasn't listening, "Why are you so angry with me?"

It wasn't an innocent question. He knew part of the reason. She had made that plain. He hoped she would tell him that it was his body she didn't want dumped somewhere. She sat back in her chair, arms folded across her chest, lips pressed flat. She knew what he was asking her, and the answer wasn't easy. She gave it in a tight, controlled voice.

"Lou, this is a murder investigation, not *The Dating Game*. You are attractive and fun to be with—in spite of your one-liner approach to life. If we'd met another time, maybe something good could happen. But you're screwing up this investigation."

"Which means that you're using your badge to keep me away. You're protecting yourself, not me. I'm not your dead partner. I'm not a cop and I'm not dirty."

She flinched, telling Mason that he had hit home. She had become the one bright light in his suddenly chaotic life. He knew he couldn't hold her if she didn't want him. But he wasn't about to roll away into the darkness.

"You're way out of line, Counselor!"

She bit off each word and spat them at him. They traded hard stares until hers began to redden and glisten. "Damn you!" she snapped and swiveled her chair around, leaving him to argue with her back.

Mason got up slowly. "Blues can find his way back to the cabin even if it's supposed to be a secret. I'll wait for you there. Sandra can stay and work with Riley." No response. He walked to the door and turned, still talking to the back of her chair. "You might want to run Vic Jr. through one of your crime computers, Sheriff. He's got to be the link to Chicago. Maybe you'll find something interesting."

CHAPTER FIFTY-SIX

Mason found Blues loading three shotguns and enough ammunition for a small army into the backseat of his Trans-Am.

"Where in the hell did that come from?"

"Store across the street," he said pointing to Smith's Hunting and Fishing Shop.

"Did you get a hunting license?" Mason asked, ever the careful lawyer.

"We're not going hunting," he said as he slid in behind the wheel. "Get in."

Mason closed the door and looked again at the armory in the back. "Well, I guess it's a nice day for target practice, huh?"

"You ever shoot a gun, Lou?"

"No. Is that important?"

Blues smiled. "All depends on how you feel about getting your ass shot off."

"I'm feeling very attached to my ass, actually."

"I'm not going to sit up in those woods waiting for Camaya to come looking for us and not have anything to offer him except coffee."

"Camaya doesn't know where we are."

"You killed one of his boys. It would have been better to kill him. He's getting paid to kill you, so he's got to find you. He'll find Kelly and figure you won't be far."

"Thanks a lot. You're the one who brought us here. If you knew Camaya would figure it out, why didn't we go somewhere else?"

"Because that won't solve your problem. He'd still find you."

"So I'm supposed to become a gunslinger overnight and call Jimmie out for a showdown?"

"You'll be lucky if you don't shoot your dick off. Shotgun's your best bet. Know why?"

"No, but I have a feeling you're about to educate me."

"A shotgun fires a pattern of shot that spreads out the farther it gets from the gun. It makes up for a lot of weak stomachs and shaky hands."

"So why does Camaya use an automatic?"

"Ain't nothin' weak or shaky about him. He's got a lot more experience killing folks. But I'll take a shotgun every time for close work. The New York City Police Department did a study of shootings involving their officers. The average distance between the shooters was seven feet. At that distance, the cops only managed hits thirty-six percent of the time."

"Lousy shots."

"Nope. Just human. A man can stand on the firing range all day and put ten out of ten slugs in the center of the target. Trouble is, the target is standing still and isn't shooting back. When it's real, anyone with a weak bladder can be a lousy shot. All I want you to learn is how to load, point, and shoot. The shotgun will do the rest."

They dragged a half dozen hay bales that had been lined against the back of the cabin over to the edge of the woods and stacked them two across and three high to create a makeshift shooting range. Blues positioned each layer so that there was a narrow ledge in front of the second and third bales. They scavenged through the cabin until they found an array of tin cans and other junk that didn't object to being shot to pieces. Blues arranged their targets on the ledges, picked up a shotgun, and started class.

"This is a semiautomatic shotgun. Once it's loaded and the safety is off, you pump it and pull the trigger. Keep pulling the trigger, and it keeps firing until the magazine is empty. Anybody who gets in the way will have a very bad day."

"That's it? Just point and shoot?" Mason asked, reaching for the gun. "This is starting to sound fun."

"Not exactly, Wyatt Earp. Don't point it at anybody or anything that you don't intend to shoot."

"Sounds reasonable. Let me have it." Mason hefted the shotgun, raising it to his shoulder and then lowering it to his waist, aiming at the hay bales from his hip.

"What about the safety?"

"If you're hunting quail, keep it on until you're ready to shoot. If a man's hunting you, keep it off. You forget to release it and you're dead. You take too long to release it and you're dead. It hangs up and you're dead."

Blues made him practice loading and unloading the gun, sighting, and firing without ammunition for an hour before letting Mason fire a live round. He paced off firing lines at ten-foot intervals from the hay bales, telling Mason to begin at the closest mark, fire three rounds, and back up to the next station.

The shot patterns on the bales vividly demonstrated the spread from each shell. As he backed up, the spread grew into an ever-widening killing field. A blue-gray cloud of acrid smoke hung in the air. Mason had learned how to load, pump, point, and shoot. He just hoped the bad guys were as cooperative as the hay bales.

Afterward they sat on the front steps of the cabin sipping cold beer they'd bought on the drive back. The sun was on the backside of the cabin, leaving the front in comfortable shade. The quiet of the woods had returned and it was hard to believe that they'd just finished their war games.

"So—what are you going to do?" Blues asked.

"Circle the wagons, make 'em pay for every inch of ground—what am I supposed to say?"

"No, man. When this is over, what are you going to do?"

"I'll treat the question as a vote of confidence. To tell you the truth, I haven't really thought about it. I guess I'll have to find a job or take up piano again."

"You'd be better off joining the foreign legion. Why do you want to keep practicing law anyway?"

"I'm not certain. I had the right motives when I went to law school. Fight the good fight. Protect the individual. But I lost the fire somewhere along the way."

"But you turned out to be pretty good at it."

"Sometimes. I lost my last case. It was one of those I couldn't afford to lose. Maybe I lost my nerve."

"Fall off the horse, you're supposed to get right back on. Maybe you should go back to the kind of practice you started with."

"And maybe I should start doing what I should have done in the first place."

"What's that supposed to mean?"

"Listen to my aunt Claire. How about you? Are you going to spend the rest of your life as an itinerant Piano Man?"

"Nah. I've been making my changes all along."

"Somehow musician and scuffling PI doesn't sound like a grand strategy for fulfillment."

Blues laughed and agreed. "You're right about that, brother. I'm tired of bouncing from gig to gig. I'm buying my own place."

"Get out! What kind of place?"

"Used to be a restaurant on Broadway. I'm gonna call it 'Blues on Broadway.' It'll be a first-rate piano joint. I'll play when I feel like it, and if I don't feel like it, I'll get somebody to sit in." He said it with the satisfaction of a man who'd figured it all out.

"Have you closed the deal yet?"

"Supposed to close in three weeks. That's why I wanted to have dinner with you last night. My place is across the street from the restaurant and I was going to ask you to look over the paperwork for me."

"How big is it?"

"The club is a couple of thousand square feet. But I'm buying the whole building. There's an office upstairs that I need to rent out. Make a nice place for some mouthpiece to hang his shingle. I'll make you a good deal."

Mason looked at Blues as he smiled and pulled on a long stem of grass he'd been chewing. Before Mason could answer, Blues said he was going for a walk. Mason watched him disappear into the woods, carrying a shotgun. He looked around for his, checked its load, and climbed back into the love seat on the porch to consider Blues's offer.

Practicing law was the only way Mason knew how to make a living. He'd chosen the profession because he believed in the law—in its central role in society—in its capacity to heal and make whole. At first, representing injured people gave shape to those values. But the practice of law introduced a different human dimension to living those values. Partners he couldn't trust; clients whose cases he couldn't win and who had nowhere else to turn. He had abandoned those values just to keep practicing when he joined Sullivan & Christenson. Some safe harbor. A desk above Blues's bar might be the right place to start over.

CHAPTER FIFTY-SEVEN

Kelly pulled into the clearing around five o'clock. Mason was inside trying to scrape more clues from the printouts on O'Malley. She came in carrying sacks of groceries for the night and no signs of baggage from their conversation in her office. Mason wasn't going anywhere, and so far, she wasn't throwing him out.

"Any luck?" he asked.

"Not yet."

"Where's Sandra?"

"She's staying with Riley until they find something."

The sacks contained K.C. strip steaks, corn on the cob, charcoal, watermelon, and more cold beer. Mason was back in the barbecue business. He built a fire and put the steaks on when the coals turned white on the outside while still glowing red on the inside. Kelly joined him and they watched the flames lick the steaks until Mason decided to test the waters.

"Any news on Vic Jr.?" he began.

"McNamara called again. He's really pushing me to bring you in."

"Bring me into what? He makes it sound like I'm a criminal."

"He isn't satisfied with the information I gave him. Says he has to talk to you personally. I told him I'd let you know."

"Great. What else?"

She hesitated to answer. When she did, Mason understood why. Amateurs aren't supposed to be right.

"Vic Jr. attended the University of Chicago. His senior year, he was charged with drug trafficking and interstate transportation of

234

a minor. Since he crossed state lines it became a federal case. And then it all went away."

"Daddy buy him out of it?"

"I don't know. But it puts him in the right place at the right time. Carlo D'lessandro runs the skin trade and the dope in and out of Chicago. He might have hooked up with someone in D'lessandro's organization and the contact followed him home to Kansas City."

"So now what?"

"I'm going to Chicago in the morning."

"Why? The money laundering isn't part of your case. Leave that to the feds. I thought you wanted to find Sullivan's killer."

"We both know they're tied together. I want to get a look at Junior's file."

"That's it?"

"No. I've still got sources in Chicago. I may be able to find out if D'lessandro is running this operation. If he is, I might come up with some way to pressure him to back off."

"How are you going to do that? Go see him and ask him nicely not to let Camaya kill the poor schmuck who wandered into this mess?"

"Lou, sometimes you make it hard to care about you."

"Well, that's just part of my charm."

"Really? If that's as good as it gets, I may bring him back here to meet you in person."

The grill was going up in flames and the steaks were sizzling on the edge of incineration. Mason rescued their dinner just in time. Later, she joined him in the love seat and surprised him by leaning her head against his shoulder. He put his arm around her, and she didn't resist when he pulled her closer. Blues came outside and wisely announced he was going for another walk.

"My dad and I built this cabin," she said, nestling against him. They were a natural fit. "It was just before he died. He could build anything—do anything. I helped him trim the trees and notch the logs so they'd fit together. Making it together made it really special."

"It is special."

"It's always been my hideout. I come here to heal my wounds."

The air was clear, the sky a starlit panorama. The love seat rocked them gently as he pulled her face to his. Finally, she breathed his name.

"Do you want to see my trapdoor?"

"I always knew you were a hopeless romantic."

He fumbled with her belt. She held his hands in check.

"No, you dope. I really do have a trapdoor. I made my dad build it in the cabin. I thought it would be fun to have a secret way out."

"Oh. Sure, I'd love to see it." Mason said, slumping against the love seat. "Where is it?"

"In the bedroom."

She giggled and spun out of his grasp, clinging to his fingertips. They made it to the bedroom, but Mason never saw the trapdoor. They began to undress each other as the moonlight cast their shadows against the wall. The bed was soft and they rolled to the center, entangled, consumed by the exquisite sense of discovery when two people make love for the first time. Part shyness, part adventure.

Mason traced the freckles on her chest with his fingertips, an abstract pattern caressing her breasts. She stroked the side of his face in a soft gesture that slid past his chest and ended with a grasp both firm and delicate. They paused for a moment, eavesdropping on the night sounds rolling through the woods, catching the sounds that didn't belong.

Soft but certain footsteps, a discreet tap at the bedroom door, Blues's cautious whisper as it opened a crack. "We've got company."

CHAPTER FIFTY-EIGHT

"How many?" Kelly asked.

She dressed with an economy of movements, ignoring Blues's presence. He kept his back to her, but Mason couldn't. Watching her put her shirt back on was nearly as mesmerizing as taking it off. The sound of shells rattling into shotgun magazines finally got him moving.

"There's a black Escalade blocking the road right where it comes into the clearing. Four guys got out, one short and heavy. He was giving orders to the other three. I figure we've got a couple of minutes, tops."

Kelly snapped her service pistol around her waist. Blues dumped extra shells into three ammunition bags, slinging one over his shoulder, handing them the other two along with their shotguns as the woods came alive with animal sounds telegraphing news of the advancing party.

The air in the cabin thickened. Beads of sweat dripped from Blues's neck. Kelly's hair was matted along the edge of her cheeks. They were wired but under control. Mason's stomach churned as he picked up his shotgun and ammo pouch.

Kelly slipped into the front room and peered out the edge of a window. The moonlight illuminated the clearing enough to make out shapes but not faces.

"That's got to be Camaya standing next to the Escalade. I don't recognize the others," she whispered over her shoulder. "They're at the edge of the clearing. There's about a hundred feet of open space between them and the cabin." She crouched below the window line and scooted back into the bedroom. "They'll see us if we climb out the windows. We'll go out the back way," she said, opening the closet door. Blues started to roll his eyes until Mason explained.

"Trapdoor. Every high-class cabin has one."

Kelly knelt and pressed down on a plank in the center of the closet floor with her right hand. The other end rose, revealing a steel ring that she grasped with her left and pulled up. A two-foot-square lid swung open on hidden hinges. She rested it against the wall of the closet. Holding her shotgun and ammo bag, she dropped into the crawl space below the cabin and disappeared. Blues went next, followed by Mason, who crouched and pulled the trapdoor closed over them.

Kelly was on all fours against the base of the rear wall, running her hands along the stones that formed the foundation for the cabin.

"Got it," she said, pushing open a square section of rock that swung outward. She slipped through the opening and, an instant later, stuck her head back in and motioned them to follow.

Running close to the ground, Kelly led Blues and Mason across the open field behind the cabin, not stopping until the woods camouflaged them. They turned around in time to hear automatic fire ripping through the inside of the cabin.

"Bastards!" Kelly said.

"What now?" Mason asked.

"My Trans-Am and Kelly's pickup are out front, so they know we're here somewhere. Once they clear the cabin, they'll come looking for us."

Blues was calm, somehow satisfied with their predicament. His eyes shone as he shifted his weight lightly from right to left like a boxer keeping loose before the first bell, sweat trickling off his face. He was ready.

Kelly put a soothing hand around Blues's arm as she drew both men near her, focused on the fight they were about to have.

"Lou and I will circle around to the north. Blues, you take the south side. They won't find the trapdoor, so they've got to come out the front. If we can catch them in the open, we can take them. Don't shoot unless they don't give us a choice."

Moving slowly to make as little noise as possible, Mason and Kelly threaded their way through the trees, watching the open space around the cabin for signs of company. There was no path to follow. The moonlight couldn't penetrate the tangled vines and thorny bushes hidden in the dark that grabbed at their legs and feet. The few minutes it took to reach the front of the cabin could have been an hour.

Through the trees, Mason could see the yard in front of the cabin and imagined its oval shape to be a clock, the cabin at twelve o'clock. He and Kelly were hiding at three o'clock. The Escalade was parked in the mouth of the drive at the six-o'clock mark, engine still running.

Camaya leaned against the back, taillights lighting his face with a red glow. Blues's Trans-Am and Kelly's pickup were parallel parked at the edge of the grass, clockwise from the Escalade. Mason guessed Blues was somewhere between nine o'clock and midnight.

From inside the cabin came the sounds of reckless searching. Cursing followed the crash of furniture upended and glass broken. Mason knew they were looking for both him and the disks. He was glad that he was outside and that the disks were safe with Riley and Sandra.

"The angrier they get, the better off we are. It'll make them careless," Kelly whispered.

When they were through kicking the front door off its hinges and stepped outside, Mason and Kelly eased to within a few feet of the clearing and crouched behind a mound of limestone boulders.

"Are you going to invite them to surrender?" Mason asked.

"I doubt if they'll RSVP. If they start shooting, I'll return fire first. That way, I can reload when it's your turn."

Mason's throat was dry and tight, but his grip on the shotgun was slippery and wet. He marveled at the odds that he would be waiting to kill someone who was waiting to kill him for the second time in two nights. He was no more skilled with a shotgun than he was with a toilet-tank lid. Only this time, he was ready; willing to level the gun, squeeze the trigger, and watch a man die. That was the true marvel, he realized. The night before, he hadn't thought about killing, only surviving. Now all he thought about was killing.

CHAPTER FIFTY-NINE

Three men stood on the porch. Camaya raised his arms, directing one of them to return to the Escalade and the other two toward the woods on either side of the cabin. Kelly steadied the barrel of her shotgun on the rocks. He matched her movements from his spot two feet away.

"Shit!" Mason hissed as one of the killers started toward them.

"Shut up and watch the other side of the woods. I've got this."

Despite Kelly's order, Mason couldn't take his eyes off the killer moving toward them. As he got closer, Mason could see his gun. It had a triangle-shaped frame stock, a pistol handle, and a short barrel. It reminded Mason of the guns favored by bad guys in every action movie he'd ever seen.

He was close enough now that Mason could see his wide forehead, mushy nose, and hard-set mouth. There was no trace of fear, nerves, or regret.

Kelly jabbed Mason in the side, pointing to the south side, the gesture reminding him of her order. Mason watched Blues's target take his first steps into the trees before stopping and crumbling to the ground. Blues was good, but not good enough to smother the sound of the man's startled cry.

Mason glanced to his left to see if Camaya had heard his man go down. Camaya took a cautious step forward, now flanked by the third gunman. Kelly spoke in a voice loud enough for her man to hear but not loud enough for Camaya.

"Freeze, or I'll blow you in half!"

"Fuck you, bitch!"

The killer fired first, but Kelly made good on her promise, two blasts tearing into him, twisting his body and shredding his chest. His finger clung to the trigger of his gun as he fell, exhausting his clip.

One of the rounds found the propane tank mounted near the side of the cabin. The tank erupted in a blinding ball of fire, the shock wave knocking Mason and Kelly to the ground, the limestone boulders shielding them from the molten shrapnel.

Dazed, Mason raised his head. Kelly was sprawled facedown in the dirt. Mason crawled to her. She was conscious, her hands digging into the soil. He rolled her over, pulling her into his arms. Tears ran down her soiled cheeks as the flames swept through her cabin.

Above the roaring blaze, Mason heard more automatic fire. He looked in the direction of the shots and saw Camaya riddle the tires on the Trans-Am and the pickup from the open passenger window of the Escalade. As they sped away, Blues ran after them, emptying his magazine, his shotgun useless at that distance.

Kelly stiffened, clotting off her tears. She and Mason were stunned by the power of the blast but otherwise in one piece. The searing heat from the fire drove them from their rock pile. Once clear, she called out the rest of the Pope County Sheriff's Department, the fire department, and Doc Eddy.

Blues and Mason walked the quarter mile to the county road to wait for them. Kelly stayed behind, a lone silhouette framed by the inferno devouring her hiding place. Incandescent shadows swarmed through the trees like extras in a low-budget horror movie before evaporating into the black sky.

The rescuers and the rescued worked through the night stamping out the few burning embers that had drifted into the trees. By daylight, the fire had consumed itself.

Brilliant tracers of pink and orange crept into the morning sky as the last tendrils of black smoke drifted away.

Soot stained and weary, Blues, Mason, and Kelly poured themselves into a deputy's car and joined the procession back to town. Tow trucks dragging the Trans-Am and the pickup bounced along, bringing up the rear.

Riley and Sandra, their faces pinched with fatigue, were waiting in front of the courthouse when they pulled in. Sandra was stretched out on the wide stone handrail using her arms for a pillow. Riley lay across the stairs like the hypotenuse of a triangle. Mason had the feeling that the morning wasn't going to get any better.

"Hi, honey, I'm home!" he called out with more good cheer than was fair.

He figured the one who answered was probably still alive. Sandra rolled off her perch and reeled Riley to his feet.

"You folks okay? The deputy told us what happened when you called in," Riley said.

Kelly walked into Riley's waiting arms and he held her, rubbing her back. She pulled away a moment later.

"A little shell-shocked, Riley, that's all," she said. "Any luck?"

"Well, I've got an answer, but it's not the one you expected," Riley said. "There's nothing else on the porno disks."

"What do you mean?" Mason asked.

"The only thing on those DVDs is people doing the horizontal mambo and switching partners faster than you can say 'Swing your partner, do-si-do.'"

"That doesn't make any sense. There has to be something else. You'll just have to keep looking until you figure it out. It's been a long night. We'll all get some rest and start fresh this afternoon."

"I'm sorry, son. There's no point in it. I spent half the night looking, and there just isn't anything else there."

Mason took a deep breath and shoved his hands in his pockets to keep him from shaking Riley until he made some sense.

"What in the hell are you talking about? People are getting killed for those damn disks, and you're trying to tell me it's all a big mistake? What the fuck is that supposed to mean?"

"Son, no one's getting killed for the skin flicks. Now, Johnny Mathis—that's a different story entirely," he said.

CHAPTER SIXTY

"Johnny Mathis?" Kelly asked.

"Yup. It's not a commercial CD, like an album you'd buy. Somebody copied the songs onto a blank CD."

"They put it in a CD case from a Johnny Mathis album to make it look like the real deal," Sandra added.

"I was playing it on a boom box while I was fiddling with these other disks," Riley continued. "Right smack in the middle of my wife's favorite tune, he hit that high note—kinda like a warble— then it cut out. Nothing. So I got to wondering about Mr. Mathis and I decided to run some tests on his CD."

"Riley found two documents that had been imaged onto the CD. We printed them out," Sandra said, handing copies to Blues, Kelly, and Mason.

Each document consisted of a single page. The first listed the shell companies O'Malley had set up to borrow money from his bank and identified the owners. Sullivan owned half of each of the companies. O'Malley owned the other half. The document would have made St. John's case against him.

"These must be the documents Sullivan wanted you to destroy," Kelly said to Mason.

"I don't think he wanted me to destroy anything. I think he was just testing me to find out which side of the line I walked on. There was no way he could know if every copy of this had been destroyed. Especially if it had been imaged onto a CD. Besides, he wasn't the only one who knew about this. O'Malley knew. They were partners. What's on the other page?"

244

"Another list," Sandra said. "I recognize the names of some of the companies involved in the fixtures deals. But there's also a list labeled 'accounts.' Each account is a combination of letters and numbers. I don't know what they mean."

Kelly scanned the second document. "It's a combination of bank account numbers and passwords. Offshore banks in the Cayman Islands use the codes to identify account holders and give them access to their accounts without using names. When I was with the FBI, we spent a lot of time breaking these codes down so we could trace laundered money."

"So break these down," Mason said. "It's the key to the fixtures deals. We'll follow the money and find out who started all of this."

"It's not that simple. You just can't hold the numbers up to a mirror and read them backward. But this is another reason for me to go to Chicago. I've got friends there who can decipher them."

Kelly led the way to the Home Style Cafe on the west side of the square for breakfast. The restaurant was filled with regular customers who made it part of their daily ritual. The men in denim shirts and blue jeans were stretching their last cup of coffee before starting their day. The storefront was dusky brick, unchanged for the last forty years. Kelly and Mason slid side by side into a booth while Sandra, Blues, and Riley chose the counter.

"Why do you think Sullivan imaged those documents onto a CD with Johnny Mathis?" Kelly asked.

"He was hiding them in plain sight. Anyone who found the CD case would see the Johnny Mathis label and think it was nothing important. If they opened the case and saw a disk without a Johnny Mathis label, they might get suspicious and listen to it. There was enough music on the CD to make most people assume there wasn't anything else on it, but it took a true fan like Riley to listen long enough to find the documents."

"I respect the man and his music," Riley said from his seat at the counter.

Mason continued. "Sullivan knew that St. John had him cold when St. John served the subpoena on him. The fixtures documents were his trump cards. Sullivan was going to offer a trade to St. John. Somebody else found out. They must have been looking for the documents when they broke into Sullivan's house last month."

"And Harlan was going to try his own version of let's make a deal. Now they're both dead," Kelly said.

The sun flattened out against the water-spotted window. Kelly rested her elbow on the ledge, chin cupped in her hand, her eyes set on some distant place. The sad weariness Mason had first sensed in her had spread in the hours since her cabin burned. She hadn't talked about it and didn't have to. It was the last link to her father. He'd died long ago, but now he was truly gone. Mason tried to comfort them both by holding her close. She pulled away, her melancholy smile telling him that he was not what she needed right now.

Breakfast passed quietly. She explained that her chief deputy would handle the investigation while she was away. Another deputy would drive her home to clean up and pack and then take her St. Louis, where she'd catch a Southwest flight to Chicago, getting there in time for lunch. She left the tip and said good-bye.

CHAPTER SIXTY-ONE

There was a Holiday Inn two blocks away with a vacancy, and Mason's plastic was still good. He showered and slept past noon, too tired for nightmares. It was Friday and he counted on the latest set of clothes he'd just purchased to last through the weekend or his insurance settlement wouldn't see him past Labor Day.

By two o'clock, he was all dressed up with no place to go. He drifted back to the courthouse and Kelly's office, figuring that Blues and Sandra would turn up eventually. Nobody told him not to, so he camped out in Kelly's chair.

He was about to go looking for Blues when a file clerk walked in with a fax from the community blood bank. Like all faxes, it had a bold *Confidential* stamp across the cover sheet. Like all people who were tired of getting shot at, Mason ignored it.

The second sheet was a copy of the blood bank's laboratory test from September 1987 for Richard Sullivan. The lab data were medical hieroglyphics to him, but the narrative report couldn't have been clearer. It was 95 percent certain that Richard Sullivan was the natural father of an unnamed child, then aged ten. The mother was Meredith Phillips. The report was addressed to Dr. Kenton Newberry of Rogersville, Kansas.

Mason finished writing the information on a yellow pad just as Blues and Sandra came through the door. Judging from the creases in their jeans, they'd all been on the same schedule.

"Trans-Am's got new wheels and is running fine," Blues reported.

"Well, Chief, got any bright ideas for the rest of our summer vacation?" Sandra asked.

"Yep. We're going home."

"Pardon me. But unless I'm missing something, we came down here to hide from Camaya—and now we're going back to Kansas City!" Sandra said. "Should we just paint a target on our backs or would a *Shoot Here, Stupid* sign be better?"

"We haven't done a bang-up job of hiding. Besides, he won't look for us there if he thinks we're still down here. We're the only ones who'll know where we're going and we won't tell anybody, now, will we?"

The mildly accusing tone came out without premeditation.

"No, we won't!" Sandra said, bristling at the implication in Mason's voice. She turned and walked out.

"Hey, where are you going?" he called to her.

"To the bathroom. Do I need an escort?" she replied over her shoulder.

"What's that all about, man?" Blues asked when she was out of range.

"I don't really know. I didn't intend for it to sound that way. But she sure took it personally. It just seems kind of odd that Camaya found us so easily."

"I told you he'd come looking for us, and he'd figure you were with Kelly."

"Yeah, but how did he know where Kelly was?"

"She's the sheriff, for crissakes! You look for her at the sheriff's office."

"Well, unless he keeps tabs on ex-FBI agents, how did he know she was the sheriff down here? St. John didn't even know that."

The more Mason talked, the more he warmed up to this latest thread. "Even if he knew Kelly was in the Ozarks, the location of her cabin was practically a state secret. Somebody sure as hell had to tell him how to get to it. And back at the warehouse, Sandra didn't bat an eye when that black Escalade pulled up."

Blues got his clenched-jaw cop look as he chewed on the possibilities. "And she didn't complain about being stuck down in that basement all night with Riley."

"Maybe I'm just grabbing at shadows. But we don't know where Camaya is or how much help he's got. If he stayed in the area, chances are he'll watch the roads back to KC. I've got a different route in mind."

Mason told Blues about the blood-bank results before showing him a road map he'd dug out of Kelly's desk. They were about 180 miles south and east of Kansas City. They would take Highway 54 west across the state line into Kansas to Highway 169, then head north on 169 to Rogersville, a small town about sixty miles south of Kansas City.

It was roughly the same distance to Rogersville from the lake as from the lake to Kansas City. It would take three to four hours to get there. Mason didn't know what they would find there on a Friday night, but he doubted anyone would be watching for them along those roads. They agreed to say nothing to Sandra about their route. They would stop in Rogersville for dinner. Mason hadn't gotten any further in his thinking when Sandra reappeared.

"Okay, guys. I'm ready," she said, all trace of hostility gone. "I hope your moms told you to go to the john before going on the highway."

"You betcha!" Mason said. "Come on, Blues; I'm not stopping every ten minutes for you."

As they were walking out of the bathroom, Mason noticed a pay phone tucked in an alcove between the sinks and the urinals. He told Blues to take Sandra to the car and he would meet them in a minute. He pretended to have forgotten something in Kelly's office, and on the way back out stopped to talk to the sheriff's dispatcher, a greasy-haired kid, probably not yet twenty-one and barely winning the war on acne.

"Were you on duty last night when Sheriff Holt called in from the cabin?"

"Sure was! That must have been one hell of a fire!"

"Lucky thing the troops knew how to get there. I never could've found the way on my own."

"Shit, man!" he said laughing. "Nobody knew how to get to that cabin. The sheriff had to damn near talk the lead deputy all the way in. We all knew she had the cabin, but she was mighty private about where it was."

"No kidding?" Mason's stomach tightened with a cold shiver, and he changed the subject. "How do you keep in touch with Sheriff Holt when she's on the road?"

"Age of the cell phone, man."

"Mind giving me the number? I may need to get in touch with her."

"No problem," he said as he scratched it on a piece of paper and handed it to Mason.

Mason started to leave and stopped. "Just one last thing. I was wondering, do you have any pay phones around here?"

"Yeah. There's one in each john."

"Thanks," Mason said and headed for the car.

Sandra was in the front seat, riding shotgun.

CHAPTER SIXTY-TWO

Mason couldn't explain his sudden suspicion of Sandra, yet he couldn't shake it, and her passive aggressive response didn't help. He would have preferred ducking her usual barrage of sarcasm and threats than the uncomfortable silence that filled the car. When he turned to look at her, she made a point of staring out the window, not bothering to ask why Blues was ignoring all the highway signs pointing to Kansas City.

Looking back, he realized his doubts began when she told him about her medical background. She knew enough to poison Sullivan. At the warehouse, Camaya threatened him, not her. Tying her up could have been for show, her escape planned rather than fortuitous. And Camaya couldn't have found them without somebody telling him where to look. He wondered if paranoia made him a clear thinker or just paranoid.

They chased the afternoon sun through the rolling, wooded Ozark hills, across the state line, and into the grassy knolls of eastern Kansas. Highway 54 beckoned westward to the broad, endless plains.

Mason had once driven that road all the way to Liberal, Kansas. Eight hours of seamless prairie, thinking about the pioneers who had dared to cross that land 150 years ago. There must have been moments when they looked in every direction, finding nothing to reveal where they were, where they'd been, or where they were going. Swallowed by their surroundings, they had to press on or go mad where they were.

He was beginning to understand what that felt like. He couldn't

251

go back, and it was impossible to know whether he was headed the right way. By the time he found out, it could be too late.

An hour and a half later, Blues pulled into the parking lot of a Kentucky Fried Chicken restaurant in Rogersville, Kansas. After his diet the last few days, those red and white stripes and tantalizing choices of original or extra crispy beckoned Mason.

A weather-beaten phone book dangled on a steel cable from beneath a pay phone planted in a corner of the asphalt parking lot. While Blues and Sandra went inside, Mason lingered at the phone, checking the local listings. There was no listing for Dr. Kenton Newberry. Meredith wasn't listed either. She may have married, died, or moved away. There were ten different listings under Phillips. He tore out the page, hoping that one of them might be her family.

Blues and Sandra sat opposite each other in a booth. He was eating and she was watching. Mason slid in next to Blues and reached for a chicken thigh. That was as close to dinner as he got.

"Okay, Boy Scouts. I've been good and kept my mouth shut. But I've had enough. Either I get some answers, or I'm out of here."

She didn't have to raise her voice. Sandra had one of those tones that sliced right through you.

"We just thought it would be a good idea to take a different route home in case anybody was watching for us," Mason said, hoping it was the question she wanted answered. Wrong again.

"I'm not stupid, Louis, so don't patronize me. We're having this wonderful bonding-in-the-midst-of-danger experience and you all but accuse me of tipping Camaya off about the cabin. Now, what is that bullshit all about?"

Blues was making quick work of the mound of chicken, gravy, and mashed potatoes on his plate and was not going to bail Mason out. The teenager wiping the counter overheard Sandra and dropped his dish towel, the snap of boiling oil and sizzling chicken fat the only sounds in the Colonel's house. He thought of every witness who'd blown his credibility by stalling an answer to the tough question and knew his was draining away.

252

"I don't know," he said without looking at her, his bad start getting worse. "Somebody had to have tipped him off and you weren't at the cabin when they came for us. I didn't mean to imply anything. It just came out that way. I was out of line. I'm sorry."

She chewed her lip for a moment, eyeing him, then took a deep breath and nodded. "Okay, since we're all friends again, tell me what was so interesting in that phone book you vandalized."

Blues moved on to the biscuits, the cashier wasn't moving, and Mason wasn't fast enough with a response because he didn't have one that wasn't a lie she wouldn't see through.

"Listen, Sandra . . . ," he stalled.

"No, you listen, Louis! I saved your ass at the warehouse! Or did you forget how we got untied? Blues, Kelly, and me—we're the ones saving you—not the other way around. And now you treat me like a suspect! You don't even have the nerve to accuse me to my face."

She shoved the bucket of chicken in his lap and stormed out. Mason knocked it onto the floor as he followed her outside.

"Wait a minute! Where are you going? What are you going to do?"

"I'm going to do what I should have done in the first place, Louis. Handle this on my own."

She walked across the street to a truck stop, waving at a trucker about to pull out. He stopped long enough for her to climb into the passenger seat of his eighteen-wheeler. Blues joined Mason as the rig headed north.

CHAPTER SIXTY-THREE

On the way to Kansas City, Mason scanned every tractor-trailer rig they passed, looking for Sandra, alternating between feeling guilty for goading her into leaving and relieved that she was gone. When he felt guilty, he kept his eyes open for rape victims lying abandoned on the shoulder of the highway. When he felt relieved, he concentrated on what he would do next.

Blues left him to his thoughts until they reached the southern edge of Overland Park, the biggest of Kansas City's suburban bedrooms.

"You make up your mind yet?" Blues asked.

"About what?"

"Whether you want to let trouble keep finding you or whether you want to start running the show."

"I'm tired of running—that's why we came back. I've got a short list—Pamela Sullivan, Scott Daniels, and Angela Molina. You got any preferences?"

"You've been set up. Scott picked you to investigate the firm because he figured he could control you. When you picked Sandra to help you, he knew that he was screwed."

"There's a big difference between trying to control the investigation and committing a murder."

"One's the beginning and the other's the end. When Scott found out you had the disks, he told the wrong people. Maybe he knew what he was doing and maybe he didn't. Either way, you'd have been just as dead."

Mason didn't want to confront the possibility that Scott would let him be killed. He could live with the O'Malleys being crooks. He could handle some unknown bad guy sending a slimeball like Camaya to punch his clock. These were people he didn't know or care about. They presented problems that he would find a way to solve. But betrayal by a friend was another story. He was loyal to his friends and expected no less of a commitment in return. It seemed a modest standard in a world too often covered with shifting sands.

They stopped at a sporting goods store, where Blues bought two boxes of .45-caliber ammunition.

"Scott has a lot of questions to answer," Mason said when they got back in the car. "He was in on the fixtures deals from the beginning. But he wouldn't know what rock to turn over to find Camaya, so he's got to be reporting to someone higher up."

"If he's scared enough, he might talk to us," Blues said.

"Then we'll give him a chance."

Mason dialed Scott's home number. His wife answered.

"Gloria, it's Lou Mason. Is Scott around?"

She didn't answer at first. When she did, she struggled to keep her composure. "No—Lou. He's been working late—every night."

"Friday nights too? You think he's still downtown?"

"He called a little while ago—and said he was going for a swim and before he came home."

"I'll try him there. If I miss him, tell him I called, okay?"

"Lou—what's happening? Will we be all right?"

She started to cry. He remembered the dead, flat look in Scott's eyes the last time he saw him and thought again about what Scott had done to him. Mason owed Scott nothing, and he wouldn't lie to her.

"I don't know, Gloria," he said and hung up.

"Any luck?"

"Not home. His wife is on the edge."

"They have any kids?"

"Yeah. Three." Then Mason felt sick as he remembered one of those loose threads, the elusive piece of the puzzle. "And the oldest is diabetic. Let's try the Mid-America Club. Maybe we can catch him while he's still wet."

When Blues stopped in front of the Mid-America Club, he turned to Mason. "You got a plan? Or you just going to ask him to write it out nice and neat for you?"

"I'll ask nicely, but he's going to write it down."

"This isn't a game. You know that?"

"You forget I already killed someone?"

"Just wanted to make sure you didn't forget." He opened the glove compartment and removed a blue-steel revolver. "It's a Sig Sauer .45 caliber," he explained as he loaded the clip, slid the safety to off, and handed it to Mason. "Just in case he doesn't understand nice."

Mason looked at Blues and the gun. A freak blow to a stranger trying to shoot him was one thing. Hiding in the woods with a shotgun to protect himself against a killer was doable. Pointing a gun at a friend, even one who'd betrayed him, was in a different league.

"Listen to me, Lou. Nobody is who you thought they were—at least not anymore. Blood changes everybody—there aren't any rules. Don't use it if you don't have to. But don't take the chance you won't need it. I'll catch up to you."

Mason got out and stood in front of the revolving-door entrance to the club, shirt untucked to cover the gun stuck in his waist, pressed flat against his belly and pointed at his crotch. He was more afraid of tripping than anything else.

As the door spun around depositing him inside, Mason began to fear something else—his own anger. Knowing that someone wanted him dead scared him at first and still did. But his anger balanced his fear, giving him a chance to do what he had to if he was going to live. And that made him afraid of who he would be if he did survive. The gun was fast becoming an easy answer. Mason's growing sense of the inevitability of that answer—and his acceptance of it—was terrifying. Blues was right. Nobody was who he thought they were anymore, including him.

CHAPTER SIXTY-FOUR

Scott was alone in the pool, doing the backstroke, his long arms looping rhythmically overhead like twin paddle wheels, his legs knifing through the water. Mason watched from the deep end as Scott swam away, staring back at him as if Mason was a stranger.

Mason waited for his return lap, and before Scott could tuck, turn, and swim away again, he grabbed him by the hair and slammed his forehead onto the edge of the deck. Scott grunted and slid backward into the water. Mason slipped his hands under Scott's arms and pulled him out of the pool and onto the deck, where he lay, coughing and bleeding.

"Jesus Christ, Lou! Are you out of your goddamn mind?"

"Pretty fucking close, buddy. Swimming is a dangerous sport. You should get out of the water before you get hurt."

Scott sat up, holding his head in his hands. Blood trickled through his fingers, pooling on the floor. Mason tossed him a towel, yanked him to his feet, and shoved him into the locker room.

"Come on, let's check the damage."

Wooden lockers lined three walls and filled a half dozen aisles furnished with benches. One wall was all mirrors and sinks split by a doorway that led to the toilets and showers.

Scott leaned on Mason, woozy from the blow, as Mason leaned him up against the wall by the sink and cleaned the cut. Mason wrapped a bath towel around Scott's neck and gave him a hand towel to hold against his forehead. When the bleeding slowed, Mason sat him on a bench and propped him against a locker. He pulled a bench from another row of lockers parallel to Scott's and sat across from him.

"So how long have you and Vic Jr. been using the firm to launder money?"

"You're not just crazy, Lou. You're out of your fucking mind!"

"I just want to get out of this alive. And I don't much care if you do. Help yourself and answer my questions."

Scott laughed. "You don't have it in you, Lou. Give it up and go away while you still can."

Mason stood and grabbed the ends of the towel around Scott's neck, choking him. Scott clawed at the towel, but Mason twisted it tighter and whipped Scott's head against the locker, reopening the cut over his eyes. Holding the towel with one hand, Mason drew his gun and jammed into Scott's cheek, his finger tightening around the trigger. Bug-eyed, Scott blinked as blood ran into the corners of his eyes.

"Now, Scott, I'm not having a very good day. Frankly, I'm more than a little edgy. Been doing some really weird shit. Help me out, will you? Talk to me. It calms me down. Okay?"

"Okay, sure, just put the gun down, please."

Mason let go of the towel and sat on his bench, lowering the gun to his side. "I'm not going to ask again."

"Okay, okay. It was Vic Jr.'s idea. He got hooked up with some mob guys while he was in college in Chicago. They bailed him out of a jam and he agreed to help them out."

"How?"

"Laundering their money."

"So why did you get into it?"

"Money. They let Junior take a cut, and Junior needed Harlan and me to cover the deals, so we got a piece too."

Mason wasn't surprised that Harlan had been involved. The fixtures deals must have been the source of the unreported income that caught the attention of the IRS.

"That's what the fixtures deals were for?"

"Yeah. Quintex bought the fixtures and leased them back. The lease payments were the dirty money."

"What were the fixtures for?"

"Strip joints and porno shops. The rent was pumped way up to provide the cash flow."

"And the fees for work that was never performed?"

"We had to get the money out of Quintex, and the firm was the easiest place."

"But how did you get it out of the firm?"

"Consulting fees paid on behalf of Quintex."

"To whom? Who's behind the whole thing?"

"I don't know who got the fees and I don't know who was running the show."

Mason grabbed the towel again.

"Okay! I knew but I didn't know. Sure, it had to be the mob but I never heard any names. Please, Lou! I'm telling you the truth!"

Mason let go. "Tell me what you did know."

"We always dealt with a Chicago law firm. They had power of attorney. The principals were never identified."

"Who got the consulting fees?"

"Don't know. We just made out the checks to corporations and mailed them. Everything went to a post office box."

"Angela had to cover the billings for you. You had to cut her in. And you had to pay the money back out. Seems like a lot of trouble for the amounts involved."

"The firm was only a piece of it. We set up separate corporations to contract with Quintex for phony services. Ran a lot of the money through them. Harlan thought it would be fun to run some through the firm since O'Malley was Sullivan's client."

"Harlan?"

Mason thought of that gentle man getting a kick out of setting up Sullivan's biggest client. Every partner has his secrets, Mason realized. Harlan's secret must have been that he hated Sullivan.

"Oh yeah, Harlan," Scott said, reading Mason's mind. "He hated Sullivan as much as the rest of us. The more you needed him, the more you hated him."

"Enough to kill him?"

Scott's shocked expression was genuine. "No way! That was just a lucky break."

"Where were you before the poker game?"

"I don't know. I mean, I don't remember."

Mason slapped him hard across the face with the back of his hand.

"Lying violates your oath as a lawyer. You don't want me to report you to the bar association, do you? Now, tell me where you were before the poker game started."

Scott looked away, letting out a resigned sigh. "Angela and I had a thing going. We rented a ski boat and went for a ride. Let me tell you, it's not easy to screw in one of those boats. But Angela's something else."

"Why didn't you use O'Malley and Sullivan's condo? You had to know about it."

"Sure, but I didn't want to run into Sullivan. Angela and I didn't need the publicity."

The bleeding on Scott's forehead had slowed, his eyes were glassy, and his nose was pink and runny. He slumped against the lockers, no fight left in him.

"By the way, how's the family? Have you introduced Angela to the wife and kids?"

Scott shook his head, his voice weak, unable to summon any outrage. "You're a real prick, you know that, don't you?"

"And how's your oldest—the one with diabetes? Must be tough, all those injections."

"Since when do you give a shit about my kids?"

"Since right now."

"You want to know how he's doing? He's fine. We control the diabetes with diet; no shots, no insulin."

CHAPTER SIXTY-FIVE

In spite of everything, Mason was relieved at Scott's answer. Whatever else Scott had done, unless he had another source for insulin, the odds were against him having murdered Sullivan.

"I'm glad to hear that. Did Sullivan know about Quintex?"

"Not until St. John's subpoena. That's when Sullivan started digging into the Quintex files. He must have figured it out, because Harlan and I were supposed to meet with him Sunday night after the retreat."

"Did Sullivan tell you that he knew?"

"He didn't have to. He told us about the subpoena and St. John's target letter and said we needed to talk about the work we'd been doing for Vic Jr. That was enough."

"How could you have kept it from Sullivan and O'Malley?"

"Sullivan only cared about his own work. He gave me Quintex and forgot about it. Junior convinced his old man to do the same thing. Said he needed a chance to prove himself."

"If Sullivan was on to your scam, that's a good motive for murder."

"Yeah, but I didn't do it and I don't know who did," Scott said, raising his arms and dropping them in his lap, signaling his surrender.

"Why did you and Harlan leave so early Sunday morning? And don't tell me it was to get ready for your closing."

"We wanted to search Sullivan's office to find out how much he knew. I got there before Harlan. He called me when he found out that Sullivan was dead."

"Who did you call from the office that afternoon to talk about Sullivan's death?"

"How do you know about that?"

"Angela bugged your office, you schmuck. You were screwing her, but she was fucking you."

Scott shook his head. "I trusted her."

"Imagine that. Who did you call?"

"It was just a number and a voice. No names."

"And you didn't find the disks?"

"Didn't know about the disks on Sunday."

"When did you find out about them?"

"At Sullivan's funeral. Angela told me she walked into Sullivan's office the week before. He was talking to O'Malley about having the records they needed on a CD. Angela was worried that some of our legitimate work for O'Malley would get screwed up and, with Sullivan gone, he'd fire us. None of us could afford to lose O'Malley's business."

"You mean she didn't know what was on the CD?"

"If she did, she didn't say anything about it. She was just looking after the firm's biggest client."

"So how did you know there was anything on the CD?"

"I didn't know for certain. But it was the only thing that made sense. I knew Sullivan had the information and I couldn't find it anywhere else. Everyone in the office knew you had the disks."

"So you told your anonymous business partners I had the disks even though you knew it could get me killed?"

"I didn't know!"

A husky voice interrupted. "Sure you did."

It was Jimmie Camaya, standing at the opposite end of the benches, pointing a pistol at them, a silencer screwed into the barrel. Mason tightened his grip on his gun, holding it next to his thigh out of Camaya's view.

"How do you do it, Jimmie? You always show up just when I'm getting to the good part."

Camaya flashed his serpentine smile. "You just got bad luck,

Mason. I came here to tell Scott about his retirement. Looks like you both can have a going-away party now. Too bad I didn't get here before Scott got so talkative. But it don't matter since you're both dead."

"If it doesn't matter, then let me hear the rest of it; maybe you'll learn something."

Mason turned back to Scott, hoping to distract Camaya long enough to gain the edge he needed. "Jimmie says you're lying, Scott. Says you knew they'd kill me? Is that right?"

"I don't know which one of you is crazier!" Scott shouted. "I didn't want you to get hurt, Lou, but I was in too deep. They told me to get the disks back—"

"Or else?" Mason asked.

"Or else Scott would end up like your partner, Harlan Christenson," Camaya said.

Scott's face froze. The unspeakable meaning of what Camaya said hit Mason head-on.

"You told them Harlan was being audited, and they were afraid he'd make a deal with the feds and turn all of you in, so they killed him," Mason said.

Scott didn't answer, but Camaya did.

"Julio snapped that old man's neck like it was a chicken's leg. You should have got there early, like Scotty here did. He had a front-row seat."

Mason listened in disbelief. The tears rolling off Scott's face and the retreating look in his eyes said it was true.

"He made me watch—," Scott said. "So I wouldn't forget to do what I was told."

"And then you took Julio out with a goddamn toilet! What a fucked-up world, huh, Mason? So, Scott, you want to go first this time or watch another one of your friends die?"

Camaya pointed his gun at Scott. Mason estimated the distance between them at about ten feet.

"Jimmie, do me a favor, come a little closer, will you?"

"Why?"

"Better odds at seven feet," Mason said, raising his gun and firing three quick rounds.

Mason didn't know which round hit Camaya, but only one did, the others shattering the mirror behind him. Camaya squeezed off a shot as he fell to the floor, wounding Scott, who toppled onto Mason, knocking him off the bench. Mason looked up to see Blues standing over Camaya.

"He ain't dead, but he sure bleeds a lot."

CHAPTER SIXTY-SIX

Camaya wheezed from the round that caught him in the right side of his chest, pressing a towel Mason gave him against the wound, slowing the bleeding.

"Hey, Mason," he whispered in a feathery voice. "Why'd you shoot me, man?"

"Gee, Jimmie, I don't know. Seemed like a better idea than letting you shoot me."

"Aw, man! I was gonna shoot Scott—I hadn't made up my mind about you."

"Yeah, how come?"

"Friend of mine wants to talk to you—besides, you was gettin' to be good company."

"Who's your friend, Jimmie?"

"Man—you wouldn't believe me if I told you."

"Try me."

"No way—it's all I got to deal with—"

He started to gag and cough blood just as the paramedics arrived. Mason went to look for Scott when they started talking about establishing an airway.

Camaya's shot had grazed Scott's shoulder. One of the paramedics was cleaning a crimson furrow along his upper back when Mason found him sitting mannequin-like on a bench, expressionless as an EMT tended him.

"Scott," Mason said.

"Forget it, buddy," the EMT said. "The guy is zoned out."

"What do you mean? Is he in shock?"

"Way past that. The shrinks got a name for it. I call it 'zoned.' Sometimes they come back. Sometimes they don't."

He finished bandaging Scott and unfolded him onto a stretcher. Scott never blinked as they rolled him out to the elevator.

Harry Ryman questioned Mason in one corner of the locker room while another detective quizzed Blues in a different corner. A forensics team methodically gathered evidence, taking photographs and measurements to preserve the scene. An hour later, they were ushered downstairs through a gauntlet of reporters. Their police scanners had picked up the report of the "Mid-America Club Shoot-out," as one overheated journalist dubbed it. Mason managed a tight-lipped "no comment" before their squad car pulled away.

The homicide squad room was a collection of grimy steel desks, gunmetal gray chairs, and matching filing cabinets overstuffed with the statistical residue of the city's violence. Mason sat in a chair next to Harry Ryman's desk while Ryman banged away on his keyboard.

"You leave out any details you want me to know about, Lou?" Harry asked him when he finished typing.

Mason had told Harry almost everything. He didn't tell Harry that he'd killed one of Camaya's henchmen with a toilet. That was too twisted a road to go down.

"I hit the high points, Harry. When can I get out of here?"

"Pretty soon. It'll be up to the prosecutor to decide whether to charge you with anything, but I don't think he will. It's a pretty clear case of self-defense. You might get some heat for carrying a weapon without a license, but that won't play too good. You'll come out of this a hero."

Mason shook his head. "That I don't need."

"There is one other thing. Couple of nights ago, we got a call about a dead body in a warehouse down in the West Bottoms. Only thing was, there was no dead body. We found some blood on the floor at the front of the warehouse and some more in a bathroom in the back. Turns out the warehouse is owned by this Victor O'Malley you been telling me so much about. You got any clues for me on this situation?"

"Sorry, Harry. I can't help you with that."

Harry studied him closely. "Your aunt Claire and me got something nice going. She cares a lot for you. Talks about you all the time. Don't do anything that might mess that up for any of the three of us. Are we clear?"

Mason nodded. "We're clear, Harry."

"Try that sofa over there. They'll be done with Bluestone pretty soon."

Mason moved to the faded, dust-soaked couch and closed his eyes while he waited for Blues. He didn't expect to sleep. He just wanted to hide for a few minutes.

The hardened footsteps of cops and perps played an uneven cadence on the linoleum floor. Tired questions and angry answers swirled around him in a haze of faded aftershave and street smells. A door slammed but Mason didn't peek until he heard a familiar feminine voice.

"No good pencil-necked son of a bitch!"

Sandra Connelly tripped over Mason's outstretched legs, unable to catch herself before falling onto the sofa next to him.

"Bad day?" he asked.

"Are you the victim or the suspect?" she asked. "Never mind, I don't care." She started to get up, but he grabbed her arm.

"Hold on. What the hell are you doing here?"

She yanked her arm free and stood up. "Touch me again, Louis, and I'll perform your second circumcision."

"Just a little off the sides, please." Mason was scrambling, but she hadn't left yet. It was progress. "I plead temporary insanity. I don't blame you for walking out. I won't blame you for leaving again. And I'm sorry and I'm glad you're all right. Sullivan's illegitimate kid was born in Rogersville, Kansas. The mother was named Meredith Phillips. She's not in the phone book but her relatives might be. I'm here because I shot Camaya. What are you in for?"

"Depends. Burn any of your friends at the stake today?"

"Close. Camaya made Scott Daniels watch Julio kill Harlan.

Scott got the message and gave me up. How was your day?"

"Lousy. Angela is dead," she said, and she sat down next to him.

Mason couldn't respond. For a minute, he thought he would join Scott in his twilight zone.

"The cops think she committed suicide, but I don't buy it," she continued.

Images of Angela flashed in Mason's mind; lover to Sullivan and Scott, amateur spy, embezzler, manipulator. Whatever she was, she was a risk taker, not a quitter. He couldn't picture her taking her own life.

"How did she die?"

"Some kind of overdose. They won't know for certain until they do the autopsy. It just happened tonight."

"Who told you?"

"Nobody. I was the one that found her."

CHAPTER SIXTY-SEVEN

Sandra's anger softened with the telling of the story. "I told you I would figure this out myself, and I decided to start with Angela. I went to that bar she took you to, The Limit, and waited. She showed up around eight."

Mason glanced at the classroom clock on the opposite wall. It was one a.m.

"She was alone," Sandra said. "I told her that if you figured out the wiretaps, the wrong people could too."

"Thanks for the endorsement."

"She was really shaken when she heard what happened to you at the lake, and she started to talk. She knew from the wiretaps that Sullivan had the goods on Scott and Harlan and that he was keeping the information on a CD. She wanted the disk for blackmail and guessed that the information was on one of the CDs you had. So she copied them."

"Then the bad guys would chase me, never knowing she had a copy. She could blackmail them, and they'd never know what her sources were."

"Exactly."

"Scott found religion tonight too." He told her what happened at the Mid-America Club. Sandra gave him a sympathetic look that showed more compassion than he gave her credit for. "Is that all Angela told you?"

"She said there was something else that she didn't want to talk about in public. She said she was meeting someone else at nine, so we agreed to meet at her place at eleven. When I got there, she was dead."

"So why do the cops think it was suicide?"

"No signs of forced entry, no visible signs of violence. I found her slumped over her PC with a suicide note on the screen. The cops found a syringe in her bathroom that they think she used to overdose."

"What did the note say?"

"Something about Sullivan exposing her to AIDS and not wanting to die that way. I tried to tell the cops that she wouldn't have killed herself, but they like the easy way out."

Before Mason could ask another question, Blues joined them, nodding a noncommittal hello to Sandra.

"You done?" he asked Mason, who nodded his reply. "Then let's get the hell out of here."

"Any news on Camaya?"

"Yeah, he's gonna make it. Scott's been admitted to Western Missouri Mental Health."

Blues didn't say a word when Sandra walked out with them. Mason was glad that Camaya would survive. He preferred the threat of Camaya to more blood on his hands.

A weak storm front had coasted through the city while they were inside. The air smelled wet, and tepid steam rose from the pavement beneath the streetlights. Ghost clouds draped the moon as they walked to the cars.

"Mine's this way," Sandra said to Mason, motioning to a parking lot across the street. "We've had a rough ride, Lou. We both could use some company."

Mason needed some company, but not Sandra's. "I can't. But thanks."

She forced a bright smile. "That's okay. Say hi to the sheriff for me."

Blues dropped Mason at home, where he found his TR6 in the driveway. "Did you arrange that?" Mason asked.

"I been too busy to worry about your damn car. There's a note on the windshield."

Mason got out of Blues's car and pulled the note from beneath the windshield wiper.

"It's from Harry Ryman. It says, *We traced this car to your neighbor, who says she sold it to you. Claire made me get it back for you. Be glad she don't ask for too many favors.*"

Blues shook his head. "You should have been dead at least three times in the last two weeks, man. Somebody is looking out for you."

Mason watched him drive away before going inside. His empty, forlorn house couldn't slow the spring in his step as he bounded inside, buoyed by the return of his TR6. The message light was blinking on his answering machine. He realized he hadn't been home in days. The first ten messages were from reporters promising a flattering exclusive. Mason was in the fast lane of his fifteen minutes of fame. The last was a message from Kelly. She left a number for him to call and ended by saying she missed him.

He called the number, tapping his fingers against the kitchen counter until she answered.

"Hi, it's Lou."

"I know who it is, you dope," she said softly. "I recognized your number."

Mason warmed at the sound of her voice. "What's the latest?"

"You made CNN. Are you all right?"

He filled her in on the details of the shoot-out, answering her pointed and professional questions.

"Now it's your turn," he told her.

"I've still got some friends in the bureau's Chicago office. They let me have a look at Vic Jr.'s file. He was busted in 1996, just like the computer records said."

"Could you tie him to D'lessandro?"

"He was represented by Caravello and Landusky. That's the same firm that represents D'lessandro and that signed off on the fixtures deals."

"Seems like too much of a coincidence."

"The FBI got involved because he was transporting across state lines."

"Drugs or girls?"

"Both. And you don't do that in Chicago without D'lessandro's permission."

"So, that's it? There's nothing else to tie Vic Jr. to the mob?"

"Maybe—not exactly—I don't know for certain."

"What aren't you telling me?"

The line was lifeless for a moment, and then she answered, raising more questions.

"My partner, Nick, busted Vic Jr. I was off that weekend and he was working alone. He claimed that he got a tip, thought it might be a link to D'lessandro, and ended up with Junior."

Her voice was heavy with sadness and uncertainty. Her partner—and dead lover—had arrested the son of Sullivan & Christenson's biggest client. Then he ends up gut shot on a sidewalk in Kansas City, Junior disappears, and Mason becomes a moving target. No matter how he arranged these pieces, he couldn't make them fit.

"Did D'lessandro make Nick dump the case against Vic Jr.?"

"I don't know. But a week after the bust, McNamara took him off the case and reassigned it to himself."

"Gene McNamara? St. John's lapdog?"

"The same. I told you, we were all in Chicago at the same time."

Sandra's chaos theory was in full bloom, bumper cars in a major pileup.

"What about the bank accounts and passwords?"

"I'm still working on it. I'm on the Southwest flight that gets in at five fifty-five Sunday night. Will you pick me up?"

"No problem."

"Lou, be careful. This isn't over yet," she said.

CHAPTER SIXTY-EIGHT

Mason got up before dawn, too wired to sleep. After a run and a shower, he decided it was a great top-down day and took the TR6 for a drive. He headed south, through the suburbs and into the country, following the same route he'd taken six days earlier to Harlan Christenson's farm, shutting out everything except the sun and the breeze until he pulled into Harlan's gravel drive.

Mason had missed Harlan's funeral, so he'd come to the farm to pay his respects. Harlan was the one partner who had reached out to him, whose friendship seemed genuine. When he came to Mason for help, he still had a chance to find a way out, but Mason didn't pay enough attention. Mason knew he'd carry that burden for a long time.

He left the car in the drive and went for a walk through the pasture that surrounded the farmhouse. The pond he and Harlan had fished in was a quarter of a mile away, surrounded by cottonwoods. There was a break in the trees at one end of the pond and a small dock that hung over the water. Mason found Harlan's fishing rod lying on the dock. It wasn't baited, but he cast the line into the water anyway.

At least three of the people connected to Harlan's murder had been accounted for. Julio was dead, Jimmie Camaya was in the hospital, and Scott Daniels was somewhere over the rainbow. None of that meant that Harlan's murder was solved. Whoever had given the order, whoever had set Vic Jr., Scott, and Harlan up in a money-laundering scam, whoever had ordered Mason's death— was still in business.

Camaya was the best bet to nail Harlan's real killer. He'd use the identity of his boss to make a deal with the U.S. attorney, a fact that wouldn't escape his boss and would, for the moment, make Camaya a bigger target than Mason, unless his nurses were good with a gun.

But none of that explained Sullivan's murder or Angela's suicide. Angela's confession to Sandra fit with his theory that the two murders were only indirectly related. Whoever killed Sullivan had set in motion everything else.

Angela bugged the offices to get something on Sullivan. After his death, she hit pay dirt with the CDs and decided to set Mason up as the fall guy and watch what happened. Only she never got the chance to cash in. Suicide made no sense for her. She'd already taken all the big risks. She may have been scared when Sandra told her about the shoot-out at the lake, but Mason couldn't believe Angela was frightened enough to kill herself.

If she was murdered, her killer was more likely to have also murdered Richard Sullivan than Harlan Christenson. Death by lethal injection was not part of Camaya's repertoire. In any case, he was digesting a .45-caliber slug when Angela died. Sullivan died by lethal injection. Mason caught himself humming "Will the Circle Be Unbroken?" as he walked back to his car.

CHAPTER SIXTY-NINE

A short time later, he stopped in front of Pamela Sullivan's house. He was going back over ground he'd already covered, but he didn't know what else to do. A *For Sale* sign had been recently planted in the front yard.

Pamela greeted him dressed in a purple and yellow tennis warm-up suit. Judging from the boozy fragrance that hung over her, Mason doubted she would be hitting the courts anytime soon. Her face was puffy, her hair barely brushed. She wasn't wearing makeup. Her eyes were slightly glassy. She was racing her demons to the bottom.

"What can I do for you, Lou? Did you come back for something else?"

"I just wanted to talk, that's all."

"Well, come on in, then. I'm long on conversation."

She took him through the front hall, past Sullivan's study, and into the kitchen. There was a bottle of wine on the kitchen table next to the morning paper. She fumbled in a cabinet for two glasses.

"Nothing for me, Pamela. It's a little early."

"Well, in my case, it's a little late." She poured herself a full glass. "My husband left one hell of a mess," she said, pointing to the morning paper.

The headline read *Shoot-out Widens Law Firm Scandal*. A picture of the shattered locker-room mirror with Camaya sprawled on the floor promised more gory details on the inside pages.

Mason scanned the article, taking small comfort in the correct spelling of his name. There was a sidebar about Angela's death. The coroner hedged his preliminary conclusion of suicide pending an autopsy.

"I've been in the middle of the whole thing, Pamela, and I still don't believe what's happened. I hope it's about over."

"So do I," she said, the wine feeding her melancholy. "I'm heartbroken about Scott. Mostly for Gloria and their kids."

"He probably didn't intend for it to go this far—it just got out of control. Actually, I think your husband was on to Scott and Harlan and was going to confront them."

"And probably demand his cut! Oh, don't look at me that way, Lou," she said as he picked up his jaw. "The man was a shit. I don't think he would have cleaned house."

"Did he ever talk with you about what was going on?"

"No. He made it clear early in our marriage that business was off-limits. I never made an issue of it."

"I don't mean to pry, but there are some questions I need to ask you."

"You won't offend me. I'm past that."

"Why didn't you and Richard have children?"

She sighed and looked over his shoulder, through the window, and back to another time.

"We tried. I got pregnant twice and lost both babies with miscarriages. The doctors said I shouldn't try again. Richard said it wasn't my fault, but he never forgave me. That's when he started cheating and I started pretending not to notice."

"Had Richard been married previously?"

"No. What are you getting at?"

"Richard fathered a child back in the late sixties by a woman named Meredith Phillips. I've seen the results of the paternity test."

The last of the color drained from her cheeks. Mason saw the ache for her own babies in her moist eyes.

"I didn't know," she said softly.

Mason believed her. If she'd been a client, he would have stopped and come back another day. But he didn't know if there would be another day, so he pressed on.

276

"You knew that Richard was HIV positive?"

"Yes."

"Did you discuss that with him?"

"He told me and said he'd take care of it, like it was a problem for a client."

"Weren't you concerned about being exposed?"

"We quit having sex years ago." She hesitated and then added, "Richard didn't want me, but I needed to be wanted. You don't always find that where you think you will."

"Did Richard tell anybody else that he was HIV positive?"

"I don't know. We never spoke of it again."

"Did you tell anyone?"

"Diane dropped some papers off a few days after he told me. I must have looked like a wreck because she asked me if something was wrong and I just started bawling like a baby—about everything. I made her promise not to repeat anything."

"Was Richard treating himself for the virus, maybe injecting medications?"

She nodded her head with a dry, humorless laugh. "He said he didn't trust the doctors and that he'd found a source for a drug the FDA hadn't approved but was supposed to be a miracle cure. I told him he could live a normal life for years and begged him not to try black-market drugs."

"But he did anyway?"

"At least he thought so, but he was being taken. It was nothing but saline solution. The police found a vial of it when they searched the house."

"Do you know who he was getting it from?"

"I have no idea."

Mason thanked her for her time and she walked him to the door. This time, as they passed Sullivan's study, he noticed the computer on his desk.

"By the way, did Richard do much work on his computer?"

This time, her laugh held genuine amusement. "Are you kidding? He had to have that damn PC and every other new gadget that came out, but he never learned to use it. The man couldn't type if his life depended on it."

The doorbell rang just as Mason turned the knob. It was Diane Farrell. A new Diane, she had makeup on, her hair was washed and styled, and she was wearing a lively blue-and-yellow floral-print dress.

"Diane, darling! You look marvelous." Pamela said. "Diane just turned thirty-something. We don't keep an exact count. I gave her a day of beauty and a new dress. Doesn't she look fantastic? Happy birthday, dear."

"And many more," Mason added as he walked out.

CHAPTER SEVENTY

Mason sat in his car in Pamela's driveway, studying the names on the page he had ripped from the Rogersville, Kansas, phone book. There were ten ending in Phillips: Anson, C.J., Donald, Harry, Keenan, Martin, Missey, Opal, Vernon, and Wyatt. It was ten o'clock. He could make Rogersville by eleven.

The addresses were a crisscross of numbered streets and dead presidents. Anson lived at 227 Jefferson and Wyatt at 1634 Roosevelt. The others were evenly distributed between Republicans and Democrats. Once he figured out where the party lines were, he figured he could find them easily enough.

On his way, he called Blues. "I'm headed to Rogersville to find Meredith Phillips. I need you to track down Angela's autopsy results."

"You think I'm running a bar and you've got a tab?"

"We'll settle up when this is over. I'll call you if I find Meredith."

Most small towns are laid out with Main and First as the north-south and east-west dividers. If you can count and tell your right from your left, you can't get lost. Rogersville was no different except that the presidents weren't in chronological order. Fillmore and Hoover were back-to-back. Maybe the city fathers just had a wry sense of humor.

Anson Phillips's house was the third from the corner, west side of the street, on a block lined with heavy-limbed oaks leaning over the center of the street in a green canopy. Well-tended lawns, one-car garages, and sturdy wooden front stoops spoke to the longevity of the neighborhood.

Mason parked in the driveway behind a late-model white Buick, a car the size of Brazil. His TR6 looked like a mutant exhaust pipe protruding from its tail end.

Anson was as round a man as Mason had ever seen. He filled the width of the glider on his porch, work boots not quite touching the ground. His head perched like a paperweight on his shoulders, with no visible support from his neck. Eyes, nose, mouth, and ears melted into a pie-pan face. He was a denim-wrapped doughboy given too long to rise. Mason bet he hadn't seen his feet in years.

"Morning," Mason called out from the driveway. "You Mr. Phillips?"

"What you want, boy?"

No one had called Mason a boy in years. He liked this guy already.

"Help. I'm looking for a woman named Meredith Phillips. Last I knew, she lived in Rogersville. You're the first Phillips in the book."

"What d'ya want with her?"

"I'm a lawyer from Kansas City. She may have a child who's inherited some money."

"Don't know her. Might try Vernon Phillips. That family's been around here a long time."

No one was home at Vernon's, so Mason spent the next hour running down the rest of the Phillips clan. Only a few were home and none of them as helpful as Anson. He decided to try Vernon again.

This time there was a car in the driveway, a lime green, road-worn Chevy with a *Baby on Board* sign hung in the rear window. It was littered with Happy Meal bags, two car seats, and a scattering of diapers and baby wipes.

A chorus of bleating kids sang their demands from the other side of the screen door. A loose-jointed girl no more than twenty, her right hip jutting out to hold the rheumy-eyed infant glued to her side, answered Mason's knocks.

Stringy maize-colored hair hung over her narrow forehead as

she examined him with defeated, washed-out eyes ringed by dark circles. She ran her tongue over chapped lips, while another toddler clung to her T-shirt, dragging it off one bony shoulder. The sour stench of soiled diapers followed them to the door.

"I'm looking for Vernon Phillips. Is this his house?"

"Yeah," she said, pushing the older child behind her and tugging her shirt back over her exposed dull gray bra strap.

"May I speak to him, please?"

"He don't live here no more. I'm renting from him."

"Do you know where I can find him?"

She disappeared for a minute and returned with a scrap of paper on which she'd written an address, 1860 Lincoln.

"Do you know Mr. Phillips?"

"Sure, known him all my life. We moved in across the street when I was five."

"Did he have children?"

"A girl, Meredith."

"She's the one I really need to talk to. Do you know where she lives?"

"No place. She's dead. Killed in a car wreck 'fore my folks moved in."

From the back, Mason heard another wailing voice cry out. The toddler bolted while the baby spit up. She didn't have to say good-bye.

CHAPTER SEVENTY-ONE

Eighteen-sixty Lincoln was the address of the Loving Hands Convalescent Center, a low-slung, U-shaped building made of sandblasted brick. Heat waves radiated off a playground on the south side. Overgrown weeds had erupted through the asphalt, wrapping around the legs of a steel jungle gym. It was the only landscaping. A faded tire hung from a chain in the center of an otherwise empty swing set.

Mason parked in the circle drive next to a barren flagpole. The plaque embedded at its base declared that the alumnae of Lincoln Elementary School had donated it in 1953. A pair of oversized, pale pink cupped hands had been painted over the entry beneath the gracious claim that those inside had cared for loved ones since 1985. He wondered if any of the alumnae had reenrolled at their alma mater, proving again that life is a circle.

Airplane propeller–sized fans stood in the lobby blowing antiseptic flavored air down each stuffy hallway, though the breeze passed by the closed doors of the patients' rooms.

He shuddered, remembering when his aunt Claire dragged him to a nursing home to visit her mother. He was six. His grandmother was ancient. She lay in bed, near death, her hair fanned out around her head.

Claire had patiently brushed her hair, working out the tangles. He had looked into her cloudy black eyes sunk deep into her face. Her skin had been brittle and translucent, like looking through tissue paper into her skull. Her parched lips had been shut, silencing the voice that used to sing him to sleep, her gnarled hands lying uselessly at her sides. She had smelled like the stuff that the cleaning lady used to clean the toilets. He never went back.

Vernon Phillips lived in room twelve on the north wing. So did three other people, each cordoned off by a peach-colored vinyl curtain suspended from a track along the ceiling; four to a classroom, each bed with a view. Probably a lot less crowded than the days when kids roamed the halls.

A clipboard with an erasable surface hung on each classroom door, listing the occupants and their bed numbers. Vernon was bed number three. Each patient's space was furnished with a chair for visitors. Sandra Connelly sat in Vernon's.

"About time you got here, lover boy. I almost gave up on you," she said as she stood.

Sandra had an inexhaustible capacity for the unexpected. She had made it plain that she was doing her own investigation. Still, he was surprised to see her.

"Sorry to keep you waiting. I had some other stops to make."

"Tell me all about it."

"Later. How's Vernon?"

"Like all vegetables. Not good company."

His chart hung from a hook at the end of the bed. The top page contained the admitting information. He'd been there five weeks following a stroke. Mason put the chart back and looked at the figure lying in bed.

He was propped up, placing them in his line of sight. His gaze passed through them, through the walls, and kept going. Ragged gray stubble covered his chin and peppered his mottled cheeks. A loose-fitting hospital tunic lay over his chest and upper arms. His Adam's apple bobbed rhythmically, the only sure sign part of him was still with the living.

Mason couldn't take his eyes off of him. Vernon knew the answers to Mason's questions, but they were locked inside him. Mason sat at the foot of his bed, staring at him, weary at another dead end.

"Let's go," Sandra said. "Maybe you'll come up with another

bright idea." Mason didn't move. "Come on, it's not your fault. We'll come back on Monday and check the city's birth records."

"Good idea. But I think I'll stay a while. He might come around."

"Yeah, and the first thing he'll say is 'Lou, good to see you. Let me tell you about my daughter.'"

Mason looked at Sandra, feeling the harshness in her, trying to figure out why she was risking her life to solve this case. He decided that she thrived on the combat. It was all about winning.

"Stranger things have happened. I'll call you."

"Don't count on it."

She waited for him to say something. He ignored her, content to watch the old man's breathing. Sandra waited in silence for five minutes.

"You damn well better call, Louis," she said and left.

Twice over the next hour, an aide came in to turn Vernon so that he wouldn't develop bedsores. She was a copper-colored Hispanic woman, jet-black hair, broad, flat features, and strong hands. Vernon had had eight inches and a hundred pounds on her in his prime. Even now, he retained most of his bulk. Yet she rolled him effortlessly from side to side, massaging his flanks to encourage his circulation. She spoke no English. He hoped for Vernon's sake that Medicare didn't ask for her green card.

At three o'clock, she returned with a syringe, rolled up Vernon's sleeve, and gave him an injection. Smiling at Mason, she moved on to her next patient.

Curious, he picked up Vernon's chart and studied the doctor's orders. Vernon was diabetic. He called Blues.

"What'd you find out about Angela's death?"

"Insulin overdose, just like Sullivan. Cops canceled the suicide."

CHAPTER SEVENTY-TWO

Now he knew how Sullivan and Angela had been murdered. Vernon could tell him who and why, but he wasn't talking.

Mason stood at the edge of his bed, staring at him, feeling like an idiot. What did he expect Vernon to do? Listen to a list of suspects and blink once for innocent, twice for guilty?

The Loving Hands people provided a nightstand for each patient's personal items. A copy of a *Kansas City Star* newspaper lay on Vernon's. Mason picked up the newspaper to check for the date. It was two days old. Vernon had had a recent visitor.

Mason dropped the newspaper in the trash can next to the bed and saw a Bible that had been hidden beneath it. The Bible was bound in black leather, *Phillips Family Bible* embossed in small gold filigree letters on the spine.

Tommy Douchant's family also had a Bible embossed with the family name. He remembered Tommy showing him the family tree on the inside cover that traced his clan back five generations. *Be there, baby,* Mason prayed as he picked up Vernon's Bible.

And so it was written. Vernon Phillips and his wife had been married in 1956. Four years later, a daughter, Meredith, was born. She died in 1990. Beneath her name was the inscription Alice, born to Meredith July 3, 1977. Alice made no sense. There was no Alice. Mason went back to the beginning, to Vernon and his wife. He read her maiden name. Then he knew.

He said good-bye to Vernon and tucked the Bible under his arm. Promising himself that he'd return it when everything was over, he drove straight to Blues's house, struggling with the last hurdle in solving Sullivan's and Angela's murders. How to prove it? A brilliant trial lawyer once told him not to bother him with the facts, just tell him what the evidence was. Now he knew what the evidence was, but he wasn't certain that he could prove the facts.

He flashed back to the chalkboard at The Limit announcing the symposium on alternative AIDS therapies. He conjured the haunting image of Sullivan injecting himself, thinking it was some experimental AIDS treatment, not realizing he was killing himself. The killer had watched from a safe distance, not wanting to betray any undue interest, content in the knowledge that Sullivan would die by his own hand.

And that would be the killer's defense, that somehow Sullivan had made a terrible mistake. Whoever Sullivan had bought the phony AIDS meds from had made the mistake.

There would be no confession. Too much was at stake. The killer knew that, at best, the circumstantial evidence was as thin as yesterday's soup. Mason would prepare the same way he prepared for trial. And that meant tying up a few more loose ends.

Tuffy's barking announced Mason's arrival at Blues's house before Mason could knock on the door. Blues was standing at his kitchen sink, cutting slices from a fresh peach. Tuffy pawed happily at Mason's side until he scratched her ears.

"Peach?" Blues offered.

"Pass. Here's how I think Sullivan was murdered."

Blues listened, probing, picking, and ripping at any weakness. When Mason finished, he dropped the peach pit in the sink and wiped his hands on his shorts.

"I believe you. But you can't make it stick."

"Why not? It's all there."

"On Sullivan, maybe. But where does Angela fit in?"

"Murdered the same way. Insulin overdose." It was clear to him, why not to Blues?

"People get shot every day. Don't mean it's the same gun. If you're right about the killer, why take out Angela?"

Mason sagged under the weight of the question. "Angela told

Sandra she had something else to tell her about besides the money laundering. Something she could only tell her in private. It must have implicated the killer. Did the cops find anything at Angela's apartment?"

"Harry Ryman told me they turned the place upside down. Nothing."

"I thought you guys didn't talk to each other."

"We don't. He's helping you, not me."

Mason's phone rang. He answered, listened, and hung up."

"Who was that?"

He looked at Blues, shaking his head. "That was the hospital. Man, I've got a new client."

"Who?"

"Jimmie Camaya. He's out of intensive care, and he's asking for me. Says he won't talk to anybody until he talks to me."

"Where is he?"

"Truman Medical Center," Mason said. "I'm guessing a private room with a cop on the door."

"You better take something just in case Camaya is feeling frisky."

Blues disappeared for a moment before coming back carrying a pistol he handed to Mason.

"What is it?" Mason asked as he held the gun.

"Thirty-eight caliber. Good enough for close range."

"Camaya can't be dangerous. I already shot him once. Plus the cops will be there."

"Somebody might be hanging around the parking lot waiting for you to come visit. Stick it in your waistband in the small of your back. Less chance you'll shoot your dick off."

CHAPTER SEVENTY-THREE

Blues followed Mason out to the driveway and tossed Vernon's Bible onto the passenger seat of the TR6.

"Don't leave the Good Book lying around."

Mason drove away, uncertain whether he would agree to plead for justice and mercy on Camaya's behalf. He alternated the lawyer's litany that everyone was entitled to a defense with Claire's corollary that he didn't have to represent everyone.

When he arrived at the hospital, Mason got a text message from Kelly.

D'lessandro owns Vic Jr. Sending crew to clean up after Camaya. Be careful.

He tapped his reply.

No doubt. No surprise. No shit.

A uniformed officer sat outside the door to Camaya's hospital room. He nodded when Mason identified himself and motioned him into the room.

Camaya was sitting up in bed, a drain sticking out of a bandaged hole in his chest and an IV line plugged into his arm.

"Hey, Mason, how do I look, man? It ain't much, but it's all I got."

"What are you? The new Jimmie Camaya, repackaged and user friendly?"

Camaya's laugh caught in his throat as he winced. "Don't make me laugh, man. You're killin' me."

"Well, you don't look bad for a guy with a hole in him who's looking at the death penalty. What do you want from me?"

"To talk. That's all, just talk. Thought you might help me do some business with the boys out in the hall."

"You forget that I shot you and I'm going to testify against you?"

Camaya dismissed his objections with a wave of the hand. "Old business. I think we can help each other."

Mason walked to the window, looking at nothing in particular. Camaya laughed again and Mason turned around.

"What's so funny?"

"You're packin', aren't you?"

"I'm what?"

"Packin', man. Carryin' a gun. Man, you kill me!"

Mason flushed at the absurdity of it all. Camaya was recovering from a gunshot wound and surgery and Mason had a gun to protect himself from him. He laughed too.

"Yeah, Jimmie. I've got a gun. So don't get out of bed. How'd you know?"

Camaya's good eye narrowed, matching the other, as he drew his lips back, baring his teeth, almost hissing his words.

"You killed Julio and shot me. Lost your cherry big-time. No turning back now. Shit like that changes you forever. You walkin' the walk now, and that piece belongs right where you got it."

Mason nodded.

"Feels good, don't it, Mason?"

The door swung open. No knock. Just company.

Franklin St. John and Gene McNamara could darken a room like a solar eclipse. They cast the biggest shadow on Camaya, who flipped from snake eyes to wide eyes.

Mason assumed that Camaya was a coward at the core, like all bullies. But he didn't expect him to fold before the interrogation started. Particularly since he was holding a great trump card, the identity of his boss. Mason didn't have anything to say, so he waited for somebody else to kick things off.

"What are you doing here, Mason?" McNamara demanded.

"Jimmie invited me over to watch TV."

"Showtime's over, wiseass. Take a walk."

"No, thanks. Jimmie and I are going to watch an *American Idol* rerun."

Mason couldn't help but do the opposite of what McNamara wanted to him to do. It was a petty way of showing him up—and probably not too bright—but he couldn't help himself. To make the point, he sat on the edge of the bed, facing McNamara with his back to Camaya.

"Mr. Mason," St. John said, "we have to question Camaya. You can come back during regular visiting hours."

"Franklin, you forget that Jimmie is entitled to have his lawyer present for any questioning."

St. John smiled. "And you're his lawyer. How convenient. Jimmie, do you really think the judge is going to let the man who put you in that bed and whose testimony is going to put you on death row represent you?"

"Nothin' but the best for me."

"I'm truly sorry to hear you say that, Jimmie. I thought you had better judgment."

"I'll make you a deal," Mason said. "I'll tell you what you want to know and you'll tell me what I want to know."

"Mr. Mason, you know what we want from your client. We want to know who hired him."

"Come on, Franklin. You already know that. It was Carlo D'lessandro. Mr. Chicago Mob. No, what you want is for Jimmie to roll over and testify against D'lessandro. And, if he agrees, you'll give him a nice new identity flipping burgers in Bumfuck, Montana. How's that sound to you, Jimmie?"

"I ain't flipping no fucking burgers, man. No way."

St. John let out an exasperated sigh. "Mr. Mason, you are more than an inconvenience. What do you want?"

"A history lesson."

"On what subject that wouldn't exceed your limited grasp?"

"The migratory habits of Chicago mobsters."

St. John looked at McNamara, who nodded. "Begin, Mr.

Mason."

"Why did you take Nick Theonis off of Vic Jr.'s case?"

McNamara lost his snarl as if he'd just been hit across the nose with a newspaper. St. John's eyes fluttered in a momentary panic. Neither had expected Mason to bring up their dirty laundry.

"Sorry, time's up," Mason said. "No answer? I get to go again. Vic Jr. was small-time. How does he hook up with a mob mouthpiece like Caravello and Landusky?"

The corners of St. John's mouth began to quiver as he and McNamara exchanged glances. Mason was getting warmer. He loved body language. Still no answer.

"Somebody had to refer Junior to Caravello," Mason continued. "Somebody who could be certain that the case against him would evaporate and that he would show the proper appreciation. Nick Theonis could have done that. Screw up the bust just enough to get Vic Jr. off. Then Vic Jr.'s lawyer tells him that Mr. D'lessandro has a small favor to ask. He wants to use Daddy's bank to launder money."

CHAPTER SEVENTY-FOUR

Both their faces went taut, their eyes narrowing, boring in on Mason. McNamara held his arms at his sides, balling his hands into fists. St. John crossed his arms, hiding his hands in his armpits. Still, neither man spoke.

"You guys must have known that Theonis was dirty, but you kept him in play. Then Theonis gets whacked and you lose control. Bet that was a tough one to explain to the organized crime boys in the Justice Department."

McNamara broke their silence. "You're full of shit."

St. John pressed himself against the wall.

"That's an artful response, Gene. Your ass was on the line. What did you think you were doing with Theonis? Turning him into a double agent?"

Mason had released the brakes on Sandra's bumper cars. All he could do now was wait; let them try to restore order. St. John composed himself and sat in a hardback chair on the opposite side of the room. McNamara held his ground.

"You're to be congratulated for doing your homework, Mr. Mason," St. John said. "Or perhaps it was Sheriff Holt. No matter. Nick Theonis arrested young O'Malley. The case involved drugs. We suspected that Theonis was dirty, and we removed him from all drug cases while we continued to investigate him. Quite simple."

He brushed his hands together. End of story.

"Then why bring Theonis and Kelly to Kansas City?" Mason asked. They didn't answer. "Theonis had compromised both of you. You didn't know which side of the street he was really working, so you had to hold on to him in the hope he'd help you nail D'lessandro without giving the bureau a black eye."

"We take care of our own problems. Privately," McNamara said.

"Except D'lessandro took care of it first. He had Jimmie hit Theonis. I guess he didn't want Theonis working for two bosses. Or maybe it was just a salary-cap problem."

"Are you admitting that your client murdered an FBI agent?" St. John asked.

"Not me. I'm just thinking out loud. You guys interrupted us before Jimmie could tell me a thing. Here's the way I see it. You lost Theonis but you still had Vic Jr.'s old man. He was already under the microscope for his banking problems. You figured he was also in on the money-laundering scheme. You planned to pressure him to roll over or his son would take the fall."

"An investigation has its own life, Mr. Mason," St. John said. "We just follow it."

"But you screwed up. O'Malley wouldn't cave. So you tried to squeeze his lawyer. Then somebody killed Richard Sullivan and you were fucked again."

"If you mean by that that we ended up dealing with you, I would quite agree," St. John said.

"And everyone says you have no sense of humor, Franklin. Sullivan's murder knocked everything off track. You had threatened to prosecute Sullivan so that he would put pressure on O'Malley to cooperate. If O'Malley wouldn't give up his son to save himself, did you really think he'd do it to save his lawyer?"

"I didn't care," St. John answered. "Richard Sullivan was involved in the senior O'Malley's bank fraud and he knew about the money laundering. We were negotiating a plea bargain when he was killed."

"So you must have known that Vic Jr. was washing the mob's money through the law firm with the help of Scott Daniels and Harlan Christenson and that O'Malley had nothing to do with it."

"Apparently so. Sullivan had proposed giving us the evidence on his partners and Vic Jr. in return for a free pass for himself and O'Malley."

"So that's why Sullivan didn't tell anyone about the subpoena for the firm's records. He was going to give you the records, claim ignorance of the money laundering, and let Scott and Harlan take the fall along with Vic Jr. Did O'Malley know what Sullivan was doing?"

"A detail in which I had no interest."

"With Sullivan dead, you were stuck with Vic Jr. to make the case against D'lessandro, but he disappeared. Harlan Christenson is dead and Scott Daniels is going to be the next poster boy for electroshock therapy. Camaya is your last chance."

"It pains me to admit that you're right."

"There's one thing I still don't get," Mason said. "How did Jimmie find Kelly's cabin?" Mason asked the question, almost forgetting that Camaya was lying in bed behind him.

Camaya answered. "I found a map in Theonis's apartment after—"

"That's enough," Mason interrupted. "Don't confess to anything yet."

The door to Camaya's hospital room flew open. The police officer that had been on guard was shoved inside and onto the floor, his hands cuffed behind his back. Two men dressed in black, silenced pistols drawn, followed. One was tall, the other about Mason's height, only broader. Both had the slack appearance of men who aren't impressed by much and who care about less.

"Hey, Jimmie," the taller man said. "You don't look so good."

Camaya sat up, using Mason as a shield. "Feel better than I look, Tony." Mason could feel Camaya's labored breath on the back of his neck.

"Carlo said we should come down. Check on you. If you was feeling bad, he said we should put you out of your misery. So how you feelin'?"

McNamara made a poorly disguised move for his gun.

"Hey, fat boy," Tony warned. "Don't be stupid. Gino," he said to his companion, "get this dickhead's piece."

Gino shoved McNamara against the wall, grabbing his gun. McNamara offered no resistance when Gino yanked his wallet from his pocket. St. John's face twisted with disgust, though he remained silent.

Mason felt Camaya's hand slide under the back of his shirt onto the butt of his gun. He couldn't move without giving Camaya away. He hoped Camaya knew which side he was on.

"This guy's fucking FBI," Gino said after opening McNamara's wallet.

Tony turned to St. John. "And who are you, J. Edgar Hoover?"

"You should see him in a dress," Mason said.

"Shut the fuck up," Tony told Mason. "Jimmie, you got all these visitors. Carlo don't like that. He's worried you might talk to the wrong people. Maybe say the wrong thing."

St. John couldn't keep his mouth shut. "My name is Franklin St. John and I'm the United States attorney. Put your guns down. You're under arrest."

Tony laughed. "Jimmie, where did you get these guys? And who are you?" he asked Mason.

"I'm Jimmie's lawyer."

"So that's the way it is, huh, Jimmie?" Tony said. "You got your lawyer, the FBI, and the U.S. attorney in your room all at the same time. Smells like you're selling out. I guess we got here just in time."

Gino pulled St. John from his chair and shoved him against McNamara, leaving them huddled in a corner next to the window. He took a step back, keeping out of McNamara's reach and keeping his pistol pointed at the two of them.

Camaya lifted the gun from behind Mason's back and nudged Mason with the barrel. Mason edged forward until he was on the edge of the bed, the balls of his feet pressed to the floor like loaded springs. He braced his hands against the mattress for added leverage.

Tony stood at the door, about five feet in front of Mason. Gino was closer to Mason, but at an angle to Mason's left. He knew that

Tony would shoot him before he got close to him, but he'd have a chance with Gino if Camaya took care of Tony.

"Listen, Tony," Mason began. "This isn't working out like you expected. You probably counted on the cop outside the door but no way could you figure on an FBI agent, the U.S. attorney, and me being here. You kill everyone in this room and your boss is going to catch so much heat you'll never be able to go home again."

Tony considered Mason's comments. "It is the way it is, pal. Lots of people end up in the wrong place at the wrong time. I guess this is just your time."

"Last chance," Mason said. "Put your guns down and give up or Jimmie will shoot you." Both gunmen laughed. "Don't say I didn't give you a chance."

Mason stood up, stepping toward Gino and drawing Tony's attention away from Camaya. Tony froze in astonishment at the gun in Camaya's hand long enough for Camaya to shoot him in the face. He was dead before he hit the floor.

Mason leapt at Gino but not before Gino shot McNamara. Gino had weight on his side. Mason had surprise and desperation on his. And he fought dirty. Mason grabbed Gino's gun with his left hand and Gino's testicles with his right, squeezing both while he drove his head into Gino's neck.

The gun flew out of their grasp as they toppled onto the floor. Gino slammed his knee upward, breaking Mason's grip on his crotch, and wrapped his hands around Mason's throat. His fingers were crushing Mason's windpipe and cutting off his breath. Mason straddled Gino as the bigger man held Mason at arm's length, strangling him.

Raising his right hand from Gino's chest, Mason jammed his forefinger into Gino's eye, puncturing the outer surface until he felt the hard socket against his knuckle. Gino's piercing scream nearly shattered Mason's eardrum as his grip on Mason's throat gave way. Mason withdrew his bloody hand, leaving Gino's eye dangling alongside his nose.

Mason staggered to his feet. McNamara lay on the floor,

moaning but alive. St. John had wet himself and assumed the fetal position.

"My man! My main man!" Camaya crowed, waving Mason's gun in the air.

Mason snatched the gun from him and grabbed him by the throat. "I'm not your man, you miserable piece of shit. Now, call the nurse!"

CHAPTER SEVENTY-FIVE

Sunday started with a steady rain pinging against Mason's windows as he lay in bed long after Harry Ryman's last questions stopped reverberating in his ears. It was welcome white noise, something to concentrate on when he felt Gino's blood trickling down his arm again.

Bright flashes of light sparked against his eyelids when he clenched them against the jarring array of mortal images he had collected. Snapshots of Sullivan's bloated corpse, Harlan's gargoyle death mask, Julio's pulverized face, and Gino's mutilated eye dotted his mental landscape like unholy billboards.

He had slipped so easily from a world of rules where uncivil conduct toward an adversary was grounds for sanction to one in which blood ruled and the only sanction that mattered was death. He doubted whether he could return to his old world without a part of him remaining in his new one.

Dawn, gray and misty, found him pounding the jogging path around Loose Park, two blocks from home. Breathing raggedly, he tried to outrun the demons that had become his new best friends until he dropped facedown in the grass, cool and wet. The rain ran off him as he rolled onto his back, squinting skyward, looking for an opening in the clouds. With no epiphany in sight, he trudged home to find Anna Karelson camped on his doorstep, dry and nosy under her umbrella.

"For pity's sake, Lou, you'd have to look better to die!"

She had bed head and she hadn't found her mouthwash yet. Her candy-striped housecoat, loosely tied at the waist, was playing peek-a-boo with her heavy bosom.

"Early morning isn't your best time of day either, Anna. It's just the rain. I'm fine."

"In a pig's eye! My two-week-old bananas have better color than you do."

"Look, Anna. I appreciate your concern, but I'm really okay. I promise to look better after I clean up and get some rest."

"Well, Mr. Celebrity Lawyer, I wouldn't plan on getting any rest today if I was you."

"Meaning?"

"TV trucks and reporters have been banging on your door since you left this morning. I told them you took a cab to the airport. But they'll be back; that's for sure."

Mason had one more rock to turn over before he was ready to go to the cops with Sullivan's and Angela's killer. If the media started shining their light on him now, he'd lose the privacy he needed.

"Anna, mind if I shower at your house?"

"Lou!" she said as she blushed and clutched her gown to her chest. "Jack's still asleep!"

"Don't worry, I'm a quiet scrubber." He ran upstairs and grabbed clean clothes, a black Windbreaker, a Beaver Creek cap, and Vernon's Bible. "Drive my car around the block behind your house," Mason said when he came back and handed her the keys to the TR6. "I'll be in the shower."

Anna came in through her back door, dripping and cursing Mason as water ran off her neck and between her breasts. "Honestly, Lou, I don't know why I let you talk me into these things."

He was sitting at her kitchen table, tying his shoes while scanning the front page of the morning paper. McNamara would live. St. John announced that his investigation into organized crime would continue.

"That's what neighbors are for, Anna. I owe you one."

Mason glanced out her living room window. Camera crews for the local affiliates of the major networks were setting up shop in his front yard, their logos emblazoned on the rain poncho of each crew member. The clock was running on his fifteen minutes of fame.

Mason kissed Anna on the cheek and went out the back door, cutting across lawns to the next block and his car. It was eight o'clock, early for house calls. Mason hoped he wasn't too late.

CHAPTER SEVENTY-SIX

Pamela's newspaper was still in the driveway and there were no lights on in the house. It felt as though more than twenty-four hours had passed since he'd last knocked on her door. Vernon's Bible lay heavily against his side, protected from the rain by his jacket, as he leaned on the doorbell. Five minutes of chimes brought protesting footsteps that stopped on the other side of the peephole in the door.

"Lou, what are you doing here at this hour?" Pamela asked in a voice muffled by the thick oak door.

"I've got to talk with you. It's very important."

"I had a late night. Can't it wait until later, or tomorrow?"

"Pamela, please open the door. I can hardly hear you."

Mason hoped that it would be harder to send him away face-to-face than separated by the heavy door. The dead bolt slid back. Pamela pulled the door open enough to peer around the edge. Mason stepped sideways through the narrow opening before she could protest.

She had the same puffy-eyed, just-rousted-from-bed look as Anna Karelson had. He could taste the stale, smoky aroma that hung on her, and he could smell the booze in her sweat. She hunched her shoulders inside the velour red robe she had zipped to the neck. She was close enough to rock bottom to touch it with her tongue.

"I'm sorry to barge in on you like this. I know who killed your husband. I thought you would want to know."

She slumped against the door, pushing it closed, as she covered her mouth with one hand, her eyes asking questions that she refused to speak.

"I don't want to go to the police until I'm certain," Mason continued. "There are a few details about Richard's past that I need to clear up. Let's talk in the study."

Mason led the way, not giving her the chance to object. He hoped that taking charge in her own house would keep her off her guard. The study reeked of Pamela's long night. She didn't smoke. Mason wondered who did.

The sofa cushions had been left in casual disarray, with two of them piled at one end. Pamela sat on the sofa, holding a cushion in her lap, her arms wrapped around it. Mason chose the wingback chair opposite the sofa, setting his jacket next to the ornamental letter opener on the small table next to the chair, the Bible tucked inside the jacket.

A dark walnut butler's table separated them, adorned with an empty wine bottle and two glasses turned on their sides. Two streaked glasses, one with lipstick on the rim. He pretended not to notice. It wasn't any of his business if Pamela skipped the grieving-widow stage and jumped into friendly arms.

Pamela squeezed the cushion in her lap as if she were trying to pull herself inside it. She hadn't uttered a sound since he'd told her why he was there. Not even a monosyllabic "Who?" The silence was so puzzling that he decided to wait her out and make her ask him who did it.

Smiling at Pamela, Mason stood and began a quiet survey of the books lining the shelves behind Sullivan's desk. He had a theory that you could learn a lot about a person by the books they kept. Some people kept them for show, while others intended to read them someday, though they never would. Still others read them, loved them, and took comfort in being around them. The bindings on Sullivan's books were crisp and virginal. Having them was what counted. Not knowing them.

Mason stopped in front of a volume half-hidden by the vertical molding at the end of the middle shelf. The top half of the letters in the title was visible enough along the book's spine that he could read *Rogersville H.S. 1973 Yearbook*. He sat down in Sullivan's desk chair and began leafing through the book. Pamela was still mute.

"Did you and Richard get back to Rogersville very often?" Mason asked, looking at Pamela as she rocked back and forth on the sofa. Her eyes bore down on the intricate pattern in the Persian rug as if the answer could be divined in the weave.

"Pamela, over here," he said, breaking her spell. She jerked her head up and raised her lids halfway in his direction. "Did you and Richard get back to Rogersville very often?"

"Not in years."

Mason found Sullivan's senior class picture and index of achievements. Crew cut, shiny cheeks, cocked, arrogant smile, head tilted at a jaunty angle. Look out, world, here he comes. Lettered in track and cross-country. Choir. Junior Achievement.

"Why not?"

Flipping through the pages, Mason ran his finger under the names beneath the pictures, stopping at Meredith Phillips's photograph. Pageboy, wide nose, wider face, crooked smile, square chin. Unremarkable, yet vaguely familiar. Home Economics Club.

"No reason to," she said to the floor. "We wanted out."

The girl in the photograph next to Meredith's had long dark hair tucked behind her ears, bangs pulled across her forehead, oval face with perfectly aligned teeth, dimpled cheeks. Cheerleader, Homecoming Queen. Pamela Phinney. Mason looked up. There was no doubt. Pamela Phinney Sullivan lay back against the couch, her eyes raised to the ceiling.

"You knew Meredith Phillips?"

"We were best friends," she said softly.

"And you didn't know about the baby?" Some best friend.

"Best friends in high school—not later."

"What happened?"

"She and Richard dated all through school. No one could figure it out. Great-looking guy and the homely girl."

"No competition. Maybe Richard was insecure in spite of his

good looks."

"Maybe. Anyway, she was a small-town girl. Richard and I couldn't wait to escape."

"And you ended up with Richard."

"I chased him for four years in high school. That's why Meredith and I were best friends. She kept me close to Richard. Back then, he was loyal. But I got him in the end."

"But not before he and Meredith had one last stroll around the park."

"No—not before."

"And you didn't know about the baby until I told you yesterday?"

She hesitated an instant before answering. "Not before—"

"Not before what?" Diane Farrell asked, one hand on her hip, the other on the entry to the study. She was wearing a half-buttoned man's pajama top that fell to mid thigh and, nearly as Mason could tell, nothing else.

CHAPTER SEVENTY-SEVEN

Pamela paled and shook at Diane's appearance, growing smaller behind her pillow. "Diane—please don't do this to me."

Smiling voraciously, Diane walked toward her. "Pamela dear, I told you last night that I wasn't like the society lesbians you cheated on Richard with." She stood in front of Pamela, reaching down and stroking her hair. "You didn't tell me we were having company for breakfast."

"I was in the neighborhood."

"Pamela, you're ruining my new dress under those pillows." She reached behind a cushion and extracted the wrinkled dress Pamela had given her on her birthday.

"Please, Diane—no," Pamela managed, her lips barely moving, her face downcast.

"But, Pamela, it's all I've got to put on. After all," she giggled, "I didn't pack my overnight bag."

She shook the wrinkles out of the dress and looked at Mason again. "If you don't mind, Mason. I'm a little modest around men."

Nodding, he stood and turned his back, placing the yearbook on the credenza behind Sullivan's desk. Trusting that Diane had her eyes on Pamela, he set his smart phone down and turned on the voice-recording app.

"Okay, Mason, you can turn around. I'm decent."

"Not by half," he said as he pushed Sullivan's desk chair back, blocking her view of the credenza.

"Mason," she said, sticking out her lower lip in a mock pout, "I sense your disapproval. How provincial. This is the new millennium."

"Leaving someone their dignity never goes out of style."

"Noble horseshit. Now, tell me what you and Pamela were talking about. She seems to have lost her spark. Probably needs a drink to get her motor going."

"I was asking her if she knew where you worked before you came to the firm."

"You came here at eight o'clock on Sunday morning to ask Pamela about my work history? You can do better than that."

"Actually, I've taken up genealogy. I'm trying to figure out if pathological behavior is a generation-skipping phenomenon."

He returned to the wingback chair and picked up his jacket. She held her ground by the sofa, warily appraising his comments, calculating her response. Pamela's muted sobs were buried in her pillow, the undercard to the main event about to begin.

"In that case, my family wouldn't interest you."

"Why not?"

"Every generation has been pathological," she said without a trace of humor.

"Tell me about them. Maybe I'll change my approach."

"Oh, Mason, you're being so coy. Why don't you ask me what you really want to know?"

Diane sat next to Pamela, draping her arm around her. Pamela froze at the gesture, then shook her off and stood, smoothing her robe and glaring at Diane, who smiled serenely in reply.

"You should leave her alone," Mason said to Diane.

"She's a big girl. She can make her own choices."

Pamela moved to the windows and turned to look at Mason, her eyes searching the room as if to find someplace else to go. Diane smiled at her like a mother encouraging her shy child. Pamela sighed and made her way back to the sofa, accepting Diane's outstretched hand.

Mason ignored Diane's triumphant grin. "What did you do before you came to the firm?"

"Really?"

"Really."

"I went to school. Penn Valley Community College. Paralegal degree with distinction."

"And before that—where's home?"

"No place special. A little town you've probably never heard of."

"Family?"

"None anymore."

"So your first job was with Sullivan?"

"You are a quick study, Mason. I'll bet you're terrifying on cross-examination."

"I like to let things build. What did you think of Sullivan?"

"He treated people like dirt, but I didn't have a problem with him."

"The two of you must have had a special relationship."

Her eyes flickered for an instant. She leaned forward, legs crossed, her chin cupped in one hand, elbow resting on her knee. She was studying. Diane was no fool and wouldn't allow him to trap her easily. But Mason knew more than she could suspect, and he was better at this than she was. And she was living on lies, which made for a foundation with deep faults. Not the kind that would withstand much stress. Her outrageous treatment of Pamela told Mason that she felt safe—beyond his reach. Now doubt was creeping in, filling the faults and pushing them into wider cracks.

"I knew what he wanted and I did it."

"Including figuring out what Scott and Harlan were doing with Quintex and the phony fees?"

She sat back, leaving her legs crossed at the ankles, arms extended across the back of the sofa. "Including Quintex. Sullivan asked me to check into it. I put it all together for him. Including the Cayman Island accounts. It wasn't difficult. Scott and Harlan weren't very clever crooks."

"But why hide it on the Johnny Mathis CD?"

"That was my idea. Nobody listens to Johnny Mathis. It was the perfect hiding place. All I needed was a scanner and a CD burner.

Sullivan didn't want anyone to know he had the information. Except for the U.S. attorney. But I guess he didn't get the chance to rat out his partners and poor Vic Jr.," she added with a quick laugh.

Mason connected the last dot. "You knew Sullivan was going to make a deal with St. John?"

"I figured it out. It was the only way he could avoid going to jail," she said with a thin-lipped smile.

Pamela tried to shrink farther into the sofa, but Diane clamped her hand on Pamela's thigh, keeping her close.

"Why did Sullivan revoke his will?"

Diane shrugged. "He changed his mind about the charities. The codicil gave him time to decide what to do with the money."

It was a practiced reply. The kind that is believed if repeated often enough but doesn't make sense to anyone else.

"Then why not keep the will and change the beneficiaries? Revoking the will means he dies intestate, the estate pays huge taxes, and the heirs get screwed."

"There would still be plenty for Pamela."

"And for any other heirs."

"They never had children. You should do your homework, Mason."

"Oh, I have, Diane. I have. They never had children, but Sullivan did."

"So the kid gets a share."

"How did you know there's only one kid, Diane?"

CHAPTER SEVENTY-EIGHT

She reddened, stood, and walked toward the bookshelves. Mason gripped the arms of his chair to keep from cutting her off before she noticed his phone. She stopped at Sullivan's desk and took his seat.

"He said something about it once, a long time ago."

"What did he tell you?"

Her eyes filled with the memory. "That he'd gotten some girl pregnant a long time ago but didn't find out until years later. Once he found out, he paid support but never saw the child."

"That must have been torture for you. To be right there in front of him and realize he didn't know you."

"You don't know what you're talking about! Pamela, get him out of here. We don't have to listen to this!"

Mason glanced up at Pamela, whose face was a furious mask. Diane pushed the desk chair back against the credenza. Her eyes were wild. Mason reached in his jacket and opened the Bible in his lap.

"Pamela, there's an old man lying in a nursing home in Rogersville. He's in a coma. His name is Vernon Phillips. This is his Bible. His family tree makes interesting reading."

"Where did you get that?" Diane hissed, her body taut, ready to spring at him.

"Homework, Alice. When did you take your grandmother Diane Farrell's name? Were you just being clever or did you want Sullivan to figure it out on his own?"

"My mother loved him, gave herself to him, and he pissed on

her—on both of us!" she screamed. A lifetime of venom contorted her face.

"He paid child support."

"Money! She didn't want his money! She wanted him! But Pamela, beautiful Pamela, got him. And we got nothing."

"You couldn't stand that he didn't want you—didn't even want to see you," Mason said, driving each nail slowly. "When did Meredith tell you about him?"

She was startled at his use of her mother's name. It was another invasion of her life. Mason was Sherman marching through Georgia, and he was just warming up.

"Did she tell you Daddy was dead or that she didn't know who your daddy was? Or maybe she didn't tell you anything at all. Then one day, you found a check from a man you'd never heard of before."

Diane/Alice bolted from her chair, leaning hard on the desk. Mason had scored a direct hit. The words poured out of her in a torrent.

"When I was thirteen, she wrote him a letter begging him to acknowledge me. He sent it back unopened with a check. My mother left it out where she knew I would find it. That's how she told me!"

"And working for him was your way of getting even? Wasn't it worse when he didn't recognize you or your name? Surely he must have remembered Meredith's mother?"

"My grandmother died when my mother was young. He'd have never known her."

"But still, not to recognize you at all. There had to be some family resemblance."

Mason shook his head sympathetically. Pamela stood as still as Lot's wife as he moved from his chair to the arm of the sofa. He couldn't predict what Diane would do if he kept pushing her, and he wanted more mobility.

"When did you finally tell him?"

"Last January."

"Just before he revoked his will. What was his reaction?"

"He told me to keep my mouth shut and my billable hours up."

"That's it?"

"We made a deal. I told him all I wanted was my inheritance. I didn't care if anyone knew, so long as I got my share."

"Why not make you a beneficiary in the will?"

"That was too public an acknowledgment. This way, if Pamela died first, I'd get everything as the only heir."

"How were you going to prove paternity?"

"He took a blood test when I was ten. That's when he started paying child support. And I made him sign something."

"Where is it?"

"It doesn't matter."

Mason remembered that Angela had told Sandra that there was something else she wanted to talk with her about.

"Angela found it, didn't she?"

Diane's face softened and then hardened again as she sensed where he was headed.

"Mason, I'm getting tired of this."

She stepped away from the desk. He stood as she reached behind the Carl Sandburg biography of Lincoln and turned around, holding Pamela's gun.

"Oh shit," Mason said.

"How right you are."

CHAPTER SEVENTY-NINE

"You don't need the gun, Diane," Pamela said.

"Don't tell me what I need, Pamela. If you'd have left my mother and father alone, none of this would have happened."

"Richard chose me—that's not my fault!"

"Not your fault! Ha! Mother told me how you seduced him. How did it feel to be seduced by his daughter, sweet Pamela?"

"I've been a greater fool before and no doubt will be again. But there's no need for a gun."

"Tell him that," Diane said, waving the gun at Mason.

"What is she talking about, Lou?"

"She killed Richard and Angela. Now she's trying to decide whether to kill us."

Pamela stepped toward her. "Diane?"

"You're a pathetic whore. You stole my father. Over there, on the couch, where I can see both of you," Diane commanded, directing them with the gun.

Pamela complied, clutching a pillow in her lap.

"How did you know about the gun?" Mason asked.

"Pamela told me. She told me everything."

"Including that Sullivan was HIV positive?"

"That was rich. It renewed my faith in God."

"But threatened your inheritance. AIDS is a very expensive way to die. But if you killed Sullivan, you'd get your money and your revenge."

"It was a good deal for both of us. We'd both stop suffering."

"So you told Sullivan that you had access to experimental

drugs through the gay community and, as the loving daughter, you wanted to help him."

"I told you he trusted me."

"And you let him shoot himself up with saline until you were ready to give him the fatal dose of insulin."

"My, my. You have done your job, Mason."

"The nursing home doesn't seem real careful about its drugs. Lucky break that your grandfather ended up there."

"It didn't matter. I would have found something to give him."

"How did you get him to inject himself?"

"The day before the retreat, I told him I had something new, very powerful. He begged me for it. I made him wait until Saturday night at the lake."

"And you just watched him kill himself."

"It was a dream come true."

"You might have gotten away with it if you hadn't killed Angela too. How did she find out about you?"

"The wiretap on Sullivan's phone. She tried to blackmail me for a share of my inheritance."

"So you went to her apartment. But how did you do it?"

"It was easy. I stabbed her in the neck with a dose of insulin. It's very quick that way."

"And left the suicide note on her computer."

"I thought it was a nice touch."

"Actually, it was stupid. Angela didn't know Sullivan was HIV positive. Other than his doctor, you and Pamela were the only ones who knew. Too many bodies, Diane. You can't cover all your tracks."

"I can try. After I shoot you, I'm going to help sweet Pamela put the gun in her mouth. A messy murder-suicide should at least muddy the waters."

Diane began walking toward them as Mason stood up.

"Sit down!" she screamed.

There was no way out. She was too far away to try and disarm her, but she was close enough to shoot them both. Mason decided to at least put some distance between him and Pamela.

"Sit down!" she screamed again as he moved toward the desk.

"Diane," Pamela replied wearily, "the gun isn't loaded."

Diane and Mason stopped in their tracks. "What?" he yelled at Pamela. "Were you waiting for a sign from God to tell me?"

"I wanted to know everything," Pamela said. "There have been too many lies. She wouldn't tell the truth if she thought the gun wasn't loaded."

Diane threw the gun at Pamela, striking her on the shoulder, and charged her, screaming. They rolled on the floor in a tangle of arms and legs, knocking over the butler's table. Mason pulled them apart, but not before Diane raked Pamela's face with her nails, opening ugly wounds. Mason held Diane with her arm twisted behind her back until her breathing steadied, while Pamela called 911.

Diane sat in the wingback chair while they waited for the police. The doorbell rang and Pamela left to answer it. Mason had his back to Diane as he listened to the recording of their conversation, turning around just as Pamela and the cops came in the room.

They all stared at Diane. She was holding the ornamental letter opener that had fallen on the floor during her wrestling match with Pamela. Diane waited until she had their full attention before plunging the letter opener into her neck.

CHAPTER EIGHTY

Diane punctured her jugular vein. The cops did what they could and the paramedics did more. She lived long enough to be pronounced dead in the emergency room.

The clouds were breaking up when Pamela and Mason left the hospital. It had been two weeks since he had identified Sullivan's body at the lake. For the first time, the air was clear.

Pamela thanked him for the ride, for everything, she said. Mason promised to check in on her, but it was a promise neither of them wanted him to keep. It's too hard to become friends after you've been stripped naked.

Mason believed that Pamela must have suspected Diane. At least that she was Sullivan's daughter. Yet she allowed their relationship to become dangerously intimate. Perhaps had even encouraged it.

He'd read that some people stay in abusive relationships because they think they deserve it. Maybe Pamela knew what she was doing with Diane—punishing herself for taking Sullivan from Diane and her mother. He couldn't wait for Jerry Springer to do a show on women who sleep with their stepdaughters who kill their husbands to get even with their fathers for abandoning them.

Sunday evening, Mason met Kelly at the airport. Other friends and lovers streamed past them, embracing one another, grabbing luggage, moving on. Mason and Kelly stood for a moment, holding hands, measuring where they were. She clutched him briefly, brushed his lips, and said she was glad he was all right. The intensity of the last two weeks had locked them together. Both sensed that the grip of those days was loosening. They had a quiet dinner, dancing small steps around the future.

"Blues is buying a bar," he told her. "It comes complete with office space upstairs. I'm thinking about becoming his first tenant."

"That's great. Really great. You'll be happier on your own."

Mason knew that she was talking as much about herself as about him. She'd buried her partner, exhumed his memory, and had to bury him again. Another part of her had been lost when her cabin burned.

After dinner, they drove to the Plaza and parked in front of their fountain. The top was down on the TR6. The air was close, thick with humidity. Bugs danced in the fountain's spray. Cars filled with teenagers sauntered past, rap and rock bellowing from open windows. Mason and Kelly smiled ruefully at each other, realizing that the magic had been in the moment, not the fountain, and the moment had passed.

Mason read her thoughts. "Nick was dirty, Kelly. That was about him, not about you."

She sighed deeply, rubbed her hands in her lap, and nodded. "I didn't see it," she said. "That is about me." A thin tear leaked from the corner of her eye. Mason reached to wipe it away. She took his hand. "The cabin was my hiding place, Lou. I hid everything there, including my feelings for Nick, for you, and for myself. I've got to rebuild before I can decide what I want."

Mason dropped her at her hotel. Kelly stepped from the car, leaned back in, and kissed him. He watched her walk away until she disappeared through the revolving door.

The next day, he returned Vernon's Bible to him. He was unchanged. A new nurse was caring for him and told Mason that he could last for years in that condition. He almost promised that he'd come back to visit, but he was tired of making promises meant to be broken.

When he got home, he called Webb Chapman. "Any news on the safety hooks?"

"I was getting ready to call you. The test results came back today. Several of the hooks have blood on them. One of the blood samples matches Tommy's blood type. You need DNA tests to prove it was Tommy's blood, and that's not cheap to do."

Mason quickly calculated how much money he had left from his insurance settlement. "Do it."

"Have you told Tommy?"

"No. I want to be certain first."

Blues on Broadway opened the week after Labor Day. It was a straight-ahead joint. No cutesy memorabilia from funkier times. A rectangular-shaped mahogany bar dominated the center. Glasses hung in racks from the ceiling. Single-malt Scotch got premier billing on the shelves behind the bar. Black leather booths lined the walls, and a handful of matching round tables dotted the floor.

Blues's Steinway grand piano, its ebony wood buffed to a high sheen, sat a foot off the floor on a stage barely big enough for it and the big man who played it. Mason had an office upstairs and a part-time job tending bar.

Sandra Connelly dropped in one afternoon as he was wiping glasses. Her auburn hair was shaped, shortened, and highlighted for fall. A glistening diamond hung from the center of a gold necklace. She stood in the doorway, silhouetted by the sunshine.

"Come on in," Mason told her. "You can sign up to be a charter regular."

"What do I get? My own chair at the bar?"

"Any seat that isn't taken."

"Suits me. Give me a glass of your best house wine. And don't open a fresh gallon on my account."

Sandra had been at the center of a fierce recruiting battle among the major law firms in town. She didn't discourage the soft exaggerations of her exploits by the media and leveraged her high profile into a corner office and a fat paycheck. Mason admired her ambition but didn't envy her. He poured and she sipped.

"Victor O'Malley just wrote my firm a check for a hundred thousand dollars."

"Still paying for work his lawyers didn't do."

"Cute, for a bartender. This one is the real deal, Lou. I'm his

317

lawyer. St. John is still going after him."

"Any word on Vic Jr.?"

Sandra turned serious. "No. The cops assumed that Camaya killed him. His father wants me to keep looking. I came by to tell you something else."

"What's that?"

"Camaya escaped from the prison hospital last night. It looks like he had outside help."

"I'm not worried. Jimmie and I have an understanding."

"All the same, watch your back. Are you going to spend the rest of your life tending bar?"

"Nope. I'm just helping Blues. The DNA tests on one of the Philpott safety hooks turned up Tommy's blood. I'm going to file a motion for a new trial next week. Then I'm going to hang my shingle out in an office upstairs and see what comes through the door."

"Just remember, Lou. My door's always open." She left him a nice tip.

Mason wandered upstairs to his office. Tuffy was curled on a rug next to his desk chair, waiting for her ears to be scratched.

He settled into his chair, swiveled around to look out his windows onto Broadway. His office was in a part of town the mayor described as "in transition." He felt the same way. There was nothing fancy about the office—just the basics. Blues had given him an office-warming gift. It was a metronome. He told Mason to just listen to the beat. It was good advice.

THANKS

Thank you for adding *Motion to Kill* to your library. This is an exciting time to be a writer and a reader. The indie revolution has given writers the chance to connect with readers in ways that were never imagined before.

The next novel in the Lou Mason series, *The Last Witness*, will be available soon as an e-book and POD. Enjoy the opening chapters I've included beginning on the next page, and stay in touch.

Find out more about Joel Goldman at http://www.joelgoldman.com

Follow his blog at http://www.joelgoldman.blogspot.com

Sign up for his newsletter at http://www.joelgoldman.com/newsletter.php

Follow him on Twitter at http://twitter.com/#!/JoelGoldman1

Follow him on Facebook at http://www.facebook.com/joel.goldman

ACKNOWLEDGMENTS

A number of people were instrumental in helping me with this book the first time it was published as a paperback original in 2002. From the beginning, my wife, Hildy, and my children—Aaron, Danny, and Michele—supported me. Many people, including my sister Susan, my cousin Merilyn, and my friend Dan, read and reread the early drafts, adding their enthusiastic encouragement. My agent, Meredith Bernstein, gave me a chance and became my good friend.

The e-book revolution has given this book and the others in the Lou Mason series a second life. I've updated the book but kept the story intact. It's like getting a do-over with one of your kids!

I'm thankful for all those indie writers who have shown me the e-book way, with special thanks to Lee Goldberg (http://www.leegoldberg.typepad.com/), Paul Levine (http://www.paul-levine.com/), and Joe Konrath (http://www.jakonrath.blogspot.com/).

Thanks also to Steven W. Booth (http://www.gosmultimedia.com/) for formatting this book, to Jeroen ten Berge (http://www.jeroentenberge.com/) for designing the cover, and to Eileen Chetti (chetti@optimum.net) for a superb copyediting job.

Enjoy this excerpt from *The Last Witness*, the thrilling second novel in Joel Goldman's series featuring Lou Mason...

CHAPTER ONE

Jack Cullan's maid found his body lying facedown on the floor of his study, his cheek glued to the carpet with his own frozen, congealed blood. When she turned the body over, fibers stuck to Cullan's cheek like fungus that grows under a rock. His left eye was open, the shock of his death still registered in the wide aperture of his eyelid. His right eye was gone, pulverized by a .38-caliber bullet that had pierced his pupil and rattled around in his brain like loose change in the seconds before he died.

"Shit," Harry Ryman said as he looked down on the body of the mayor's personal lawyer. "Call the chief," he told his partner, Carl Zimmerman.

Harry knew that Jack Cullan wasn't just Mayor Billy Sunshine's lawyer. He was a social lubricator, a lawyer who spent more time collecting IOUs than a leg-breaking bagman for the mob. For the last twenty years, getting elected in Kansas City had meant getting Cullan's support. Anyone doing serious business with the city had hired him to get their deals done.

Harry guessed that Cullan was in his early sixties, dumpy from years spent avoiding physical exertion in favor of mental manipulation. Harry squatted down to examine Cullan's hands. They were smooth, unlike the man's reputation. Cullan had a Santa Claus build, but Harry knew the man couldn't have played St. Nick without asking for more than he ever would have given.

Harry had been a homicide detective too long to remember ever having been anything else. He knew that the chances of solving a murder dropped like the wind chill after the first forty-eight hours. If time weren't a powerful enough incentive, a politically heavy body like Jack Cullan's would push his investigation into warp speed.

He gathered his topcoat around him, fighting off the cold that had invaded the study on the backside of Cullan's house. The windows were open. The maid, Norma Hawkins, said she had found them that way when she arrived for work at eight o'clock that morning, Monday, December 10. The heat had also been turned off, the maid had added. An early winter blast had locked Kansas City down in a brutal snow-laced assault for the last week. Cullan's house felt like ground zero.

"The chief says to meet him at the mayor's office," Zimmerman said, interrupting Harry's silent survey of the murder scene.

"What for?" Harry asked, annoyed at anything that would slow down the investigation.

"I told the chief that somebody popped the mayor's lawyer. He told me to sit tight, like I was going someplace, right? He calls back two minutes later and says meet him at the mayor's office. You want to discuss it with the chief, you got his number."

Carl Zimmerman had grown up fighting, sometimes over jabs about being a black man with a white man's name, sometimes to find out who could take a punch. He and Harry had been partners for six years without becoming close friends. Harry was older, more experienced, and automatically assumed the lead in their investigations, a batting order he knew that Zimmerman resented. That was Zimmerman's problem, Harry had decided. Zimmerman was a good cop, but Harry was a better one.

Harry wanted to get moving. He wanted to interview the maid, figure out how long Cullan had been dead before she found him, and backtrack Cullan's activities in the hours before he was murdered. He wanted to talk to everyone Cullan had been with during that time. He wanted to search Cullan's home, car, and office for anything that might lead him to the killer. The last thing he wanted to do was run downtown to promise the chief and the mayor that they would solve the crime before dinner. The next-to-last thing he wanted to do was deal with the chip on his partner's shoulder.

"Here," Harry said, tossing the keys to Zimmerman. "You can drive."

CHAPTER TWO

Lou Mason read about Jack Cullan's murder in Wednesday morning's *Kansas City Star* while the wind whipped past his office windows overlooking Broadway. In the spring, Mason would open the windows, letting the breeze wrap itself around him like a soft sweatshirt on a cool day. Wednesday morning's wind was more like a garrote twisted around the city's throat by Mother Nature turned Boston Strangler.

The story of Cullan's murder was two days old but still front-page news. The reporter, Rachel Firestone, wrote that Cullan had been at the center of an investigation into the decision of the mayor and the Missouri Gaming Commission to approve a license for a riverboat casino called *The Dream*. *The Dream* had opened recently, docked on the Missouri River at the limestone landing where nineteenth-century fur traders had first thought to build the trading post that became Kansas City.

Cullan's client, Edward Fiora, owned *The Dream*. Whispers that Cullan had secured *The Dream*'s license with well-orchestrated bribes of Mayor Sunshine and of Beth Harrell, the chair of the gaming commission, had circulated like tabloid vapor, titillating but unproved. The reporter had dubbed the brewing scandal the "Nightmare on Dream Street."

Mason put the paper down to answer his phone. "Lou Mason," he said. When he'd first gone into solo practice, he'd answered the phone by saying, "Law office," until one of his clients had asked to speak to Mr. Office.

"I need you downstairs," Blues said, and hung up.

Blues was Wilson Bluestone, Jr., Mason's landlord, private investigator, and more often than Mason would like, the one person Mason counted on to watch his back. Blues owned the bar on the first floor, Blues on Broadway. He never admitted to needing anything, so Mason took his statement seriously.

Mason double-timed down the lavender carpeted hallway, past the art deco light fixtures spaced evenly on the wall between each office on the second floor. One office belonged to Blues, another to a PR flack, and a third to a CPA. They were all solo acts.

He bounded down the stairs at the end of the hall, bracing one hand on the wobbly rail, his feet just brushing the treads, making a final turn into the kitchen. The cold urgency in Blues's voice propelled him past the grill almost too fast to catch the greasy scent of the Reuben sandwiches cooked there the night before. A sudden burst of broken glass mixed with the crack of overturned furniture and the thick thud of a big man put down.

"Goddammit, Bluestone!" Harry Ryman shouted. Harry hated bars and Blues too much to pay an early morning social call, especially on a day that would freeze your teeth.

Mason picked up his pace, shoved aside the swinging door between the kitchen and the bar, and plunged into a frozen tableau on the edge of disaster. Blues stood in the middle of the room surrounded by Harry Ryman and another detective Mason recognized as Harry's partner, Carl Zimmerman, and a uniformed cop.

The beat cop and Zimmerman were aiming their service revolvers at Blues's head. Another uniformed cop was on his knees next to a table lying on its side, surrounded by broken dishes, rubbing a growing welt on his cheek with one hand and holding a pair of handcuffs with the other.

Blues and Harry were squared off in front of each other, heavyweights waiting for the first bell. Harry's dead-eyed cop glare matched Blues's flat street stare. In a tale of the tape, it was hard to pick a favorite. Though half a foot shy of Blues's six-four, Harry had a solid, barreled girth that was tough to rock. Blues was chiseled, lithe, and deadly. Harry carried the cop-worn look of the twenty years he had on Blues.

No one moved. Steam rose off the cops' shoulders as the snow they had carried inside melted in the warmth of the bar. The wind beat against the front door, rattling its frame, like someone desperate to get inside. Blues was spring-loaded, never taking his eyes from Harry's.

Mason spoke softly, as if the sound of his voice would detonate the room. "Harry?" Ryman didn't answer.

The uniformed cop on his feet was a skinny kid with droopy eyes and a puckered mouth who'd probably never drawn his gun outside the shooting range and couldn't control the tremor in his extended arms.

Carl Zimmerman was a compact middleweight who held his gun as if it were a natural extension of his hand, no hesitation in his trigger finger. His dark face was a calm pool.

The solidly built cop Blues had put on the floor had gotten to his feet, his block-cut face flush with embarrassment and anger, anxious for redemption and ready to take Blues on again. He took a step toward Blues, and Carl Zimmerman put a hand on his shoulder and held him back.

"You're going down, Bluestone," Harry said.

"I told your boy not to put his hands on me," Blues answered.

"Officer Toland was doing his job and I'm doing mine. Don't make this worse than it already is."

"Harry?" Mason said again.

"This doesn't concern you, Lou," Harry answered, not taking his eyes off Blues.

"That's bullshit, Harry, and you know it."

Harry Ryman was the closest thing Mason had to a father. He and Mason's aunt Claire had been together for years and had been unconventional surrogates for Mason's parents, who had been killed in a car accident when Mason was three years old. Blues had saved Mason's life and was the closest thing Mason had to a brother. Whatever was going down didn't just concern Mason. It threatened to turn his world inside out.

Harry said to Blues, "I'm gonna cuff you. Everybody gets cuffed, even if we have to shoot them first. You remember that much, don't you, Bluestone?"

Blues looked at Mason, silently asking the obvious with the same flat expression. Mason nodded, telling him to go along. Blues slowly turned his back on Harry, disguising his rage with a casual pivot, extending his arms behind him, managing a defiant posture even in surrender. Harry fastened the handcuffs around Blues's wrists and began reciting the cop's mantra.

"You're under arrest. You have the right to remain silent. Anything you say can and will be used against you in a court of law. You have the right to an attorney. If you cannot afford an attorney—"

"I'm his attorney," Mason interrupted. "What's the charge?"

Harry looked at Mason for the first time, a tight smile cutting a thin line across his wide face. Mason saw the satisfaction in Harry's smile and the glow of long-sought vindication in his eyes. He had always warned Mason that Blues would cross the line one day and that he would be there to take him down; that the violent, self-styled justice Blues had employed when he was a cop, and since then, was as corrupt as being on the take. As much as Harry may have longed to make that speech again, instead he said it all with one word.

"Murder." Harry held Mason's astonished gaze. "Murder in the first degree," he added. "You can talk to your client downtown after we book him."

Mason watched as they filed out, first the two uniformed cops, then Carl Zimmerman, then Blues. As Harry reached the door, Mason called to him.

"Who was it, Harry?"

Harry had had the steely satisfaction of the triumphant cop when he'd forced Blues to submit moments ago. Now his face sagged as he looked at Mason, seeing him for the first time as an adversary. Harry thought about the battle that lay ahead between them before responding.

"Jack Cullan. Couldn't have been some punk. It had to be Jack Fucking Cullan." Harry turned away, disappearing into the wind as the door closed behind him.

About The Author

Joel Goldman is an Edgar and Shamus nominated author who was a trial lawyer for twenty-eight years. He wrote his first thriller after one of his partners complained about another partner and he decided to write a mystery, kill the son-of-a-bitch off in the first chapter and spend the rest of the book figuring out who did it. No longer practicing law, he offices at Starbucks and lives in Kansas City with his wife and two dogs.

NOVELS BY JOEL GOLDMAN

Motion to Kill

The Last Witness

Cold Truth

Deadlocked

Shakedown

The Dead Man

No Way Out

PRAISE FOR
JOEL GOLDMAN'S NOVELS

Motion To Kill

"Admirable . . . high tension . . . fierce action scenes carry the reader toward an electrifying dénouement."
—*Publishers Weekly*

"Lou is a fascinating protagonist . . . fans will set in motion a plea for more Lou Mason thrillers."
—*Midwest Book Review*

"The plot races forward."
—*Amarillo Globe News*

"Lots of suspense and a dandy surprise ending."
—*Romantic Times*

The Last Witness

"Fast, furious and thoroughly enjoyable, *The Last Witness* is classic, and classy, noir for our time, filled with great characters and sharp, stylish writing. We better see more Lou Mason in the future."
—Jeffery Deaver, author of *The Vanished Man* and *The Stone Monkey*

"*The Last Witness* is an old-fashioned, '40s, tough-guy detective story set in modern times and starring a lawyer named Lou

Mason instead of a private eye named Sam Spade. There's a lot of action, loads of suspects, and plenty of snappy dialogue. It's a fun read from beginning to end."
—Phillip Margolin, author of *The Associate* and *Wild Justice*

Cold Truth

"Wanted for good writing: Joel Goldman strikes again with *Cold Truth*. Kansas City trial lawyer Lou Mason doesn't shy away from the hard cases. Always working close to the edge, he worries that he 'was taking the dive just to see if he could make it back to the surface, gulping for air, beating the odds, wishing he had a reason to play it safe.'"
—*Kansas City Star*

"Joel Goldman is the real deal. In *Cold Truth*, Lou Mason goes his namesake Perry one better, and ought to make Kansas City a must-stop on the lawyer/thriller map."
—John Lescroart, best-selling author of *The First Law*

Deadlocked

"In his fourth novel, attorney-turned-author Joel Goldman delivers a well-plotted legal thriller that takes an insightful look at capital punishment and questions of guilt. *Deadlocked*'s brisk pace is augmented by Goldman's skill at creating realistic characters and believable situations. Goldman is among the legion of strong paperback writers whose novels often rival those in hardcover."
—Oline H. Cogdill, *Orlando Sun Sentinel*

"A certain death penalty case and execution is the catalyst in Joel Goldman's legal thriller *Deadlocked*. The fourth Lou Mason case is the best and most thought provoking, and when the action starts, it is a real page-turner delivered by a pro."
—*Mystery Scene Magazine*

"Lou Mason's best outing. . .very satisfying and highly recommended."
—Lee Child, *New York Times* best-selling author

Shakedown

"Here's why . . . mystery lovers should put *Shakedown* on their nightstands: Goldman, a 'nuthin' fancy' kind of writer, tells a story at a breakneck pace."
—*Kansas City Star*

"Goldman's surefooted plotting and Jack Davis's courage under fire make this a fascinating, compelling read."
—*Publishers Weekly*

"*Shakedown* is a really fine novel. Joel Goldman has got it locked and loaded and full of the blood of character and the gritty details that make up the truth. Page for page, I loved it."
—Michael Connelly, *New York Times* best-selling author

"*Shakedown* is a chillingly realistic crime novel—it's fast paced, smartly plotted, and a gripping read to the very last page. Joel Goldman explores—with an insider's eye—a dark tale of murder and betrayal."
—Linda Fairstein, *New York Times* best-selling author

The Dead Man

"A masterful blend of rock-solid detective work and escalating dread, *The Dead Man* is both a top-notch thriller and a heart-rending story of loss, courage, and second chances. I loved it."
—Robert Crais, *New York Times* best-selling author

"The Dead Man by Kansas Citian Joel Goldman is a rock-solid mystery with likable, flawed characters. I would have enjoyed it even if it had not been set in Kansas City, but scenes such as Harper looking out over Brush Creek or eating in the Country Club Plaza added to the pleasure."
—*Kansas City Star*

"The Dead Man is one of those rare novels you will be tempted to read twice: the first time to enjoy, and the second to appreciate how Goldman puts the pieces together. The hours spent on both will be more than worth it."
—Joe Hartlaub, Bookreporter.com

No Way Out

"Sleek and sassy, *No Way Out* is a page-turner that keeps going full speed until the very end."
—Faye Kellerman, *New York Times* best-selling author

"Goldman spins his latest yarn into a clever, complex tangle of chain reactions between six families of characters whose lives are intertwined by blood, grief, lust, desperation, and even love. The fun, of course, lies in the untangling. . . . If you like to blink, you may want to skip this novel."
—*435 South* magazine